BEING WERE

By C.C. Guice

The First Born Saga

Book One

Copyright © 2008 by C.C. Guice

Cover art by Benjamin Ezra Cremer

ISBN 978-0-6151-9187-4

To my God who provided the platform
To my Family who encouraged me to climb
To my Friends who pushed me and called it a dive

~Prologue ~

In the beginning, that which is and had always been looked upon the vast void that was, and was not pleased; so it was that the spark of all things, which are and were, was created. Of this spark also rose up the First Father and the First Mother, and from them came that which we are.

Now the First Father and the First Mother came to displease that which had created them, and they were cast down. We that had become of them, however, had not displeased, and were not, therefore, cast down. . . . We remained as we were; in the image of our Creator.

Now that which had created all things, loved all things, and was displeased also that they had fallen from grace, and sought to provide for them a way to redeem themselves.

So it was that we that had become of the First Father and the First Mother became absorbed, viewing this strange punishment the Creator had set down that is being human and those attempts that were made to return to His divine grace. Hence in our fascination we did not yet question what we were. . . .

Many an age passed and we began to wonder at ourselves, being neither limitless as that which had created us, nor so limited as humanity which passed constantly before us.

We called to that which was and had always been, asking of Him, "What then shall we be?" Yet we heard no answer. So it was that we have remained what we were . . . neither Creator nor human, neither angel nor devil, neither animal nor plant, but things ever changing, ever learning. . . and ever listening for an answer. . .

Introduction

The Realtor could hear the phone ringing in his small office as he approached the door. He had been anticipating this call since the previous evening. He hadn't held out much hope for a sale the day before, when a young man appearing to be no more than twenty-five, although of obvious means, had looked at the old house on Elm Street. Then he had received a call that evening, telling him to expect another call the following day, and that a man would meet with him and buy it. He had been shocked, even doubtful, but ecstatic nonetheless.

He had long ago come to realize that the realty business here wasn't what it could be in a town this size, with most of its historical three-story houses having been converted into apartments or duplexes. These could be rented out month to month or even by the week but no longer suited the prospective buyer of a family home. The town had adapted itself to house the students that came through it in droves throughout the year. The majority of these houses were minimally maintained, limping through time on wobbling legs, to make their landlords the easiest dime possible.

Those students they housed were more interested in such things as "the million man marijuana march" being conducted in the town's streets or whichever pub crawl was occurring next, hence they left the realty section of the paper relatively unnoticed. After the employment and events sections had been read, this town's paper was generally discarded. Therefore the showing of the house, original as it was and for sale not rent, to someone of this age group was a rare event, and should it prove fruitful it would be even rarer. So he said a small prayer this was the call and that he wasn't going off on a wild goose chase.

He fumbled with his keys a moment before managing to get his excited fingers to work them into the door. Finally gaining entrance, he threw the door wide, stepping forward and grabbing the phone from the desk in one motion, just as the answering machine was about to take the call for him.

"Hello...I...Johnston Realty, may I help you? Yes sir, I can meet you there in ten minutes...Yes sir," he said.

The Realtor held the phone for a minute more trying to order his thoughts. He had bought the house years ago, and no one had seemed genuinely interested in it in all that time. Then, here in the span of twenty-four hours, it seemed to have become a hot item. He would never understand this town.

He slowly put the receiver back in its place and stepped back through the door, turning the knob and locking it behind him as he went. Walking back to his car, he again went over the recent events. Nothing had changed in the property value. The house was still run-down and badly in need of paint. Was he missing something?

Getting into and starting his little white four-cylinder, with its little dent in the rear bumper, he realized he didn't really care. He'd never drive anything else if he thought too long on it. Make the sale, get the money, and move on.

He couldn't help it though; the entire length of the short drive, he kept thinking he had missed something. Pulling up to the house, he saw the brand-new, beautiful, black convertible coupe first and his doubts began to fade. It had to be just a rich out-of-towner with big dreams, like he'd once had, and money to blow on a summer fixer-upper.

Turning off his car and climbing out, he took yet another of many deep breaths he would take in the next few hours and silently thanked God for such an exemplary day. If the house fell short and couldn't sell itself, maybe Missouri's current weather would. The "Show Me State" might show you every kind of weather in one week, but today she was showing off.

The Realtor approached the steps of the old three-story Victorian slowly, feeling again, as he always did with this place, an odd discomfort and awe, as if the man on the porch were not the only one watching him. It was probably an amazing place once, with its towering gingerbread façade and huge bay windows. When he'd first seen it, his imagination had run rampant with visions of the perfect Victorian style bed-and-breakfast, but that had never happened. This place had always made him dream of bigger, better, more beautiful things while somehow making him feel he had no right to them.

The man waiting for him was becoming impatient, shifting his weight restlessly. He realized he had been gazing about at the house, lost in these thoughts, and hadn't even taken the final step up onto the porch.

"I'm sorry to keep you waiting." he said, shaking his head slightly as if that would clear it, and extending his hand. "Been waiting long?"

The corner of the man's mouth twitched a little, not unkindly, but more just not of a mind to be amused or distracted at the moment. The man gripped the realtor's proffered hand briefly.

"Keys?" The prospective buyer had a deep, rich voice and hopefully pockets to match.

The Realtor wasn't a greedy man, he just had bills to pay, and getting this house sold would do a lot of that.

"Yes, yes," he said.

Again the Realtor fumbled with his keys, and finally came up with the right one. He put the key in the deadbolt first, then the knob. Giving the door a shove, to open it wide, he stepped back to allow the intriguing man to enter ahead of him.

The door more moaned than creaked, as it gave view to a once beautiful foyer. Again he was assailed by the sudden sense of mixed awe and discomfiture, as if he were an unrepentant sinner in some holy place. He reasoned with himself that it might be why he never did the necessary work on the house, to make his dream bed-and-breakfast. Or even after disregarding that dream, what kept him from doing at least what repairs that might have allowed him to have sold it sooner. Admittedly he had never had the extra cash resources but he might have found them had he truly wanted to.

The man had already entered and was standing in the foyer with his hand on the wall to the right of the door. This wall had obviously held a large picture or mirror for quite some time, because the man's hand was resting in the center of a large dark square, accented by the pale walls that surrounded it. One could see the taste of an era that had lavished exquisite beauty on every surface it could, by this square of wallpaper that had been shielded from the ravages of time. The man appeared to be quite lost in thought.

Assuming that the discoloration of the walls was about to hurt his chances at the much-needed sale, the Realtor quickly said, "Sir, the lady who owned the place before it went up for auction had a large portrait or something that had hung there for a long time. I'm sure a fresh coat of paint will fix her right up."

The man's lips again twitched and the Realtor suddenly realized the man had obviously known this. Feeling quite silly, he began to search his mind for any small facts he might have managed to retain about this particular house over the years. He was hoping that he could relate them now and alleviate his feeling of stupidity.

The Realtor was shocked out of his mental stock-taking by the man's sudden question, "Will you take a check?" When the man's unexpected question was met with only stunned silence, he had added, "Obviously there is no need for the deed until after the check has cleared."

The Realtor snapped to. "Yes, yes of course, that will be perfect." Then he added, "But don't you want to see the rest of the house?"

The man now let loose with a chuckle, revealing a full set of perfect pearly whites. This gave him the appearance of a happy young boy who just won a very exhilarating race, dropping years from his eyes and already young visage.

"No need," he replied.

A few minutes later the Realtor drove off, in his soon-to-be-traded-in little white four-cylinder car, glancing again at the check on the seat beside him. Taking a deep breath he said to himself once more, "I will never understand this town." Then with a little laugh he added, "Or the wealthy."

Alone at last with his new home, the man raised his hand back to the wall with its darker square of beautiful covering, and took a deep breath. A few moments later he removed his hand slowly, as though it pained him to do so, and walked forward into what was once a very elaborate dining hall.

The room spanned the depth of the house and ended in two beautiful glass doors that looked out onto what had once been an amazing garden. It was overgrown now and most of the original inhabitants had given up blooming long ago, but he could still smell the flowers in his mind. He went slowly to stand before these doors and stood there a moment, envisioning it for a time as it had been, then just as slowly he turned and walked back to the center of the room. There he seemed to become rooted for some time, just breathing in the place, absorbing it as he swayed slowly from side to side, shifting his weight from one foot to the other.

This place gave him a peaceful feeling and he couldn't resist smiling to himself as he finally began to move through the rest of the house, touching the old oak frames that edged its doors and running his hands over the bricks of the fireplace in the den. He could almost feel the heat the hearth had once created, even hear and smell the wood that had once crackled within it. He wandered through his new home in this slow, almost entranced manner, up the stairs and into every room. He peeked into every closet, turned on every light switch, sink tap and shower, and pissed in every toilet.

This was his now.

He returned at last to the dining hall, with its view of the garden that

9

would be again, and stood once more in the center. He began slowly shifting his weight again, swaying as he had before to some internal tune that sung in his heart when he was pleased.

Suddenly his right foot went through the aging board as he shifted once too much in the same weakened spot. Slowly, gently, as if to keep from inflicting further harm upon this wonderful place, he withdrew his foot. He knelt down to examine the damage and, seeing that some of the wood had fallen through, he reached into the hole to retrieve it. When he pulled his hand free he was holding the old plank almost gently. With it still in one hand, he peered into the hole to see if any more pieces remained.

"Ahhh," he said, almost victoriously, reaching his hand into the hole once more.

Resting back on his haunches, he examined a large old leather-bound book in his other hand, and a huge grin produced slight dimples not seen very often of late. It appeared to be a journal or diary covered in dust and cobwebs.

He sat there for a moment with one hand full of old planking and a dusty old book in the other, smiling like an idiot. Anyone observing his actions today might have thought him half-mad. At the very least they'd have had their previous suspicions, that he was a consummate eccentric, confirmed. Lucky for him, the only one there to bear witness to these oddities was the daddy-long-legs he had rousted. That one, however, was more interested in returning to the hole he'd just been so rudely pulled from, than in reporting to anyone a madman had just moved to Springfield.

The man, however, wasn't thinking of any of that just then; he was more interested in his find. Wiping the dust off of it onto his expensive slacks without a second thought, he held it almost lovingly, as though it were some holy relic and it would disappear were it handled too roughly. His new home had provided him a little extra prize.

Suddenly he resumed his previous childlike manner, all toothy smiles, this man who had reminded the Realtor so much of the young boy winning the race. Falling backward onto the floor he crossed his legs, opened

his prize and began to read the following...

The Journal

Part

1

February 8th 1996

~1~

Father Paul

My name is Angelica. I lived and died in Scotland nearly five hundred years ago. This is my journal and I warn you now that this is a private recollection of my life. It is not some lost manuscript of a fairytale love story or an epic record of some forgotten battle, so if it is not for you mayhap you should choose to put it back in its grave to await those it was meant for. What I write here will only have to be dismissed as the mad ramblings of some poor soul, unless you were meant to find this or know those of whom I speak and know the truth of what I say here. In the latter case, I trust you will pass my final words on to them with all my love.

I have thought many times of writing this to you: my loves, my friends, my family, and been afraid, but my desire to remain is fading without you and I am torn. That ever-insistent refusal of my soul to cease its existence is present still, even now after centuries of looking for you. Once more it makes me wonder if the past might be best left there and I should save my sanity by escaping it. Yet I convince myself I can still remain in some form through this pen, that the page will someday carry me back into your hands, and I pray, "That be enough, let the rest be over."

So very long ago…all of it and too terribly far away, I don't know where to begin. I feel the madness creeping back on me as I allow the ghosts of things past to come and be logged and put in order. These memories

13

seduce me and just as I am bound to put them down you may not be able to. Know then that my intent is not to wound with my recollections but to leave this as what balm it may be. I pour my very soul into the ink to remain for those I love, should they find it. Should they find me, as I have failed to find them. Some things written they will have known, others I will make known now, but know that all of it is here only through my love of you and my soul's insistence that I allow it some way to continue, if only through these words.

I suppose I should start then, where I feel it actually began: not with my birth, but rather with my death. I was murdered, you see, though I hold no grudge now against those who murdered me. They did me a service in the end and though it is not actually that coming of age moment, when I lay bleeding on the banks of some forgotten lowland stream, of which I wish to write to you now, I feel you will need to know how such came to be, to fully understand all that I tell you here. There is much about my life that would seem fantastic were it not so easily shadowed by what came after, but then I am getting ahead of myself now, aren't I?

Times were very different then, you see. The year was 1523 and the Lowlands of Scotland had come to be our home, my mother's and mine. I had realized when I was very young that, as a midwife and healer, my mother would only sometimes be met with respect. Most often, though, there was a feeling of fear and avoidance from the people of the villages that we lived near to.

We had never stayed in any one area for very long. The longest was having been near to Oban where my mother and I had gone to a market. We had happened upon an elderly priest and I had pointed to his hand. He had a festering cut on it. I do not remember if I ever learned how he had suffered it. I only know it went far to change my life. I also know my Mem was a very brave woman. I look back and I know what risk she had taken. She had offered him advice on how to make a poultice that could help to heal it. I had been only aged six years then, but I could easily see his surprise, written openly upon his face.

He had thanked her and asked her another question. Then he had

14

invited us to his parish for a meal. Mother rarely turned down a meal, but this was a priest of the Church and it gave her pause. I think it was my having taken his good hand in mine that made her go ahead with her acceptance. Looking back I think she might have been more than a little frightened, but she hid it well. That was Father Paul, and he was a kind man whom I came to learn later was also an extremely exceptional one. I think it was his presence there, and my need of such a figure in my young life, that caused Mem to choose to remain there as long as we did.

He would invite us over again and again to dine, each night repeating the original offer, and eventually I think some unspoken bargain was struck. My mother would sometimes take him herbs and teas and care for him by doing small chores. In return he began to teach us to read and write, always with the theme of God's redeeming love at the root of our lessons. We would talk for hours about religions throughout history, the gods of other places, and then his own. My mind was constantly filled with visions of the Greek gods, Roman gods, and Norse gods all hard at work to shape the earth.

I came to know him more as a historian, a teacher and collector of knowledge, more so than a priest. Though he would always come back somehow to telling us of the One True God, he never condemned my mother or our way of life. He seemed to only want to learn and teach. He would question my mother often on the old ways of Erin and the teachings of the Druids. He was always writing little notes to himself. Then he would say simply, "But you do know there is but One True God." Mem would dutifully tell him yes, and he would seem to be satisfied he had fulfilled his calling.

Sometimes we would speak for hours of the New World, so recently discovered, and so full of promise for those such as we. That it was at the end of the world, and tales told of no end of hardships, did naught to discourage us. Often we would dream of all we might be able to accomplish if given such breadth of freedom as it seemed to offer. Only the actual improbability of our ever being able to travel so far could put us off our verbal dreaming, turning our conversations back to the more attainable goal of understanding different religions, where they had come from and their impact on man throughout history.

It was not, I think, that my mother did not believe in his God, for they spoke as comrades, not combatants, as he made each concept easy to grasp. We would pray together often and we even attended Father Paul's services on occasion, when he would speak to all the people of the village en masse. I think it was more so that she sometimes blended the old ways with the new, which caused the villagers to look on her with also blended feelings.

I was nearing my fourteenth year when he passed on, my mother and I at his side. Some of his last words to us were strange coming from one such as him.

"Go now from this place, seek you somewhere far from here," he had whispered, "for another will come to take my place and he will study my writings and records, and come to know and share in the gossip of these people. Things grow worse for such as ourselves swiftly, and if I am not condemned as a heretic, you surely will be."

There was genuine fear in his voice then, and it crept into my being as his words sunk in. You see, I had gotten used to when I would see the women that had sought out my mother for her help, whether it had been for a poultice or potion, or to help with the birthing of a child, that they would not call out to her in greeting at market. There had always been whispers, but they would be calmed when Father Paul was near. Now I saw there would be no one to shield us from these things.

I recall it happened quickly; quite soon I was hearing the word "witch" more than "wise woman" or "midwife," and the importance of this was frighteningly clear. It seemed Mem was somehow being blamed for Father Paul's death, though it had been obvious to all, in the harsh light of truth, that his years had merely came to claim him. Yet truth back then nearly always disappeared in the shadow of superstition, and both, often too dark to examine closely, became hard to separate.

Though those desperate ones would still arrive in the night, looking over their shoulders for fear of being seen, and she never begrudged them her skill. When they were in need they would come and she would help them, otherwise they would avoid us completely, talking behind their hands and making the symbol of the cross over themselves, fueling the darker superstitions of curses fulfilled in poisoned teas and therefore further shadowing the facts of old age.

So we did indeed do as Father Paul had advised us. Soon after his passing we gathered what little we had, leaving by the second week's end. As the whispers grew louder, we began again to wander. Once more my life became the constant toil of gather and avoid, serve and heal, but remain always at a distance. Only now I had the gift that is education. I had been taught to read and write and to figure numbers. I had been taught the histories of many peoples and this was all given me by one who also gave me hope. This gift, though, turned out to be a blessing and a curse.

Mem, too, taught me. She would tell me how it had not always been the way it was now, regaling me with the most beautiful tales of the old ways. I could understand then that in some ways we had become different, more something to be avoided or at the very least our actions understandably misconstrued as history dictated would happen. We still gathered herbs and lived off the land, for the most part, keeping to ourselves in the woods. We stayed on the outskirts and cared for the sick others would avoid. We only came to their towns to trade or purchase when it was most desperately necessary, while others had come to know no other means. So yes, I understood the how of it but this could not cause me to agree with it. My education told me it was normal but my heart cried that it was not fair. We were still of the same stock, we hurt, we bled, we prayed. We were good people who cared for others, even if they cared not for us.

I had gone many a night to our hovel, for you could call it nothing else, with a heavy heart and at times even angry. I would fall on my pallet beside my mother, aghast at some new pettiness or rudeness imparted to us. When the trivialities that could induce normally kind people to such behavior had eluded my grasp yet again, as always Mem would tell me the same thing: "The people fear what they cannot grasp, and the knowledge I carry, passed down to me, as I pass it to you, frightens them. Do not turn from them when

17

you can help them, and your reward will come."

Still, at the end of the day, no matter where we went, when the herbs had been purchased and the birthing was done, "midwife" was still made to sound as a curse. "Wise woman" was forever whispered under the breath of those turning their heads, as though they had not sought out our help the night before. I simply learned to pretend it mattered not and take my heartbreak to bed.

I never thought that hatred would go so far that avoidance would become violence. Somehow I thought that in the end truth would shine through, eradicating superstition, that someday they would see we were not much different and served good purpose. I used to be quite the dreamer, as they say.

So I would repeat Mem's words to myself frequently when the dream felt most unattainable. I would try to let her conviction put me at peace with things as she seemed to be, but the litany of repetition merely put me to sleep, and I would wake up with my heartbreak still in my pallet beside me giving Mem cause to feel the need to tell me again a few evenings later.

One evening I came home very upset. I remember it as clearly as all the other things that changed me forever.

"Angelica," she said, "must I tell you yet again?"

"No," I had pouted.

"What is it this time, love?" she sighed.

I knew she was tired and had worked hard all day, but I had to tell someone and she was always the one to tell. So I had begun to pour out the awful events of that day.

I told her how when I had gone to the stream early in the morning, to avoid the cruelty of the village girls as was my way, and to do our laundry in peace, that there had been a young man there already, tossing small flat rocks across the waters' surface. I told her how beautiful it had been when he had smiled at me, and that he had spoken to me at the stream. While I washed our clothes, we had talked, as if I were any other girl. How my heart had sung when he had complimented my hip-length black hair and dark eyes,

18

instead of holding them out to be dreadful oddities or proof of my mother's having league with the devil. I told her how we had talked not about any differences we may have had, but rather of all the normal things in our daily lives that made us alike. I then told her how, when the girls of the village had been heard coming up the path to our little spot, he had flashed me this beautiful smile.

She had interrupted me then. "Why is this so upsetting to you? Men will find you attractive, and you them. It is a natural thing," she said, "if not even a little late for a girl your age." She seemed so encouraged it was like salt to a wound, for she was often assailed with guilt that our way of life had never provided sufficiently fertile ground for such interests to blossom in me; guilt which I often could not understand, for she had not made the people change their view of us.

"But...," I tried to begin again.

She started to cut me off, continuing, "You've been a woman, full capable, three summers past, and not yet over the broom...," a speech I had heard often, and which had never brought any results. I know now that it was not merely the lack of properly fertile ground, but also the bloom my soul sought had not as yet been discovered.

I guess she must have read something in my face, because she took a deep breath and said instead, "What is it, my Little Angel?", and she called me that only when she saw I was truly upset.

I felt my eyes start to well up, as I so rarely would let them do. After all we went through on a daily basis, this should have been nothing to me, but it was. I couldn't help it.

I said, "He smiled at me so sweetly, Mem, and then turned to run into the brush before the other girls would see him, and he called to me over his shoulder, saying, 'Terrible thing your mother's a witch, pretty one!'"

Mem began to cry as well, and I had never seen this. It made me cry all the more. I knew then that we would move again. When people began to openly think of us as witches and what we did as witchcraft, we would have no choice. The rise of the Church's witch hunts had caused my mother's original flight from Ireland, and would continue to see us always moving. I had wondered again what it might have been like in the time of the Druids, when a woman who knew and did what my mother did would have been revered.

I tried then to console her, saying that it was not her fault, why should she cry for me, that I suffered only what she suffered, even more so than I and for longer, but this didn't help at all. If anything it made her cry even harder. I was distraught now that I had brought my mother to this and I threw my arms around her and started to rock her gently back and forth. I began chastising myself for my selfish need to share with her my daily pains.

We stayed like that for some time, she in my arms weeping like the child and I taking the role she had for me so often throughout the years, trying to comfort her as she had always done for me, and failing miserably.

Sometime later I realized I had rocked her to sleep, and my feelings of guilt were only slightly subdued. I gently laid her back on her pillow of clean clothing and pulled her blanket over her. I leaned down to place a kiss on her forehead and her eyes came open.

"You do not deserve this, my Angel, I must tell you the truth," she said.

Her voice sounded aged and her eyes were so swollen, I felt myself wanting to cry again.

"Not now, Mem," I said softly. "Whatever truths or bits of knowledge you have within you, to make things easier for me to bear, can wait till tomorrow; now is for you to sleep."

"Not those kinds of truths, love." Something about the way she said it, or maybe it was the way her voice cracked, scared me.

"W-what, what is it?" I was truly afraid for some reason now.

"You are not my daughter," she whispered.

"What?" I knew I had to have misunderstood her or that the stress of the day, or life as a whole, had finally had its way with my sanity.

"You heard me full well, and I do not jest about it. 'Tis a hard enough thing to tell you, do not make me repeat it." She snapped then, she sighed sadly and somehow appeared to shrivel.

Mayhap the world had become too heavy momentarily for Atlas to hold, for it suddenly seemed to be tipping over. Or mayhap it was just the walls of the hut, coming together to squeeze the air from my lungs, and push my heart into my throat. I felt suddenly that I was meant to be plucked from the world to reduce its weight on a tired god and my hut was to be the strangling means by which I was taken from it, because nothing felt right with me. Nothing was right. When I could focus again, not only my vision but my thoughts as well, I asked her as simply as I knew how with the only word I could find.

"Why?" I breathed.

"Why are you not my daughter? Why have I raised you to believe you were? Why am I telling you now? Which 'why' shall I answer first, love?" She had softened her tone toward the end and I realized later, though not just then, why she had been so sharp before. She was preparing herself for what she felt would be my inevitable disdain of her.

So I stared but saw nothing, breathed in but felt as though no air could find my lungs. Mem truly did appear to have shrunk, to be accommodated within the shriveling space of the hovel we had been confined to. I wished I could somehow do the same, as I watched her shaking hands knotting the blankets in her lap while unraveling my world. I found my strength limited to barely being able to listen, dumbfounded, as a wise woman, who was questioning her wisdom rewrote my past.

~2~

Wise Woman

"It was in the spring of the year 1506 in Down of Ulster," Mem began telling me. "I was huge with pregnancy myself, being close to my own time, but out in the wood anyway as I was in need of herbs for another woman's impending birth. This woman had come to me the night before asking for a potion to bring her labor to her, as she said the child had been too long within her. I had given the required potion to her with direction to take it when breaking her fast in the morning, and I knew she was to be delivered soon.

"My husband had recently been lost to me, his precious sea having claimed him for her own. I had begged him not to go that dreadful night, tried to tell him what sign the moon had shown me, but that is another tale mayhap for another time. It meant, however, that I could not send him for these herbs, as I might have. Nor could I rely on his support in the raising of our child. I, most assuredly, could not risk loosing the earnings of my own hands now. So I had gone to do this gathering at a time when I might not have otherwise.

"Darkness had already fallen when I had finally come upon the lus-nam-ban-sith (the fairy woman's plant) I had searched for, the moon's light having not been sufficient to aid me in completing this task, with any kind of swiftness. I always keep this flower with me, as you know, when attending a birth in the case a woman should begin to bleed from within.

"Suddenly I heard men's voices raised in anger and a baby screaming. I recognized one of the voices as belonging to the husband of the woman I was to help this night. I froze and listened in terror, as the cause of their anger became clear, as did their intentions. The husband was furious, for his wife had had a hard labor and I had been absent from my small farm when he had gone there to retrieve me. His voice rose above the others, enraged that I had not been there to help her.

"She had died in the birthing and they had found her then with a fairy child, its fairy heritage being proven by some mark I could not see. I could hear him saying angrily, "See, it is of the fairy", to the other men then again blaming my absence at the birth, as having allowed this horror to happen.

"Their plan unraveled as my terrified mind grasped onto every word. They would leave the child in the clearing just beyond me, on the fairies' knoll, for the fairies to reclaim. Then they would return to my farm and wait for me and he would take his vengeance for his wife's death. Then they would return in the morning and claim the true child, after the fairies had found their mistake and given them back the human child.

"I was frozen with fear as they left my hearing, headed in the direction of my farm. I became even more terrified envisioning what they would do if they found me. Some of the more atrocious ideas they had been voicing began painting horrors in my head.

"Then suddenly I felt my own labor pains come on me. The child on the knoll began screaming to the heavens for a human touch, and I was trying not to make a noise at all. My pains took me hard to my knees and, for what seamed like an eternity, I stayed there waiting for them to subside, but it seemed they would not. I was thinking I must not deliver here, in the wood, where they might find me.

"The abandoned child's cries were destroying every thought I was trying to compose, as I heard them weakening, and knew that it would not survive the night. The cries seemed to do me as much damage as my labor. I managed to get back to my feet and go to it, wondering what about it had made the men so sure it was fairy. Wondering what had given them cause to leave it exposed to the chilling night's cruel hours.

"I came to the knoll and looked down, just as another racking pain dragged me again to my knees. The child was so small and pinched, red and purple blotches of color had risen in its face from crying, but even in my pain it seemed to me that nothing about it was less than human that I could see.

"Its cries were becoming so very weak and I was torn amongst many thoughts: That I should gather my strength and leave this place quickly, gaining as much distance from the men as possible before they returned. I had to give birth to my own child in some relative safety and it was not being patient with these needs. That this child would not survive were it not retrieved by someone with warmth and food soon. Why had my own man been so insistent on going out that fateful night to sea, leaving me now so alone?

"Yet I was most definitely not alone, the child's weakening screams were keeping me constant and painful company. I could not think. With this one crying and my own nearly unendurable pain, my thoughts refused to congeal.

"Then some unconscious urge reared up within me and I gathered it into my arms, without thought. Suddenly all my worries disappeared momentarily as it quieted and cooed and nuzzled my breast. There was a strange moment of quiet within me, an instant of awesome peace.

"This child was you, and you were so small and purple and near to giving up I suddenly wanted to scream at the world, for the strange twists of reasoning that had brought this upon you.

"Then my pain came hard on me again. That same cruel world I was just then abhorring swept back in on me with all its force. I squeezed you to myself, burying my face in the bundling that wrapped you, and finally letting out a scream of my own.

"I brought my own child into the world, but my child did not scream. My child did not even breathe. I held your now calmer form to my chest with my up-drawn knees, holding my own daughter up to examine her.

I put my finger in her throat to see if anything blocked her cries. I frantically shook her that she might wake and breathe for me. I could not understand. Nothing made any sense to me."

I felt myself falling backward into an awful memory: the first day I had ever seen my mother cry. The day she had seemed to not know how to stop. I saw her again, rushing toward me with her swollen eyes, no longer showing their beautiful blue, her swollen face all black and purple, and all the little rivulets of blood. It was not the blood coming from her mouth, though, that scared me so, it was the anguished wet words. She had said that the goddess had turned her eyes from her. She could as well have said death has come for me for the meaning seemed the same.

She had been broken then in heart and body, stumbling blindly, with me tucked up under her chin, into the cold night. I had been bundled quickly against her body from the biting cold, but as she ran with me, a chill still began settling within my young heart. A droplet of her blood had fallen into my hair; it seemed to become rooted there, seeping through my scalp and growing quickly into inescapable fear. My mother kept keening even when I thought she would have no breath to spare, crying out, repeating "Danu!" Making the earth mother's name, that I had been taught to cherish, sound at one point a curse, at another a plea, and still others barely a name at all, merely a sound that became a sob.

I could hear again my father's voice, echoing as it had then, calling down curses and obscenities, damning her for a witch, renouncing her as she refused to renounce the old ways. I could hear the hounds, feel again the fear of being found. I felt once more, as I had then, as my mother had, escaping with me into the bitter and uncertain night: abandoned by any god that ever pretended to care. I was truly alone in a world that had no conceivable concept of fair. Only then I had had my mother.

Mem continued, "I began to sob then even harder, holding my daughter up to the night, praying to any god that would listen for her life, but none did. My daughter was cool and lifeless. I could not shield her. I could not save her. I could not be for her a mother as mine had been for me. Again

I wanted to scream at all of heaven, this time for her. I would have, calling back those awful men, to put me from this world and all it misery.

"You probably saved my life just then. As I felt something wet on my chest, the moisture of my milk had come, and you had found my breast. I looked down in shock, pulling back your covering to view your face while holding my own child away from you, as if I had thought you might bring it further harm. I saw, with uncomprehending eyes, good color coming into you as you quietly fed from me.

"Sometime later, when you were sated and sleeping, I realized I had set my own still child aside and lost myself in watching you. I sat there at that knoll with you and marveled at myself, at my own actions, thinking that I should hate myself, but then I also marveled at you and how anyone could abandon such a small angel and I could not.

"I found that all thoughts of discovery had momentarily been lost, in awe of you. Yes, you were small and wrinkled up, but your hair was thick on your head even then, black as my own, soft curls begging to be smoothed by a mother's hand. I caught myself as my hand moved to your head, smoothing it, realizing my own thoughts.

"Suddenly things came clearly to me, a million swirling thoughts at once. I understood then what had happened. Your mother had not come for the potion because you had grown within her too long. She had come because she needed you to come out from her early.

"I remembered her husband had gone to England some nine months before, having to make his pledge to the King to keep his lands, and had only recently returned. She had obviously played him false in his absence. The rich texture and blackness of the hair under my fingers spurred on my thoughts. So that it would seem you had been conceived a full nine months before, you had paid the cost, being forced from her early by my potion, so her husband would think he had sired you before he had left.

"I did not know whether it was your smallness or your dark hair that he had held out as proof, but I now understood both. Our hair color was rare in that area but made perfect sense if her husband was not your father.

26

I had ideas as to who your sire might truly have been, but I had no time then to consider them. It came back to me suddenly that the men would return, mayhap even before dawn, and I could not be here when they did.

"I was very distraught, heartsick over my own daughter's stillbirth, and not thinking very clearly. My thoughts then were more a jumbled mess than true thoughts, memories and ideas jumping about and forming conclusions. At some point it came to me that I could pass you off as my own, as all had known I was soon to be delivered as well. Then it also came to me it would not matter, as I had to leave this place in any case. Or I would meet with one of the horrible fates I had heard being tossed about, like what should be had for dinner.

"With all these realizations came the one that I knew I would keep you. I knew that I could not now just leave you for the hours and night to claim, not knowing what I knew, not feeling what I felt. You might not have survived it and I *knew* that *I* would not, if I had to leave two children behind for this dreadful night swallow up.

"I named you Angelica and I made you my own. For if all the gods I had prayed to would not give me back my own daughter, they had at least left for me an angel in her place.

"I removed your own bundling from you, replacing it with my shawl. I then wrapped my own still child in it and laid her in your place. My mind had begun working quickly and I knew I could not risk going home. I must go with only what I had. I gathered up my herbs from the brush where I had hidden whilst the men had spoken, and fled with you as fast as my aching body would allow. I came at dawn to the neighboring village and I went around it, keeping well from view. When at last I could go no further, I slept under a tree well into the woods, where none might find me.

"I lived then on berries and whatever else I could find, until I came to a village I felt was far enough removed from my own that none would recognize or remember me. There I went and sold what remedies and herbs I had collected, and bought better food to keep up my strength and yours. I saved what monies remained of these brief stops until I had come to Dublin of

27

Leinster and bought passage then to Scotland.

"The ever-increasing severity of the "witch hunts" of this place being known to me, I knew I must be careful to never be thought of as such. That is the true reason I left Ireland. I did not think of many of the things I should have or could have done back then. I was merely thankful you had survived and I had survived and we were together. I went about the business of daily life, gathering herbs, making poultices and potions, earning my way, and above all raising a happy, healthy daughter. It all began to fade and slowly be put from my head until now.

"Mayhap I should have left you. You may have survived until the men returned, but without a mother's milk and my herbs probably not much longer. I do not know for sure that he would have ever realized he was not your father. But as you've grown I have become more assured he was not, and think he would have as well. I do not know exactly what he may have done or what consequences you would have suffered. I am sure, however, that your true sire would have met a fate far worse than the one they had planned for me, for he could not have escaped being recognized as your sire as the years have progressed in your visage. To this day I can wish that one no harm, but what fate I prevented you, I know not.

"Mayhap I should have at the very least told you these things when you were of an age to comprehend them, but I convinced myself there was no need. Each time the matter rose in my mind I would tell myself it was not the right time. I see now I should have at very least provided you with some choice as to how to proceed with such knowledge."

She sighed again and sat up to better look me in the eye. "You do not have to live with the fear any longer, or pick up and move your life at every drop of the word 'witch.' If you wish, I can direct you to the man I am sure now is your father; for he was also mine, this has become undeniable as you have grown to be so much like me. He denied my mother and hence me, but I choose to think it was only out of fear. These are hard times, especially for those trying to maintain favor with the King, to keep their lands.

"I have not had words with him since I was a child. If you wish, though, I will write for you a letter; mayhap he will accept you. You need only never let him know what you have learned from me that might leave you also named a witch. You can claim your heritage and settle there with a nice young man, hopefully nicer than the one you met yesterday."

She had added that last with a short attempted laugh, and that had made my lips form a smile my mind had no part of. Not because it was not a thing that would be amusing to me, but because my mind hadn't yet gotten to that part of the conversation. I was still somewhere a few sentences behind and trying desperately to catch up, hoping it would all somehow make sense once I had.

My mind was still reeling with all she had told me. I stared at her hands as she knotted them up again in her blanket and I tried to absorb all she had told me, but all I could think was how could she not be my mother? My mother is my sister? I was a foundling found by my own sister? My sister had lost a child and I had never known? It was all too outrageous, like some badly concocted Greek myth I'd have laughed at anyone having ever believed was truth had it not just come from Mem's lips as such. Having no words for what I was feeling, I took her hands into mine and held them; attempting, I think, to settle my thoughts as I settled our hands between us, stopping the twisting of her hands as well as my mind. She again began to cry, raising my hands to her cheek as though begging for forgiveness.

Finally I pulled my hands free and wrapped my arms around her, whispering the only words I had. "Don't cry, Mem." Then, with a short little laugh of my own, I added, "He was quite an ass."

She put her arms around me then as well and we both laughed and cried, slipping easily back and forth between the two. I was thinking things like how we had always laughed and joked more like sisters. How the Fates could play such strange games with people's lives. Understanding was dawning finally, as to why she'd always felt guilt over my unwed state. Yet confusion still reigned over other things, when sleep came to bless me with its comfortable oblivion.

~3~

Changeling

The next day when we awoke, we did not speak of the night before. There was an unspoken agreement between us that in spite of everything there is love and it is enough. She went about her work of making potions and poultices and other healing wares. I went out to gather the herbs and flowers that she had raised me to recognize as those we could use to make them. We could speak more about those things past when the stuff of the present had been seen to. I held her to no blame and she knew it, which was enough for then. So life began as usual that morning, both of us about our daily routines, having no notion how drastically they would be changed or how unusual my life would become.

In my gathering that day I found myself wandering aimlessly, occasionally picking those things that were obvious, much as I allowed my mind to wander and settle on some random thought it found to ponder. I tossed those nearly accidental discoveries of flower or root carelessly into my basket. I was not really hunting them out, or paying the attention to my duties that I should have.

I lost myself in the feel, of the morning-moistened grass between the toes of my bare feet, and the songs the birds offered to me in greeting as I entered their world. My mind floated as freely as the songs they sang, somehow remaining unfettered by the knowledge that the trial of another move was imminent; more interested at the moment in organizing my newfound knowledge of my birth into something mildly resembling a short life history.

So between going over and around everything I had learned the night before and contemplating dew and song birds, it was with a little shock that I realized I had somehow made my way back to the stream that had started it all. I heard the girls before I saw them, but they had already seen me, and it was too late to turn around. There could be no avoiding what I knew was to come.

"What?" one of them called out. "You think you are one of us now? Just because Collin took pity on you and spoke to you yesterday, doesn't mean you can just come here whenever you like."

"It wasn't pity," I threw back.

Too late I realized I was only going to make this worse. Pride does indeed come before a fall.

"You think he would truly want anything to do with a witch?" she said, stalking toward me. "Remove your accursed spell from him."

She was a short girl, a little on the heavy side, with large breasts that were currently puffed up further by her indignation. This wasn't our first meeting and I braced myself for what was sure to be another harsh encounter.

"I am not a witch and it is all beside the point as I want nothing to do with him," I said.

I had spoken just as loud as she had and the other girls began to titter. They reminded me of a bunch of hens waiting for the grain to be thrown. Too late I saw that I was only arousing their fear and hence hatred of me to even greater heights with my angry tone.

"Oh! You're too good for him? You think you're better than we are?" she screamed then.

I think her actions were born of the fear my next words would be a spell and indignation at the thought her perfect Collin was being insulted. Suddenly she lunged forward, tore the basket from my grasp and threw it to the ground. She followed it with her eyes, pride at her own daring and the

31

dawning fear of the possible repercussions showing plainly on her round little face. Then she began to laugh, nervously at first, then with emboldened joy as I too just stared stupidly at the mess.

I don't believe I even thought about it. I just suddenly swung as hard as I could at her laughing face. I remember clearly the rose-colored spot on her cheekbone where my hand seemed to be drawn. My fist was closed, as if of its own accord it had chosen to mimic the men I had seen at the market, striking each other repeatedly while people cheered and placed bets on who would fall down first.

It felt great but hurt as well. I remember looking down at her with her beautiful light blue dress, crumpled up around her thighs, seeing her oh-so-enviable blond hair all in disarray, and feeling wonderful that all of it was splattered with mud from the stream's bank. Feeling wonderful about the look of shocked anger and hurt on her face and the fact that I had put it there. I remember thinking I hoped the blood at the corner of her mouth meant she would lose a tooth. I didn't get to think about it too long, though. All of hell seemed to have been let loose after that and I could not think.

I was hit hard in the side as one of the other girls knocked me down. Pain exploded in my head as it met with something very hard, not the soft mush the other girl had fallen into. Then I realized there was more pain trying to make itself known to me in the red haze of my head. The girls were hitting me and kicking me, and some of them had other things besides their fists and feet to do it with. They were releasing upon me all the pent-up hatred and discrimination caused by being raised during such unenlightened times.

Then it was over; silence closed in on me and suddenly I was thinking again. How it wasn't right that I fell on the hard thing. That the mud had not been there to cushion my fall as it had hers. That now my dress must be just as muddied as hers and my hair just as mussed and dirty. When would it be my turn to receive the fates' favor?

The red haze in my head slowly faded to white and I just kept thinking how it wasn't right and it wasn't fair. How I should have won that fight and the other girls should have stayed out of it. How Mem was going to be very angry I even let it escalate that far. How Collin should never have been here yesterday and Mem should never have to cry. How babies should never be left alone in the night, and finally that the light shouldn't be so bright when I was face down in the mud.

Then I realized I was dying or dead already because I certainly couldn't be breathing this mud, and then nothing was right, and nothing was fair. I knew then with a clarity that nearly broke me that it would never be my turn because the fates didn't care. The fates where just another concept, like fairness and normality, that didn't really exist. The light suddenly felt as though it were pulling me away and that wasn't right either because I didn't want to go anywhere right now. I had grown numb and that was wonderfully comfortable and I had no intention of moving, especially toward something so intrusively bright.

"This can't be the end," I thought.

But the light just got brighter and pulled harder. "I won't go!" I cried out inside my own head, growing angry with its insistence. "I will not let this be all there is. I have to get back to Mem with all the herbs and flowers. I can't die here, like this. I still have too much to learn, too much more life to live. Seventeen summers is not enough. I have to get up and pick up all the flowers. I want to find love someday. I want to see the New World. I want to know things. I want to wash this mud off me."

But the light kept pulling on me.

"No! No!"

I screamed it over and over, enraged now that such a beautiful light could be so deceptively evil. It was vile in its purpose to pull me from this life that I had barely begun. It reminded me of the boy with the beautiful smile and the mean words.

"This can't be the end, I will not believe it!" I raged.

I whirled if you will, within my consciousness, for there is no better way to explain it, turning my inner vision away from this light and what it meant to take me from. I faced then the shadows that were left behind me, which were created by what I now refused to face.

"Then it is not," said a soft, deep voice from the darkness before me.

If I had been in my body then I would have jumped from my own skin, so great was my shock. I tried frantically to see into this darkness and find the owner of that beautiful voice, ready to turn my rage upon it as well, should it too be of a mind to remove me from this world.

"Who are you? What are you? If you are Death, I will not go with you! I will get up!" I cried, frightened yet determined and definitely not in my right mind.

But I could not move to flee either the voice or the light and this injustice too enraged me. To be brought to this state of helplessness made me want to howl at the heavens all the more. I wanted to scream about reality's total disregard for any human sense of cosmic fairness.

"You are correct," said the voice, smooth and caressing, calming me almost instantaneously. "There is no such thing as fair. But there is in you a force of will strong enough to step outside the need to care, and you may forge your own form of fairness from there."

"What? What are you?" I asked.

"Do not fear me, I would never bring you harm," said this beautiful voice. "I merely came in answer to your soul's plea. If you do not choose to accept this as the end, then I will show you how it needn't be, and be your guide on a different path. Yours is a soul which wields a force of will the universe will bend for, *is* bending for even now; the sort of soul that sings to my kind, a song as eternal as we are."

My fear had begun to fade while he was speaking, as had the infuriating pull of the light. Yet I was unsure as to the reason for my level of comfort with the unseen voice, fearing it would be a faceless voice luring me into a hurtful trap rather like a smile spitting hateful words. So I held back the surge of relief that tried to overwhelm me at his confirmation that I need not end my existence here.

"What are you?" I asked again. I searched all my learning for what this voice might be if not Death himself, and I tried to focus my mind's eye in the darkness once more, to distinguish some face for the voice, but my efforts came to naught.

"What I am is known by many names in many places, but the names are of no consequence," he replied. "The abilities we have been gifted with are the thing of import. Yet if you must have a name, I prefer Changeling."

It seemed that I could sense him smiling, and I slowly realized I had unwittingly begun to accept the comfort exuding from him, letting it wash my anger from me. I found I was forgetting my own mistrusting thoughts of mere moments before as it came to me that I was in the spirit, and so then must he be. If his spirit had any malice in it for me, I felt none, and should not I be able to? My fear ebbed as had my anger, but only briefly.

"Like a Bisclavaret, a Garwal?" I said, suddenly slightly fearful again. I had heard tales of such beings, turning from man to half-man or less, mixed with wolf, and losing all sense of themselves. These Lycanthrope or Werewolves were a blight on Mother Earth.

"No, those are a cursed breed, I am something more," he replied.

"I do not understand," I said.

"Come, walk with me, and I will explain things as well as I may."

"But I can't move," I said, turning again my mind's eye to look toward my body.

My spirit shrank back appalled, as I saw myself in this new way, looking down from above, seeing the broken and bleeding form that I had made mine for as long as I could remember. I was fearful again. No longer did I even think to fear this unseen voice or its intent; now I feared for me, for my state.

"I can't move," I repeated. "I can't…"

A new sadness began to envelop me, and I felt a slight tugging of the light upon me, in response to it. Then I felt his presence come close beside me, even before I heard his voice, near to where my ear should have been.

"Will you give up now? Where is that will that told heaven it must wait?" he said.

I felt his soul then, and knew it to be strong and beautiful, somehow

35

wonderful and familiar. I could not think then why I had ever thought not to trust him, as it surrounded me and then for one brief moment became one with mine. Then he was beside me again, his presence an even greater comfort than it had been before.

"Now," he said. "Make it happen. Tell those parts of the universe that are yours to rearrange themselves, fixing the form they make up and stand themselves up."

"I don't understand." I said. I was feeling like a child, once more at Father Paul's knee, begging for an explanation.

"Do you believe me?" he asked very softly.

"Yes," I replied honestly. "But I do not understand."

He seemed to sigh and then he said, "I can see merely believing will never be enough for you, you will be forever about the why of things, won't you?"

He laughed then and what I felt, on hearing it, was unspeakably beautiful and comforting to me. "We are all made up of the same things," he continued. "We are all energy held together by will: the universe, that rock under your head, your body. You made that energy bend to your will when you refused to go into the light, the light's will being that you go with it. Your will proved to be the stronger force.

"When you chose to begin this life, your soul exuded a kind of magnetism over the universe," he said. "As it came into this realm, it bonded itself to its first small piece of that energy. That original piece is your 'Yelm,' as I call it, or your anchor in this world. As your will to be or live grew, so did that magnetism. More of this energy was drawn to you as you grew, seeking to 'live,' if you will, by being part of you, and one with your soul. It bowed to your will, to be a part of something."

He laughed a little again then continued. "Now all you have to do, in essence, is tell that energy that was yours, that it is yours still, a part of you that must obey you. You have the will, I have seen it, heard it, as the beauty of it sang to me."

He seemed to smile again then. "I know this is a lot to take in, but obviously you are not one to go on my simple word and 'fix it' as I told you."

I sensed his amusement and I also was amused, realizing I had wanted things explained in detail all my life. If you said the sky was blue, I would say, "yes, but why is that?" Mem had always said I was strong-willed, and lived too much for the questions. She would be laughing at me now, or maybe not. I left this train of thought for a better one.

"So we do not ever have to die?" I asked.

I was more than amused, I was happy, no, ecstatic, with no words for how much. Mayhap it was my turn after all.

"Not so long as you have the will to live, but come, walk with me in reality. You will find that same will to live which makes us survive the light, also makes us dislike this form of non-being, which is being absent from our bodies." He paused briefly, then added, "Do you believe me?"

"Yes," I replied again.

I might ask a lot of questions, but that didn't lessen my faith in his answers.

"Then you have all you need. Now let us walk," he said.

"But where's your body?" I asked, realizing I could see no one else below me other than myself.

"Do not worry about my form, worry about yours," he said, and then he was gone.

I felt suddenly alone and I missed the comfortable company his soul had provided me. I looked in wonder at my body for a moment, thinking about all he had said.

Then I did it. I told my body to stand up and right itself, and looked on in awe from this strange perspective. It stood up and my mouth and head ceased bleeding, and the scrapes and cuts closed themselves.

Then I willed myself back into my body, and this in and of itself was even more astounding, because it took not even the forming of the whole thought, and there was no pain in me. I felt great to be 'home.'

"Where are you?" I called out.

My mouth felt foreign yet familiar at the same time. I had a new awareness of myself and the energy coursing through my body, making it up, of the air I forced from lungs to make the words.

Then I felt a strange pull. It felt much like the light had, but more like something wanted my parts, my energy or body, not my soul. Instinctively I told them to remain with me, and I felt them obey.

Suddenly he took form before me and I knew it was he. He was as familiar to me as my own soul. I wondered only briefly if this was because of our souls' bonding, no matter how briefly, when we had been in the spirit.

~4~

Greek God

"My apologies," I said.

It was the only thing I could think to say. I looked down at my dirty and bare feet, embarrassed I had been caught staring. I was feeling like a silly milkmaid who had never laid eyes on a man before.

He started laughing then, and it was a wonderful sound, it cut through all the anger and pain of the last twenty-four hours, and made me forget it all. Suddenly the stress of life was lifted like a great burden from my shoulders, as I too began to laugh. We stayed like that for a while, the perfectly dressed and well-manicured gentleman and the bedraggled and muddy barefoot girl.

Visions I had pictured as Father Paul had spoken while giving me my various lessons had been given perfect form before me. All male deities I had ever envisioned were blended together and made flesh all at once. Here was jet black hair, shiny and cropped short, falling forward flat against his forehead. Perfect onyx orbs perched in a fringe of lashes any girl I'd ever known would have cheerfully killed for. Here were high arching brows, hovering over a perfect straight nose which pointed out amazingly full lips. These lips now twitched in a strong, squared jaw, under cheekbones that were so high and pronounced, that they left a slight hollow between his cheek and jaw line, which dimpled slightly as he grinned at me. Here was a Greek god if ever there had been one.

"That's not really how you look, is it?" I asked suddenly, as a suspicion began to grow in me, that maybe this Greek god was too perfect.

"Yes, it is." He said it almost as though I had insulted him and, looking down at himself, apparently checked for flaws. "I have looked like this since the year 340, when Alexander the Great ruled my world, excepting the change in wardrobe, of course."

"340?" I repeated aghast. "Alexander the Great?"

"Do you really look like that?" he said, pointing at my torn and soiled skirt, and ignoring my shock.

"Ye gods, you're old!" I looked him up and down again, trying to make it all work in my head.

"Why thank you," he said sarcastically, bowing over his arm in a manner unknown to me. "Now fix your dress."

"In the same way?" I wasn't sure if the control I had over my own being extended to my clothing as well.

"Yes, it is a part of you, in that it is in contact with you and made up of the same energy. You have no power over that tree to change it," he said, pointing at an old oak in the field behind me. "Or the stream," he said, pointing to my left at the stream where my life had so recently altered course. "You cannot make it do other than it does, you cannot change the direction of its flow. You can, however, borrow energy or substance from all of it, drawing it to yourself and making it a part of you or your clothing. Everything is energy, just remember that, or shall I explain it better?" he said, then laughed again, having fun with it.

"How do I do that?" I asked.

"Do what?" he laughed.

"The drawing energy from them?" I replied, trying not to get sidetracked by being drawn into his laughter.

"You will it, just as you willed your own parts to mend themselves. Your will is the stronger force. Yours being a more powerful magnetism, the universe will bend as it did back there." he said, nodding his head in the direction of the stream.

He had an odd way of making me think of Father Paul and my mother, as I will always think of her. So adept was he, at turning from the laughing comrade to the earnest teacher, then back again. One moment intent on making all these things clear to me, the next making light of the fact he had done so. I took it then, as everything else he told me, and stored it in my mind. With little effort I did as I was told I could, and fixed my clothing. I was still admiring my handiwork, when he turned to move past me, gesturing as he did so for me to follow him.

He did not compliment my ability when I had finished, or even look at me again for a while; he seemed lost in his own thoughts. I took it as a good thing he didn't feel he needed to check my work, knowing I would have done it and well. I fell into step beside him as we began walking toward the old oak tree, in the field he had pointed out just a moment before.

In some recess of my mind I knew that this would be highly frowned upon. Wandering off with some strange man you'd barely met was not an accepted practice for a young woman. But he neither felt like a stranger to me nor did I fear he would do me any of the harms to be feared by a young lady putting herself in such a position. Of course there was also the fact that I was very used to being frowned upon as well.

We walked in silence for a moment as I tried to digest all that he had told me, this being mixed in with all the other recently revealed things in my life, combining to make it quite some time before I realized something else: that though I felt I had known him all my life, I didn't even know his name.

I felt rather awkward then, as I was trying to think how to ask. I was saying to myself, *"Good sir, though I'm walking alone with you, to some unknown destination… what is your name?"* The English accent my inner monologue sometimes used when I was nervous or found myself in a stressful situation and the absurdity of it all made me feel a round of giggles coming on. I think I might have been very close to what is now referred to as a nervous breakdown, but entirely too distracted to care.

Then it came to me to say simply, "My name is Angelica, but Mem sometimes calls me Angel."

I was thrown off when rather than telling me his name in return, as I had hoped, he made a strange comment.

"Yes, it would be," he said. Before I could think too much of the possible reasons for his response he added more appropriately, "I am Demosthenes, but Baylor calls me Demon."

He had pronounced it *Day-moan*, making the *d* sound more like *th*. He made his introduction with a repeat of his strange bow, and I abandoned all other thoughts for one that made me, quite suddenly and unexpectedly, laugh outright.

He looked up at me then, confused by my obvious mirth. "What is so amusing?" he asked.

"A Demon and an Angel took a walk in a field, and talked about the universe and how to control it," I said, in my best and most proper English, as if beginning a tale for him. He didn't seem to understand until I pronounced his name as he had "Day-moan" then again as "Demon," and he too began to laugh.

We walked along comfortably. I felt quite at ease with him, as if I were simply taking a long walk with Mem. We each slipped into our own worlds for a time. I was enjoying the feel of the sun, my black hair absorbing the heat, when another thing occurred to me about the longer version of his name. Delving into the chest of knowledge bestowed upon me by Father Paul, I found its origins.

"So you *are* Greek!" I said, triumphantly, as I recalled my earlier private comparison of him to a Greek god. Suddenly realizing how that might lead him to guess at that previous train of thought or cause him to ask why this should have pleased me, I added, "That is how they bow, isn't it?"

"Yes," he replied, sobering, "though not so much now."

I was quite pleased with myself for having covered my tracks so well, until I thought that he might ask me how I could have known this. It had been a bluff, for I had not and hoped fervently he wouldn't ask. It dawned on me then, noting the sadness in his voice, how truly old he was despite his youthful appearance, and how much loss he must have suffered in that time. Not only his entire family would have aged and passed on, but his entire world. I felt awful suddenly, for being so happy, and I looked for something to talk about that might not remind him of the past.

Then my mind flew backwards again. "Baylor? Who is Baylor?"

He thought for a moment before answering me, which seemed odd when he answered simply, "A friend, you will meet him."

I didn't want to stay too long with this, or cause him to remember any possible disturbing things that could be responsible for his brief pause. My mood was too good, the day too beautiful, to be spent in solemn contemplation. So I quieted for the moment, until I might think of some safer thing to discuss.

We had reached the tree that had been our apparent destination and he motioned for me to sit with him, so I did. Leaning up against it and gazing upwards he soon pointed out to me a small sparrow-sized female crossbill, with feathers a dull greenish yellow.

"Do you see how delicate she is, how light?" he said. "Be like her."

"Be delicate and light?" I asked, very confused now and trying to decide if I should take insult.

"No!" he laughed. "Be the bird."

I was still confused but at least I knew now I had not been insulted.

"Be a bird! But she is so small," I said.

He sighed again and smiled his amusement. "Envision yourself as the bird. Tell most of the energy that is yours to control to leave you for now, keeping your Yelm. Never, ever, discard your Yelm, for it is your anchor. Keep also whatever else you need to attain her shape, and become like her. Tell the energy left to make for you a form like hers."

I took this too for storage, and did as he had said. Then suddenly I found myself, for the second time that day, viewing the world from a new perspective. I now found myself breast-deep in grass that had moments before barely been able to tickle my ankles. I looked up at him to exclaim my wonder and all that came from me was a chirp. This amazed me all the more

43

and I wanted to share my excitement, to tell him how wondrous it was.

Suddenly I was sitting beside him as myself, saying, "…is amazing!"

He started laughing again and I was in even more shock, if that was possible, that I was again human.

"Don't do that when you're flying," he said when he could finally talk again. "It hurts."

"Don't do what, what did I do?" I exclaimed. "Why am I human again, I didn't *make* myself human again."

"Yes you did," he said, smiling, and again explaining, "you wanted to speak to me, to speak to me you had to be human, and your energies responded to your wants. That is actually a very good thing if carefully controlled, and an impressive response time from your energies as well."

"Oh!" I was still thinking about this when he told me to try again, and this time to think about how my wings worked, and to try to fly.

The flying was not as easy as the changing, I must add, and I was becoming quite frustrated as I kept hopping into the air with little success. Finally I tired of listening to his laughter and once more I resumed my natural form and punched him in the arm playfully. "You are enjoying this far too much," I said. "What are you not telling me?"

"I apologize," he laughed again, appearing not in the least genuine. "It's just so…so..," he fell off, obviously at a loss for how amusing he'd found it, and simply began laughing again.

"Why can't I do it? Stop laughing, tell me!" I was trying not to laugh myself, his laughter was so contagious, but at the moment I was on a mission and he was keeping something from me that would help me complete it.

"All right! All right, I give!" he said, holding his hands up to ward off any further blows, as I raised my fist threatening to punch him again. "When you are thinking of the bird and being her, think also of having her natural instincts. Like how to use your wings and understand which calls mean danger is near, or there's food here."

"Ohh! You're awful!" I said, and punched him anyway. I quickly took my newly-learned form and flew away before he could catch me. Which, I tell you, didn't work very well, as he too took the form, only with the bright orange-red plumage of the male of the species, and flew after me. He never came so close as to harm me, or force me from the sky, but always close enough to let me know he could.

We played like this well into the afternoon, pausing only to eat some berries he led me to. I became quite easy with this change and it felt more natural as the day wore on. I think he soon noticed my confidence, and felt the lesson was ready to be ended, for he led me back to the tree and there resumed his form.

"Come down now and talk with me," he said.

He had changed his attire to suit our surroundings a little better. Now he sat in a worn kilt of mostly blue and green shot through with yellow, bare feet and a loose shirt open across his chest. He looked just as comfortable in the attire of a peasant as he had in that of an English gentleman. He reminded me of Collin then, the boy at the stream, and I pushed this thought from me quickly, knowing in my heart Demon would never be so cruel. He might enjoy a good laugh at my expense, but never by virtue of bringing me pain.

I returned to the tree and I too resumed my natural form and sat beside him. We rested with our backs against the old oak. I could feel its rough bark against my back, through the soft linen of my blouse. Smelling the fresh clean scent of him and of the air itself, all my senses were alive. I was assailed by a great feeling of joy at just being. At last I spoke, as he seemed to be mulling too much over what to say, and saying nothing.

"You said you heard my soul call to you. Were you far away?" I asked.

"Yes," he said simply.

Again there was a long pause.

"Did you come by flying then?" I tried again.

"No, at my age, with great distance, it is sometimes easier to simply throw off the burden of form, traveling more quickly incorporeal, and

45

drawing to yourself a new form when you have arrived."

"At your age, sir," I mocked playfully. "One would think you'd be long dead and buried."

"That, you wretched little poppet, is not what I meant." He grinned, slight dimples appearing suddenly to charm me. "I meant that with greater age comes greater power over, or stronger magnetism with the universe and all its energies. It seems to slowly lessen its resistance to us; either that or we simply become less aware of it. We can hear a call such as yours from a greater distance. Also we can abandon our energies knowing we can exude enough force at our destination to pull together a new form when we will. So it is simply a quicker way to travel." He elbowed me lightly, "My age," he repeated, then snorted.

"Then that was the pull I felt at the stream before you appeared," I said as realization dawned.

"Yes," he replied.

Again, silence. Something was bothering him, I could tell.

"Were you at home then, when you heard me?" I said, as I tried again to start a conversation.

"Yes and no," he smiled. "I was with Baylor, hunting; we are going to have roasted rabbit tonight."

So that was it. Suddenly it occurred to me that he was planning on my remaining with him for dinner, and didn't know how to ask. I was stunned and began trying to think of a delicate way to decline. He had done me a great service this day, saving my life, or rather giving me a new one. I didn't want to seem ungrateful, but I had to return home soon.

"I would love to have dinner with you, it sounds delicious, but I must be returning to Mem soon with all her herbs and flowers," I explained, hoping he would not be insulted.

"You can't think you can just run home each night, after your lessons with me, and none will be the wiser," he said, sadly. "You are different now, not even human, and someone will surely notice. You do not yet know anything you must learn to survive amongst the normal humans without them knowing you are changed. You are one of us now, part of a new family."

His answer shocked me. I had not considered any of this. It wasn't just for dinner, it was for the rest of my life, or something like that.

"How will they know?" I said.

I was stubbornly trying to deny what I was at the same time realizing I knew in my heart to be true. My own mind began spitting answers at me long before he could have, and much more vehemently. I knew very well I could not just go home tonight and everything would return to normal. First I was not a human child but a fairy's spawn, then not my mother's daughter but rather her sister, and now I had come full circle back to not even human at all. As it all began to sink in, I must have bowed a little with the weight of it, because he put his arm around me to comfort me.

Then he said, "You could fall and cut yourself and without your even meaning to, heal by will of a thought you didn't realize you'd had. Just as when you changed from bird to woman to speak to me. Now that your mind knows it can do these things, they can occur due to a subconscious will. You must learn more fully what you are, what we are, and how to control such things, and that takes time."

"I do not mean to sound harsh, or put this on you so suddenly," he said softly. "I wanted to find a way to tell you which would make it easier for you to accept. I can tell you truly though, it is far better than being found out, and having your own people turn against you in their fear."

These were all things I think I had already seen. I thought then of some accident such as he described, leading to both Mem and myself being put on trial as witches. My mind shrank back from the thought of any harm being brought down on her due to any action of mine. Just the fact I had brought her to tears by forcing my pains upon her the evening before was more than I wanted to have ever been responsible for. She had survived so much misguided abuse in her life already. I could not bear to be the cause of any further suffering by somehow confirming and reinforcing the people's worst fears. Mem would never be made to suffer if I might in any way

47

prevent it. My shoulders began to shake slightly as tears of realization found their way into my eyes.

"Come with me and let me be your guide in this new life," he whispered.

He gave my arm a squeeze, pulling me closer, and I felt more than just the nearness of his body as my head came down on his shoulder. I felt a closeness of our souls and I was again very aware of the strange comfort his mere presence gave me. I knew then, and accepted it. I would go with him. I had to. Not only because I would never want to draw the Church's or the people's undue attentions down on Mem. Not even simply to be with him as my mentor, because it was necessary. I realized, I think even then, that my soul would give me no choice; it had found its flower, and would not now leave it by the wayside. Love had been planted, with or without my conscious knowledge, and it would bloom. It would just take me a while longer to recognize and accept it.

"There is one thing I must do first," I whispered. He sighed and gave me a soft smile as he heard my acquiescence.

"What is that?" he asked.

"I must take Mem her flowers."

~5~

Foxglove

I explained to him what I needed to do and waited under the tree for him to return with pen and parchment for me. It had taken me some time, but I had decided this would be the best way to leave Mem. She would know it was by choice and not by force. I wanted to put her mind at ease, but I could not bear to see her cry were I to tell her face-to-face that I must leave. Nor could I chance an accidental discovery that could bring harm on her, by some mistake on my part.

He had said that I could tell her that we had met somehow, fallen in love, and we were going off to be married. I had told him that Mem would never fall for that. As he had noted himself, I was not one to go without questioning things, and neither was she. I had said that even if she did believe, due to the mere fact she had wanted to hear it for so long, it would only lead to more troubles. She would surely haul out the broomstick then and there. That is when I told him I could take no risk, as her actions were already very questionable in many eyes, and he must carry this plan out for me.

All things considered, I could find no better way, and though it pained me greatly, I told myself I would return when I was sure no harm could come of it. I could still feel Demon's presence beside me, as if the tree had retained something of him, and I leaned back against it to take what comfort that came.

I felt his return as I saw a large white owl come into view with my basket. He had retrieved this from the stream bank, and held it clutched in his talons. He dropped the basket gently to the ground. Then with a slight pull, drew enough extra energy to become himself again. He didn't say anything, as I pulled from it a small piece of parchment, quill and small ink pot he had found for me.

Then at last he said, "Do you need anything else?"

It was nearing dark now and I told him the last thing I would need.

"The what?" he had asked me, in confusion.

"The fairy woman's plant," I translated. "You might know it better as foxglove."

At that he had nodded and, as he went off to get it for me, I began the unwanted sadness of telling my mother good-bye.

The basket of herbs and flowers, with a letter and the foxglove on top of it, was the first thing she saw. She had opened the hut's small door the following morning and the owl in the tree above it would have sworn she knew even before she read the letter. She had picked up the foxglove and held it like a child. Eyes swollen, with obvious lack of sleep and tears, gazed on it with love.

Then she had read:

My Dearest Mother of My Heart,

I pray you know my love for you has diminished not in the slightest of amounts, and my memories of you will never be tainted with anger, for what you did, you did with pure heart and love for me. You have been to me   the best mother a child could call out to heaven for, and I hold no contempt for the manner in which you became that mother.

Know also that though my path in life has been irrevocably altered, and no longer follows yours, that I do not turn away from you, but turn now only as a new

and wondrous course is shown me. You have taught me
well and I will hold those teachings dear now, as I allow
my proud wandering heart to guide my feet.

        With My Eternal Love, Your Daughter, Your Sister, Yours,
Angelica

    It wasn't until she had read the letter through twice that her
shoulders began to straighten and she seemed to make peace with the flower,
placing it just within the doorway on a pillow of clothing that hadn't been
slept on the night before, and closing the door.

    The owl flew off then, silent as it had come, and any that marked its
passage or thought it odd that it was out by day, went unnoticed by it. It was
lost deep in its own thoughts.

    When Demon returned to me that morning, telling me all that he had
seen and done and thought, a little of the guilt was lifted from me. I knew
then that she had accepted, if not fully understood, what I had chosen to do,
seeing that I had decided to leave her only to pursue a new and wonderful
life.

    "You seem to have an odd way of bringing comfort," he had said to
me.

    It seemed an odd thing for him to say of me, for though I had
thought it of him many times, I didn't see how it could be thought of me at
that moment. I said nothing, walking silently with my own thoughts,
wondering if mayhap I should have done it differently. I supposed he might
have said it merely to urge me forward by simple virtue of hearing and
following the sound of his voice.

    We began to walk away from the small bracken of trees we had
made camp in the night before, leaving behind all I knew and the woman that
had made me hers seventeen years before.

    "You were well-named, though no ordinary Angel," he said. "It fits
you. Why foxglove?"

For the first time I considered that maybe I was not the only one who drew comfort from our being together. Then I thought he may have only been referring to what he saw of my mother's response to my form of good-bye, so I made no remark. I began instead to look at all the animals I caught glimpses of here and there as we passed, trying to save a picture of each one in my mind.

I realized I was not being companionable in my silence, and that he had tried to begin a conversation, asking me a question in an effort to return to the easy friendship we had shared yesterday. I told myself this was a new adventure, just another move. That I should treat it as a gift, not a curse, as I had before I'd realized I must leave Mem. I told myself lots of women left their families to begin new lives and I should put my chin up and enjoy this. The mental self-scolding began to work and my mood also started to lift.

"Because she was looking for it when she found me; now I have given it to her in my stead," I said, finally answering him.

"You are a foundling then?" he asked.

"Yes," I said, "in a sense."

"Please explain," he said with a little laugh.

I too found the irony in that he was now the one asking for explanations. So I told him what I myself had only just recently learned. Once I had begun talking, I was quickly through feeling sorry for myself. I was a very blessed individual and knew it well. When I had finished my tale, I realized I too had explaining I wanted done, and now was as good a time for questions as any.

So I said then, "Can anyone resist the light and become one of us? There must be hundreds of us."

"No," he replied. "Not really, there are a few of us, but ever since the rise and wide spread acceptance of Christianity, most go willingly into the afterlife. For they have been told a loving God awaits them with rewards and a life in paradise. Even before that it was a rarity to find a soul that refused to accept that its time here was over. Some know no better than to meekly accept whatever life hands them, even be it death."

We had walked for miles the night before, and many more already today. I had no real concept of how far we were from where it had all began, but the scenery was slowly changing. The familiar rolling fields of heather were becoming more hilly and rocky as we went. I was still considering his answer when he continued.

"Not all are chosen, even if they do resist," he said. "If I had found your soul to be evil, or your purpose for continued life to be vile, I would have left you."

He said this with such purpose that I had no doubt of it.

"What would have happened then?" I asked.

"You either would have given up eventually, and gone into the light, to face whatever judgment awaited," he replied, "or the light would have given up, and you would have been in the spirit then, left here without form until something happened to bring the light again to you."

He paused then to climb up unto a rock, as our path had taken us to the rocky foot of a mountain. I knew then that we had come officially into the Highlands. I had never more than looked at these mountains as a view on the horizon, and I realized we had left all I had known far behind. He reached down to offer me his hand and I took it, amazed by his easy strength as he pulled me up beside him.

"You live up here in the Highlands?" I asked, trying to divert my mind from thoughts of strong hands. I might have been seventeen, but I was still very inexperienced with where my thoughts might be trying to go. This was made even more disturbing to me, coupled as it was with the fact we were alone and he was still holding my hand.

He said simply, "Yes," and, releasing my hand, he turned to continue slowly upwards.

"So it is you who chooses to change them? They can't just change?" I continued, trying to return us to our previous topic, as soon as my mind would go back to it.

"Well, both are necessary really," he replied, "the person with the will for change and the Changeling with the changed soul. A changed soul blends with the soul of the willful one and it is then changed as well. Without this blending the energy that *is* form will no longer recognize the soul as something to form around."

He paused again briefly, then said, "The Changeling that hears a call such as yours would decide if the soul wishing to remain were worthy."

"And so evil Changelings are never made?" I said, working to keep up as the way became steeper.

"They are not supposed to be, not under the Code." He seemed not the least affected by the climb, nor did he sound as though he believed the Code prevented it completely.

"What is the *Code?*" I asked.

"It is a set of laws, set down by a Council of Elder Changelings in Rome," he said, smiling to himself, obviously reflecting on something amusing. "'That we may live peacefully with humanity…chirp," he intoned this with a gusto that made me think that he must have heard it much the same way. Then continuing in his normal tone, he added, "They are important, some of them anyway, and it would be nice if they were followed."

"Like the Ten Commandments then," I said, understanding. "Tell me them."

"Well, I can give you some of the better points but… 'One should never force a soul to become a Changeling should it wish to go, or bring harm to a human to force them to choose between staying or going,'" he laughed. "This is not a perfect translation, by the by, the Code is old, and very long-winded, like most of the Elders themselves. "'One should never take from another Changeling those parts that make it whole,'" he continued, still smiling, "'Never mix forms or invent forms. Never allow it to be known what you are to any, other than those being changed. Never change the mad or deranged. Never change the vile and wicked. Never bear children.' A few more, blah, blah, chirp, chirp," he ended, expressing an obvious lack of interest in the rest.

"Wait!" I interrupted, panting my way up to a stop beside him, "why not?"

"Why not, which one?" he laughed, stopping also and looking at me.

"The 'no children' one," I said, trying to catch my breath, as this had been one long hard hike, and I was not unused to long walks.

"What would you give birth to?" he asked. "As a Changeling you take many forms; what would the offspring be? Besides," he added, "it's never been done, to my memory, which goes back quite far, as you have enjoyed reminding me. I wonder if a new soul would even attach itself within a Changeling?"

This seemed to intrigue him, and he turned then, walking again up the hillside, apparently lost in thought and still smiling. I was wondering how I should feel about this new knowledge, that I could never have a family and bear children of my own, when I realized I had fallen quite behind.

"Wait, slow down, Demon!" I yelled.

He stopped then, finally hearing me; either that or finally choosing to acknowledge my calls. He turned with amusement still openly written on his face, and a suspicion began to grow in me.

"All the smiles and laughter, there is something else amusing you, what are you not telling me this time?" I asked.

"Nothing, it is only that I would have expected you to be trying out all the new animal forms you can take now," he replied. "It would be easier."

"But then we couldn't talk," I cut in, finally panting to a stop beside him again.

"Like that goat," he continued, pointing up the hillside, and ignoring me. "It's not panting!"

He slapped my arm playfully with the back of his hand as he turned and bounded forward. Changing so smoothly that, just as his hands should have touched the ground, they became hooves and propelled him swiftly up the side of the mountain.

"Aghh!" I huffed, as I too changed and took after him.

The day and the journey passed quickly then, with his leading me steadily upwards, and my simply enjoying the feel of four strong legs carrying me sure-footedly along. By mid-afternoon we were half-way to the top. He had stayed slightly ahead of me most of the day. Once more I found myself allowing my mind to wander, mulling over all of the recent events.

He had made his way to a beautiful clear spring, wonderfully hidden in a copse of trees. These were growing stubbornly out of the side of the mountain, holding on for dear existence, much as I had done the day before. I marveled at their will, remembering what he had taught me of all things' will to survive. I was seeing things in a new and amazing way that left me in awe of the smallest of details.

Once there, I watched as he turned back into himself. Cupping his hands under the surface of the water and leaning forward to take a drink. I felt a strange raw joy at just being alive to bear witness to such things. Suddenly I felt a childlike impulse and I could not resist the urge. To be honest, I don't think I even thought to try. He may have forgotten as the day passed, but I had not. Slipping quietly up behind him, I lunged, pushing his head into the water.

"You're the wretched one!" I yelled triumphantly.

He came up sputtering and laughing, throwing water over his shoulder at me. I began laughing as well, feeling wonderful and extraordinarily alive. I think I had never felt so many wonderful things at once. I think that moment was my closest brush with what one would call a happy childhood memory.

"It did go easier, did it not?" he said finally, as we sat facing each other, still dripping, by the stream.

"Yes, it did," I admitted. "But you could have just as well said 'we can talk about this when we stop for a drink,' rather than amusing yourself at my expense."

"Yes, well, it's always good to practice every new form you encounter; you never know when it could become useful. And of course," he added, "it's always good to laugh."

With that he fell forward into the water, disappearing as he went. I leaned forward to look for him. I could feel his presence was near, but I could not see him. I had a suspicion, though, that he just might be of a mind to appear, and pull my face into the water in payment for my earlier trick. So I didn't therefore lean too far forward.

Suddenly I saw a small fish dart into view, and then I was staring at his calves, water dripping from him onto the top of my head, and I heard him say, "You're no fun."

"Just too smart for you," I said, looking up at him, as my thoughts were confirmed.

"Well come in anyway, you might as well try being a fish. At least there are no sharks here." He took the defeat only somewhat gracefully, and again disappeared.

"Sharks?" I thought, but followed this time, and again time passed swiftly.

I enjoyed the feel of the water on my scales and the pull of the water through my gills. I thought then how it was a good thing he had told me earlier to include some of the creature's instincts in the change; because I would have drowned, while being absorbed in the feeling of gliding through the water, and forgetting then to breathe. I loved the water and did not want to leave it. Swimming had always been a joy to me, even as a normal girl.

Later as we sat again on the bank, letting the dying rays of the sun dry our hair and clothes naturally, I asked him, "What brought you to live here?" I gestured with a nod of my head meant to indicate not only these Highlands, but also all of Scotland itself.

"That is a long story, and one probably better told by Baylor. Why don't you ask him when we are all well met and fed?"

At the mention of food I was reminded that I had eaten not much more than berries as a bird. On those three occasions, when I'd been left to my own devices, I had kept myself busy learning various bird forms, eating what delectable little treats my bird instincts led me to, while waiting for Demon's return.

As he'd gone to accomplish the tasks I'd set him to, before I would leave with him, I had busied myself with the perfecting of them to avoid brooding on what I was about to do.

Now the thought of the roasted rabbit he had mentioned the day before caused my stomach to begin rumbling.

"Well, I can see we'd best be about getting home," he said laughing, as we both looked toward my belly.

~6~

Odin

We left the spring just after sunset, after sitting quietly for a time and enjoying the view. The sun had dropped like a tired child from the sky, into Mother Earth's comforting arms, to sleep through the night. I thought then that I had become a sponge, absorbing all things, even as the great mother did. For I wanted to keep it all forever; every wonderful thing I had heard and learned, every amazing sight I had been blessed to view, all of it that should have now been beyond me but would now be a part of me forever. I was in love with being alive.

As we took to a path, marked only in Demon's memory, the moon arose nearly full, a bloated greenish-gray orb, come to keep us company. I was tired and hungry, and again chose to make my way as a goat, hoping this last bit would pass more quickly in this manner and I wouldn't be so aware of these now more trivial things.

It was still a few hours till midnight but a chill was setting in. Not only our newly achieved elevation but the moon's lesser heat caused the earth to cool. I found that I was glad of the goat's thick coat. Demon had emerged from the stream, after our lesson in swimming as a fish, clad as before, still wearing only a worn kilt and a simple white shirt.

I was beginning to wonder whether or not it provided any warmth at all, or if he was simply not bothered by the cold, when suddenly our steadily upward track turned into a flat grassy expanse, dotted here and there with a stubborn tree or boulder. We had reached a plateau which went a few hundred meters before the mountain again went straight up ,and I forgot about the chill, and his kilt, as I was suddenly awestruck.

Of course I was very aware, with the goat in me, of the bountiful supply of sweet grasses. More so, though, was my woman's mind, thinking how a great house should stand here. Built to nurture its inhabitance with its beautiful setting, taking in the glory of the sunset I'd witnessed from below for an eternity. Reminding any that ever stood where I did now, that surely there is a God, and he is most definitely an artist.

I followed Demon as he walked in silence across its depth, toward the sheer face that ended it. I had begun to wonder how we would continue up, whether we would fly or if he would reveal yet another hidden path, when the face of the mountain began to move. I stepped back in shock and wonder as what had appeared to be a sheer rock face turned out to have an entry-way. Behind this well-hidden door stood Odin, with his hair on fire.

That was truly my first impression, as my religion-soaked mind reached desperately for an explanation. They do last, first impressions, and as the largest man I had ever seen came out from the cave with its cleverly fashioned entrance, I knew then I had now stood before two gods. He was a full head *and* shoulders taller than I was and I am not short, standing to five foot and seven inches when myself. Now granted the first impression was received from the perspective and stature of a goat, but that made him no less massive in truth.

His hair was a huge mass of red and gold catching light from the interior of the cave. This gave the impression his hair was ablaze. It was full of mixed sizes of braids. Bits of it were tied with leather thongs. Some of it was simply loose strands, but all were falling well past his shoulders and blending into his beard, which was done in much the same way.

I say "done" not because it appeared that way to me by any means, but because I came to learn later that he wasn't inattentive to his hair and beard. He meant for it to be this way. It wasn't unattractive; by any means, to my way of thinking it was rather quite a pretty mess. He was clothed much as Demon was, in the same worn plaid and holding a large wooden spoon. Not exactly what I thought the god Odin would have had in hand, but I'm sure you can see the cause of my sudden inability to move.

"You nearly missed the feast of rabbit, Demon." His voice was the deep baritone expected, only not as loud as I would have thought. "But I see you've brought a goat."

At this I bleated, jumping backwards and sideways. Odin, as I was still thinking of him, raised an eyebrow, looking askance at Demon, as I too looked to Demon for protection from this hungry god.

"This is Angel," Demon said, gesturing toward me without looking back, and I felt a surge of relief.

"You named the goat?" came back the confused baritone.

"No? Oh! Great gods, Angel, remember yourself, please." he said, turning to look at me, as I stood there on four shaking legs. "This is my friend, Baylor."

Relief and embarrassment collided headfirst within me, so it was that a red-faced, barefoot young girl appeared. Now it was Baylor's turn to jump back.

"Gods, you two!" Demon seemed torn between smacking some sense into the both of us and falling down in a fit of laughter.

It took him a moment to settle with amused disapproval before saying, "Baylor, you act as though you've never seen a change, and you," He turned on me then, and adjusted the level of disapproval, so it now far outweighed the amusement. "You can never freeze up like that, that was too much instinct and not enough good human common sense, which can get your body killed." He then softened his tone, adding, "He can be rather intimidating, though."

So it was that I met Baylor. Though our introduction was highly irregular, we were at last "well-met," as Demon had put it, and soon to be well-fed.

Baylor ushered us into the cave, which was no dingy cramped hole in

61

the earth. It was rather a huge well-lit cavern, much like a huge throne room of stone. Demon strode in, and feeling quite obviously back at home, threw himself face down across a chaise lounge. This sat to the left of a great circular hearth in the cavern's center. From a huge pot, hung from a chain above it, came the most appealing aroma I thought I'd ever smelled. My stomach rumbled loudly.

Baylor looked askance at my stomach. "Ye gods, did you not feed the lass?" he threw over his shoulder at Demon.

He was moving about with a swift grace I found amazing for a man his size, taking a bowl and filling it with the aromatic stew.

"She's been a Changeling for only two nights and a day. I doubted she'd have the stomach for a good hunt," Demon shot back tiredly. "And I'm not the cook, you are. Besides," he added, in sheepish defense, "we had berries."

"Berries," Baylor snorted, as he motioned for me to take a place at the table.

The table sat to the right of the hearth and directly opposite Demon's prostrate form. Baylor sat the large steaming bowl in front of me, quickly adding to my bounty a small loaf of bread, a hunk of cheese, and a mug of chilled ale. The last of which was not as delicious as the rest, but then I'm not one for ale, and the food was amazing.

I ate quickly, shoveling great spoonfuls of the delicious stew into my mouth, with little notice for the huge man hovering over me like an old mother hen, until I heard him again reprimand Demon.

"The poor thing's near starved," he said, taking the bowl from my hand as I finished drinking down the last of the broth, and promptly refilling it.

No retort was forthcoming, and as Baylor put the newly refilled bowl in front of me, he said, "Seems you've exhausted the poor old man. He's fast asleep."

He pulled a chair up opposite me and sat down quietly. I started the second bowl in silence, realizing Demon probably had not slept since even before coming to find me, and I was feeling slightly guilty for it. I had been the one to ask him to take the letter to Mem, while I slept what little I could, not sure that I was up to the task. I wondered then also how he had stayed awake, let alone been so attentive throughout my lessons and endless questions.

"He is a good man," I said wholeheartedly. "How long have you been friends?"

I could tell by the way they had spoken to each other that it had been for quite some time, but I was not in any way prepared for the answer.

"Ach, coming close now to fifteen hundred years," he replied.

"Oh my..!" It was all I could manage for a moment, trying to grasp so much time, then finally I added, "Then you must be a Changeling, too."

"No." His short answer had stunned and confused me all the more, but not so much as when he continued. "We haven't yet figured what or why I am for sure, other than, perhaps, still suffering my mother's curse. I do change, only it is into something that is both man and wolf," he said sadly. "But the fullness of the moon controls it, not I."

A Werewolf! So this had been the reason for pause when I had asked Demon who Baylor was. He had not wanted to frighten me. I had been obvious with my fear when I had asked Demon if he was a Lycanthrope, and he had not wanted to frighten me. I was confused more so than frightened at this point. The tales I'd heard of these creatures were not coinciding very well with what I had learned of the ability to shift shape.

"But I don't understand. How?" I asked.

My confusion met with a sense of compassion for this huge sweet man beside me, swiftly erasing any sense of prejudice instilled by those legends I had been raised on. I liked him. I could see that he was kind and gentle despite his size. I was swiftly coming to think of him as not only Demon's friend, but my own as well. He had a way of putting one instantly at ease. All these things combined to leave me at a loss for words. The sadness in his eyes told me he had no answers, so I let my questions die on my tongue, not wanting to pain him further with what memories they might resurrect at

63

this time. He had taken me in, made me comfortable in his home, fed me; I would not now bother him with my inquisitive mind.

I finished with my food and looked around then to see where I should take my bowl to be washed. I was again astounded by the sheer size of the place, and its delightful mixture of raw and refined beauty. There was no specific date to be made out for when the place had been furnished, as it held furnishings and decorative items from further back than I could have recognized and some that appeared very new. All over there was a sense of elegance created by each thing's individual beauty.

The walls were hung with tapestries and huge paintings. These covered many eras in history. Some depicted knights engaged in battle with dragons, others such ordinary things as a maiden industriously at work at a loom. One, which I especially liked, was of a goddess reclining on a chaise lounge, much like the one Demon was now sleeping on. She was being fed delicious-looking grapes by perfectly depicted cherubs. The furniture had much the same appeal, not speaking of any one era, but all of good taste and quality.

A huge bed, with four posts reaching for the ceiling, supported rods hung with thick, dark blue velvet drapes to hide the sleeper from view. This was surrounded by such things as a mirror set on legs, which allowed it to stand free, and a tall chest for the storage of clothing. Combining this, with all of it being set toward the rear of the cavern, gave the impression of an elegant bedchamber with see-through walls. I had never seen anything like this place, or a finer sleeping arrangement.

Many little groupings began to make themselves clear to me. Like for instance, Baylor and I were in a "dining hall," with no walls to make it a "hall." You must also understand how difficult it was for me to come to these conclusions, comparing what I was seeing to pictures painted in my head by others. For no matter that I had wandered with my mother constantly, we had never lived in more than a single room hut, or been invited for any length of time into more than a parish. When we had been in any better structure it had been rare; only to attend a birth, so I had not had much opportunity to view such beauty with any kind of leisure.

So I looked, stared actually, then I noticed a rack of drying herbs over the hearth and instinctively went over their names in my head. I don't know how long I had looked around or what expressions had crossed my face. Mayhap my lips had moved slightly when reviewing the herbs or I had done so for overly long. In any case I had obviously given myself away.

Whatever the reasons, Baylor said, "You are a healer?"

I'm not sure if it was that I expected him to toss me from his home or if I was merely so used to people's looking down their noses at us, that my answer had come so stiffly.

"Yes," I replied.

"Wonderful!" he said.

I was shocked by him yet again, as he seemed so happy to hear it, and appeared as though he hadn't noticed my tone. I was instantly contrite. Demon and he had showed me nothing but the utmost kindness, even more so now as he continued speaking in his soft tone, making no note of my blush.

"Healers are a dying, or at least retreating, legacy of the Druids," he said. "And it is good to see that their teachings still exist in these harsh times."

"Yes we have been lucky, my mother and I." I said, thankful he had so politely let my rudeness slide off of him.

"Demon said you've only just been changed, and yet you are here with him, having left your home and what family you may have for a new life. You arrived at our door with naught but the fur on your back, comfortable in a different form than your own, and not one complaint other than that made by your empty belly." He smiled at me then, and it occurred to me that he too was a truly handsome man. "Takes quite a strong lass to do all that. I wouldn't call it simple luck."

"I thank you," I said from the heart, narrowly avoiding another blush.

"Your kind, healers, they remind me of my people long ago. Before Christianity came to our lands and the Druids still lived among us in great numbers. Teaching us better things than how to build churches and give money to priests." He sighed, bowing his head a little. "Don't misunderstand me, I don't think Christians are evil people," he said looking up again, trying to be clear. "Quite the opposite really. I think they are, for the most part, a very good people, with good intentions. It is only that I think some have found a love for the power to be had in the teaching of it, and misplaced their God in that process."

"So you believe in God, I mean One True God?" I said, trying to understand him and being reminded of Father Paul yet again.

"Yes, of course I do," he said, and smiled again. "I think most everyone does, no matter what name they call Him."

I'm not sure I truly understood him, even now, but I knew he was a good person and that we would become good friends in no time at all. In fact, I felt we already were. I picked up my ale then, for even though I wasn't fond of the taste, my throat felt parched.

It was chilled, and after taking a cool swallow, I asked, "How do you keep it so cool?" I nodded to indicate my mug as I set it down.

"There is a small stream that flows from the top of that chamber there," he said, pointing.

He had pointed to an opening in the wall behind me, where I had not yet looked in my perusal of the place.

"It flows cold all year round, though more so in the winter," he added.

I got up to see this other chamber he spoke of and he followed behind me, explaining more.

"It comes in here," he said as we entered another room. Though not nearly as large as the first, it was huge, and he was pointing up at a small hole near the ceiling. Here a slight, but steady flow came out.

"It pools up here." He indicated the miniature pond taking up most of the room's floor space. "And drains out here," he said, as he pointed again, this time walking in the direction he had pointed.

I followed and noticed the floor sloped slightly downward, and at this end I saw where the stone of the floor had been cut away to allow for the pool to drain into a natural fissure in the earth. I stared at it all in amazement for a while before I noticed a wall, built just under the surface, at the far end, close to where we'd entered.

I walked back to this and was staring at it in wonder. I was trying to grasp why the wall had been built and why the floor of the pool on the smaller side was smooth and the larger side was littered with grapefruit-sized smooth stones. When he answered the questions I couldn't quite form, I was even more amazed.

"We built the wall, to separate the cold water we use for drinking and keeping things cool," he said, "from the water on the other side. This side we toss heated rocks into, to warm it for bathing."

I was still drowning in amazement at the pure genius of it, when he answered another question I hadn't yet asked.

"When Demon and I met and came to be living here together, he had a great appreciation for bathing and cleanliness," he said, "which he soon prevailed upon me to adopt."

He started laughing then and his laugh too, was a wonderful sound, rumbling and deep. "I'm talking like him now," he said before he continued. "He said I stank, to be honest, and if I didn't fix it myself he'd fix it for me. I believed him. So I gave it a try. I liked it, a lot, it is very relaxing. So we've made improvements to our bathhouse over the years."

I was silently agreeing with his statement, thinking how clean and wonderful- smelling Demon had been. Remembering how I'd noticed his scent whenever he'd sit beside me or when he'd held and comforted me, as I came to terms with the necessity to leave my mother. Thinking how I too had a great love for the water, I was caught off guard by a sudden yawn and jerked my hand to my mouth, remembering my manners just in time.

"How *did* you meet?" I asked, once it had passed.

"That is a long story, one probably better told by Demon, and you, lass, need some sleep. New adventures or no, you're no good for them without your rest."

"But," I began, thinking it unfair, both had conveniently and seemingly too swiftly denied me the story.

"No buts, come now, we've forever to talk and you're for bed," he said.

He turned then, letting me know further protest would fall on deaf ears and walking back into the main chamber, left me little choice but to follow him. He led me to a large wooden box set off to itself, with two small doors. These opened and closed toward each other, providing entrance into it. It was about the same size and shape as my hut had been.

"This should make you feel right at home and bring you a peaceful rest," he said.

He opened it to reveal that it was one large bed. Only instead of the velvet drapes, the other I had seen had, this one had doors to shield the sleeper from view. It was covered with fresh-smelling sheets, of a white material unknown to me, and looked extremely inviting. I put my hand out to see if it was as soft as it appeared to be and it was even better.

"Feathers and silk," he said, once more reading my mind, as he seemed so good at doing. "Demon has a taste for the finer things of life," then he added, looking at me, "and I've known him to travel quite far to get them," He seemed to be stating what was becoming quite obvious, by all the beauty surrounding us, but there might have been more my tired mind just wasn't grasping.

"Up you go," he said, pulling on a lever I had not seen and releasing from below the doors a small hidden step.

I realized I had no argument left in me as feathery softness called me to sleep. I hopped up, relishing the way it felt as the bed fluffed momentarily and then molded beneath me.

"Sleep well, lass," he said, as he began closing the doors, and I felt the comforting closeness of it lull me.

It did indeed make me feel quite at home. The nearly endless energy I had felt mere moments before seemed to seep out of me to bury itself in the feathers with me. I turned my head, nuzzling into the softness of the pillow, facing the slowly closing doors, though not of bundled clean clothing, this pouch of feathers was a very acceptable head rest.

"Baylor," I said sleepily, just before the doors clicked closed. "You're a good man, too."

I felt sure he'd heard me as sleep came to claim me.

~7~

Goddess

I was dreaming that I was the goddess of the painting, only instead of cherubs feeding me grapes as had been depicted, it was a demon. I was not frightened by this in any manner; actually, it made me exquisitely happy. There was a joy in me I felt would bring me near to bursting where it to grow in even the merest amount. The demon leaned toward me, whispering words I couldn't hear but whose meaning was clear, and a sense of excitement bloomed in my breast and began to seep throughout my limbs. This demon had the feel of Demon's soul, and I was oddly contented within my being as we laughed at some private joke. We were very comfortable in each other's nearness, and the unseen but present gathered in my dream were not party to the cause of our private amusement.

The demon then became Demon in truth, as I knew it had always been, and again leaned toward me. My feelings of happy contentment swiftly became more excited anticipation; his closeness was now making it difficult for me to breathe. He held a plump grape up to my lips and I playfully nipped it from his fingers, sending its juice spurting onto my chin. He smiled, an amazing smile, which spoke volumes of things I didn't understand, yet aroused the strange feeling within my stomach, to even grater intensity.

Demon then lowered his head slowly to mine, licking the juice from my chin, then the corner of my now trembling lips, finally running his tongue

70

across them where they met in a dawning smile of my own.

I awoke with a start, the dream and my surroundings combining to leave me very confused and shaking for quite some time. I lay very still as my body slowly returned to feeling like my own and the tightness in my belly began to fade. I think I started to realize even then that I was falling in love with Demon. Yet I had managed to push it deep within a shadowed corner of my mind so that it could not confuse me further.

It then came quickly to me where I was, as I thought of Demon. I heard Baylor and him speaking from somewhere in the vast chamber. Though I couldn't make out their words, it gave me a wonderful sense of happiness to hear their voices.

I wondered about washing and thought of the pool Baylor had shown me, but I was feeling unexpectedly shy, due to the dream, I supposed. I abandoned the thought of asking to use it as quickly as it came. Instead I concentrated on making myself as clean and appealingly scented as Demon had been, giving this order to my form without much thought.

I took care with my clothing that morning, having found I liked the feeling of the silk I had slept on. I fashioned my clothing of it. I made an over-dress in the deep burgundy of the robe worn by the goddess of the painting, and a blouse of a pure clean white. I took such care out of a deep want within me to please Demon, but I convinced myself it was because he was my teacher. I told myself I wanted his approval of my skill, not my appearance, not wanting to spend too much time thinking about any other possible reasons, with the dream still fresh in my mind to confuse and disturb me.

I remembered then that I had a goal this day, and swiftly now began running my fingers through my long hair, in a useless effort to untangle it. I didn't think to merely will it to untangle itself. My mind had now moved on to other things it wanted to learn today. So it was that I emerged from my bed falling only slightly short of appearing very well-kept.

I was still running my fingers through my hair when Baylor looked up from the table where they were sitting and drinking wine and greeted me.

"Well, don't you look bonny this morning, lass," he said, gesturing for me to sit as he stood and pulled a chair out from the table for me. "Did you sleep well?"

I'm not sure even now whether it was the fact he had said I looked bonny or his reminding me of my dream that had made me blush, but I quickly bowed my head. I allowed my hair to hide my face and the traitorous evidence of my instantaneous discomfiture the blush had been.

"Yes, I was quite comfortable," I said at last.

I hoped that I had managed to appear only to be adding a gesture of acquiescence to my verbal answer. Whether I had succeeded or not, neither of them seemed to take any notice, as Demon merely took another sip of his wine and Baylor stood and turned to do something in the kitchen area, as it were.

I forgot about it in any case, as Demon then said, "Good morning, Angel, you have done well." Looking askance at my attire, he added, "You like silk, then?"

I was pleased that he noticed and approved. Raising my hand to my breast, feeling the material again, I said, "Where did you find it?"

"China," was his unexpected reply.

"China," I repeated.

I had heard of the place and knew it to be very far away. I realized Baylor had not been jesting in the slightest when he had said Demon would travel as far as he must, to find fine things.

Baylor returned then with a bowl of boiled oats swimming in butter, cream and sugar and set it before me along with a spoon and, surprisingly, a brush. Again he had amazed me.

"Thank you," I said, looking up at him and smiling.

I didn't know which I wanted to make use of first. I looked from the spoon to the bowl, then the brush, then back to him, smiling again and thinking him a wonderful man. I then spotted the painting, which had held such influence over me lately, hanging on the wall behind him. So forgetting my present dilemma, I picked up the spoon.

"Which goddess is that?" I asked, nodding my head toward it, before I took a spoonful into my mouth.

That had been a mistake, as I found it suddenly hard to swallow.

Demon said, "The goddess that was my betrothed."

I managed to get the mouthful down, but the delicious taste went unappreciated, as a strange feeling twisted within me. I had assumed it was just some painting of a goddess, searching my mind unconsciously for any likeness of her to any thing Father Paul had ever taught me, never thinking it would be of someone Demon had known and loved.

"You were married?" I asked.

I chided myself for thinking he hadn't been, or not thinking as it were, and for even allowing it to affect me as I will now admit it had. He was nearly two thousand years old, of course he had been in love before, and I was being a silly girl for letting the thought of him being in love with someone else disturb me. After all, I had no claim to him, did I?

"No, she died before we were wed, and before I was changed and could save her," Demon replied slowly.

There was deep sadness hidden behind his calm response and I felt worse now for my previous feelings of what I now recognize as jealousy, as they were quickly ousted by compassion.

"I am sorry," I said, and I truly was.

I ate in silence for a moment, wishing I had never brought it up.

"Her name was Sera, actually Seraphim," he said unexpectedly. "You remind me very much of her. You were both aptly named."

He seemed to be at peace with speaking about her, or maybe he was only hiding the hurt better now, but either way I realized he was not holding a grudge that I had brought it up.

Baylor had refilled their goblets and brought me one as well, resuming his place at the table. Finishing my meal, I took a sip, finding it to be more to my taste than the ale of the night before and quite wonderful as well. I sipped again and began to swirl it, gazing into its depth. Then I raised it approvingly.

73

"Very nice," I said, tipping my head toward my raised glass.

"Roman," Demon said, dipping his head in a mock bow, acknowledging my approval.

"The food was marvelous as well," I said, turning then to Baylor.

"Scottish," he said, copying the bow Demon had made, with a grin, and then falling into a fit of laughter.

What could have a moment before passed for a strange new breed of gentry enjoying good wine and food had quickly disintegrated into a scene of three young fools laughing themselves to tears. These were the times that built in me the foundation of what was to become my acceptance of them as my new family, I revel in these memories as some of my best, even now, and though they are far too few, they mean everything to me.

When at last we were subdued and Baylor had refilled our glasses, I realized, having them both at the table with me, that there was no time like the present for my questions. So, picking up my brush, I looked from one to the other.

"So, now," I said, applying the brush to the ends of my hair first, "which of you is going to tell me how a Greek Changeling came to be in Scotland, wearing a kilt no less." I looked at Demon, raising my left brow, indicating his choice of clothing. "And then somehow became the best of friends with a Werewolf," I added, looking now to Baylor. "And if one of you tells me that another person, not present here, can tell me the story better I will hit you both. I have been stayed by that excuse twice now and will not hear it again."

I held the brush up as proof I had the weapon to carry out my threat. They both stared at me open-mouthed for a moment, and then looked from me to each other. Demon burst again into uncontrolled laughter, and Baylor followed suit. Each time one seemed on the verge of gaining control, he would catch a look in the other's eye and begin anew. I was beginning to wonder if they would ever stop and whether or not I had missed something, when both questions were answered. Demon being the first to find his voice, he looked again at Baylor.

He said, "Did I not tell you she was a wretchedly willful little poppet?"

"Ugh!" I swatted his arm with my brush indignantly. "You say strong-willed like it's a bad thing. It allowed me to resist the light until you came, did it not?"

"Aye, that she is, but it did allow you to hear her from here," Baylor added, taking up my part, if only to avoid the brush.

"Whose friend are you?" Demon demanded, holding his arm and feigning being crushed, both emotionally and physically.

"Should have stayed home," he grunted. "Only a jest, gods!"

Demon raised his hands quickly to ward off any more blows, as we all laughed again.

"Well?" I said.

Refusing to be forestalled any longer by either of them, I looked from one to the other still holding up the brush. Demon turned again to Baylor.

"Why'd you have to go and arm the woman?" he asked.

Baylor shrugged his shoulders, saying, "How was I to know my brush could be a lethal weapon?"

"My dear, naive boy," Demon replied, in a very good imitation of an English lord, "even a smile can be a lethal weapon when a woman wants something."

I realized I had won then, as they both sighed and looked at each other again. It seemed they were in some silent debate as to where to begin the tale and who should begin it. I'm not sure by what means they resolved the issue, but it was Demon who finally spoke.

"I guess I should begin." He sighed again, then smiled, quietly accepting what he seemed to think of as the burden of being the storyteller. "It was, I believe, in the year 70." he looked toward Baylor, who quietly nodded his agreement. "The one that had made me what I am had long since abandoned me. Believing, I suppose, that he had taught me all I needed to know of what I was, and having grown tired with this world, he had ascended..."

"Ascended?" I interrupted

"It is a kind of death for a Changeling, I think, what the tired ones do. When one has lost the desire to live corporeal on the earth, whether from the sheer length of time it has done so, or because of some great pain it does not wish to live with, one will sometimes throw off the burden of retaining any kind of form," Demon replied in his teacher tone.

I believe my raised eyebrow told him I would require more of an explanation, because he sighed and continued without my having to ask him to do so.

"A Changeling can remove itself to another plane, which is neither heaven nor hell. I believe it is more a kind of non-being, while still being self-aware. I would think it would be much as when I become incorporeal to travel quickly over a great distance. In this way, by retaining only their Yelm, they escape the pain and monotony of daily life, without entirely giving up their existence."

I was absorbed and he knew it, as he continued then with this explanation, saying, "Rather than take the time and discomfort of allowing their bodies to age and die real deaths, avoiding somehow any small or involuntary change that would revitalize the energy that makes them up. That would only force them to begin again the natural process of aging and dying. It is often an unachievable thing to let go the will to exist for a Changeling and so ascension is the easier choice when one becomes tired of living."

"But they still are? I mean, they do not cease to exist. Ascension is not *really* dying, right? So they can come back then from this?" I asked, intrigued.

"I would think it more, just not *living*. Coming back, that, I do not know. All I know of ascension is from the one that changed me, and what I could learn from the Elders of the Council. I do not know if my Master even truly knew of what he spoke. My mentor was by far the oldest and wisest Changeling I have met to this day, having come up into Egypt, as he put it, 'before time was even time.' He may or may not have done it and returned but he did not say so, and I have never met another that has.

"Can one be *forced* to ascend?" I was full of new questions now, the original ones having been completely forgotten.

"It has been said, but again I don't know for sure," Demon answered.

"But a Changeling *can* die the other way?" I said.

"If they manage to age within one form, never changing it in the slightest," he replied. "It is the constant revitalization of gathering and releasing and rearranging our energies both old and new that makes us immortal. In all my years, I have only met one who achieved a natural death. I stood by his side as he went into the light, should he, in the last moments, decide to remain with us, and need my help, but he did not look back."

This was an incredible revelation to me. We were immortal! Yet we could die if we chose to. I could not fathom why one would though, it was all too glorious; other than not being able to have children, I saw no flaws in the beauty of the gift I had been given. As I finished brushing my hair and thought about all he had said, I nearly forgot my earlier purpose.

So it was with some embarrassment that I heard him say, "Now if you've no new questions, I will continue with the answering of the original one."

Baylor snorted in amusement, though I know he had been just as absorbed with the sidetracking of the conversation as I had been, and I narrowed my eyes at both of them before retorting.

"Please continue," I said.

So it was that again Demon sighed as though he had half hoped I would let him out of the telling, but now realized there was no real hope for such a reprieve. Taking up his wine he took a small sip and swirled the remaining contents idly, as if they reminded him of what he was to tell. Then he began for the second time, softly slipping into the tale and losing his teaching tone somewhere along the way...

~8~

The Council

"I suppose it actually started long before the year 70," Demon told me. "With the great sense of loneliness my mentor's ascension had left in me. Not so much so that I had ever thought to ascend as well, but creating a void within me that needed filling. It was due to this growing state of loneliness that I left the great city of Athens, and the home I had been unable to fully return to at least within my heart, and made my way to Rome.

"I was hoping to eliminate some of my sadness by leaving behind that place that was so rich with memories for me: the house that was no longer a home, the city which was no longer mine. Yet still I could at any turn of a corner, on any of its familiar streets, easily be reminded of those friends and times now so far beyond my grasp. I had allowed these ghostly remembrances to haunt me for far too long and knew I would be driven mad by them where I not to find a safe refuge.

"Once in Rome, a new sense of hope took root in me quickly, as I found only new things down its every road. I was at once surrounded by things familiar, but in no way so much so as to bring me pain or assault me with terrible memories. Also I found the unexpected pleasure of companionship. I discovered this on the very first day there, while enjoying the Trajan baths.

"I had gone there, as most did, to enjoy the company of others and to be in society again for a time. I had stayed late into the evening, listening to the conversations of those around me, and learning the secrets of this new place. Feeling like the young aristocrat that I had been, only without the sadness of a well-known family name being dropped within my hearing.

"When the baths had closed for the evening I had returned in secret, sneaking in under cover of darkness to be alone, to sit in the cooling pools and enjoy my newfound sense of well-being. I was quieted within myself, feeling I had been a part of something again for a while. Contentedly absorbing the events of the day, I began thinking that I had made a good choice in coming there. I think I even thought to somehow begin again, start some semblance of a life in this new place, and let what all had come before slip quietly from my mind.

"It was then, with my mind freed of its constant hurts and full of the joy found in that day's wonderful distractions, that I had felt the presence of other Changelings. They were not only here at my very location, but throughout the city, going about in no guarded attempt to go unnoticed by others of our kind. I briefly toyed with the idea of shielding my identity as one of them: that is, from the ones I sensed entering the bathhouse. I had been taught I could, and most often should, do this by projecting absolutely nothing. My curiosity won out, however, and I remained where I was for easy discovery.

"They had padded into the bath on the silent paws of the huge black cats they had taken the form of. A matched pair, both, beautifully made. I knew them to be panthers, as my teacher had seen to it. Insisting that I learn more creatures' forms than at times I thought my mind could contain, he was adamant that I should learn every name, instinct and habit, of every thing I ever had opportunity to observe.
It took their panther noses' not but a second to turn toward me, scenting me, and I could tell they had not expected anyone to be present here.

"But then it seemed to take them a bit too long to realize I was not as they had assumed at first, a mere human. I knew then that these two were not schooled as to the full extent of their abilities and must be very young.

They also had not been cautioned to make use of their new abilities always, shielding themselves from such easy discovery, for I had caught them quite obviously and completely off guard. This should not have been possible had they been older and properly taught.

"They appeared to be trying to determine if they should leave, and quickly. Yet being quite confused and not having done so already, they realized they had lost the opportunity to do so with any chance of successfully escaping me, should I wish to harm them. I think they recognized by my demeanor that I had no fear of them, and this in turn instilled more in them of me. I took pity on them.

"'I will do you no harm,' I said.

"The young woman was the first to take the chance." He paused in his narration and smiled at me, and I thought I must remind him of her. He continued, "She was the first to disregard any thought of retreat, and resume her natural form before me. She appeared not much more than fourteen. When she had done this, with no move coming from me to belie my word, the other too took his natural form. They had stood before me then at the edge of the pool, trying to appear brave. I marveled at them then, for they were twins and charmingly beautiful.

"Hence, I came to meet Adonia and her brother Adreal, the two youngest and newest members of what I would come to learn was a small closed society of Changelings living within the city of Rome. These two had never met another not born to, or rather changed by, the approval of this society as a whole, and seemed to not even know it could be done. I found that their fear of me had not been caused so much by the fact they were young and unprepared and I could have easily done them harm, but rather by the fact I existed at all. We talked of this and many other things, well into the night.

"It was decided then, after much coaxing on their part, that I must meet the 'Elders'. So that I might learn more and so might they as well. I did not know fully what I was getting into but I felt well overdue for a new adventure. Had I not just been thinking of a whole new life? So, finally, I had agreed.

"'All right!' I had said, allowing her to grasp my hand and pull me from the pool into their world.

"It was just a few hours before dawn when we took to the sky. We flew over the city and came down into the gardens of a grand villa, nestled in its heart. They took me through this beautiful place, at too great a speed to fully absorb its beauty. Its wide white arches, marble floors and columns, went almost unjustly unnoticed, as we headed directly to a well-appointed chamber deep within the heart of the house. Here I was to meet a member of this 'Council' they had spoken of, which set down the laws all Changelings lived by, or so these two had believed, until meeting me.

"It was with a great show of consternation on their part that they were nearly instantly sent from this room after giving brief excited explanation of my presence there with them. This Elder had immediately optioned to speak with me in private, telling them it was well past time they were in their beds, citing how they had obviously avoided them the entire night as proof. Thus I was left quite alone and feeling suddenly the stranger in a very strange new world.

"He was a thin man, obviously a scholar of some kind, if his desk was any indication. He also appeared to be highly agitated, furthering my feelings of discomfort. I realized too late that I might have just followed two very beautiful children into a trap of some sort and that they might not have been as untrained as I had previously thought.

"'Come. Sit,' he said, indicating the chair opposite him. 'The twins say you had no knowledge of our society, or of the Council and the Code. How is it, then, that you were blessed? Who laid the blessing upon you?'

"Everything was happening so quickly. Out from the baths and over the city, through the gardens and into the house. I wanted to compose a happily nervous little ditty about it all. There was more of my kind, lots more. Yet my joy was slightly tainted, for it was also quickly made obvious to me he was not as happy to have met me. No trap had been sprung, at least, and as the little tune I had been thinking to compose in my head quieted, I

81

decided I would at the very least gain some knowledge as well from this venture. He was used to being in a position of authority, as I noted he had demanded answers without preamble, and I realized we would have to get a few things straight between us were we to ever hope to get along.

"I stood where I had been before, not having taken the seat he had pointed at. I did not intend to be gone over with a fine-tooth comb by him, to ascertain my worthiness; if that were his plan I could make my farewells to the twins and leave. I wanted to be clear with him that I had not come to him seeking acceptance, nor was I asking for a place in his little world. I was very intent on making it clear that I was not a child and had existed for a very long time without bowing down, as was obvious he was used to. All of this I told him and more.

"I told him that, if anything, I was seeking to make a friend of my own kind, not to find a guardian, for I had no need of one. I said that I had come here merely to please the twins, for they had proven to be such as were the kind I sought. I added I had meant merely to amuse myself and them and perhaps pass some pleasant time. But above all I allowed my tone to convey my opinion of his rudeness in questioning me, without so much as a nod of his head to pass for greeting.

"'My deepest apologies. Your arrival, even your mere being, comes as quite a shock, please forgive me, my intention was not to offend,' he had said.

"He had seemed to shrink back into his chair as I had spoken. He appeared now to be only a confused and frightened middle-aged man, having a lot of thoughts trying to work themselves out too quickly in his mind. I think he realized sometime during my pointed speech that his best hope of getting any answers from me, was to begin again, only this time as equals. Polite, equals, he was nothing if not astute and willing to do whatever it took to learn what he wanted to know.

"'My name is Edsel,' he continued. 'I am very pleased the twins prevailed upon you to grace our home and meet with me. Please do sit down, and forgive my earlier lapse in manners.'

"I allowed his attempt at humility to suffice and this time took the seat as he had asked. I had things I wanted to know as well, like how this little community had managed to thrive amidst the hustle and bustle of a major city, with no harm having come of it, and above all my never having heard of it.

"'I am Demosthenes,' I told him. 'And I will excuse your shock, though I'm not sure I yet grasp the cause of it, realizing I too have many questions eagerly awaiting answers.'

"So we began again, each obliging the other with what information we could. I told him what I knew of the one that had 'blessed' me, as he called it, but the answers did not seem to ease his mind. I merely knew he had most usually appeared in the masculine form. I had no acceptable description that I could guaranty was a true form to relate, as he had seemed quite masterfully at home no matter which form he took. I had no name to give him, as I had called him only Master or Teacher. This all was a great disappointment, but he listened quietly as I told him also how I had been changed. We discovered that, lacking a good bit of ceremony, it was in much the same way he had.

"He then told me how the Council had risen up out of a need to provide order, and reduce the numbers of those being blessed. There had come a time when faith in an afterlife spent in paradise, which could be guaranteed by a priest at the local temple for the right coin, had come into question, a time when this easily won salvation was rapidly coming into question, being replaced with confusion. It seemed every one had lost faith. All were made to wonder whether their gods were even gods at all or if the man called Jesus was the son of the One True God. The people feared him and killed him but the damage had been done, in more ways than one. There was no more guaranty in far too many minds, just more uncertainty and a lot of fear of the now unknown.

"The Changeling population had begun to grow at an alarming rate. Too many were refusing to go into the light that blinded them to an unknown future and destination. Some were being created which should have never

83

been allowed to live as long as they had as humans, let alone be granted a second blessed chance. For enough currency a murderer would be given the blessing. It had become a trade, so to speak, the new guaranty, for the same old coin.

"So the Council had been formed, with the oldest and most powerful coming together to establish laws and to enforce them as well. Forming a strong enough combined will, to cause the parts of energy that made up those that were evil, to flee them, inflicting enough damage to send them and those that had blessed them into another realm.

"His telling of a forced ascension intrigued me and though, I was skeptical, I questioned him more about it. Discovering that, according to him, not only could one *will* their own energies to and from themselves, throwing them off by choice, to ascend, as I had already known, but that the Council had found a way, by combining their wills and exerting them as one, to force a soul to ascend. Hence control of the problem had come quickly with such ruthless force behind it. I hid my skepticism and listened intently as he continued.

"He told me how then the Elders had chosen one blessed child each, and taught them all they knew. They had sent these chosen ones out into the world to enforce and teach the laws they had established, seeing that none were blessed by any but themselves or without their joint approval, to ensure the problem would not arise again. It was with pride he said that nearly forty years had passed in peace. Not a single evil or unworthy soul had been blessed since the Council had been formed.

"I began to see now why my presence had so agitated and disturbed him, and why he had asked the questions he had. I also understood how it was that I had not heard of them. They had sought out only the unworthy ones or they that had obviously made themselves well-known and hence had not found me, and being otherwise a closed society had not made their presence known for those such as myself to have spread the word. They worked quietly, so quietly in fact that they missed those such as me, erroneously coming to the conclusion they were the only ones left.

"I felt for him suddenly. Not because I now believed this tightly structured and strictly governed society was the best thing for humanity or Changelings, or even wished its influence to spread to encompass all countries, as was obviously its goal. Others, as well as myself, had done quite well without it. We were not running about blessing undeserving souls, just because some Council had frightened the will to, out of all of us.

"I felt for him because he truly thought any other way would lead again to a disaster such as the one this Council had come together to prevent. He had no faith in his own people's abilities. Like the twins. I suddenly realized that it wasn't that they were merely young and unschooled, as I had previously thought, but purposely left unknowing. He would probably never even bother to teach them how to know which souls were fit for change and which ones would be better to let pass on. He simply would never teach them how to change anyone else.

"I thought then how all these blessed ones, were not to my reckoning blessed at all, they were shielded and left in ignorance. Told what was right to think and do, and what was good or vile, becoming merely extra arms and legs and eyes for a select few that had elected themselves.

"Rather than being taught how to ascertain for themselves, they were guided. I now saw a value in the Council, as a safeguard of sorts, but feared what it might become: a school of unlearning, the unexpected second downfall of our race. I believed if another disaster was to come, it would be because of this. This mass ignorance was what I saw as the biggest danger.

"I saw disaster in the possibility that someday the Elders may not be around to guide, as my mentor was no longer. The young ones would then become lost, having never been taught how to find a path by themselves. Not in what he did, I didn't think it even remotely possible another Changeling would set up shop in a market somewhere in Europe, if one of the Council's spies were not there to stop him, and begin selling passage to an alternate afterlife.

"We talked openly about all these things well into the evening, alternating between rank disapproval of the other's opinions and grudging

85

appreciation of their idealism. I showed him my views and tried to see his but admittedly, come late afternoon, after many attempts, we still could not see eye to eye.

"'Will you stay and dine with us?' he had asked unexpectedly.

"His question had thrown me off a little, as I would have thought he'd want me gone before my ideals could become contagious among the younger ones, such as the twins.

"'It would be my pleasure,' I accepted.

"I had realized, quite unexpectedly, that I wanted to continue our conversation and indeed was enjoying it. For certain I had no better plans and could find no good reason to decline. So we dined or rather talked and argued our points all the way through what should have been dinner. Right after which, while enjoying a glass of wine, I made a horrible mistake.

"'What is the Code, exactly?' I asked.

"I soon found myself wishing I'd bitten off my tongue instead of used it. He had launched himself into the quotation of it with a gusto that belied the very boring, longwinded and often repetitious body of it.

"With, 'Let all that be Blessed come to know and hold true...'

"I began to pay much more attention to my wine than was necessary as he went on and on and on.

"Chirp... Chirp, chirp...

"I slowly came to notice that there were birds chirping in time with his never-ending quotation and looked then over my shoulder to see that the twins had come to roost in the window, somehow having done so without his taking notice. They had begun chirping in time with his words, mocking him in their own way. I hid my amusement by taking another drink.

"Now as I have told you, some of the laws are important," Demon said, as again he looked up at me, raising his glass and sipping. As though the memory of having done so then demanded he do so now, he added, "And one would do well to live by them but some were either amazingly stupid or should have never had to be stated in the first place. Any idiot would have known some of them," he said, continuing then with his story.

"'...mate with a beast of the field, or fowl,' Edsel was saying.

"I heard him say it but thought I had to be misunderstanding him. Mayhap I had drunk too much wine without having noticed, but then,

"'Abomination...,' he continued.

"'What was that?' I had demanded, cutting him off. 'You actually have a law forbidding mating with animals?'

"'Yes!' he said indignantly. 'It is an abomination.'

"'Well yes, I quite agree that it is, but have you no faith in good common sense that you must have a law for every little thing?' I replied, equally indignant.

"The two birds in the window were tittering with amusement now and he suddenly took notice of them and sent them off, saying, 'To your chambers, the both of you!'

"And off they flew into the night, leaving me quite alone once more to deal with the insanity. Suddenly I was frantically searching my mind for any likely diversion from this mess I had gotten myself into.

"'I just thought that I might be able to help you, in possibly discovering if you know the one who made me,' I had said suddenly, hoping fervently to divert him from beginning again and someday mayhap even finishing what seemed a never-ending quotation of his precious Code. I was hoping also to avoid not only a continuation of this one but any other long and inanely stupid argument.

"'How? What have you remembered?' he said quickly.

"I was beginning to realize he wasn't actually rude, he just cut straight to the point of things and had this demanding tone all the time. I was also extremely thankful he was so fanatic at least in this instance, as it proved to be that easy to divert him and my ploy did indeed serve its purpose. All one had to do was offer a lead to one who was threatening his perfect little world by creating others without the collective consent of the Council, others like me. I conveniently neglected to mention my maker had ascended already and was no longer a threat.

"'He said once to me he had "come up into Egypt, before time was even time." If that can help at all,' I said.

"He told me that it did not, but at least he didn't start the reciting of the Code again, but rather became lost in thought for some time. He then surprised me yet again by breaking this long silence with yet another invitation. He asked if I would stay until morning and break my fast with him before I left his villa. He made no mention of leaving his city and this too took me by surprise. I could only take this to mean he was beginning to see that I was no threat, for there seemed no other reason for his continuing hospitality.

"When I came to breakfast the following morning, I was stunned to see a man I knew from my mortal life, breaking his fast with Edsel, and another man I did not know. I had paused in the portal to the room, where they were eating and talking like old friends, taking in the entire scene as best I could in my shocked state. I noticed, from the corner of my eye, the twins sitting still as death trying to avoid detection, posing as twin housecats in the corner, looking back and forth from those at the table then myself. I took in the food itself, the sweet smell of the fruits displayed and brightness of them, blending with the harsher scents of fried meats and the earthy ones of fresh baked breads. All of this I took in: Edsel, the twin housecats, the stranger, and then stranger still, a friend that should have died of old age more than three hundred years before.

"Suddenly this one, that had been a friend to me in my mortal life, looked up from his plate of various fruits and his familiar face split into a wide grin.

"'So it is you, Demosthenes,' he said happily. 'I hardly dared to hope when Edsel sent the twins to tell me of you.'

"The twins' heads moved in unison again, looking from him to me. Although I would later find it all quite amusing, I was then far too confused to enjoy the amusement their spying techniques might have otherwise offered me.

"I could not, in that moment, find words as he came around the table and, grabbing my hand, pulled me into a huge hug, which he then tried to turn into a wrestling hold, and I knew it was he. I was speechless still, for we had wrestled more times in my life than I could remember, and my heart began humming again. The little ditty began to add lines to itself: out from the baths and over the city, through the gardens and into the house, speak with the Elder don't give away the kitties, hug an old friend but don't let him win...don't let him win.

"Instinctively I twisted from his grasp and backed up, taking a wrestling stance again, still working to organize my thoughts into a greeting. I was also busy noting on a separate level that the twins were still taking everything in as well. Their heads moving always in unison, both as eager for any little morsel of knowledge as their current appearance would have said they were for a pan of milk.

"Finally finding my voice I said, 'Kynan, you live?'

"This was wonderful! We came together in another great hug, which quickly turned into a power struggle as it always had, and the one I had not recognized interrupted us.

"'If you please?' the one unknown to me had said.

"The twins looked from Kynan and me, heads moving as one toward the speaker, and then back to me as if awaiting my reaction. I felt for them then, that they should have to resort to such tactics to be a part of this meeting. I felt that they as much as any other should be able to join a table filled with fellow Changelings, especially since they had been responsible for such a meeting even taking place.

"They jerked their heads back to the one unknown, to me, as the stranger added, 'If you must wrestle about like children, be so kind as to excuse yourselves to the garden.'

"The matched pair of housecats then hissed in unison, mimicking his rudeness. I was suddenly torn between laughter at their antics, realizing in many ways they were still very young, and anger with this unknown man. As he looked in their direction as well and they bolted out into the garden, I was asking myself, when had Changelings become such a high-handed rude breed, excepting of course my friend Kynan here and the twins. I realized then, I had actually known very few besides my mentor until now, and it might be the norm and myself the exception.

"'If you are however of a mind to break your fast, please do come and join us,' he added, when we had not moved.

"I changed my mind slowly as I pulled out the appointed chair, considering that both Edsel and this one seemed very old, at least in their ways. They must think of themselves as fathers, rather than equals, until someone made them revise their opinion as I had done with Edsel. I chose to let it go, being too happy at the moment to ruin it with an argument. Slapping my friend on the back, I sat down opposite him as he said, 'The man who forgot his sense of humor at home today is Lachlan; Lachlan, this is my dear friend Demosthenes.' Kynan made the introductions and chastised the man at the same time.

"He had made wonderful use of the gift he had always had, speaking with the same easy grace that had made him such a great orator when we had been no more than boys. The two of us desperately dreaming, trying to make the world a better place, by voicing our hearts to the Senate. Chastising our elders even then, in a manner they would find acceptable and managing to make our views heard at the same time. He had been able to show disapproval of another's actions without causing a scene, even as he had so long ago when disagreeing with his own father.

"The day seemed to fly by after that, as I spent most of it alternately catching up with my old friend, discovering how he had become a Changeling not long after I had, and answering what new questions Lachlan could think up. These questions only led us into other questions and the morning quickly disappeared in a flurry of shifting conversations.

"At one point in the afternoon the conversation came back around to how I had been changed and who had done it, and again I related the tale. Telling them all again everything I could remember of my Teacher. Of course this made me miss him all the more, but I was with another old friend and surrounded by new ones in the making and it was not such a bitter thing as it could have been.

"'I was in Egypt not long ago,' Lachlan had said. 'I felt a powerful blessed one had spent much time there as its presence was still ingrained in the very sand of the place.'

"'Did you never meet this Changeling then?' I asked.

"He had looked askance at me for a moment until he realized I meant 'blessed one' when I had said 'Changeling.'

"'No,' was his disappointed reply, then, 'Why is it you call us 'Changelings?' "

"'Because we are change,' I replied, repeating my Teacher's words without thinking too much of it. 'It is what we are, it is what we do.'

"So the evening passed as well. With all of us steeped in conversations, remembrances, questions and sometimes too long answers. When the night had come full upon us and we still had not finished talking, I again was asked to stay for breakfast, and again I agreed.

"So it went throughout the week, with me meeting two more of the Council, those being named Santon and Cathmore, each of them asking more questions. Some I had answered before and others were new. As I found them to have different views of things and hence different things they wanted to know, but they were each very willing in their answering of mine as well, so I did not begrudge them the repetitions.

"The week turned into a month, and that month into another. Those turned into a year and another after that. Each night always ended with the same invitation, one that I would always find no reason not to except. They had filled the void of loneliness I had had. I felt no desire then to end our relationship as it was.

"Slowly they became like uncles to me, great, often grumpy, and very opinionated uncles, but uncles nonetheless. We had our disagreements, sometimes quarreling back and forth well into the night, but then there were also the nights when we would sit and tell stories of those things we'd done, or the people we'd had occasion to meet, that were now a part of history. Those were the times I could not seem to justify denying myself the pleasure I had found in my new life, by leaving their company.

"There were also those wonderful times when I would go off into the night with the twins, unnoticed. We would hunt or fly or swim and always afterwards they would ask me eternal rounds of questions, much as you yourself. Adreal and Adonia became a constant source of joy to me, bringing me always to laughter, often at the most inopportune times.

"When I should have been deeply engrossed in an important conversation with the Elders, I was often paying too much attention to their mockeries of it. I was constantly receiving frowns and Adreal and Adonia were constantly being sent to their room, being treated as eternal children. Though their looks might have warranted it, their age was quite beyond such treatment, and I took to answering questions for them the others would not. I knew such a thing might cause the lot of us no end of trouble, but I was not able to see that as sufficient reason not to tell them what they had every right to know. They became my brother and sister, cherished siblings; I could not find it in me to deny them.

"The years passed swiftly without my noting them, and there came the knowledge between all of us, that we would always be disagreeing on some point or other, but there would also always be respect. For the twins, though, there came also a deep abiding love."

~9~

The Twins

"It was on one of those wonderful days I had taken to spending in the garden with the twins. I was teaching Adreal more wrestling holds and listening to Adonia recite her latest poem, when Edsel appeared in a huff. I was sure then that I was about to hear how somehow encouraging Adonia to write poetry or teaching Adreal to wrestle was against the Code, when he surprised me.

"'Please children, continue without Demosthenes. I need to speak with him privately for a moment,' Edsel had said.

"If the mere fact he had been polite wasn't enough to tell me something was amiss, he had looked at me then, and I could see fear in his eyes. So as not to alarm the twins and see that they would not follow, I chose to excuse myself for him.

"'It appears as though I've broken some new law and must now be punished,' I said. Adonia giggled at this and I continued, 'Wait for me here? I shall endeavor to survive and return.'

"I winked at Adreal and he smiled back, holding his laughter in until we had departed. Feeling sure now that they would remain in the garden, I followed Edsel into the villa and down the hall to his office. Once we had entered, he closed and locked the door. There was a Changeling in the room I had not met before, taking up one of its chairs.

"'This is Piper. Piper, this is Demosthenes,' Edsel had said, making quick work of the introductions.

"He was proving that the many times I had prevailed upon him to at least make small attempts at using manners had begun to pay off, if only minimally, but more so he was reiterating my fear that something was very amiss. I looked quickly from him to the young man in the chair, finding I was the one now impatient for answers and wishing the introductions over quickly.

"'Piper has come to us with news that does not bode well,' he continued.

"He swiftly moved around to the opposite side of the desk and took his seat, then motioned that I should take the last remaining one before continuing.

"'Piper, tell Demon what you have told me,' he said at last. Then as an afterthought he added, 'Please.'

"He began refilling our guest's glass, placing one before me, and I smiled to myself. Then turning, I looked again to the man who had been asked to speak. He was shorter and of a smaller build than myself, though not by much. He had light brown, sun darkened skin, and dark brown hair falling in slight waves between his shoulder-blades, looking not at all the Pict his name proclaimed him to be. He had none of the tattooing so common among those people and look more to me to be of Celtic heritage, hailing quite probably from the Isle of Erin.

"'Aye,' Piper began. 'I had recently come into the Highlands of the north land, having left my native Erin and come across the water. I had left my home behind me for a time, only that I might travel down from there, to Londinium.'

"His accent was hard to understand at first, but it and the words themselves had confirmed my thoughts. His speech had a singsong quality I liked, almost as though he were reciting a poem rather than delivering news. I allowed myself to be drawn into them as he continued.

"'I wanted to see with my own eyes,' he had continued, 'what had become of that wondrous new town, as I had held out much hope that it would thrive. It had come to my hearing that a Queen of the Icini tribe had risen up in her vengeance and destroyed both Londinium and Camlo-Dunum, the place you would call Colchester, I believe. After the slaughter of the Druids by the Romans had turned so many to her, and word of all her other smaller victories over those invaders spread, she was hailed as the Queen of the Celts. This signaled to me a change for all of Britton forever.'

"He had paused briefly here then said, 'Now I am Celt through to my soul and I'll not begrudge her revenge, or the acts that avenged the Druids as well, what was done to her and to them was deserving of no less. The Morrighan saw to it that she had vengeance and rightly so. It is only that I am a Changeling also and must witness these oft-ended attempts at progress with great sadness and I can see no end of it now. So it was that I longed to see with my own eyes how horribly these progresses had been put back.'

"This cause for sadness in him was one well-known to me as well, having watched myself, as many a human progression had fallen under a warrior's heels, necessary or not, rightful or no. I nodded my understanding, encouraging him to go on with this tale.

"He accepted this gesture with a sad smile and continued, 'It was then among these people, a people so much still as I had been, I began to long for a simple cup of mead and a good tale. I had found a place along the road where such was served for coin. I entered the place, just sitting in quiet, listening to my language from someone else's voice. I had lived in seclusion for far too long and found myself now being ensnared by its simple beauty.

"'I had meant to be on my way quickly, having only the one cup,' he continued, 'but it had not happened this way. The afternoon had worn. The aroma of the stew that had been slung over the hearth fire had become a living thing, winding its way into every nose. All around me, they were eating and drinking their fill. Talking, laughing, all of it weaving a spell around me, I couldn't seem to force my legs to lead me away to the loneliness again. On the third cup, I reckon it was, I actually began to pay attention to the words and not just the sound of them, in the conversation that was going on behind me.'

"Piper had looked me in the eye briefly, to be completely clear with this next part as he lowered his voice. 'Now I don't make a habit of eavesdropping mind you, I try to stay away from humanity for the most part,' he said. 'And wouldn't have then, but I had heard "change shape" and "wolf man" and I couldn't help it, my curiosity had been piqued.'

"'So I called for just one more cup and focused my hearing behind me. From what I came to understand, there has come a curse of some kind among some of the Celts of the Highlands.' He had lowered his voice yet again so that I was forced to lean forward as he continued saying, 'Causing them to change, but into half-wolf, half-man, not one or the other as we do, and only when the moon was full. They are said to go berserk, killing livestock or any other things to come into their path. These unfortunate souls would remember nothing of it when they'd wake. They would find themselves naked, in their fields or someone else's, with not one idea what they'd done or how they came to be there.'

"I had looked at him in disbelief saying, 'I mean no offence, but are you sure you were not just gone in your cups and misunderstanding? One does not change without thinking and meaning to do it, and half shapes are forbidden.'

"'Ach, no offence taken,' he replied. 'It would take more than a few cups of mead to make one mistake the fear in their voices. I would not believe it had I not heard it for myself. It was enough to convince me that they at least believed it. When I asked one of them to have a cup with me, and tell me what they were talking so earnestly about, he said he couldn't stay any longer as the moon would be full that night, and he must be getting home to his family. I tell you there is not a Celt alive to turn down a cup offered in turn for a tale, unless there is a damn fine reason for it,' he said.

"He had given a short laugh at his last assessment, looking down at his own glass. Edsel again refilled it and we both looked uneasily at Piper as he took another long swallow.

96

"Then he continued soberly, 'I then thought of the Council. She who had changed me, before she went her own way, leaving me to mine, had told me of it. She had said that came I to any troubles I could not right myself, and she could not be found, that I might turn to them. She said you were still very young but seemed to have knowledge of certain things.'

"'The one who blessed you knew of the Council?' Edsel asked.

"'Yes, she had told me you had solved a great problem for Changelings years ago, and in any case,' he said, ignoring my objection to being assumed a member of the Council and turning back to again speak directly to me, 'she seems to have disappeared quite cleanly from this earth some time ago, and so I came here. Roman or Celt, we are all Changeling, and this seems to be in need of addressing as Changelings the other things can be set aside in deference to that.'

"I was considering all the Celt had said when Edsel began voicing his own musings aloud.

"'Lachlan has gone back down into Egypt, to nurse his obsession with the old one he can never find,' Edsel was saying. 'And he has once again taken Kynan with him, as you know.'

"He was speaking to me, not really simple musing, and his tone was too polite. I knew already in what direction his mind was headed, so I took pity on him and saved him the trouble of asking.

"'Yes, and I too am well overdue for a new adventure,' I said, to make it seem my idea. 'I think I will go into these Highlands and see for myself what these men Piper spoke of were talking about. If there is any truth to it, it could, well and truly, be a disaster such as you are constantly on the lookout for.'

"I smiled again to myself. Edsel had become so predictable to me. Now he would invite Piper to dine with us and plague him with endless questions. He would want to know more of the one that had made Piper. That one having at least known of the Council, he would be dying to know why she had not told them of blessing him. How she had escaped being reported to them by their network of spies as one who was 'blessing' without their blessing. I watched him as he relaxed back into his chair, obviously feeling a small part of the weight being lifted from his shoulders, and considering his next move. I thought then how I would miss him, he had truly become a friend to me.

"Thinking this suddenly reminded me of the twins, and I almost changed my mind instantly. I wondered how I would ever be able to leave them. In this situation, with no real guide, I had become enamored of my role as their elder brother and mentor. Yet I somehow managed to convince myself that the Council had not as yet failed in its protective role, though its means might often disturb me. They had survived years before my arrival and they would survive another few months. Surely I would only need to be gone from them for but a few months?

"When I went back out into the garden, they were subdued and I knew instantly that they had listened in. I chastised myself then, angry with myself that I had been so intent on deciphering Piper's accent and grasping everything he had told us. Between that and his new Changeling presence to distract me, I had not thought to discern if theirs was close by.

"I knew full well they did not know, as I, how to disguise their presence. None of them seemed to. So I berated myself all the more for not having prevented their eavesdropping, that I might inform them better in my own way.

"Adreal took the blame, as was his way, stepping toward me first.

"'I'm sorry I disobeyed, but,' he began, and then he broke into tears, unable to finish his sentence.

"Running up to me, he wrapped his arms around my waist. I nearly changed my mind yet again, having to force myself to be firm in my conviction, as Adonia too began to cry, and came to hug me.

"'Please,' I begged, 'don't cry, you know how tears destroy me.' I wrapped my arms around them both, adding, 'Since you were listening in you must realize how important it is that I do this.'

"'But why you?' they demanded in unison.

"'Because there is no one else here to do it, all those capable of handling a mission such as this are on one already. You know how fond Edsel is of expanding one little rumor within his mind. He will mull it until it is pulled so far out of its proper proportions that it becomes the veritable uprising of hell, needing to be squashed immediately. This sounds as though it could truly be a problem, a Changeling problem, and does bear looking into,' I said.

"They had smiled a little at my assessment of Edsel's character and I felt I was making some small progress in making them understand my decision. At least they seemed willing to dam up their tears for me.

"'Besides,' I added, 'it's not like I will be gone forever or that you're going to die anytime soon. If I don't go, Edsel will let it swim in his mind until he becomes impossible to live with, and we don't want to live with him in such a state until one of the others returns.'

"I tweaked Adonia's nose and squeezed them both once more as they began to sniffle back their tears in earnest. Adreal released me first, wiping his long, white, grass-stained sleeves across his nose. Then Adonia stepped back, tears still wet on her face, and looked up at me, staring me deep in the eye.

"'Swear!' Adonia, always the brave one, demanded.

"Adreal's sharp intake of breath and quick glance around told me that swearing must too be against the Code. So taking it one step further, to prove my sincerity, I put my hand over my heart and looked them both in their eyes.

"'On my soul,' I intoned solemnly.

"Both of them took in great breaths and looked around, making sure none of this had been witnessed. I too scanned for any presence, not wanting to have placed them in the path of any possible punishments with my rank disregard for so many of the rules they must live by.

"My promise to return seemed to satisfy them, for they now seemed a bit more contented, though not as they had been before Edsel had come for me. I wanted them to be happy always, laughing as they had been. For the briefest of moments it came to me to take them with me. Yet I knew this would never be permitted and I might only be putting them in danger, for I had no idea what might await them where I was going. I did not know, for that matter, what awaited me.

"Having thought of putting them in danger made me again think of all the things the Council did not see fit to teach them. I decided then that I would teach them all the things the Elders would not, and damn the consequences. No time now for the little answers here and there; I knew them to have strong, beautiful souls that would not misuse the knowledge. I would assure myself that should the Council fail or fall, they could survive without it, even thrive, and I would do so before I left them. I had no other choice I would consider.

"So it was, when darkness came to claim the city, and I had assured myself Edsel was fast asleep in his bed, I came to them in the chamber they shared and, waking them, bade them return with me to the baths where we had met. They had come quietly and unquestioningly with me through the villa, seeming to know already what I meant to do.

"Once we had arrived at the baths and I had assured myself with all my available faculties that none were within a distance to observe or hear, I began to tell them all that I am also going to be telling you right now, so listen well, Angel."

I had been hypnotized by Demon's voice as he spoke. He had ceased long ago to use his teacher tone and hence I had become lost in the tale. Since he had been speaking in this quiet manner, at such length, his use of my name nearly made me jump from my skin. His tone had suddenly become almost teacher-like again, as he seemed lost a little in the memory yet determined too that I learn something more from this tale than merely how he came to meet Baylor.

I nodded, wide-eyed and silent, to prove I was indeed listening closely as he had just instructed. He continued, "I told them how so many things that a Changeling did would begin like reaching out in the dark for something you knew would be there. When your hand met it you knew what it was, its shape and texture would be familiar. One might not know what one was even looking for, but when found, it was recognizable immediately.

"I explained to them how many things would begin with the soul, not the mind. Like if they needed to know whether or not a Changeling were near. They could reach out in a way with their soul, much like scanning the horizon with blind eyes. If their souls came near to another changed soul, they would know it, feel it, no contact need be made nor should it. If the soul were vile or mean-spirited they would instantly sense that too.

"To avoid such a soul, I told them, there were many ways, but best was to pull back their soul immediately and to begin to think of nothing, nothing at all, becoming a blank spot essentially. So that should that other soul take notice you had come near to it and begin searching in kind, it would sense nothing.

"I told them should they come upon a Changeling such as that, in the flesh, unexpectedly, as they had myself in those very baths so long ago, that if for whatever reason they had relaxed what I said should be a constant vigilance and awareness, and should such a one try to do them harm, that their best course would be to throw off all the energy that gave them a form it could do damage to. They should flee in the spirit to some place far-removed, willing new form to take shape around them when they were safely away. I warned them that it is always far easier to gather a new form to you if you have never allowed harm to come to the energies that have submitted to you before.

"Should they, however, choose to stay and engage in a battle, they had to keep their wits about them. They must remember it is all about inflicting pain, be as quick and ruthless as they could possibly be. Inflict so much damage so swiftly and repeatedly, so that their opponent would be forced to flee its flesh, leaving them alone. Make it so that the other Changeling must leave its form behind, so that it could not heal that form fast enough but rather have to escape it to escape the pain. They must make the encounter into a constant barrage of agony, so that the other Changeling could not possibly repair or heal its form quickly enough to do harm to them with it before they rendered it useless again. 'Be ruthless,' I told them.

'There is no good way to fight, only quick ways to win.'

"I told them how once in a while they might 'hear' a soul 'singing' out to them, whether or not they were even looking or listening for one. It would be so beautiful and alluring to them that they would be in awe of it and be hard-pressed should they try to resist looking for it. This would be a soul that begged for change, which denied conventional belief and did not want to end its time here. A soul refusing to believe it should have to. These souls appeal to ours because they have a force of will so much like our own. Our souls respect and admire this quality, they cannot help but be drawn to others like themselves.

"It *is* beauty and it *will* sing to you, it has a beauty very hard to deny," he warned me, as he had the twins so very many years ago. "But you must be very careful not to come into contact with it, not to be seduced by it, not to bow to its will to remain. You must first look very closely at it. Examine it, to be very sure that it is worthy to be a Changeling. For once your soul makes contact with another, it is changed, and there is no changing it back. You must be positive that it is good and pure, and I trust that you will. Yours, like the twins', is, and like recognizes like. Just as your will is going to recognize these kinds of souls on hearing them, and draw you to them.

"The twins told me they had heard such a thing before but had been warned that these were a kind of siren to the 'Blessed,' an evil seduction set out by vile forces to draw them in to their destruction. I had to then explain to them why the Council had chosen to tell such lies, that they were not evil because of this, merely afraid of too many things and unable to trust when they should. I asked them not to judge the Elders but to try to understand their reasoning, and I explained those reasons the best I could, while not agreeing with them myself.

I then spent the remainder of the night showing them one form after another and how to use them. Constantly thinking I was forgetting something, as I had tried to condense over three hundred years of learning into one single night, I tried desperately to assure myself I was leaving them well prepared.

"I would ask them repeatedly, 'Have you any questions?'

"They would nod each time that they did not, and I knew I had confounded them with so much information at once. So great was the desire in me to make sure they would be able to handle whatever came, I could not stop myself.

"You and I have time, Angel, and I will explain these things again at greater length to you if you need me to," he told me. "But the more I had thought about it the more I knew the things Piper had said needed to be investigated, and soon. Also the more I explained the Council's methods and reasons behind what they had done, the more I knew I must go.

"I did not know if maybe a Changeling that should have never been made was running rampant in the Highlands. Having spoken to them about what to do, should they come to meet a Changeling with an evil soul, reminded me such things did happen occasionally, for whatever reason. Once in a great while a mistake was made and vile creatures were created.

"Having gone so long without meeting one, maybe even a part of me had become soft with the belief the Council's goal had been attained, and none were made that would willingly bring harm to anyone. Maybe I simply could not fathom a Changeling willingly helping an evil soul to remain in this world. Either way my teaching of them had taught me something.

"Rather than mocking Edsel's constant vigilance, I should have kept mine as well, as I had warned them to do. I could not sit there, in the protective lap of the Council, like a small contented dog. Doing willingly with myself what I had scornfully told Edsel he should not do to these young Changelings on our first meeting. In allowing myself to be shielded from the realities of life, I had been; I had been allowing myself to be shielded.

"They were realities, and could not be so easily escaped, bad things happened that should not, and were possibly happening right now in those Highlands. I could not, in good conscience, pretend that all was well. Simply because all was well here with me, as I happily enjoyed the company of my precious twins, did not mean all was well elsewhere.

"Morning was coming far too quickly as I again tried to think of any further warnings or advice. Grasping for anything I could tell them to keep them safe and I think they saw, on my face, my worry for them, and took pity on me.

"'We will be fine,' Adonia said then.

"She consolingly placed her hand to my cheek and gifted me with one of her beautiful smiles.

"'Yes,' Adreal agreed.

"Following her lead he stepped to my side, stretching up taller to put his arm across the back of my shoulder.

"'Besides,' he added, 'as promised, you will not be gone forever.'

"He was reminding me as subtly as he was able that I had given my word to return. They were acting like such adults, it near did me as much damage as had they begun to cry again. Knowing they were putting on their bravest faces to save me worry broke my heart all the more.

"'Come then,' I said.

"I took Adonia's hand then in mine, and put my arm around Adreal as he had me. I walked them from the bath silently, praying I had done right by them, that I would be able to return and walk with them this way again.

"We took to the air again, and it brought me some small measure of much needed joy to see them shifting through many of the new shapes I had taught them, with so much easy grace. They might have been young still, both in age and in the change, but they were truly skillful beyond any number of years. They went through each new form never loosing speed or altitude. I was very proud of them and my pride too near changed my mind.

"You will find I am sometimes a sentimental creature and returning to that garden, just before dawn with them, I was reminded keenly of our first meeting. That garden had become ours, a haven apart from the world. It was our wrestling arena, our poetry recital forum, our place to dream out loud where the gods might hear but the Elders wouldn't bother. I wanted it to be that way forever.

"I painted it as a picture on the canvas of my memory, every flower,

104

every fruit tree, and every color to remain with me, as it was right then. I embedded each and every scent. Above all, I ingrained within my heart and mind, the twins. All the way down to the tiniest of details.

"The way Adonia was pushing the hair from her face because a breeze had come up and blown it forward, each jet strand shimmering nearly blue in the rising sun. The way Adreal was scuffing his foot in the short cropped grass and did not seem to know what to do with his hands, except hold them behind his back so that I would not see him wringing them. How none of us knew what to say but were saying it all perfectly well. I captured it all. So that I might return there in my mind, whenever I had a need for what peace such a memory could bring me.

"'Until we swear again?' I asked, wording it so they would know I would never forget my promise.

"Adonia took a step forward. As always the first one, keeping her poise and refusing to cry for my sake. She stood on her tiptoes and placed kisses on me, one to each cheek.

"'Until we swear again,' she said.

"Then Adreal came up to me also, stretching up to put his arms around me. This he did in much the same way they had witnessed Kynan do, when that one and myself had been reunited. Both of them were being so strong, I was afraid I would be the one to cry.

"'Until we swear again,' he agreed.

"Then he had released me. I could not stay one moment longer. I kept the picture as it was. I threw off the energy I had carried as my own for so long, so that it would remain there with them, pieces of me all throughout our garden. Leaving it where they would be able to feel my presence long after I had gone, and take what comfort they could from it, when they would.

~10~

Werewolves

"And that is how a Changeling of Athens ended up in Scotland," he said. "The kilt? Well, it is comfortable; if you think it an odd choice of attire you should see what I used to wear."

Demon ended his tale with a short laugh, pushing away from the sadness that seemed to have built at the end of it as he pushed now away from the table, stretching his arms high up over his head.

I couldn't help thinking how beautiful he was, not just his body, which was indeed very nice, displayed as it was just then in all its perfection before me, but his heart as well. I had learned more than just how he came to be here in his tale. I had seen deep inside of him. He was thoughtful and kindhearted and, yes, sentimental as he had admitted.

Baylor had gotten up and stretched as well, and like witnessing a yawn I could not help but follow suit. When I had finished I looked at Baylor, as he turned to walk into the adjoining chamber to retrieve more wine.

"Do not think you've gotten out of telling me your part of this," I called.

His shoulders slumped as he disappeared into the other chamber, throwing over his shoulder to Demon, "And she's a demanding little wench as well."

"I still have your brush," I countered.

"Ha!" Demon said, pointing triumphantly at Baylor, as he reentered with the new bottle of wine.

"And now, whose friend are you?" Baylor rejoined.

I started laughing then. They were like two overgrown children and it did my heart good to see them in this way. They might not share blood with me, but I knew then they would make me a wonderful family just the same.

"I still want to know how you two came to meet and be friends," I said.

Trying the new tack of pouting this time, I stuck out my lower lip.

"Ahh! Then that would still be Demon's tale, for it was he who found me," Baylor said triumphantly.

With this he bit his tongue between his teeth and made a face at Demon then strutted passed both of us, with the wine and his goblet, both in one large hand, like a rooster proud to have just awakened the sun. The only thing out of sorts with this perfect impression of the cocky foul was the fact he was gingerly rubbing his posterior with the other as he went.

"But before Sir I'm-not-the-longwinded-one, begins telling tales again, might we remove ourselves to softer seating," he said. "My arse is killing me."

My cheeks were killing me as well, both sets, as I followed Baylor, glass also in hand, still laughing, passed Demon in search of the softer seating he led us to. Demon was left standing, hand to chest as if he'd been stabbed, a mock look of betrayal on his face at being referred to in such a way. We made our way to a grouping of mixed padded chairs, settees and chaise lounges, including the one Demon had fallen onto to sleep the night before.

I went to this one without thinking, until I sat down. Unexpectedly I could feel that he slept here often, it was full of him somehow. I had to admit to myself, I liked being close to him, even if just in a residual way. I had leaned against the old oak pulling the feel of him from it when he had left me that first night. I did so now, pulling it from the place he so often slept. I did not, however, allow myself to think too much about what this might mean at that time. The memory of the feeling my body had woken up with that morning left me confused and uneasy, not something I wished to consider just then.

One must also understand that it might have seemed obvious to anyone else that he was a very attractive man and that my hormones were finally waking up, being extremely late sleepers, as I have figured out now. I had the distinct disadvantage then of having just been made a Changeling, with no one to tell me this was not a Changeling dilemma, but a life one; merely a part of growing up. Granted I might have asked Demon if these feelings were due to the fact our souls had made contact and his had changed mine. Indeed, I wanted to know if it was a feeling all Changelings felt for those who changed them and became their mentors, but I could not bring myself to ask. It was all too mixed up, and I was almost embarrassed even thinking about him guessing at my dream.

Baylor had placed the wine and his goblet on a table near me. He had begun scooting and pulling different pieces of furniture about. Then he would turn in a circle a few times and move another piece. He was reminding me very much of a huge hound looking for a comfortable way in which to lie down. Finally he seemed to be satisfied with the new arrangement, and turned to take one of the seats that faced me.

Demon then came to join us, walking toward his normal spot, which had somehow avoided being moved. As he noticed I had taken it he paused. Just as I thought I should move and give it back to him, he veered right, taking the one opposite it. We all had, in this new triangle arrangement, a clear view of each other. I saw then there was reason behind Baylor's odd behavior after all.

"More wine, anyone?" Baylor asked.

"My good sir, are you trying to see me soused?" I said aloud.

I froze, instantly confused as my normally silent, English accented inner monologue, which usually remained in the confines of my head, popped out in public. I glanced quickly at Demon and then at Baylor, who both seemed as shocked as I was. Embarrassed, I was about to apologize when I started laughing instead, and they quickly joined me.

It seemed we laughed endlessly back then.

When at last we had again subdued ourselves, and had been sipping our wine in comfortable silence for some time, I looked expectantly at Demon saying, "Well?"

"Well, what?" he asked, in mock ignorance.

"Come now," I coaxed, bottom lip jutting forward again in an exaggerated pout. "How did you come to meet Baylor?"

"I went looking for Werewolves and found one. I liked him. We're friends. The end!" Demon attempted.

He was trying to keep a straight face, but failing miserably.

"Not fun!" I cried. "Must I get up from this comfortable seat and find Baylor's brush?"

"I've hidden it," he said, looking smug.

"Please," I begged. "You did so well with the first part."

I added this hoping to appeal to his ego. I'm not sure which tactic had worked. Or if he had simply decided he had nothing better to do with the day, and would rather tell me than hear about it forever. As he would have, and I'm sure he knew it. Whatever the case, I got my way and relaxed back into the soft padding that felt of him, losing myself to his voice as he started to speak again.

"I wasn't even sure I had reached Scotland at first," he began, "as traveling incorporeal can often be a tricky thing. I knew I had crossed water not too long before, as it has a different feel to it, even in the spirit. I drew form here in the Highlands and looked around, both with my eyes and the other way in which I've told you we can do. Nothing came to me in either case and I simply began to walk.

"When my feet became tired or began to hurt, I would change into another form and continue. I went on in this manner for two days, before I came upon the spring that we stopped at, where you learned to be a fish. I had decided then that it would be an ideal place to rest. It was well-hidden and yet I could see for miles around me. I took then the form of the wolf, as it had been much on my mind for the obvious reasons. I sharpened my sense so that I would be aware of anything that might approach, and I slept. It is in this manner that I spent the better part of three weeks, going about all over these Highlands hunting for any sign of these 'Werewolves,' as you called them, until I was too tired to continue. Then taking the form of the wolf, I would rest there.

"I had decided when I had taken my form in the Highlands that I would in essence work my way from the top down. Since in all this time I had found not one sign of any thing out of the ordinary, I was preparing to move down into the foothills. I waited one more night. I was thinking that if I found no sign up here during that night's full moon that I probably never would.

"I could then move on, with my conscience being as clear as it could be, knowing I had searched as thoroughly as I knew how. You must realize I did not even know exactly what I was looking for. I had begun again with all of my senses and abilities to scan for anything out of the ordinary, when suddenly, I felt a flash of something *almost* like a Changeling in the heights above me, but then it was gone. I wondered if it had even happened, for I now felt nothing at all.

"I knew a Changeling could shield its presence from detection by thinking very hard of being and appearing to be nothing. I thought then that maybe my scanning for it had been felt, and it had shielded itself in this manner. This made no sense to me, however. The presence I had felt appeared as quickly as it had disappeared, and why would one seeking to hide its presence have dropped its guise in the middle? It had been almost like starring at a wall and a painting appearing on it, but before I could discern what it depicted, it had vanished.

"I took again the form of the wolf and went further up the mountain, heading in the direction from which I thought this feeling had come. I heard a fearsome battle taking place above me, even before I reached this plateau. When I came up onto it, I froze. It was only luck that I was hidden. A good thing, for I could do nothing then, but stare.

"There before me, shown clearly by the glowing fullness of the moon, were two huge beasts such as I had never seen. They stood upon their hind legs, knees backward, with tails protruding much like a kangaroo standing tall..."

"Kangaroo?" I interrupted.

Demon sat his glass down and quickly obliged me with an illustration, changing into one of those amazing creatures he had called a kangaroo, then changing back into himself just as quickly. I was amazed even more then, if that were possible. He retrieved his wine, and picked up where I'd cut in, acting as though nothing out of the ordinary had just occurred.

"They had huge bulging muscles across their bellies, backs and arms, like enormous gladiators. Yet from the shoulders up they were huge raging wolves, and they were covered from head to toe in fur. They tore at each other with both fangs and claws. Their great snouts were snapping furiously, and their growls and howls of pain were splitting the night in two. One was more massive than the other was, and it appeared that his wounds healed more quickly, almost instantly. The other's wounds did not heal, or at least not nearly as fast enough to be perceptible and I knew the larger one would be the victor.

"They had battled in this manner until nearly dawn, when the smaller of the two, being worn down and greatly wounded, let down his guard for not but a moment. I stood in awe as the more massive one moved in instantly, snapping his huge jaws closed on the other's momentarily exposed neck. Raising his large misshapen and clawed hands to the other's head, the stronger one twisted and tore it from his opponent's shoulders. The smaller one had dropped lifeless to the ground, his blood pouring freely forth.

"The victor had then thrown back his head, howling out at the moon. It was a most painful sound to hear. He was holding his opponent's head high, like an outrageous token of love to that unyielding orb. Then the howl had disintegrated into an incredibly mournful sound, as he lowered the head slowly as though his token of love had been declined. I watched as the horizon turned pink and this Werewolf dropped back onto his haunches. He was still clutching the other's dismembered head, but there came a gentleness in his manner that made the scene, impossible as it seemed, even more grotesque, as he sent up another howl that spoke volumes of both anger and pain.

"Then when I thought no further strangeness could occur; that I could bear witness to nothing more outrageous, this huge beast changed into a near equally massive man. Naked, and bowed over in the dawns faint light, his anguished howls became human sobs of unthinkable pain. He held the head still in his now human hands, and this head had also become human. His cries slowly took enough form to resemble words and I realized that he cried to it for forgiveness, repeating over and over two words.

"'Forgive me!'

"I could not move as I was confounded by all of this, and neither my mind nor my body responded to my need for answers. I could only listen as the man gained some measure of composure, and slowly began forming whole sentences that I could understand. He told the soul of the man to go to its rest and be at peace, that he was sorry to have brought this upon him. He even vowed to honor the man with a proper burial.

"He stood then and not one visible scratch could I see upon him. He picked up the smaller man's dismembered body gently and carried both pieces close to himself, reminding me of a small, heartbroken girl, who having recovered her torn rag-doll from the village boys now sought to return both pieces to her mother to be repaired. He shocked me further as I watched him walk straight up to the sheer face of the cliff, open what appeared to be a hidden door cleverly fashion into it and disappear inside. When he reemerged he was clothed in a tartan of tattered blue and green shot through with yellow. He held a crude shovel in one hand and cradled in the other, like a huge child in swaddling, was the body of his fallen foe, wrapped in a coarse woolen blanket.

"Then, carrying this body just as though it were merely a sleeping child, he walked to the far edge of the plateau. Here I had to strain my hearing to know if he would say more. I was amazed again when, after having dug a hole and placed the man in it, he said, 'May what god watches over you speed you to a better place and forgive my spreading this plague among our people.' I remember this quite clearly for it echoed in my head as he began to fill in the hole.

"So if you think your first impression of Baylor had you frightened, you can imagine my state of shock.

"It took me some time to compose my mind and try to begin to think clearly and rationalize all these things. I thought throughout the day about all that I had witnessed. I wondered how such a thing was possible for, in all my years, I had neither seen nor heard of anything such as this. I wondered as well at this particular one's awareness, even when a Werewolf. For Piper had told us they were unaware of what they had done when they awoke again as humans. This one had seemed to know he had killed someone or something and been saddened greatly by it, howling miserably, even before he became human again. He had also appeared to feel responsible for this other Werewolf's having been made.

"I sat in contemplation the whole day through, wondering if it could be that he was indeed responsible, being as he had healed almost instantaneously and been so much more powerful that the other. I knew that among Changelings the older ones grew to hold a greater sway over the universe. This one might too be very old, having had greater healing power and awareness. Therefore he could in some way have been the other's creator.

"I still did not know any better what to think when he again reemerged from the mountain. Then an idea took shape inside me: to simply ask him outright what I wanted to know. I had great faith in my ability to protect myself should he attack me, but somehow I didn't think he would there was something about him, whether it be the rage that he had so obviously felt when he had killed the other Werewolf, or simply the way in which he'd cried and then buried him, that told me I could speak to him. I just had to figure out a way to approach him.

"I had to make him want to talk to me, but how? Then I figured, why not? What more harm could come to a situation so messed already? The Council wasn't here to say me nay, and would I really care even if they were? I would show him I too changed shape, so he would feel safe to trust me, and talk to me about how this had happened to him. I would also make it clear I was not evil or in need of a swift death. I knew he couldn't kill me, but I'd seen him at work and I didn't like entertaining the thought of his trying to.

"Now I had a new dilemma, for I could not think what form I should take. Not a wolf; that thought died immediately. I needed something that he wouldn't fear and so kill, or try to, in self-defense, but what? I contemplated this for some time as well, before it came to me to take the form of the stag.

"I could not be sure, but I thought I had once been told his people revered it for some reason. So that was what I did, I took the form of the most beautiful stag I could imagine, a 'Royal', and walked out from behind the boulder, where I had spent most of that day deeply submerged in thought.

"He was hard at work chopping wood under a tree, and had not noticed me as I crossed the plateau. I was nearly to him when he looked up. I don't know what I had expected; actually I don't think I had thought about this part at all. The initial reaction had not been important to me, only the end result, and again he shocked me.

"'Edana!' he cried, dropping his axe and falling to his knees. 'Forgive me; I am doing all I know to set it to rights!'

"I didn't know what to think but I had to continue with my plan. I couldn't guess why he had reacted like that. I had to move. I could not allow my mind to run off into a world of new questions. I turned into myself copying his mode of dress to put him at least that much at ease.

"'I am...' I began.

"I got no further than that before he had his axe back in hand and was flying at me with amazing speed for a man his size.

"He was yelling, 'What have you done to my Edana?'"

"This was not working out at all as I had planned. I was to walk up, change, say, 'I am a Changeling. You seem to have a problem that involves some kind of change. I want to help. Might we talk?' and that was to have been the end of it.

"The plan I had concocted had not involved me doing what I was just then, hurriedly yelling, 'Wait! What? Who is Edana? For god's sake man, put down that axe before someone gets hurt!'

"He stopped just short of cleaving me in two. The axe frozen mid-swing, still held ready to complete its job.

"He said, 'You don't know my Edana?'

"'No, I do not, and from the looks of it I don't believe I want to,' I said, looking at the axe and then to him. I raised one eyebrow and said, 'Might we talk in private, without the axe?'

"He had laughed then, a great booming sound from deep in his belly. He turned and threw the axe so that it struck the tree he'd been working under, planting itself deep in the bark.

"'If you do not know Edana, then we are well met,' he said then. 'I am called only Baylor.'

"He stuck his hand out and I took it, admiring his grip. A gladiator trainer, or 'lanista,' would have given an entire herd of goats for this man.

"I couldn't help it, I allowed myself to be sidetracked and asked him, 'Who on god's great green earth is Edana?'

"And that, my dear, begins Baylor's part of the tale," Demon ended.

Leaning forward to grab the wine from the table that was between us, and refilling his glass, he grinned to himself.

"Your turn to entertain our Angel," he added, turning to Baylor, still looking smug.

"But you were doing so well!" Baylor's attempt at using my tactics didn't work out as well as it had for me, as Demon just laughed at him.

"There is no way that is working on me this time. 'But you're the better hunter, you're the better fisherman, you're the better...,'" Demon said.

"I caught onto your game years ago."

Demon sighed contentedly and leaned back on the chaise lounge he occupied opposite his usual one, which I had taken, putting one hand behind his head. With the other he held his wine balanced on his chest, swirling it gently.

"Besides, you're the better storyteller," Demon then added, laughing.

Baylor leaned forward and refilled his glass as well, cutting his eyes at Demon, as he put the wine back on the table.

"Should have buried that axe in you after all," Baylor said, and then we all laughed.

"Well, if we must continue the whole day through with telling you tales then you must provide us dinner," Baylor told me. "Leftover stew may suffice for our luncheon, but I'll not have it for my dinner as well."

"Well said!" Demon agreed.

"Fine, but you can do the hunting, providing the meat, 'since you're so good at,'" I replied sarcastically, turning to Demon.

"Ahh," he countered me. "But you must test your wings. I think we shall have to see who the better hunter is."

"Leftovers, anyone?" Baylor said.

Exiting rather too conveniently from the conversation, Baylor made the offer as though he would be serving up some rare treat, which it had been, the night before, but I wasn't sure how it would be now. I realized I was hungry though, and added my assent to Demon's.

"Why should I have to learn to hunt, with you two big strong men around?" I said playfully.

His serious tone when he answered was quite unexpected on the heels of our recent jesting.

"Because sometimes the unexpected happens and I want you prepared," he said. "You must always be learning everything you can. Know that you can never rely one hundred percent on anyone but yourself."

Baylor returned just then, with another small table held before him. On it there were three large, steaming bowls. I said nothing more about it and neither did Demon as we all ate our meal in silence. The stew had simmered over the dying embers of the hearth all night and this morning. If it were possible, I thought it even better now, than the first time. I said as much to Baylor who smiled his acceptance of the compliment.

My mood lightened again with his smile and I found I could contain my own curiosity no better than Demon had so very long ago. I finally decided to give up trying to patiently allow him finish his meal, as he seemed to be silently nursing each bite, making the one bowl last as long as possible simply to delay me. Just then he tilted it to sip off the last of its contents.

"Well, then," I said happily. "Who was Edana?"

He laughed at me then, Demon joining him, and I had to laugh at myself as well, but not for long. He was indeed a marvelous storyteller and I was quickly swept away into another world created for me by his deep baritone.

I wish I had his voice here, so that you might feel and hear and smell, as I did, a Scotland that had disappeared long before I was born. A Scotland filled with romance, glory and bravery in battle that to this day fires the imagination, a wild country that created heroes and legends with the same easy complexity with which it wove its family tartans, brought back to life as could have only been done by the soft brogue of one who'd been there.

Part
2

February 9th 1996

~11~

Druid's Word

"Edana," Baylor whispered.

It meant so many things if one were paying attention, as I was. The one word spoke volumes.

"She was the love of my life...but not always. Before that she was the eternal bane of my young existence, and before that just another child born in my village nine months after a raid. We always had that in common, the rest just came with time."

"Where to begin?" he sighed again, and again I felt a great sadness and compassion for him.

"You do not have to tell me anything more if it pains you," I told him, not wanting to dredge up painful memories for him, simply to ease a curiosity in me.

"No," he said. "This is all many lifetimes passed and I have made peace with it. Besides," he added, "all must earn their supper, as old Sara would say." He gave a soft, short laugh then, some memory having tickled him. Then he said, "I just don't know where to start."

"Then start where you started, nine months after the raid," I said, and he picked it up. So began Baylor's tale:

"I never really thought of it as a hard life,' Baylor said. "Though I suppose looking back on it, it truly was. Now I live in relative ease, with fresh

119

water easily accessed in the next room, a friend and companion who can hunt down any prey in the harshest of seasons, and not a soul to fear.

"Growing up was very different. There was always a shortage of good red meat. Fresh water had to be carried from the stream for every task, and there was always a sense of fear. Resting just below the surface, waiting for you, should you mistake yourself for being safe.

"Our small fishing village had been raided often, old Sara would tell me, and I was going to grow up big and strong, a powerful warrior, and it *would* be stopped.

"And I believed her. It became the theme of my boyhood.

"She would send me off to find one of the few men our village still had, telling me that I must learn to earn my supper.

"It made no sense for the longest time how searching out old Conner with his one arm, and his spending the day regaling me with tales of war, should earn my supper. Until one day, secluded in his small hut, he displayed for me a chest of weapons. He pulled this elaborately carved chest from beneath the rough planking and padding of straw which served as his bed. The weapons he took from it were made of a silver metal, and very fine. I was thinking when I saw these things how they didn't seem to belong in this place. Until he said that all the stories he had told me were his stories, and he was going to begin to show me how to use these weapons, as he had done. He put one of them into my hand.

"'A sword,' he said, 'made of iron.'

"I hadn't known how important this was then but I was awed nonetheless. I sat in his small hut with the last of the sun's efforts streaming through its one small window. A single ray cut through the smoky haze created by his small fire and shimmered back into my eyes from off this metal. I was spellbound.

"When I returned to old Sara that night, I was all enthusiastic energy, bouncing around her as she prepared our meal. I told her what he had said and how he planned to teach me how to use these wonderful weapons he had shown me. I was still giving to her a very detailed and awestruck description of each of them when she set my dinner before me.

"'I'm going to be the greatest warrior,' I told her, barely noticing my food.

"Then she had stopped my rampant excitement, saying, 'Baylor, I am going to tell you something now, it is high time you knew it.'

"That was when I came to learn how it was that she felt learning the art of war was earning my supper. I was seven years into my life then, but I grasped it all with a vengeance, literally.

"She told me how before I was born a Druid had come to live in our village, a priestess, one of those that our people revered. The village had come together and built for her a place to live, honored that she would choose to live here with them, and teach them. She had lived in this very hut we now lived in, and been loved and respected by all our people. She had been in our village for many years and nursed and nurtured the people through many a recovery, from many a raid; earning every day all our people had given her.

"One night the air had grown thick and heavy and the sky had darkened with an impending storm. The entire village had begun the quick tasks of battening down in preparation, every person doing their part. All had been hurriedly going about these tasks and none had seen the raiding party coming. They were caught unaware, not having thought a raid would occur so soon before a storm, and having been preoccupied with their preparations for it.

"The people had run about frantically in the darkening dusk, scattering in all directions: the men trying to find their women and hide them away, the women, in a frenzy, trying to find their children, and the children screaming and running in all directions, in the near blackness that was descending.

"The raid had been swift and savage. Many of the men lay dead or dying, others would be useless if they did survive. This is when Conner had lost his arm, trying to protect their Druid. Many children and most of the younger women had been stolen away. The village was set ablaze and there was much crying and keening, as some found their loved ones no longer

121

among the living, or found them not at all.

"It was through this scene of chaos and raging flame, she said, she had seen the Druid limping to the water's edge. Blood had been dripping from her mouth and one arm was held, useless, close across her body. Her dress had been soiled and bloody, torn nearly from her body. She had not stopped until she stood with her feet in the water. It had lapped hungrily about her calves, whipping itself up into a rage to match her own. The Druid had stared blindly out to sea. Then she raised her voice up in a great keening wail.

"She had called to the heavens and the long departed men, 'I will have vengeance for this night, painted in blood by the son. The moon shall bear witness, and he will protect us all. So I will it, so will it be!' Silence fell all over the village, like the torrent of rain soon to follow. The sky let loose a great clap of thunder, and her form was illuminated suddenly by lightning. Then came the rain, as the sky broke open, and all knew she had put on all of those departed a great and horrible curse.

"Their Druid was normally such a quiet, peaceful woman that this had frightened many beyond what they would admit. All knew, deep down, that the Druids were more than healers and historians, teachers and leaders of festivals. All knew their Druid had just become far more before them. None ever said a word about it, as her belly began to grow. They kept their own silent councils or at least kept them to whispers in the dark hours of the night. Much quiet contemplation was devoted to whether their Druid had meant the sun, or a son, when shouting her curse, but none would be sure until she gave birth. All knew it was indeed a curse though, and that this curse's fulfillment was coming soon no matter which was to be the case. They were both terrified and hopeful at the same time, within that knowledge.

"She had searched out old Sara when her time had come upon her, telling her, 'I will not survive this night, as my vengeance has grown too big inside me and consumes all my strength to sustain itself and its purpose.'

"She had told old Sara to raise her son up well, seeing that he was trained and taught, so that he might fulfill her word and always protect their people. So it was, old Sara told me, the Druid who was my mother had died, as she had said she would, bringing forth the son. She had whispered only, 'Baylor,' as I had come far too large, kicking and screaming with rage, into this world, seeming to know already what I had come for.

"Old Sara had kept me then, and did as she had been asked, and raised me. I had been called 'Baylor' and nothing more, as it had seemed my mother's final wish.

"'You are your mother's vengeance and the protector of our people,' she told me. 'Finish your dinner and go back to Conner, learn all that he can teach you, and then find another who can teach you more.'

"I had sat in awe as she had spoken, knowing every word she spoke was true. I had always known that I was different. The other children of the village had never let it escape my attention, especially young Edana. Always I would hear something whispered, sometimes even hollered, when I passed the other children. That let me know that my feet were too big, or my head, or some other thing was not right about me. Most of the older people of the village had always just stayed clear of my path and now I knew why.

"Edana was always the worst, always the one brave enough to come running into view yelling, 'You're a curse, mum said!'

"Then she would dart off again, screaming as though I would chase her. I never did, before or after I had been told she was not wrong. I had always just continued on my way, going to see old Conner as I had been told. Even this I knew was a difference in me. Any other child would have taken after her and thrown her to the ground, squishing mud in her face, rather than continue on single-minded as I always had.

"I think mayhap now that her mother ought to have taken better care to see she was truly sleeping, or out of hearing, when gossiping with the other women of the village. But that is all just the path behind me now, and she too must have had a great need to believe I would serve vengeance, on her behalf as well, for had she not suffered, as my Druid mother had? Had she not also been left the burden of a child the same night she'd been stripped of the loving help of a mate?

"I began my training then in earnest, with a vengeance, you might say. Every day I would go to see old Conner, and every day I would swing the sword until I could no longer even lift it.

"Listening, as he would repeat again to me, 'He was taller than I by a hand's span, with hair and eyes as your own. You will know him.'

"It became like a battle cry within my heart, as I would be haunted with visions of this man standing above my helpless mother, beating her, forcing her. Envisioning Conner lying nearly unconscious, unable to help any longer, as his severed arm lay beside him and his life bled out. I could see my people running and screaming amid the flames. I could smell the fires and the fear.

"You must understand, the time in which I grew up was one ripe for raising a child up like this. Whether it was the Romans knocking insistently upon the door to our lands, or the constant raids by other clans and peoples that they feared. There was always a curse or hero for the people to believe in. Something to give them hope, that they would have their revenge for the injustices done them. It was not so different even some twelve hundred fifty years later, when the people had turned to William Wallace. So I grew up full of the knowledge I would avenge my mother and protect our people always. I was born to be a great hero and serve vengeance.

"It was also near this time, when I had begun training with the sword, that another Druid came to our village. Again we came together as a people and built for him a dwelling place. So it was that my nights were filled with the stories of Cuchulain and the mighty Red Branch, the doomed love between Deidre and Naisi, and the Queen, Maev.

"With my arms aching and hands blistered, I would come around the fire with the others. To find my purpose made even stronger within me, as his voice would weave for me tales of others who had done things, much as I was born to do. He would encourage me in my goals with smiles directed pointedly at me across the fire, and I knew I would be a great hero and protector much as Cuchulain had been.

"He also took it upon himself at this time to take Edana under his tutelage, telling her to cease her constant torment of me. Telling her I was destined for great things. He began teaching her the uses of different herbs in healing, and the histories of our peoples on a deeper level. Training her mind to retain all of it for the future teaching of our people and we were proud that she had been chosen.

"To be singled out by him for instruction in the Druid's path, was an honor, and she was full of this knowledge. I am not saying she came to feel she was better than the other children of the village, only that she took it quite seriously, as well she should. She no longer spent her idle time playing and teasing as she had done. Rather, it was that she was often secluded with him somewhere in the woods or on the shore, always learning something.

"He was a kind man, appearing to me to be very old, but then to me gray hairs were only for the very old and his was all silver. It was always glinting in the fire's light. It was long like that of a woman and blended most times with his great long beard. So that sometimes, when he was speaking to us as we surrounded the fire, I would think that a spark would jump up into it and set him ablaze. I would chastise myself harshly for having such an unkind thought about such a good man, though I suppose it was merely the active imagination of a young boy.

"So my life went: with my days spent in learning the arts of war, swinging axe and sword till my arms felt they would fall from my shoulders, and my nights spent sitting in rapt attention around the fire, listening to the Druid's words. Calluses came to replace the blisters and my arms grew used to their constant labors, no longer bothering me into the night. My purpose grew stronger every day as well, more a solid, tangible thing within me. As both Conner's teachings and the Druid's words congealed it, making it into a veritable force in and of itself.

"Until there came a day when there was nothing more for Conner to teach me and I knew my time had come to leave. So that I might continue, as old Sara had said to, in my learning.

"I went then to old Sara and told her that I must leave. Though she was saddened, she said not one word to stay me. I said my farewells to all in the village and told them that I would return. That then they would no longer have to fear anyone, for I would come back the greatest of warriors.

"It did not occur to me then that in the fourteen years I had remained there we had lived in peace without a single raid.

"It was in my fourteenth year then, that I began to wander the Highlands. I would seek out any with a reputation of skill in battle. I would convince him to teach me something more. Whether by seducing him with the grandeur of being the teacher of a hero destined to be a legend, as the Druid had assured me I would be; telling him, as I had been told, the story of my birth. This failing, I would often serve them on their land, had they any. Or do whatever labors they might put me to, to earn my lessons. I continued in this way for nearly four years. Learning what I could from any with a skill to teach me, then moving on.

"In my progress, I would come at times upon one who would rather try to steal my sword than teach me to use it better. They too became lessons, for I was never bested but always learned something, even if they had not intended to teach it. I had grown huge, not only in my body, but also in my confidence with my sword. We had become one in our quest and I gave it a name. I took to calling it simply 'Bane,' as I had the one simple name and thought so should it for my sword.

"It was after one of those encounters, which had become more and more frequent, that I came to realize I was no longer viewed and accepted by people in the same way. Whether because my size presented a challenge they could not resist or my Bane was a prize they would have at any cost. It may have been that I no longer appeared to anyone a boy in need of tutelage or simply that I was moving into rougher territory. I know not which. Only that it was at this time, and with these realizations preoccupying my mind, that I had come unaware, out of the brush. Emerging along the shoreline and in front of me was another small fishing village. The moon was full and bright above me and gave me clear view of everything before me.

"I must tell you here, that I knew. I had a surety in me that would not be shaken, even had the scene before me not been so familiar, having been envisioned so often within my head. He was here. The village was in turmoil, and he was here. People were running and screaming and I recognized the entire thing. As if reviewing a memory: the screams, the random fires springing up, the young women being tossed over shoulders and carried away kicking and crying out. These were all known things to my heart.

"He stood not but twenty paces beyond me, not but a hand's span taller than Conner, with hair very like my own. The moon gave me perfect view of him, creating a halo of fire of that hair and marking him for me. As if to say to me, 'Come, I will bear witness, as promised, take your revenge.' He stood towering over a helpless young woman as she screamed and begged for his mercy. He had none, as he kicked her then to make her cease in her cries. In my mind this young woman became the Druid that had cared for my people and been heartlessly destroyed. In my heart she became the mother I had never been allowed to know.

"I did not have any mercy within me then either then, as I came crashing toward him, bearing with me my mother's revenge, beneath her perfect moon. He saw me then in all my rage as I loosed it on him. He heard the great war cry tear out from my throat as I raised Bane to cleave him.

"'She will have her vengeance, written in your blood, by my hand!' I had yelled.

His eyes flew to mine, as he barely managed to raise his own sword and then only minimally slow my blow. In that instant I knew his eyes were mine, as well as I knew he recognized himself in me. This man had well and truly sired me, but I felt nothing good within me at this knowledge. If anything at all, it merely forced extra strength into my blow.

"Those eyes, huge now with shock, widened in surprise and then pain, as Bane broke his sword in two and continued in its path, hurrying to bury itself deep within his side, fulfilling our joint purpose. Then those eyes squinted with questions and flooded with pain.

"He fell then before me, almost too quickly to appease me in the least, his life spurting forth unto the sand. I stood before him as his soul left, that he might look upon his seed. Seeing in me what had grown of his foul plantings. I wanted him to see that the harvest stood over him and was also become the reaper. Knowing without a doubt of what I spoke as I stared down into his eyes, spitting my hatred.

"'Go now, to whatever judgment awaits you,' I told him. 'I am my mother's vengeance and have served her well this day.'

"His mouth worked, as though he would have one last word before he would leave, but failed. I didn't move then, or even lean down to hear what it might have been, or encourage those final words formation. I didn't care. I'd had my say to him and my mother had had hers.

"I went then into the heart of the village, a mighty rage still boiling in my blood. I spread our vengeance upon all those present and doing their evil to the helpless gathered there. I hacked them down like so many blades of grass, blind in my rage, leaving them to bleed out upon the sand. I swung Bane like I was some wild thing with arms that no longer grew tired, and a rage that refused to die, until the last of them lay dead.

"So it was my mother's curse upon them was fulfilled, as I left them all in pools of their own blood, where they lay strewn about as they had fallen, the great glowing orb of the moon watching, counting each of them with me. The sand absorbing what ink their bodies spilled, writing their eulogies for a long dead Druid to read.

"I cut then from each man's belt the thong that had held his weapon to his side when he was not using it, taking from them any means by which to even take a weapon into their next life. I made a braid in my hair for each one slain. Bigger ones for the better fighters, that I would remember my victory over each one, always. I tied each thong up in my hair, counting them with the greatest of satisfaction. There was in me then a wonderful feeling of joy and a new purpose.

"I took to the path that would take me back to my home and my people. I could return now, victorious, and be again among my own."

~12~

Hunting

Baylor stood and yawned then, stretching his huge hands high above his head. I was jerked back to the present suddenly and very aware once more of how huge a man he really was. I was imagining how truly terrifying he must have appeared back then, ragging through that village, and wreaking havoc on those evil men. A shiver went up my spine. Baylor noticed this and turned toward me.

"Have you a chill, lass? Do you want me to fetch you a blanket?" he asked.

The spell was broken.

He was too thoughtful and kind to be thought of overly long as simply a raging warrior. He was fast becoming a compilation of far too many conflicting things -- the great god Odin, who liked to cook; a Werewolf, who cried when he killed; a giant of a child making constant jest; and a savage warrior who told the best story I'd ever sat spellbound absorbing. Like Demon, he was showing himself to be very multi-faceted, and it all just refused to condense itself into anything more or less than just one word, "Baylor."

"No, I'm fine," I told him. "I was just so caught up in your story, it is amazing!"

"Well then," he replied, "seems I've earned my supper once again."

129

This was his reminder that I had to provide the meat for our dinner.

"Ahh! I want to know what happened when you returned home," I pouted, not ready for him to break off just yet.

"Then you'd best be about it right quick, hadn't you?" he replied.

His indulgent yet determined smile, coupled with his lifted eyebrow, told me I would get no further until I'd brought him meat. I looked then to Demon, who seemed also not inclined to move, hoping for some assistance from that one. Upon catching my eye, he took some pity on me.

"That was ingenuously cruel of him wasn't it, to leave it just so? Seems we must let him begin his precious cooking before we'll get another word," Demon said.

With that he stood and extended his hand, helping me to my feet.

"Come, let us be quick about it," Demon said. "The sooner he's got dinner cooking the sooner you'll have the rest of your tale."

Baylor put his hands then on his hips, looking very much like an upset housewife and suddenly sounding like one as well.

"You ungrateful little heathens!" he called, as we walked toward the door. "You're lucky I even do the cooking, mayhap I should only cook enough for myself."

"Ahh! But then you would be hunting for yourself as well," Demon tossed back over his shoulder. "And who then would be constantly complimenting your culinary skills?"

We heard Baylor's great booming laugh as the door closed behind us and I too began to laugh. Realizing this kind of playful argument had probably been going on between them for ages, about this same sort of thing. Demon looked down at me and smiled at my laughter, and suddenly I was very aware of his closeness and that we were alone.

I felt suddenly shy as he gazed at me and I could not fathom what he might have been thinking. My laughter died down, as my stomach tightened suddenly, and my heart jumped. I knew where my mind had a tendency to go when I was close to him and I searched about frantically for something to talk about to keep it from those wanderings. I managed then to think not only of his beauty but all the beauty around me as well.

"You know," I said, successful in my quest finally. "When I first saw this place I thought that a great house should be built here; now it seems, there has been." I nodded over my shoulder, indicating the door behind me, as I took a few steps forward then turned back to face him, adding, "This is become just a giant frontage." I waved my hand to indicate the whole of the plateau we stood upon.

"Yes, it is very beautiful," he said, coming up again beside me.

He was effectively destroying what little sanctuary I had created with the distance I had placed between us. The look in his eyes, such beautiful jet black eyes, was unreadable by me. I was on the verge of giving up, letting my mind wander wherever it would. God shouldn't have made eyes that pretty, they force little girls to wake up and become women.

"So what would you like for dinner?" he asked suddenly.

Thank the gods, he had distracted me or rather distracted me again. Suddenly I had something to occupy my mind, as I would not want to disappoint him by not coming up with an answer. I thought for a moment of the roasted rabbit I had missed before, but was not sure if Baylor would want to have it again so soon.

"Why not just fly about for awhile until we spot something," I said to him then, remembering the play of our first day, and letting it put a smile on my face.

"And you are sure you are ready for this?" he questioned me, wondering if I would be all right with the hunting and killing of another animal.

He was looking at me openly, awaiting an honest answer. So I gave it to him.

"Everything must eat," I said. Rabbits being on my mind, I added, "I may not like that some furry little bunny is going to die to fill our bellies, but if not us then some other predator. It is the way of things and I cannot deny I too enjoy having meat. I was after all created to be an omnivore. So as you said, I must learn to hunt."

He looked at me appreciatively, apparently having liked my answer. "Well then, follow me," He said.

So saying, he took the form of the great white owl he had taken before. I too did this and followed him into the darkening dusk, down the side of the mountain and back into the wood. We flew about for some time before I heard a sharp cry from him that, my instincts told me, meant he had spotted something. I had been much absorbed in the feeling of merely flying, and had not myself been hunting, as I should have been.

I watched in awe as he swooped down on the young boar, his weight as it came out of the sky sending it rolling and squealing onto its back. Then before it could gain its feet Demon swiftly changed from the owl to a wolf and tore out its throat. It had been quick and ruthless. I came to the ground allowing my claws to become feet and standing before him as myself, and I was still filled with wonder.

Then he turned toward me, his jaws still dripping with the blood of the young boar and I was suddenly afraid. I'm not sure why this had frightened me, looking back. Maybe it was just the very human, primal, instinct to be afraid when viewing such a scene and in turn being viewed by a wolf with blood dripping from its jaws. But just as his unwavering gaze was near to tearing a scream from my lungs, so intense and inhuman was it, he became himself and laughed.

I knew full well his laughter was due to the exhilaration of the hunt and he was apparently unaware he had near frightened me to death. I suddenly felt very silly for having let him. I started laughing too, only at myself. Then suddenly a new thought made me laugh all the harder, only at him.

He must have realized we were not laughing for the same reasons for he said then, "What?"

He was looking himself up and down as though he would find some fault with himself to have caused my laughter. This was the second time he had done such a thing and I wondered if there might be a reason. For now, though, my mind was more involved with our present dilemma.

"It is only that your eyes appear to have been larger than your stomach, so to speak. That thing is going to be far too heavy for you to carry!" I started to laugh again but was cut short by his response.

"That, my dear, is why you are going to help me gut it," he replied smartly.

Then he was laughing at me, and it wasn't so funny, by far, to me then.

The task was not as disgusting to me as I had at first thought it would be. Either that or maybe it was just that I had done quite well with my wolf instincts, when I had finally joined him to complete the job. Either way, it was accomplished quickly, and we were soon on our way back home. He had made his form quite unnaturally large when resuming that of the owl for the journey, and I stored this as a new little piece of knowledge about our kind. We did not have to be a creature exactly as it was in nature: we could make it bigger, faster, stronger, and I thought I must ask him more about it when we had arrived at our destination.

When we had come back to the plateau, Demon had dropped his burden to the ground beneath him. We had arrived with a few hours remaining still until midnight. When we had again taken our own forms, he lifted the young boar up in his hands and carried it the rest of the way across the space to the door, which he then kicked twice. Baylor was there almost instantly and Demon dropped the boar into his waiting hands, walking silently past him in the direction of the bathing chamber.

If I had had any doubts before that this was a normal arrangement between them, they vanished then. I was torn between seeing how Baylor prepared such wonderful meals and wanting to wash myself. Since I also had a question for Demon, the washing up won out and I too went to the bathing chamber.

This was not the most genius decision I had ever made, as Demon was standing in the hip-deep water with his back to me, naked as the day he was born. The water was not providing much cover at all. Frantically I began trying to make my body obey my mind and turn to leave, but I was far too fascinated right then to concentrate very hard on such an accomplishment.

"I will cover myself if it will make you more comfortable," he said suddenly. "Only, of course, if you still wish to join me instead of just standing there."

Thank goodness he could only sense my presence behind him and didn't actually have eyes in the back of his head. Because I am sure that was the most embarrassed I had ever been. He was covered instantaneously with a loincloth but did not look back to see what my decision would be. Again I gave silent thanks.

When, at last, I felt my face might have returned to a normal color, and I could safely join him without it betraying me, I became aware I didn't know what would be appropriate for a woman to wear when joining a man for a bath. I wanted to, not only so he would not guess at my sudden shyness or the cause of it, but also for reasons I was not yet prepared to consider. So I simply gathered my bravery to myself and chose to do as he had.

I entered the pool then behind him, wearing a brief cotton dress to my knees, like one I would have worn to bathe in a stream. Pushing my dress down as the water tried to lift it, I began the conversation immediately, hoping to eradicate any other thoughts that might try running through my mind.

"When you turned back into the owl the second time tonight, it was bigger. We can change the size and shape of things to suit our needs then, am I right?" I asked.

He turned then acknowledging not only my presence in the pool but my statement as well. He handed me a small scented bar he had been rubbing on his arms when I entered, that I might do the same. Then he began concentrating on rinsing the white lather he had created with it off of himself and said, "Yes, but you must be wary when making such changes, as they can also become a danger to you."

I was scrubbing my arms as he had and looked up then, instantly intrigued.

"A danger, how?" I asked.

Privately I was noting that this bar of soap was where he got his wonderful smell, while trying desperately to make myself return my focus to his teaching. It is rather odd, how it seems I often had two totally separate thought processes running side by side, when around him.

"If you alter the shape you must also alter the instincts," he said. "A normal owl with a normal wingspan can make use of those wings with normal instincts. Because it is something your mind invents that does not exist in nature, you cannot simply tell the energies making you up to give you the instincts that go with it. We are part of nature but if we make ourselves unnatural, natural energy doesn't know what to do and we must tell it. We also must be right."

"These energies can become the form you picture in your mind," he continued. "But they cannot give you the instincts to go with it, for they do not know them. You must then tell them something like, an owl on a larger scale, and hope for the best. I have had a lot of practice, but I don't suggest you try it alone, especially with birds, until you have gotten it down."

He grinned, for apparently he had found his own teachings amusing for a moment. Or some memory or other had amused him again. I was still considering all of this, turning to place the soap on the edge of the pool and rinse my arms, when Baylor's large form came to take up the doorway.

"Dinner is started," he said, then turned and walked away.

Demon exited the pool, coming to stand on the edge of it, clad, as usual, in a kilt and loose white shirt. He reached down his hand to lift me out and, as I finished my rinsing, I took it.

A strange look came into his eye then and he turned to leave. It was I who was now looking myself up and down to see what flaws I might have, just as he had done when first we had met in the flesh. It was sometime before I dared to join them again; I had found my shift to be plastered to my body and was greatly embarrassed. I had not, as he had done, clothed myself in dry appropriate attire on exiting the pool and I wondered if the look on his face was disappointment at my lack of skill. He had taken such pride in the skills of the twins and I wanted so much to make him proud of me as well.

Finally I gave up my embarrassment, for I could do naught to change the cause of it. I was eager to hear the rest of Baylor's story and just standing there wasn't helping. I attired myself then much as I had that morning and I simply told myself I would do better next time. I would learn from my mistakes and not repeat them, it was the best I could do. Then, putting on my bravest face, I went out to join them.

They were both smiling and waiting for me, where we had been before, freshly refilled wine already in hand. Demon handed me my also refilled glass as I walked past him, and he did not appear upset with me. So I quickly forgot the whole incident as I set about getting the rest of Baylor's tale.

"So," I said, "what happened when you went home?"

"My mother's curse took on a life of its own," he said. "Not so much at first but eventually."

"What do you mean?" I asked him, and so Baylor began the tale again, picking up where he had left off.

~13~

Edana

"'When I came at last again to the village where I had left my people, it was very much changed. New homes had been built and others rebuilt in the same places. Many of the faces I had looked forward to seeing were not there. Some of them that were did not seem as pleased to see me as I was to see them. They peered out their half-opened shutters and called no greeting at all.

"The air seemed chillier suddenly, the day not as bright. The sound of the water lapping on the shore seemed not as inviting as I had imagined it would be, yet it was the only welcome I received. I walked through the center of my village, wondering why it was that none came to greet me. I was a hero, was I not? I had done the first of my mother's wishes and now I returned to them to do the rest.

"It was then that Edana finally came out to greet me, her long blond hair swaying behind her in opposing time to her hips. She had become an amazingly beautiful woman, and though I had not really expected her, so much as others, I was very happy. I swept her up into my arms swinging her around.

"'I have done it!' I said excitedly. 'I am become a great warrior and fulfilled my mother's curse on them that were deserving of it.'

"But she said nothing in return. She did not try to pull herself from my arms but neither did she hug me back. No happy laughter or congratulations came from her lips. So I sat her down, holding her at arm's length that I might look her better in the eye.

"I asked her, 'Have you no kind greeting for me?'

"'Aye, Baylor, 'tis glad I am, you have returned,' she whispered.

"Finally she had squeezed my forearms in return and given me a beautiful almost shy little smile.

"'Only you? Why are the people not happy to see I have returned? Why have none but you come to greet me?' I asked.

"'Most are afraid of you,' she had replied sadly. 'You have become a giant in their minds and in truth.' She looked me up and down, emphasizing her words. 'Even I was frightened at first, until I knew for sure 'twas only my childhood friend, come back to me. The story of the curse surrounding your birth has spread. Some fear it, especially those newly come to live here, who have never met you in the flesh. Others, those left from your time here, feel you abandoned them in a time when you were most needed.'

"She then told me, 'In all the time that you stayed here with them, not one evil thing had occurred. Then, when you left them, they were again attacked. Now many of them are gone and they feel that, had you stayed, you could have protected them. They say your mother's curse placed made you their protection in that you were merely present.'

"Her perfect blue eyes were very sad and she appeared not at all the young happy girl that I had left, but rather now a woman aged beyond our eighteen years. She was still very beautiful to me and I wanted to understand her sadness and put it from her.

"'How then would I have become a great warrior to protect you if I had not left?' I asked her, wanting to understand the people's reasoning.

"'Those who were here then think that old Conner had taught you well enough. They think that you should have never left them,' she answered. 'As I said, they felt your presence was the protection, that no further skill was needed.'

"'And you? What do you think?' I asked her, surprised by my own deep desire to hear she did not begrudge my absence as the others did.

"I will never forget her answer. For it surprised me and made me think of things that I would not have otherwise considered. Would not have considered had they not come then from her lips.

"'I think that it was old Sara who made the mistake, not you. In telling you that you needed to go and find others to teach you, she turned you aside from your path. It truly having seemed your mere presence here was enough to keep the people safe until you had grown big and strong. Your mother never spoke of you leaving here for any purpose, even that," she said.

"'But what then of the vengeance I was to serve?" I said. 'I found those men far from here.'

"'You had learned all you would have needed to know from Conner, and eventually those you needed to take revenge on for your mother would have come here, as they did again in your absence. You would have accomplished both goals in one: protecting our people and fulfilling her curse on them at the same time,' she finished, and smiled again at me then.

"It seemed she was trying to tell me that she did not blame me. That she understood I had only done what I had been told by the one who had raised me. She seemed to merely wish to make me understand the views of the people and why it was that she was the only one standing there now to greet me.

"'Come,' she invited. 'Dine with me, and tell me all that has become of you. Put the people's fear and lack of reception at this time from your mind, and enjoy this evening with me. The people will forgive you and quickly forget and when they have heard you destroyed those who have plagued them, you will indeed be their hero. They merely need time to see things as I do.'

"So she had taken my hand and led me to one of these new places I had noted. She explained that all had gathered and had built it for her. I came to learn that she had excelled in her learning and was become a Druid herself. I asked her then about the old one who had been here when I had been.

139

"'He is with us still, though grown old now beyond most of his senses. The years have been not so kind to him. So that now, not often does he venture from his home,' she told me.

"'Who then do the people come to?' I asked.

"I was still very much surprised at the revelation that she had been accepted as a Druid. Not yet thinking that I would know her answer, even before she told me, it was she.

"We dined then in her home and spoke of the old times, laughing openly, like children again, at some of the things she had done to me in my youth before the Druid had taken her in. I would call her a harsh name in jest, not yet thinking of her as a Druid, and therefore worthy only of my utmost respect. But she never appeared to notice or take it as any rudeness. We merely became again as we had been back then, two young people talking and drinking through the night.

"We had picked up effectively where we had left off, only now as adults looking back. I had told her of my adventures and all that had taken place of note in the last four years, regaling her with tales of those people who had taught me, willingly and otherwise. The hour had grown very late as we talked of all these things, both long past and near present, which made us laugh. We had begun more frequently yawning into our mead cups than drinking from them.

"Then sobering, she told me of all that had taken place there in my absence. Not only how she had come to be accepted in a beautiful ritual that had taken place amongst a great gathering of Druids, a year ago, journeying to somewhere far into the lowlands, to a place that she did not name, but that it was during this journey that the village had again been raided. She explained I was not the only one who need feel the guilt of having been absent, when this tragedy had befallen our people. Both she and the old Druid had been away as well.

"So now not only were we both the bastard leavings of a raid some eighteen years before, but also we had in common our guilt. We confided in each other and took comfort from the knowledge we were not alone. She spoke of the many sleepless nights she had lain awake with the great 'what if' torturing her, only to find it did naught but leave her too tired to accomplish any good in the day. How she had finally had to simply set it aside if only to do right by them now.

"She then began to tell me of all those who had departed from us into the afterlife, and I was greatly saddened to learn that both old Sara and Conner were no longer among us. Conner in the latest raid, and Sara wearing herself far to thin with the caring for those wounded in it.

"The time was very late now and both of us very tired, being hard pressed to keep our eyes open. She told me that I might take the place that I had shared with old Sara, as it had been my mother's and was therefore still mine. She told me also that she would speak with the people and make things right between all of us. We would have a great feast on the morrow. I could tell them all, as I had told her, of the great victory I had won for them, and there would be joy again in our village.

"I went to my rest with many things then in my mind and it was a long time before sleep could claim me. I lay there on that pallet that had been in my boyhood a place to rest my aching arms and legs. It was now become a place for an aching, confused heart. My body was exhausted yet my mind refused for a long time to let me find rest.

"I thought of all I might have done differently, but I could not fathom how I might have been victorious over such numbers as there had been, had I not continued in my learning beyond what old Conner had taught me. I knew that if nothing else there had been in those other men a way to test the skills he'd taught me, for he had not been able to spar with me as they had. I still did not know if I had made the right decision in leaving, when my thoughts turned to Edana and how beautiful and wonderful a woman she had become, and sleep finally came bringing me peace.

"When I awoke, it was to the smells of a wonderful meal being prepared. Outside my door in the heart of the village, a great fire had been built and a huge boar hung over it on a spit. I came out to hear the people cheer, and I did not know what she had told them, but it did make my heart jump to be so well received.

"A small child was turning the spit, his feet lifted off the ground by each turn of it, and he let it go then to run to me, tugging eagerly at the bottom of my shirt. I looked down at him and it seemed he would topple over backwards as he tried to look me in the eye.

"'Can I be a great hero too?' he asked.

"His huge blue eyes were so wide with wonder and hope, that even had I thought differently, I still would have answered the same.

"'Yes,' I told him, lifting him up into the air and looking him deep in the eye, that he might know I told him true. 'As long as you have a pure heart and good intentions, bearing the needs of others above your own, you will be.'

"I meant it and he knew it. I could see his little mind taking it in store, as I had all the things I had been told in my youth. I sat him back on his feet and smiled as he nearly tripped, so eager were his little legs to get started, desperate to carry him off to tell his friends that he too was going to be a hero.

"The day passed splendidly then, with each person both known to me already and new as well, having been given, by that small boy, the courage to come and greet me as well. Much mead was passed about freely, and laughter and kind words as well. When at last the food was served there was a great sense of happiness and peace among us as we all sat around the fire.

"'Give us the tale!' someone called.

"I turned to Edana, wondering what tale she was to tell for them and if she would have the skill of the old Druid who had taught her. There was in me a sudden welling of pride then that she had succeeded so well on her path. Then I heard the same voice call out again.

"'Nay, your tale!'

"I looked then past the fire, trying to make out who was speaking, and ascertain to whom they were speaking. It was then with much embarrassment that I heard Edana as she leaned toward me. Her shoulder pushed in to mine, making me aware that I should dip my head for her to tell me something.

"'They want your tale Baylor,' she whispered.

"I could hear amusement and also pride in her voice.

"'But I do not know how to tell a tale,' I whispered back.

"Consternation and sudden shyness were mixed quite suddenly and unexpectedly within me. It made me sound like a whining child and even that, in itself, embarrassed me.

"'You are the Druid,' I tried.

"'Just tell them as you told me last night and you will do well,' she prompted.

"Her faith in me, combined with the continuous repetition of the first man's call that had now turned into a chant from all those present, finally got my voice to working.

"So I told them all in great detail, describing things then with an eye for the gore and glory that all of us so enjoyed when describing a foe's defeat. I related it as best my vivid memory of it could allow. I tried very hard to do it in the manner the old Druid had, when telling us the stories of the Red Branch that we all love so well. When I had finished there was only silence and I felt I had not done it right, when suddenly a cry rose up from one.

"'To Baylor, and the Druid's revenge!'

"And they all raised their mugs and glasses, repeating in unison, 'To Baylor, and the Druid's revenge!'

"I knew then I had done it well, and they had been there with me, as I had been there with Cuchulain. So I was back with my people and one of them again, having been fully accepted back into their lives.

"I spent the next few years as a teacher, instructing the young men how to defend themselves and the women and children. I sent a small number of them to trade for weapons, instructing them to come back only with the ones made of the silver metal, as I had seen the grater value of it firsthand. I would have gone myself but I did not want to leave my village unprotected again. So it was with great relief that I saw them as they returned again, safe and with those things I had instructed they find.

"It was also during this time that I began to fall very deeply in love

143

with Edana. We would sit and talk endlessly, whiling away the hours of the night that we should have been sleeping as the others were. We would relax most often on the shore, allowing the sea to lap at our bare feet and ankles, building little bulwarks of the sand between our toes and speaking of everything or nothing at all, well into the night.

"She would tell me things she admitted she was not supposed to tell me, and that I was to tell no other. Druid rituals were described to me that no mere man should know, but there was in her a faith that I was no mere man, and that I could be trusted. This she told me freely, with no coyness about her, the way she shared everything else within her heart with me. We nourished a closeness then that I knew I would find in no other. I knew also that someday I would ask her to be my wife.

"I realized that I must first build for us a home that would befit not only her position, in our people's lives, but in my heart as well, creating of it a worthy gift to her. It would have to be able to house many children comfortably and give her space to do her work, as I knew I could never ask her to give it up or set it aside. So I began my planning, and I would go out early in the morning cutting down the trees, harvesting the wood that I would need. I would drag it back to the village, and stow it away behind my hut, so that she would not see it. Then I would go about my instruction of the young men and my long talks with her, as though I had done nothing before the dawn.

"Sleep became a thing for those without goals. I was in love, and sleep could wait. One night while we were speaking at some length about the older Druid and his still rapidly declining health, I had interrupted her, as my mind had been wandering. I looked around me, and I could bear to contain it no longer.

"'I want to build for you a wonderful home,' I told her. 'Where would you have me put it?'

"I had waved my arm then to indicate the whole of the area around our village, the shore, the very sea. I would have built it for her wherever her heart desired.

"'But why would you build me a home when I have one already?' came her confused response.

"Her face was full of such confusion. I was amazed. She seemed not to have seen I would ask her to be my woman. I turned then to face her more fully and took her hands in mine.

"'Because I want you to be my wife,' I told her. 'And bear me sons and daughters and talk with me, as we are now, until the end of time.'

"The look of shock she so openly displayed would have made me laugh if she hadn't said what she did then.

"'But haven't you been listening?' she said.

"Sadness and proud joy warred on her face and I couldn't decide which she felt more strongly. I found that neither could she, as she continued.

"'I have been trying to tell you, if you had only been listening, that the old Druid is dying,' she had said. 'He has revealed to me a great secret. He has told me that he carries within him a blessing passed down from Druid to Druid since time unknown, and that he will pass it on to me, should I choose to take it. But if I do I can never marry, or be with a man in any way. Even you, ever again, or this will expel the blessing from me, and it will be lost to us for all time.'

"I stared at her aghast.

"'But you will not take it then,' I said finally. 'Will you?'

"'It is a great blessing and it will be lost to us if I do not,' she said. 'There is no one else he might give it to.'

"She seemed to be very upset then. I did not like to see her so distraught and I wanted to help her to decide. I wanted her to be always full only of happiness and joy, and make the decision that would bring her the most peace in the end.

"'What then is this blessing and how will you receive it?' I asked her.

"I was trying to make my face a calm mask. Where it would not show any disappointment that might sway her either way. I thought mayhap if we were to talk it through, the answer would come to us, as it had so many other times.

"'There are two ways to receive it,' she said. 'Either by being close to him when his spirit leaves him, hovering over him in such a manner that it passes through me, on its journey. Or by killing him outright, ending what he considers to be the suffering of remaining here any longer, and accepting it as it leaves him.'

"My eyes widened in shock as I forgot my goal momentarily and she hurried forward with her explanation, so as to make me understand.

"'He is in great pain and can no longer see, sometimes he does not even remember who he is or who I am,' she said. 'But when he does, he has begged me many times that I should do this for him. It is a great honor that he should even offer me this blessing, as it is being able to take the form of the stag at certain times important to we Druids. That I should even be considered for such as this is a wonder in itself, as I was not born a Druid but merely trained and accepted as one.'

"I still could not fathom any of it. I was envisioning my beautiful kind Edana standing over the helpless old Druid, knife raised over her head, ready to plunge it into his heart. I did not know what to say. I could see easily that she felt it was the greatest of honors. I had heard of those very special Druids that could change into the stag, blessing the earth where they walked. But I also could not think how she could even contemplate a life without me, as I could not see myself old without her. I just had no words. So I turned then, leaving her to decide for herself which path would be best for her, knowing I would be unable to prevent myself from trying to make her choose me otherwise.

"It was nearing dawn, when I would have been going to cut more wood, but had no heart for it until such time as I had her answer. I walked in silence and contemplation. I tried to tell myself that each person had a destiny and it was not my place to begrudge her hers. Had a Druid not also set me on a remarkable path? I would let her choose for herself. I would not allow myself to become her old Sara, steering her wrongly from it. These thoughts brought me some small peace as I headed in the direction of my bed.

"Then the raiding party came. They came from out of the hills and with great cries, sweeping into my sleeping village. I burst into a run. All of these other thoughts vanished as fast as I reached my hut. I took my sword from beneath my bed. Then I ran back to the center of the village, Bane in hand. I called out as I did this, with all the force in my lungs, for all the men I had trained. Yelling for them to take up their arms and do as I had taught them.

"I ran then to greet my enemy, with all the courage and ferocity of all my years of training for this day, to protect my people. I look back now and know that much of my ferocity was born of anger at my present situation concerning Edana, and that, most likely, is why I made my mistake.

"I had held them back.

"Meeting them, as I had, head on, a raging, flame-headed giant, come out of the dawn, I had the momentary advantage of surprising them, as they had surprised us. My size and open rage served me well. I sliced through the air repeatedly, cleaving arms and legs indiscriminately whenever my blade found them. All the men of the village then came up as a force behind me, and we quickly drove them back into the wooded edge of the village from whence they'd come.

"This was not enough for me though. My rage demanded they would not escape now, and avoid payment for their attempted raid upon my home. I would not leave them to regroup and return at some later date when I might be less prepared. I took after them in a blind rage. Never did it concern me that I pursued them alone, that the rest of the village men had given up the chase sometime before. Never did it occur to me what I was doing, I was merely acting on my anger, and not just anger with those I chased but life itself.

"I pursued them, for how much time I do not know, but they must have realized at some point that the one pursuing them was only the one, because I came crashing into a small clearing and was attacked immediately from all sides. They had lain in wait for me and prepared for this, as I had not, and I was hard pressed to defend myself. I swung Bane in a huge arc, cleaving all within its path but I felt a sharp pain erupt in my back.

"Then a moment later another pain exploded in my leg.

"I continued swinging with blind fury, my arms having been trained so that they need never stop. I hacked them into so many pieces, like chunks of fish for attracting whales. Here and there I felt new pain, it made itself known to that part of my mind that cared that I was being wounded. The part that was also irrationally trying to tell me Edana might not like my body covered with scars. I continued on though, furiously, until they had all fallen beneath my blade.

"Then, I too fell.

"Dinner smells ready."

"What?" I said. I couldn't believe he had done it again as I realized his last words had nothing to do with his story. "You can't do that!" I looked then to Demon. "Tell him! That's not fair!"

"I used to tell him all the time, but he'll only tell you nothing in life is, may as well let him have his fun," Demon told me. Then he looked to Baylor, whose face wore a very self- satisfied grin, telling him, "You are indeed a cruel, cruel man!"

But he was laughing as he followed Baylor to the table.

~14~

Cursed

When at last I'd given up my pouting, as it was doing me no good and I was only missing out on what did indeed smell like a delicious meal, I joined them. I caught a smug look still in Baylor's eye, as I sat down before the feast. He had roasted the boar and boiled various vegetables by leaving them cooking high above the hearth. It was the look that held my attention, however, it was so full of mischievous mirth and self-satisfaction just below the surface, and it made me laugh too.

"You are evil you know, I take back the 'good man' assessment of our first meeting," I said.

He too let loose the laughter he'd been holding back. "Well now, I couldn't leave you with such a badly misconstrued impression, now could I?" he replied.

He was enjoying this far too much.

"But we could leave you without meat for your supper tomorrow," I said, looking to Demon once more for support.

Baylor's response was quite unexpected.

"Nay tomorrow night," he said. "I hunt for myself and, the gods willing, find only game."

The sadness in his voice, so close on the heels of his recent mirth, threw me off my guard and it was a moment before I could formulate my next question.

"What do you mean?" I asked finally.

"Tomorrow night begins the full moon and I will become the Werewolf. I will hunt for the others, as I have done every full moon, since I found out what I am," he replied.

Demon ate his meal in silence, while I tried to, but the questions just kept coming into my mind.

"When did you find out?" I asked, and Baylor laughed again.

Turning to Demon he said, "I think strong-willed was a divine understatement, I don't believe she knows how to give up." Then turning toward me, still smiling, he added, "That is all part of the rest of the story and you shall have it tomorrow when I've gotten my rest."

I pushed out my lower lip as my attempts at getting any further information or convincing him to continue failed. Both of them started laughing then. We then finished our meal in relative quiet and I stood and gathered the dishes, having seen where Baylor had always taken them and wanting to do my part. Baylor stood also and started to help me.

"No, I'll do it," I said. Then I laughed as something else came to mind and I added, "I must learn to earn my stories."

He laughed then too and I told him as he walked away, "You'd best get your rest, I'll expect my payment in the morning."

He was still laughing when the drapes of his bed closed in again, shielding his form from view as he slept.

As I finished up with the dishes, I realized I had heard no sound from Demon in quite a while and I looked over my shoulder to see what he might be doing. He was fast asleep on his chaise lounge again and I realized I had the place relatively to myself.

Quietly I put the bowls back in the cupboard where they belonged and slipped into the bathing chamber. I entered the pool fully nude as I had wanted to earlier and washed myself more thoroughly than I had been able to at that time. I washed my hair as well and then just sunk into the water. Allowing it to float me slowly toward the rear of the pool, where the steady, slow drain pulled the soap off the top of the water and into the fissure in the floor behind me.

In this position and in this lighting I began to notice the walls of this cavern. They sparkled, seeming to wink at me from every side, almost like they too were happy. I was happy. The realization struck me like a bolt of lightning and I sat up, realizing I had quite nearly been lulled to sleep.

I could see why Baylor had picked up the habit so readily from Demon and why Demon's people had adopted it in the first place. I sat there for a long time watching as my hands began to prune. I began going over the last few days in my mind trying to discern at which point I had found this happiness. I thought that I had never been truly unhappy per se but more like I had been merely contented, having known nothing more. I was then trying to make my short life form solid lines that I could grasp and understand easily.

Wanting that one should say: this is who you were and now this is who you are, and another to say: this is why you are happy and this is when it happened, but none of this seemed possible. I could not place any such labels on any one event. So I just let it be, I was alive and life was good. I was with two wonderful people, and I was happy. That was all that mattered for now.

I exited the pool, clothing myself as I came up for the practice, and went to my bed with a deeper feeling of contentment - no, joy - than I'd ever felt, blooming within me. No dream came that night to leave me disturbed upon waking. No further thoughts of Demon and his jet eyes and wonderful scent to send my thoughts into the great unknown. I slept soundly and peacefully, blissfully unaware that life would not always be so good.

I awoke the next morning with a burst of energy, knowing I would find out this morning what had happened next in Baylor's tale and how he had become a Werewolf. I did not take nearly the same care with my appearance as I had the day before. I settled simply for a clean, blue sack-type dress, with straight lines and a sash to hold it close at my waist. I jumped then from my bed, again running my fingers through my hair, and fairly skipping to the table to meet them.

"Well then, good morning Lass, I see you slept well!" Baylor said, as he put a bowl of his wonderful porridge before me and then walked away.

"Yes, you look quite cheery this morning," Demon agreed.

"Good morning," I said to both of them. Then, "Ho…where are you going?" I said to Baylor, thinking he meant to avoid his duty this day.

He stopped in front a small table, pulling something from a drawer hidden on its underside, then turned and started back.

"Only to get my brush for you," he said, displaying the item.

"Be careful with that. I hid it from her for a reason." Demon said this as though Baylor held a sharp weapon, as he covered his upper arm protectively.

I couldn't help but laugh again, holding out my hand to receive the brush.

"I'll be nice, I promise," I said.

Then, as it was firmly in my grasp, I added sweetly, "So long as you are," looking from one to the other.

"So then," I said, setting the brush aside and swallowing my first bite, thinking that I'd brush my hair when I was done, as I had yesterday. "What happened when you fell?"

"Nay not here!" Baylor said, looking with much mock fear written plainly on his face at the hard wood of the chair beside me. "I'll tell you when you've finished."

Demon and Baylor both tried to hide their amusement, failing miserably, as I made a great show of hurriedly finishing my meal and shoving my empty bowl away from me in triumph.

I said, "Done!"

That was it, they could contain it no longer, and we all started to laugh then.

Taking our wine as we had the day before, we made our way smiling back to our selected spots. Once all of us were comfortably positioned, it took no further prompting to get Baylor started.

"I had fallen then after having destroyed all my foes, and I could not feel my legs. I tried to figure in my mind why that was. But I slipped into unconsciousness before I could remember.

"When I woke next it was with an aching awareness of my entire body well beyond anything I had felt before. I began to try and pinpoint where each pain came from and what had caused it but it all blended together. I tried then to move my head so that I could look at my body and ascertain what had happened. Pain exploded anew throughout me and again I lost consciousness.

"I don't know how long I did this, slipping in and out of awareness, but eventually it came to me that I had been grievously wounded many times. That I should be dead, but I knew that I would not die. I had been born to serve my mother's revenge and protect my people. I knew death would not come to me yet. For I had done the first, but as long as they needed my protection, I had not done the last. I was sure that I would survive this and that one of my people would come and find me here.

"I awoke again with a terrible heat burning within me and I could not understand why it should be so hot. It was dark and the trees were shading me. I was thirsting and hungry but I could not move to take care of any of these needs. Then I heard them, calling to each other, in the darkness. I knew that they would come but I would survive that as well. I would live to protect my people.

"So they came, a pack of huge wolves, devouring up the bodies of those I had slain, fighting over the pieces I had cleaved. Tearing great chunks of human flesh between themselves and fighting each other for the better portions. One of these great beasts came then toward me and I determined that I would tell him something, should he lay his teeth on me.

"'I will eat you first,' I managed to growl, through my pain and parched lips.

153

"Then I passed from consciousness again.

"I did not know how much time passed then, but when next I came to my senses I was on the outskirts of our village, and it was nearing dusk. I saw Edana coming out from the house of the old Druid, with a delicate little knife in her hand. I saw the look on her face. I knew instantly that she had chosen the path of the Druid and not my love. The little knife was still dripping blood.

"I thought then to call to her and ask her why she had not, at the very least, told me of her decision before doing this. Then I saw two men coming toward her. One of them, the one who had first called for my tale the night after my return, held in his grasp my sword, and suddenly I was very afraid.

"How had he come to have my Bane?

"I had no notion. Not of how he had come to have my blade, or how I had come to lose it, or when the last time I had seen it had even been. I could not, for that matter, even remember how I had come to be here. That is when I noticed that I was naked as the day I'd come into this world.

"I was frozen then in a state near to terror, unable to move. I heard nothing of their greeting to her, but as my mind cleared that I might make out their words, staying as I was out of their sight, she calmed and quieted them, her voice somewhat calming me as well.

"I could see that they were in nearly as much distress as I was and wanted badly to understand why the man had my sword and why I could remember nothing. Bringing them to sit in a circle around a small fire she had already built, she coaxed the news from them, while tossing her small knife into the fire, unnoticed by any but me.

"The one with Bane told her they had searched this full month past, and found me not. They had found an area in which I had obviously fought in a great battle with many men and had left these foes in so many pieces, but that the rest of the tale she would not like. These men, it appeared, had been hacked to pieces, and then those pieces had, for the most part, been eaten up by wolves. It appeared the wolves had then turned on each other, for some of them too lay in pieces about this place. They could not tell from where these wolves had come, thinking some of my foes must have turned into the wolves in the first place because no tracks led to this area. What had so distressed them, even more so than that, was that there was no sign of me other than my bloody clothing and my sword.

"There had been, however, a set of tracks, larger by far than the rest, which they had followed to a neighboring village. Those villagers had told them a wild tale of having seen a wolf larger than a man, with a coat like fire and bits of leather tied up in its hair, howling up at the fullness of the moon in a glade. They had followed one of these people to this glade and found a chunk of fur, as told they might, with a leather thong tied up in it.

"The man holding Bane looked to his comrade, who then handed a chunk of bright red hair to Edana. I was terrified when I saw its color and the leather thong tied around it. A great invisible hand took hold of my heart and squeezed as Edana turned this lock of hair in the firelight and terror too came into her eyes.

"I had listened to all of this, the terror within me growing into a tangible thing. A horror I could not shake. I knew I had become this beast they described. I knew as surely as my Edana had accepted the ability to become the stag I had been cured to become some sort of wolf. I remembered, then, the wolves, wolves I had sworn to devour first. Wolves they had found torn to shreds. I ran as if the foulest hounds of hell had been cut loose to find me. Many thoughts ran just as quickly through my head, as I heard my mother's curse again.

"'I will have my vengeance for this night, written in blood by the son!' I did not know if I was being punished for having left the village unprotected again, even if only to go after those who had threatened it. If mayhap my pursuit of them, beyond the range of our lands, after they had already flown, merely to release my anger at Edana's possible choosing of another thing over me had been deemed by the fates cause to curse me too. Maybe this had been the curse all along: that I should become like Cuchulain when he became the Hound of Ulster. 'The moon shall bear witness, and he

155

will protect us all. So I will it, so will it be!' I heard again the man's voice: 'a great wolf beast, larger than a man…howling up at the fullness of the moon.'

"I came then out into a clearing and the moon shown full above me as it had the night I had slain my sire. I tried to call out to heaven that I had done my mother's will, and was not deserving of this fate. That I would continue to do it, only let it not be so, let me not be some great horrible beast. All that came out from me was a long desperate howl.

"Again I do not know how much time passed but it seems it must have been many years. For I found myself again on the outskirts of my village, again listening as my people spoke to Edana. Only now they all appeared to have aged. The man that had always spoken before was speaking again. Only now his hair had turned to gray and his voice was weaker than it had been. My beautiful Edana was older now as well, with small wrinkles at the corners of her eyes and mouth from squinting and pursing her lips as she had so often done. The young boy with the huge blue eyes and the hope of being a hero was a young man nearer now to my own age.

"My own age, how old was I? How long had I been unaware? The questions stumbled through my already confused mind, leaving me worse off than I had already been. I looked down at myself, somehow knowing that I would be naked and unchanged. I had not aged but they had. Was this then some new facet of the curse? That not only must I live as a beast but also I would not grow old as they had, I would not die as they would? Cursed to live forever, that a Druid I'd never even met might have a guardian for her people that would outlast any foe.

"What the man was saying horrified me even more than my discovery that I was unchanged. He said that these great beasts that were both man and wolf were growing to increasing numbers, spreading like a plague throughout all of Britannia and Erin. They destroyed cattle and people indiscriminately under every full moon. Then they had no knowledge of having done so, and that if you survived an attack from one of them then the curse was also on you.

"He was saying that they were fearfully hard to kill, and an old woman among those gathered asked him how one might accomplish it. He told her that the head of these creatures had to be severed clean off, but that one must be wary, for the jaws could still snap shut and if they punctured your flesh you would be cursed. Another man raised up his voice then, adding that they became human again when killed, revealing who they had been, and that it could also be done with a blade made of silver. They began to argue amongst themselves as to who had such amounts of silver to spare and who would come close enough to it to pierce its flesh with such a blade.

"I could remain and listen no longer. Their voices cut into me worse than any blade. I could not know if I had been attacking my own people and spreading this plague and I longed to sit among them. To somehow help them and myself discover a way to make all of it right itself. I longed most of all to hear Edana's soft voice full of wisdom. To be comforted and consoled by her, receiving much needed answers, but I knew I could do none of these things.

"I wondered then if it were not my mother's curse at all that had brought this on me, but rather one of the wolves that had bitten me. Carrying with it another curse, the one of which they spoke. I ran again for a very long time, seeking I suppose to distance myself from these people I so loved yet could not be with. I came here to this plateau. I stood here not noticing its beauty, blinded by thoughts and memories, thinking only of all I had heard.

"I kept telling myself that I must remember, when next I changed into this beast, to not do harm to my people. That I must hunt down the rest of these beasts, whether I had made them or they had made me. I had to stop their spread amongst my own. I had been born to protect them, not to do them harm, and I would see that none of these others did either.

"I made my home here, placing a safe distance between us. I discovered this cavern, and eventually constructed a door. I would go out on each full moon, keeping in mind my purpose, and I would hunt down the others of my kind. Whether by luring them here, or killing them where I found them, I would keep them from growing so widespread as to harm my village. I was saddened when I had to kill them, for they were just other people like myself.

"I might have even created them during my period of non-awareness, but they had no control of themselves, and could not therefore be left in peace to do their harm. I would bury them so that their jaws, even though they became again human mouths, could not by some chance still spread this curse. I would also pray every night to whatever gods might listen, trying to strike some bargain with them that they remove this curse from me. It would appear, though, that one cannot strike deals with gods.

"I have still no real explanation as to why I truly am or how this really came to be. Be it my mother's will that I walk this earth eternally, the moon bearing witness, and changing my form into something better capable of protecting her people from a plague she had foreseen would come. Or that I had fallen victim to one of these creature's jaws, while I lay wounded in the wood, and only her curse still makes me aware of a need to protect rather than do more damage. Mayhap it is a combination of both: that though I be cursed to assume that form by the one, I am aware and of a mind to protect with the other.

"I simply learned long ago that this was my lot in life. That I was to protect my mother's people, be it as a human or a Werewolf. I have not aged in all this time, so I suppose as long as there are Werewolves among us that would do them harm, so shall I be here to hunt them and keep their numbers down. Mayhap when I have destroyed them all, if no other threat remains to our people, somehow it will be removed from me, but for now I have accepted it.

"In any case, that is why I reacted to Demon's choice of the stag in his greeting me. I had not seen my Edana in longer than I could think. I thought she had come to find me, having discovered what had become of me, and where I had made my home. When Demon had changed into himself I had thought then that he had killed her to receive her blessing, as she had done with the old Druid before her.

"Once I had found him to have no knowledge of her and therefore thought he had received the blessing from some other Druid, I was willing to answer his questions. I told him, much as I have told you, all that I know of being Were."

~15~

Full Moon

I could think of nothing to say. I felt awe and compassion, pride and pity. That a young man who had suffered such a strange and hard life had still grown to be a wonderful and caring man, my friend. That rather than turn from the people who had been cause of the curse or the Druid who laid it upon him. He had chosen to bear, with chin up, his lot in life, speaking of them with love and respect, as though in some way it was an honor to have been chosen to do it. He was so much like my Mem in this respect.

I was reminded again of the time in which he had been raised, and the stories he had been raised on. I had heard the same tales he had, only from Mem, late at night while she prepared her herbs. I had taken them in as legends, even myths, but he had known them as the recent past and representative of a way of life his people cherished. Rome had stopped short in its conquest. I had seen Hadrian's Wall with my own eyes, in my wandering.

Yet I could understand the fear in those times, within those people, of losing their way of life. How, as he had said, they had instilled in their children faith in heroes who had already been, encouraging them to become ones as well. I now had to look at these things that I had also been told in a new light as histories: the reasons behind who and what we were as a people, not as I always had before, as tales told to entertain me.

I don't know how long I sat silent in this contemplation, but when I at last took notice of Baylor and Demon they were both looking expectantly at me. Baylor appeared to be simply happy to have completed the tale, waiting to hear how well he had done it. Having no notion of the depth of thought it had taken me to. Demon on the other hand seemed to be waiting for me to give some sort of judgment on it all. When at last I spoke, they both appeared pleased.

I raised my glass then, "To Baylor, and an amazing life!"

Demon smiled and raised his glass as well.

"So you never saw Edana again?" My sense of how a tale should have a happy ending, at least in some small way, was not yet satisfied.

"Only on those occasions I would go and look in on my village, and I never allowed her to know I was there," he replied.

"You never even told her…," I trailed off, not knowing what it was my romantic sensibilities felt he should have done or said.

"Told her what? That I had survived the battle, defeating those they feared, only to become one of the beasts they feared even more in the process?" he said. "That even though she had chosen to accept the blessing of the old Druid and I was become a cursed monster, I still loved her? Why would I torture her so? I did and do still love her and it is for that love that I let her live out her life in peace."

His tone was that of a man who had accepted things as part of an unchangeable past, unsure of the right or wrong of it but knowing there was naught to be done for it either way.

"But what if she would have chosen you and only took the blessing when you did not return?" I asked, not thinking how these questions might wound him.

"What if? I have lived too many years, with such thoughts of what if," He replied. "And I have come to much the same conclusions as Edana did so many lifetimes ago. One cannot go back in time to answer them, so they are but wasted questions."

His tone had become a little more pensive than simply accepting and

I realized too late that I had encouraged a line of thinking he did not want to follow. I was instantly sorry that I had done it.

"I apologize, I...," I tried.

He waved his hand, indicating it was just as behind him as the rest of the things in his life that could not be changed. I think it was at this time that he became well and truly my brother, for I loved him then. For his strength of character and forgiving nature, for all he was now and had been. He was an incredible man. I fell silent.

Suddenly he was again just the smiling and constantly jesting friend, trying to lighten the mood.

"Well, seems I've found a way to cease her constant questions," he said, looking to Demon.

They both began to laugh at me and I reached then for his brush, which I had set on the table sometime during his tale, having finished brushing my hair. I raised it threateningly at both of them.

Demon then added, "If only by increasing her violence upon our persons."

"Oh! You are both awful!" I said, and joined them in the laughter.

There was one last question I could not resist, though risking a return of the momentary solemn mood.

"And Bane? What of your sword?" I asked.

"Oh!" Baylor replied. "I returned one night to my village. Slipping silently into Edana's home while she was absent from it, I found Bane resting beneath her pallet, wrapped in my old tartan. I took it back then, not able to resist it. We were one, were we not? That was partly why I had thought she had come to find me. I thought it having come suddenly missing would have led her to know I still lived and begin searching again for me."

He had laughed, and then added, "More likely she never noted its absence, as the dust on it was mighty thick. Or when she did, merely thought some thief had stolen in and taken it for their own. It really matters not now. Bane is still with me where he belongs. I have had him remade more than once as better metals have been discovered, but he still remains my Bane. He would have otherwise been destroyed by the sea air, lying useless beneath her bed or mayhap been forgotten only to be rediscovered by another less worthy later."

"Less worthy?" I repeated, and then added with heavy sarcasm, "Have you no faith in your own skills and value?"

He had laughed then, realizing how his last statement had sounded, and I laughed as well. I was happy my last question had not set him brooding, as I had feared my ones of Edana had almost done.

The rest of the morning passed in this easy manner, with some question or answer leading us to laughter, and we were all in a wonderful mood. We lunched on the remaining young boar, poking fun at one another and enjoying it all immensely. I had never really had friends other than Mem and Father Paul. So I did not think at this time how rare was our instant friendship and sense of ease in one another's company was. Mem had always been, more a sister sharing an adventure, than a mother leading me on one. I had approached my relationship with them as mine with her. Their total acceptance of this had combined with their own permanently young approach to life to make us all get along famously.

As dusk came I noticed a sense of unease and purpose growing in Baylor's manner, reminding me again of Mem, how she would slowly cease in her jesting with me to concentrate better on the proper mixture of a potion. So it seemed he too was starting to change his demeanor to suit what he must do this evening. As dusk settled I came back again to the subject of his curse, as it seemed inevitable, being much on our minds.

"How is it you hunt them?" I asked.

"I scent them," was the instant reply. He didn't need to ask of what I spoke.

"Scent? What do they smell like?" My mind boggled at his response.

"Rage." It was a short, simple answer but not at all easy to grasp.

My look must have been amazingly confused because he started to laugh, and as his mood had been increasingly serious as night came on, I was happy to hear it again.

"Are you laughing at me?" I said accusingly, trying to hide my own happiness at his sudden relapse of good humor.

"Nay, just your face," He said, trying to get his laughter under control.

"Well, I'm happy my looks amuse you," I replied sarcastically, deliberately mistaking his meaning and putting on an outrageously overdone pout.

So it was that Baylor was still laughing when he went out into the night, doing his duty to a Druid he never had the pleasure of meeting. I was left then without my answer but content anyway, standing deep in thought, still staring at the door Baylor had just closed.

"You do well by us," Demon said, his unexpected words, so close to my ear, made me jump like a frightened kitten.

"What do you mean?" I said, with a short laugh at my own foolishness.

"Only that usually, for at least three days a month, Baylor becomes a moody, hard-to-live-with ass. He finds no enjoyment in his life in the days of the full moon. I must thank you for providing such a nice distraction for him, for us both."

I thought then of a certain time of the month I was not so pleasant to be around and couldn't help but laugh as I said, "Well, we all have our bad days and it's I who must thank you. You have given me a wonderful gift, and you may never know how precious it is to me."

I had no words to explain the depth of joy at having made such remarkable friends and being given another incredible chance at life. So I simply smiled up at him, hoping that he would know. It seemed for one heart stopping moment that he was going to kiss me then, as he had in my dream, but instead he looked down at my bare feet.

"Do you always go about barefoot?" he said, looking up again and smiling as well.

The brief glimpse of dimples had effectively restarted my heart, if not a little too quickly.

"Yes," It was the best I could do.

"Come then," he said. "Let us use this night for the learning of things, starting first, I think, with the making of foot-ware."

With that he led the way back behind the grouping of chairs we had spent so much time in recently, to an open area with only a kind of tapestry on the floor. This rug or carpet, as he told me it was called, had come from Persia with him, on one of his many trips for the furnishing of this place. This led me then to other questions. So the remainder of the evening was spent in his showing me the forms of animals found throughout the world and the clothing of the people of these places as well. Answering questions with illustrations such as he had with the kangaroo, we spent the evening hours well entertained.

"Have you been back to Rome, then?" I asked, his having just shown me a panther's form, had reminding me of the twins.

"Oh yes, I kept my word," he said, smiling.

I think he knew I was fishing for more stories even then.

"What happened? What did the Council have to say about Baylor? How were Adreal and Adonia?" I begged.

He sighed. I suppose he gave up getting me interested in learning anything else this evening unless it was through another of his stories.

"Well, I could not stay long from the twins in any case," he said. "So I spent that first year accompanying Baylor. I was perpetually studying him and questioning him. Then eventually I came to see him more as a man with a problem than some strange creature in need of examination. I saw in him a sense of purpose and a devotion to protecting his people. I could not help but see that as purely human, if not even better. It is very hard to resist his charm and he easily became my friend before I knew he had done it.

"I returned for the first time within the year to tell Edsel all I had learned of this phenomenon, which was not much more than what Baylor has also told you, and some few things I had observed for myself. Things such as they could not be found in the traditional method by simple scanning. I explained that the problem was already being addressed by one of them and must surely come under control soon. It was when Edsel asked why I had not 'destroyed this abomination' that I first realized Baylor had become so close to my heart.

"This reference to Baylor as an abomination, as well as the suggestion that I should have killed him, caused an unexpected reaction within me. Not only had I stood up from my chair instantly, sending it crashing violently to the floor behind me, but I found myself vowing that any who tried to do this particular Werewolf harm would have to find a whole new body in which to experience previously unfathomable levels of pain with. I swore I would do them such terrifying damage as to make them wish Hades would have them before another moment could be spent in my company. Then I had launched myself into a tirade of listing his fine qualities. I found in the process of this that I had come to think of him as a friend, and though I was momentarily as shocked by my rampant defense of him as Edsel, I took it in stride and have allowed it to grow ever since.

"When I had calmed myself, I of course made my apologies for my outburst. I then began again to list Baylor's finer qualities. While Edsel had eventually taken me at my word that Baylor was a good man and obviously had no intentions of testing me by disputing the fact, the others had wanted more than goodness for reason to allow him to live. One of them, Lachlan it was, thought he should be allowed to finish eradicating the others, then be eliminated in turn. While Cathmore thought he and all the others should be eliminated outright and that they should go in force right then and do the 'cleansing' immediately. That one was thinking that they could and should discover a way to hunt them.

"My old friend Kynan had seemed torn between our old friendship and his newer one with Lachlan, thinking nothing of the actual problem. This disappointed me greatly, for it signaled a change in him that I would come to very much dislike. Santon was his usually thoughtful self, wanting simply to know more, much as had been his reaction on meeting me.

"You can imagine, being the creatures of will that all Changelings are, not to mention the tendency to be longwinded, which seems a well-fed disease among the Elders, how difficult a process coming to a decision was.

"Eventually though the Council had decided that Baylor served a purpose, in that he was destroying the others of his kind. Obviously he knew how to hunt them and we did not, so he would have to be allowed to continue to do it, at least until such time as they discovered a better way. They had agreed that he should be left in peace to do this labor. That until such time as he might show himself to be a threat as well, he would be my responsibility.

"This decision, when it was finally reached, I accepted gladly. For though I fully intended to carry out my threats, and protect this man I had come to think of as a friend, I would prefer to be made his keeper, to keep him safe, rather than take on the entire Council and risk us both. I may not fully believe in a forced ascension, but I would rather not test the theory. So he became my charge and has remained such ever since, becoming the brother of my soul in the process.

"I spent my time with the twins during these long debates, patiently awaiting the Council's decision, and knowing that whatever they decided, I would do what I thought best. I would let no harm come to Baylor. Happily, I found the twins' skills much improved, even in the short time of my absence. They admitted to using the trick of disguising themselves often, only to a new and intriguing degree. Rather than projecting pure nothingness, they would project only a cat's mind, or whatever creature they were using at the time, an idea I found fascinating. They told me that in this manner they had learned more in the one year of spying than in their entire first ten years of training.

"But I was speaking of the Elders and their propensity for wasting much time, so I will leave it at this. It was a full month before Edsel entered the garden, where I sat with the twins, to tell me of the decision. A month in which I spent the majority of my time with Adonia and Adreal, becoming more and more confident I had done well by them. After which I then said my second farewell to them, swearing again to return, and leaving once more for the Highlands and my newfound friend who seemed then to need me far more.

"Over the years I have made many visits to the Council and the twins for various reasons, sometimes to update them on Baylor's progress so that they might remain secure in their decision. In the beginning his progress was quite impressive, by the by. He would kill sometimes four or five of the others during a single cycle of the full moon. This is no longer the case though, as he seems to have thinned out their numbers greatly. Which for his sake I am grateful, for it tore at his heart when he did these things. Or be it that I was summoned to sit in Council with them through some long debate. This had actually come to happen quite frequently up until nearly a hundred years ago.

"During these times I came to notice fewer actual decisions being made on the part of my old friend Kynan and more of his simply following Lachlan's lead. In one such case, when I had been with them already, involved in some discussion I can no longer recall, a soul had sung out somewhere in the city and a vote was instantly taken. Where another's acceptance into the change or 'being blessed' hung in the balance, his vote could have made it happen.

"For some reason I could not guess, for the soul was seemingly quite pure, Lachlan did not what to give it the blessing and Kynan had agreed with him. I was greatly disgusted by my old friend's lack of heart in this. For he had always fought for the people in our senate, side by side we had many times raised our voices to make things right. That was not a right decision and I was about to leave them, ignoring the consequences, and fly to this soul, caring not for their 'so be it,' when it gave up its song and departed.

"I could not forgive Kynan for this: I had come to expect heartlessness from Lachlan, he was stuck in the old way of things, but I could not accept Kynan as his puppet, especially when it had cost another their chance at change. I was, I think, also very disgusted with myself at that moment, because I had sat there in appalled fascination as they had voted on the matter as though it were a decision as to what to dine on that evening, and allowed that soul to remain alone and unattended in the process. I too had let it go. I was forced then to reevaluate not only the Elders but myself as well.

"So I came over the years to see the Council like this: Edsel was the balance keeping the peace and trying to hear both sides of a situation, making his decisions based purely on what clarity of vision could be acquired upon careful evaluation of facts. Cathmore and Lachlan were the executioners always wanting for a quick concise decision and penalty. But while Cathmore was forthright, wanting only to preserve the peace they had created at any cost, Lachlan seemed mean-spirited at times, wanting to eliminate some that I could find no fault in. Santon was the historian merely wanting to gather the information and record in his mind the outcome. When he did put forth a view, it was usually sound and well thought out, but for the most part he only listened. And Kynan, as I've said, had become a mere puppet, a second vote voiced on Lachlan's behalf."

He sighed then, his memory of this change in his friend not being a pleasant recollection. So I thought to coax his mind forward, past it.

"You said their inviting you to sit in with them became less frequent nearly a hundred years ago. Why?" I asked.

~16~

Creating Havoc

"Nay, I said it was frequent up until nearly a hundred years ago," he said. "But that is when it ceased altogether."

He had smiled while saying this and I realized this was not a sad recollection for him, but rather that I had succeeded in my goal, moving us on to one that rather seemed to amuse him.

His statement was a surprise to me, though. For I could not see the Council, as he had made it clear to me how it felt about things, not keeping contact with him and a constant check on the situation here in the Highlands with Baylor.

"You mean to say that you've had no contact with them, in all that time?" I asked.

"Yes. We had a bit of a falling out, you might say," he said, still smiling. "I was none to polite on my final visit, nor did I leave them with the impression I cared if they did call for me again."

He grinned, showing his heart-jolting dimples once again. It was clear as ever that he cared little for the Council's ways and rules. No matter that I knew he cared for them as Changelings.

"What happened?" I was intrigued now.

"Well, for some reason still unknown to me, while attending this final and fateful Council meeting, I brought up Edana and her strange Druid ritual, the one that had transferred a blessing, which allowed her to take the form of the stag. I instantly wished that whatever cursed demon had possessed my tongue to move had gone to Hades instead of my mouth, but it was too late. They were in a tizzy already.

"Edsel was sunk back into his chair, bemoaning the Celts their strange blessings and curses, which seemed an endless source of confusion to them. Lachlan was demanding an instant explanation as to why I had not spoken up before. Telling them of this new thing, that could take only a single form, though at least fully this time. Demanding to know how and why it was given at the point of death for the bearer, not the receiver.

"Cathmore wanted to destroy all the remaining Druids that Rome had missed, 'for it will lead to naught but the vilest of ends, as we are seeing.' " This last bit Demon said deepening his voice and taking on a hideous frown, then, resuming his usual tone, he continued. "Santon had an eyebrow quirked at an impossible angle, cocking his head like a dog listening for its master's call to be repeated, and Kynan was dangling from his strings as usual, waiting for a sign as to how he should react. In essence I had put my foot in it."

I started laughing, as the picture he was painting with his words became a vivid scene of pandemonium in my mind. I had a pretty good idea of the Council by now and could only imagine how well this had gone over with them.

"Then what?" I coaxed.

"Well, I stood up in the middle of all the whirling confusion and questions, accusations and condemnations, and looked to them one at a time. Then I bowed to each of them, sarcastically sweeping my hat from my head and waving it at them. Then I turned and left the room," he replied.

I couldn't stop laughing. I could see it all in my head, and when finally I managed to form a sentence it was to ask him their reaction.

"As you can imagine, they were frantic. I had at first shocked them into silence, which is an amazing feat in and of itself," he said, and he was laughing now as well, obviously recalling the scene with clarity.

171

"Then Lachlan was yelling for me to return and explain myself," he continued. "Like I was some errant child of his that must obey. Edsel was saying 'where are you going?' repeatedly in increasing levels of desperation. Cathmore seemed to have missed my exit altogether and was still plotting out the destruction of the entire Druid culture in mumbles to himself, not realizing that the Church would quite effectively do this for him. While Santon cocked his head to the other side and Kynan, finally taking his cue that he should be angry as well, began yelling for me to return at once."

We laughed for a minute more, and then I said, "So what finally happened, what did you tell them?"

"Nothing," he said, again shocking me with the unexpected reply. "I went out to the garden to find the twins. I told them I would see them again as soon as the Elders had calmed and composed themselves, and could behave like respectful keen-minded adults, and left."

"So you haven't been back since?" I asked, still somewhat in shock myself.

"No, I went back once about fifty years ago, only to see the twins. I have not been invited back nor have I spoken again to any of the Elders. I asked the twins to relay my regards to Edsel, as I still count him a good friend, but other than that it has been simpler this way. They have stayed clear of Scotland and Ireland and I have stayed clear of Rome."

His matter-of-fact tone, which came to replace his laughter, masked what I knew was no small regret at his lack of recent contact with Adonia and Adreal. I made no further comment on this so as to keep the mood light as it had been. I was enjoying this time and didn't want to chance ruining it with somber thoughts. So my next question was on a different track.

"Have you ever seen the Changeling who told you of the Werewolves in the first place again?" I asked.

"Piper? Yes, he was the one to summon me, on more than one occasion. It seems he'd taken a liking to Adonia's poetry." He gave a short laugh, smiling.

His mirth not only led me to believe he was amused by this, but that

172

it was more than Adonia's poetry that Piper had taken a liking to.

"He was often in a position to be coaxed into doing some small task such as that for the Council," he continued. "Like me, his adoration of the twins put him at the Council's disposal more than once. Though I think he too refuses to become too deeply involved with it. Hence I do not know what became of the poetry recitals, but I do not feel it would have ever been acceptable to the Council that they continue."

Again he laughed and I knew he must approve of this other Changeling as a suitor for Adonia. For it was obvious he was quite protective of the twins and would have otherwise put a stop to it rather than laugh about it.

"I take it you like Piper, then?" I asked, knowing the answer already but enjoying the sound of his voice and the joy in it.

"Yes, he's a good man, very much in the way of Baylor; somewhat barbaric in some of his ways, but still very charming and personable," he replied.

"So, then, you approved of his courting Adonia?" I said.

Again it was an obvious question.

"Yes, of course. I would have put a stop to it myself otherwise, but my approval has naught to do with the opinion of the Council," he said, his brow furrowed a bit with the last so again I prompted him.

"What do you mean?" I said.

"Well, though the Council approved of him well enough that he was a useful tool to run errands, much as I had been, they did not find him fit for their inner sanctum. With his refusal to bend to them and thus gain their acceptance, as it were, and their refusal to allow Adonia to choose any other than one of their own, I do not foresee there having been a happy ending."

Again my romantic sense of fairness was upset. Did no one ever fall in love and get married, have lots of happy babies and live contentedly together into old age? None of those I knew had found any happiness in love. Mem's husband had died at sea, leaving her alone to forge her way through a very hard life. Demon's love had been killed and I was not about to bring it up again to find out how, but obviously this had been a horrible ending. Baylor had lost the love of his life in a terrible mixed state of confused curses and blessings. Adonia was denied a life with one who loved her and she probably loved in return. If not the fates then men themselves seemed to provide very unhappy endings for lovers. I was suddenly of a mind to avoid altogether the affliction that was love.

I must have been staring at him when all of these things were running through my mind, for when he spoke and I focused my eyes again, I was looking directly at him. "What?" I asked, blinking.

"I said, what are you thinking?" he repeated, looking amused.

I pulled my hand up to my mouth and, covering a yawn, I said around it, "That I must not fall in love."

It would not be until later that I would realize how that must have seemed: me staring stupidly at him for such a period of time then saying, "I must not fall in love."

As it stood at that point in time, I took his look of shock and surprise as merely being because of my sudden yawn and my unladylike decision to talk right through it.

"Sorry," I said sheepishly, folding my hands in my lap.

His surprise had turned to confusion, and I would laugh about this entire scene later, but for then I moved on, trying to make him forget about my lapse in manners.

"When will Baylor return?" I asked then.

We had been talking for a very long time and, though I was very comfortable being alone with him, it was the comfort that was making me uncomfortable, if that makes any sense. Then again my feelings when it came to Demon never did, so it won't surprise me if you don't make sense of them either.

It was at this point, when my mind had turned to Baylor as a source of ending the uncomfortable comfort, that he answered for himself and I realized we'd talked and laughed till dawn.

"Well then!" Baylor said, as he entered the cavern and spotted us. "I see you've woken early for once, what brought that on?"

His hunting had obviously pleased him for he did not at all seem upset. He had slung over his shoulder a brace of rabbits, which furthered my belief he'd found no other Werewolves.

"Nay, the wretched poppet kept me up, forcing tales from me on pain of torture, and I've not yet slept," Demon told him.

Demon had then grinned at me and shielded his arm, as though I would hit him. I did anyway, only on his exposed leg, just before I leaped up running to hide behind Baylor's massive form.

"He lies, I swear it!" I cried. "You must protect me, it is I who was tortured by his long-windedness! I was forced to sit for hours on the hard floor, listening to his endless babble."

I darted back and forth behind Baylor, laughing all the more each time I barely avoided Demon's grasp and Baylor held his rabbits over his head to save their being tromped in our gaming.

"You damage my rabbits, I'll thrash you both!" he said, laughing as well.

Demon paused mid-reach for me and we both then eyed Baylor in amused confusion.

"What more damage might we do, kill them again?" Demon asked sarcastically. He was barely able to finish the sentence through his laughter.

Baylor raised his eyebrow then, looking up at the rabbits as if considering this for the first time.

Then he said, "True."

So saying, he dropped them, and swiftly grabbed Demon up in a bear-like hug, wrestling him to the rug-covered floor I had just bemoaned the hardness of. I began happily cheering them on equally as they fought good naturedly to pen each other down.

They were still laughing, if not a little red in the face and winded, when at last they called a truce. Baylor cited his need of cleaning and putting the rabbits into a stew so that he might get some much-needed sleep and Demon claimed it was Baylor's strong smell of dog as reason for the draw. I reasoned they had wrestled so often they had learned to end it with some excuse or other, or it would continue for hours. For neither seemed to ever get a sufficient upper hand.

Demon then asked the question most likely out of habit and we received the expected answer: he had found no Werewolf other than himself. So we talked happily together around the stewpot until it was readied and hung again over the hearth. Demon then returned to his favored place to sleep, as Baylor too headed for his bed. I also took myself off to my bed, knowing when I woke it would be to a wonderful feast of rabbit stew and another equally wonderful night in conversation with Demon.

When I awoke they had already eaten and Baylor was preparing to leave again, but it appeared that Demon was also. I was confused and disappointed, having thought to have Demon to myself again for the evening, yet not admitting that was the cause of the disappointment. Lord, how I loved deluding myself back then.

"Are you going as well, then?" I asked.

Trying hard to keep the disappointment from my voice, I gathered up my bowl and handed it unconsciously to Baylor, so that he, with his greater height, might fill it for me, while I looked to Demon for his answer.

"Yes, you will have our home to yourself for the evening; there is something I must attend to. You just stay put and do not open the door for anyone," Demon replied.

Baylor was putting my now full bowl on the table and had his hand at my back, coaxing me to sit in the chair he'd just pulled out for me. Something was wrong and they were trying to keep it from me.

"What? What is wrong?" I asked.

I allowed Baylor to seat me but I didn't let my eyes leave Demon. I would have an answer.

"It may be nothing, don't you worry yourself," he said, too calmly, still trying to avoid telling me what was obviously bothering him.

"'Maybe nothing' is not the same as 'nothing,' and I am not worrying myself, you are worrying me. Now tell me what is going on," I demanded.

Again I was speaking as an equal, as I had so often with Mem, and again he accepted this.

"As I said, it may be nothing, but Baylor told me today that he'd seen an animal he had not recognized while he was out last night," Demon finally replied. "If it is a breed unknown to Baylor and him so long in these parts, then quite possibly it is a Changeling. If it is a Changeling, then there is also the possibility the Council has retracted its agreement to leave this matter in my hands, in which case I am going with him."

He was still speaking calmly but frightening me anyway, and I was trying to keep a brave face as he continued, saying, "Do not open the door for anyone, appearances can be deceiving, especially with us. If you sense any besides me, do as I've told you and think of nothing."

I guess my attempts at bravery were failing miserably, for he came then around the table to put his hand on my shoulder, giving it a squeeze, adding, "We will be fine. I have not survived nearly two thousand years by being incapable of protecting myself, and neither has Baylor, and he's nearly as old. We will be back in the morning."

I put up my chin then, thinking he must be right and having to worry about my state of mind could help them not at all.

"I will be here then when you return," I said.

"That's my Angel! Till morning then," he said.

Demon turned and headed for the door. Baylor followed and at the threshold, turned back to me.

"Good chin, Lass!" he called. "Don't you fret, it's not like he can be killed."

Then he was gone too.

I sat in silence, with the delicious-smelling food not even able to whet my appetite, thinking too many things at once. Then slowly it dawned on me with horrible, gut-wrenching clarity: Baylor had said Demon could not be killed, but had given me no such assurance as to his ability to survive.

I thought back then over all he had told me and remembered that though he did not age he had never said he could not be killed. If other Werewolves died by having their heads removed, could he? These kinds of questions plagued me, so much so that I pushed my food from me, knowing I would find no appetite for it.

I got up from the table and wandered around the place, busying myself by cleaning up what mess I could find. I shook all the sheets, exerting my will over them as I did so, to expel all the dust and odors from them, drawing these things out as if to myself.

I began to pray silently over and over again to myself and to any god listening, that they come back safely to me. I soon found myself with nothing left to clean and went to sit on Demon's chaise lounge, putting my arms around myself and rocking back and forth, still praying.

I do not know how long I sat like that, how long I rocked back and forth trying to absorb some sufficient amount of comfort from his couch to keep me from crying. Praying over and over the same words until they had become a kind of chant, but it seemed forever. It seemed dawn would never come. I didn't even know why I was so afraid, I just was.

The fear actually seemed to become a tangible thing; it was present and it was alive.

Suddenly I felt what I can only describe as a claw scratching through my space, just barely missing my soul. The fear leapt to my throat nearly escaping as a scream. I knew instantly that I needed to protect myself and what I needed to do. I became nothing, a great black void. Not a single thought, only the empty color, the absence of all things.

"Run Angel, hide, disappear little one, don't let it find us," cried the little voice inside me.

Black, black, black. I pictured it, I felt it, I smelled it, I became it.

~17~

Piper

Suddenly something brushed my flesh, my real flesh, not my spiritual being. The scream that I had been holding back tore loose from my lungs and I came back to myself. The void was gone, the illusion shattered by my scream.

"It's all right, Angel, it is only me," Demon said.

His beautiful face came into focus as I was brought back by his words. His comfortable presence suddenly before me caused me to cry out again, only this time with relief. I threw my arms around him, crying into his shoulder, squeezing him for all I could.

"What happened? You were quite gone from here," he said, very concerned.

He was patting my back and I was feeling like a great sniveling ninny, very stupid for having screamed out.

"I became afraid after you left and the fear seemed to take on a life of its own. Then I felt a presence pass near me, spiritually, like claws tearing through the space my soul inhabits." I tried as best I could to explain my terror and why. "It seemed to be sweeping blindly for anything to tear into. I did what you said, I became nothing. Black, all black."

"You did well, my Angel," he said.

He was squeezing me now, lowering himself onto the seat beside me with his arm still firmly around my shoulders, his other hand holding my head to his chest. "You are safe now, I am here," he said softly.

I began to calm then and quieted. Until it came to me he had said "I am here" not "we are here."

"Baylor? Where is Baylor?" I said, frantic again, as I looked up into his eyes, silently begging him to say that Baylor was here too.

"He is getting wine, in the bathing chamber. He thought it might revive you. You were quite gone, as I said, and you had us worried," he replied.

As he spoke those wonderful words, I threw my head back onto his shoulder, closing my eyes and heaving a great sigh of relief. When I opened my eyes, Demon was looking at my lips, concern and something else entirely warring in his eyes, and this time I was almost positive he meant to kiss me, but just then the source of my relief came into view, effectively becoming the source of something else.

"You've brought her back to us, I see," Baylor said to Demon, with much relief apparent in his voice.

Demon looked up instantly, appearing as though no kiss had ever crossed his mind, and I began to wonder if it had only been in my mind after all. I was extremely relieved at seeing Baylor well and with us, but also somewhat upset at the same time by his timing.

Demon stood then and walked to the kitchen area, collecting the glasses that Baylor had obviously forgotten in his haste. I thought I saw him nod his head slightly in the direction of the painting I had thought before was a goddess, but had convinced myself I had only imagined the gesture by the time he returned. It all was forgotten in any case, as the wine was poured and a more pressing question came back to light.

"Was it another Changeling I felt then?" I asked of Demon, adding, "It didn't feel like you."

I was distressed and not caring if that statement might be taken wrong or right, as the case may be.

"It felt evil, you mean?" he asked, not fully understanding but trying to.

"Yes, in a way, but more just frightening; it was unfamiliar, almost inhuman," I said.

I could do no better with my description of the feelings I'd gotten from it. So I quieted and waited for Demon to explain them for me.

He turned to Baylor then, a look of confusion mixed with something else rearranging his perfect features into a grim frown. It was not exactly fear I saw in him but more a kind of foreboding and dissatisfaction with what was obviously an unpleasant situation. When he spoke, he seemed to be addressing both of us.

"It seems the Council has taken back its previous stance of watch and wait and has sent one of their spies to check up on the situation. I found no Changelings while out last night looking, but obviously one was trying to find sign of us as well. I had hoped I was mistaken in this but I suppose it had to happen eventually," he said.

He then sighed and took the seat opposite me, as he had when we had listened to Baylor's tale. I was reminded of my own life being changed then.

"But this felt nothing like a Changeling, or at least I should say not like you. Your presence is…." I searched for the proper word and it would not come to me. "When you came to save me by the stream, I was comforted by your presence and felt no malice from you. This presence was very frightening and full of malice like it was hunting for someone- to kill them, not merely to find them."

I tried to see if he had understood me then, if I had been clear enough. He looked angry then and I thought he might have finally gotten what I had been trying to say.

"If they have sent one with instruction to kill Baylor, I will destroy it a thousand times over and they will also pay dearly for their mistake. I meant my warning to them and more so now," he said.

The look on his face made me think that I would never want to come up against him when he was angry.

"But if you had not already thought that a Changeling with

malicious intent had come here, why then would you have accompanied Baylor and told me to shield my presence if I sensed any other than yourself?" I was thoroughly confused.

"Because if one of their spies had come to see how things fared and came upon him in battle, they might think him any other Werewolf and try to destroy him. I do not hold them above interfering in that case," he said. "I also didn't want the Council to be informed I had 'blessed' one, without their mutual consent. I did not want to hear about it later. I would rather have the opportunity to inform them myself, and properly introduce you at some other time. If they have sent one that obviously intended ill in the first place, before having met either of you or speaking with me, then there is foulness afoot here."

"What do you think is going on?" Baylor asked then.

He did not seem to be afraid of this revelation either, but rather just curious as to why it was. When he asked this question, in such a manner, lacking any upset, I began to think maybe I had overreacted and there was nothing to fear.

"I do not know," Demon answered. "Mayhap Lachlan and Cathmore have swayed Edsel and Santon to their views. It has been well over one thousand years and there are still occasional Werewolf sightings and reports of attacks. I hear them, sometimes, in the taverns or markets when I go into towns for supplies. They may be receiving these reports as well and they may have been convinced to interfere by now. I would have thought Edsel would have made some contact with me first, but perhaps I have overestimated our friendship."

He trailed off, seeming to lose himself in private thoughts, and we sat in silence for some time. His silence had turned swiftly to brooding and I was beginning to feel uncomfortable. I looked to Baylor, who seemed also deep in some private thoughts, and neither seemed inclined to share these thoughts with me.

Finally I could bear their silence no longer.

"What will we do?" I asked.

The sudden break of the quiet that had settled caused both to jerk their heads toward me. Suddenly I was forced, by the look on both their faces, to revise my earlier thought. I would not want to be on the wrong side of either of them, and would hate to be the one they were thinking of when I'd interrupted their brooding.

They schooled their faces into smiles for me, trying to appear as if nothing were amiss, and this upset me.

"I am not a child. I can help. Only tell me what you need me to do," I said.

I felt then a sudden pull of energy, like the one when first Demon had appeared before me, then a kick on the door. Demon was up in a flash and I suddenly felt like the child I had just sworn I was not. Baylor stood up and in one swift motion suddenly had a huge sword in his hand and his back to me. The sword had been so swiftly retrieved from its place under his chair, where I'd not seen it before, that it appeared to be in his hand as if by magic. He had effectively become armed and my shield all within the time it took me to gasp.

Demon was already at the door and I could not fathom how he'd moved so quickly. But then everything was happening so very quickly. I was having a hard time grasping any of it. Demon threw the door wide, reaching forward and dragging the form before him into our den, and then closing the door. Just as quickly, he started laughing. Baylor started laughing as well and I was trying to see around him to discover what had happened. Demon's word explained what I could not see through Baylor's massive form.

"Piper!" he said finally.

"I see I've come at a bad time." I heard a new voice reply.

This was Piper, then? His accent though heavy with sarcasm, reminded me a little of Mem. I finally managed a view from under Baylor's arm, catching a glimpse of him for myself, wanting a face to go with the story of Adonia and the poetry recitals.

Were Changelings ever not the handsomest of creatures? I was astounded that two such beautiful men should exist in such a small space. He was maybe an inch or two shorter than Demon and just as well-muscled only on a thinner scale, with sun-darkened skin and softly waving dark brown hair falling below his shoulders. He broke into a wonderful smile that lit up astonishingly gold eyes, and I thought then how Adonia could not have done less than adore him.

"We've just had a visit from someone with obviously foul plans in store for us," Demon said, releasing Piper, whom he had obviously wrapped up in a great hug before I had managed to find a view.

Then, stepping back, he added, "But you look well."

His face turned from all smiles to a confused frown with Piper's response.

"Already?" Piper said.

It was a simple enough word but it held a thousand possibilities.

"What do you mean, already? What do you know?" Demon asked.

"Well, if you will quit behaving like Edsel used to and offer me some wine, I will tell you what I know, but you will not like it," he said, forcing another smile.

He looked then past Demon to where Baylor and I stood. As he moved to a seat near us, he called back to Demon, who was getting a glass for him.

"I know the red-headed beast with Bane," he had said, then laughed. "But will you introduce me to the beauty he seems so intent on keeping from me?"

Baylor seemed to remember himself as he laughed too, returning his sword, more slowly this time to its resting place. I was busy trying to put all of it together, thinking things like, "That was Bane? This is Piper? When did Piper meet Baylor or, for that matter, Bane?" Baylor turned and took Piper's hand, giving it a firm shake while gripping his upper arm. He then returned to his seat, leaving the introductions to Demon, who had just rejoined us.

"Piper, please meet Angelica, she has only just become one of us, not even one week ago. Angel, this is Piper, the one I told you of." He said all this while pouring Piper a glass of wine and handing it to him.

So it was that Piper raised his glass to me in salute.

"To yet another bonny Angel among us!" he said with quick wit.

Then, taking a long drink, he said as an aside to me, "Don't believe any of the bad things he says about me, he's just upset I was born better-looking than him."

We all laughed then, releasing the pent-up stress of the last few hours. I pushed all other newer questions away as we got down to the business of the old one.

"What news have you, then?" Demon asked.

He had sobered more quickly than the rest of us, bringing us back to the more serious issue of what was happening here.

"As I said, you will not like it, so you can not 'kill the messenger,' so to speak." Piper replied. "I came to warn you that the voice on your behalf within the Council is no more. Edsel is missing."

"Missing?" Demon said, sounding completely incredulous.

"No sign can be found of him," Piper explained. "The Council is in complete disarray and I fear something foul might come of it. Adonia asked that I come to you and warn you of these things, for she too felt that Santon's presence would be insufficient to keep them from interfering here. They never forgave your 'insubordination' and have often brought the matter of the Werewolves up for another vote, only to have Edsel and Santon be the only voices against them."

I was very confused by Piper's statements and was glad when Demon asked the question in my mind as well.

"What do you mean, missing? Missing how?" Demon asked, still confounded.

"His presence can be felt about the villa, but no sign of him can be found. Adonia and Adreal searched for him nearly a full two weeks before sending me to warn you that he was no longer among them." Piper's reply still did not satisfy Demon or any of us for that matter.

"He would not have ascended without a word to anyone, there must be some other explanation," Demon said.

He trailed off again into silence and I was about to ask what he planned to do, when he answered before I could.

"I'm going to Rome to discover for myself what has happened. Both of you are going with me." Demon spoke with authority, looking at Baylor and myself. "I will not risk you by leaving you alone here. I can protect you better when you are with me, and I do not like what has happened in either place. You will be safer with me."

He had said this as though he expected an argument from me and I was not at all inclined to give him one. I had not liked being alone last night and did not want to try it again for any extended length of time. It was when Baylor spoke that I knew he had not expected a refusal from me, but rather him.

"I will not leave my people at the mercy of this thing you say is a malicious Changeling, to run along to Rome with you, hiding behind your kilt like some untried youth," Baylor said vehemently.

"I do not ask that you abandon your people to it. For our departure will surely lead it away. Eventually it will find our place and see that we have departed, and it will follow. So in that case you are not running from it, but rather leading it a safer distance from your people to fight it. As for hiding behind my kilt, I hope not! I count on you to help me keep her safe." He jerked his head in my direction, continuing just as vehemently, "She is still very young and it may take us both to keep her safe."

"*She* is right here!" I said, becoming annoyed I was being talked about like a helpless kitten, right in front of me. "And *she* is expecting to be taught how to defend herself as well. I am no useless kitten. I only lack instruction as to how to use my claws!"

All three of them suddenly broke into a fit of laughter and I tried not to join them. It seems we had all had enough stress this day. It had to be released somehow. I suppose a good laugh at my expense was therefore acceptable.

"Just imagine your enemy has treated you like a 'helpless kitten' and then refused to tell you a story," Baylor laughed.

"She's quite the hellcat, never mind the kitten," Piper observed.

"If you only knew!" Demon said to him, raising his hand reflexively to guard his arm, in case I should choose to swat at him again.

"What is a hellcat?" I asked, wondering if I had just been insulted, and again they dissolved into laughter.

~18~

Chasing Rabbits

It was decided that we would all get what rest we could throughout what remained of the day, and leave that evening. We would go on foot, as Baylor could not throw off his being and travel incorporeal as Demon and Piper could. Also, Demon felt I was still too young in the change, and was not of a mind to test whether I could exert enough magnetism over the world around me to call up a whole new form. He said that those parts of it that had always been mine needed to remain near me, until he was sure that the universe would bow to me in this matter.

I went off to my bed with all of these recent events and revelations running rampant through my mind, and it was a long time before sleep found me. I was deep within a dream about a creature unknown to me. It had the body of a woman but the claws of a huge cat. It was covered all over in silky black fur ending around the shoulders, where its head became my own, but with fangs and bright yellow cat's eyes. This creature was deeply angered that a question it had asked had not been answered, and on the verge of attacking the one who refused to enlighten it.

I popped awake as a knock sounded lightly on the doors of my bed. Instantly I realized the creature I'd dreamed up had been my mind trying to explain to me what a hellcat was. I was laughing when I opened the doors, telling myself I must thank Baylor for the strange dream.

"Thank you so very much for making my dreams interesting," I said sarcastically, finding it was Baylor who had done the knocking.

He looked at me as if I had misplaced my wits, and I explained, "I was dreaming I was a hellcat, literally, and about to kill someone who had refused to tell me a story!"

He was laughing with me then as we walked to the table. Piper and Demon were already there and we ate what was left of the rabbit stew from that morning. Baylor let them in on the cause of our mirth, telling them of my dream. When they had finished having their fun with it as well, Demon asked me how the hellcat had looked. Without thinking much about it, I showed them all, illustrating for him as he had so often for me

"Careful!" Demon fair shouted at me.

Reflexively I returned instantly to my own shape.

"What?" I asked, confused by his sudden outburst.

"You can not just invent things like that! How do you know what instincts to give it? I have warned you already of the danger of such things." He had lowered his voice, so as not to be so loud with me, but I could tell he was not happy.

"I gave it no instincts," I told him. "It was merely me."

I was still confused as to how simply changing my outer appearance should have upset him. It had been to me no different than when I had changed my clothes before leaving my bed. Baylor busied himself with his own preparations and left us three Changelings to whatever argument might come.

"Oh?" Now Demon appeared to be more confused than I was, saying, "I had not thought of that."

He finished his meal then in silent contemplation and, with no further comment to me, moved with Piper to an area behind the kitchen. I was left then still confused and wondering what had caused his outburst. Once in the other area they had begun strapping on various weapons and I watched them as I ate. I noticed Demon wore duplicates of certain items and had packed an extra change of clothes. I also noted he had Baylor's Bane with him and I questioned him about this.

"Why are you carrying Bane, and the extra kilt?" I said, after swallowing another bite.

"Because Baylor will need them after tonight, he will not be a Werewolf for the entire journey." He smiled at my curiosity, and then added, "Would you like a dagger?"

He held up for my approval a beautifully ornate example of one of these.

"Nay, she's lethal enough with a brush, we'll never have rest if you give her a blade!" Baylor called from the bathing chamber.

He reentered the main room just then, holding leather bags of refreshments, looking to catch my eye. His amusement was quite obvious as I rejoined.

"Then you'll just have to instruct me how to use it properly, so I make it quick and painless for you when you leave off in the middle of your entertaining of me," I said, grinning back at him, and trying my best to appear sinister.

Piper was looking very confused by this line of banter, and Demon let him in on the cause of our constant jesting.

"Our Angel has an insatiable appetite for information," he said. "And tales of our past, with a penchant for inflicting harm upon our persons should we dilly-dally in the telling. Beware refusing her a story should she have a brush in her hand!"

Piper too laughed then, saying, "So not only a hellcat, but a curious one. It appears you've got yourselves a hand full."

I had gotten up to examine the dagger Demon had offered me and as I took it in my hand, holding it up to examine it better, I turned it in the light, putting on my best sinister look as I then turned to Piper.

"So," I said, trying hard to school my features and avoid laughing. "How is it you came to be a Changeling?"

I turned the dagger again and his eyebrows shot up as he looked quickly from one to the other of us. I could contain my amusement no longer and burst out into laughter, which Demon and Baylor quickly joined in. Piper took a moment longer to realize I was having fun with him, and then he too laughed.

We finished our preparations for the journey in unusually high spirits, considering the cause of it, and were on our way by dusk. As we stepped out onto the plateau and began to walk, I noticed Baylor seemed to be talking to himself, although no sound was coming from him. His lips were moving slightly and his darkly blue eyes seemed far off, occasionally glancing up at the moon.

I was about to comment, when Demon took my hand. I looked up at him, wondering what had brought it on, and his look told me to be silent. I soon could do nothing but, as he did not release my hand, but walked with me like this. Quietly I allowed my mind to wander, wondering at one moment what Baylor was doing, the next wondering why Demon was holding my hand. I soon decided I didn't care why he was holding it, that I simply liked it.

Then Baylor started to change and I suddenly understood why. I felt a brief flash of something familiar and then I stood in awe as a great beast rose up before me. Demon's grasp had grown firmer on my hand and he drew me closer to him. It seemed I would have fallen had he not held me in that manner. I was awestruck. In some recess of my mind I knew I should have found this sight terrifying, but it was too amazing.

There before me stood Baylor, the Werewolf, and he was beautiful; absolutely, astoundingly, beautiful. He seemed even taller, if that were possible, and the flame of his hair now covered him head to toe. The braids he always wore were woven throughout, around his shoulders and down his back. I had never seen a more amazing or beautiful creature.

He threw back his head just then, letting loose a long, low, mournful howl, and I wanted badly to cry out with him or at least go to him. Every instinct I had begged me to comfort him, or at the very least join him in his cries to the moon. I cannot describe this for you as I wish I could. Demon's grip on my hand had again tightened and again I looked up at him. His eyes seemed to tell me, 'that would not be wise' and 'I know.' I turned back then to Baylor, trying to hold in my tears. We began walking again, Demon bending slightly and swiping up Baylor's kilt and shirt where they had fallen, as we walked past them.

I have never heard a sound more heartbreaking. I could not for the longest time get that sound out of my head. His howl remained and echoed within me. To this day, when I think of a tortured or wounded soul, that howl is the sound I hear. When I let down my own guard, sometimes, like now, I can hear my own soul howl like that. It seems that Baylor had found hell's tormented voice and brought it into our world. But back then it had broken my heart to hear it from him, and to know what torment my friend was in. It also brought other revelations to me.

Baylor had kept ahead of us then, with Piper bringing up the rear. I watched his progress with mixed awe and pain. So very beautiful yet so very unfair! We started down the side of the mountain, still in silence. When we came to the steam, we stopped only briefly for a drink and then we were off again. We traveled quickly and it was not so difficult for me on the downward track. I adjusted my eyes unthinkingly to accommodate the lesser light and picked my way down beside Demon.

Demon had released my hand some time ago but I could still feel him on my palm and fingertips. I think I had known I had come to love him before this, but I was just starting to admit it to myself. I think somehow, between my friend's tormented howl and Demon's holding my hand, I had realized some things were useless to deny. You could rage at heaven all you wanted to, demanding fairness till you were blue in the face, but all you got was what you got. Baylor had gotten a curse and lost his lover to a blessing. I had gotten a heart that chose to love Demon, whether I had tried to deny and avoid it or not. So be it, it couldn't be as bad as what others got, right? I still don't understand love, or why exactly it was my heart chose him, but it did.

I was allowing myself to consider then what it would be like to have him kiss me. As I had thought he would before. Once I had allowed my

mind the freedom to roam in this direction, by admitting to myself I had
fallen in love with him, it began to run. How would his lips feel on mine?
Like they had in the dream? Only for real? And so on. Therefore I did not
notice when the track became flat and we had left the mountain behind us.

Demon put out his hand, catching mine again, and I saw dawn was
approaching. I realized then we had walked all night, none of us speaking.
We had all been lost in our own private thoughts, following silently behind
Baylor. I didn't know what the others had been thinking, but I blushed now,
as Demon's hand on mine reminded me where my thoughts had been.

I had not even thought about the fact we were most likely being
hunted by an evil Changeling or that I should have been alert to any possible
attack. I had not scanned, even once, for the presence of any that might have
tried to do us harm. I had been stupidly daydreaming about Demon, and his
returning these feelings I had finally admitted to myself I had for him. The
dagger in my sash and its purpose there had been forgotten completely. I
had just begun silently berating myself for this, when we were attacked.

It came from the brush in front of Baylor and it was met with a
ferocity I can only say was breathtaking. It appeared to me it had tried to
leap past him in a line for Demon and myself, but was stopped in mid-leap by
the force of Baylor's strong right arm, sweeping out before it. It was
something between a man and a bear, to my mind, and when it recovered
itself it turned on Baylor, seeing it would have to defeat him to move on to us.
Demon was trying to push me behind him but I was not having it, and his
intense following of the fight prevented him from forcing the issue with me.

They fought back and forth and it appeared Baylor was inflicting the
most damage by far, as the other kept pulling fresh energies to heal itself. I
was amazed how Baylor made such use of every aspect of himself. His claws,
his teeth, his size and strength all were weapons he used with extraordinary
skill. I stashed this all away in my memory as I watched, eyes huge with
amazement. Then Baylor reached out and took the other's head in his hands,
tearing it clean from its shoulders, just as Demon had described him doing to
defeat the other Werewolves. The body dropped and the soul fled.

"What in all of hell was that?" I managed.

"A Changeling that just discovered it would need to be more than a quick healing gorilla to eliminate our friend Baylor," Demon replied, with unlikely good humor.

"But it did not appear to be after Baylor, Baylor just got in its way," I said.

Demon seemed to consider this for only a moment, then disregard it.

"Why would the Council send a spy to eliminate one of us?" he said. "No, it is Baylor they fear." He ended with a confidence I did not feel.

"It will return and mayhap with others now that it knows how formidable of an opponent it is up against," Demon said a moment later. "I sensed that one easily but they will be more careful in the future. You must also be on the alert."

That last statement was, I knew, based on the fact I had been near sleep-walking and he'd had to grasp my hand to stop me from walking headfirst into the situation. I again reprimanded myself harshly for my daydreaming, and vowed not to repeat the mistake.

"We will make camp here and Baylor will take the first watch. Baylor," Demon turned now to Baylor to make sure he had heard and understood. "Wake me when you have changed back and want to sleep. I will leave your clothing and weapons here."

He laid the items he had spoken of on the ground at Baylor's feet and Baylor looked at them. They made a brief eye contact and I wondered just how intelligent and present my Baylor really was when he was a Werewolf.

Piper had already entered the brush, from which the gorilla had come, and was looking intently around. I followed Demon into it as well and saw Piper change into a badger and curl up under a hedge. Demon then turned into a large black wolf and looked up at me expectantly. I changed then into a wolf as well, copying him. I sharpened my senses as he had said he had done when resting, so as to be very alert. I was determined I would not let him down again.

He turned a few circles in the small space provided in this brush and lay down. There was not much space left after he and Piper had made themselves comfortable, and I convinced myself it was for this reason that I curled up next to him to sleep.

I awoke a few hours later as Baylor's massive form came into the brush. Demon was no longer beside me and I was aware I missed his presence at my back. I said nothing as I stood, still in my wolf's form, and made room for Baylor to lay himself down as comfortably as possible in the small space. I then turned again and, pressing my back into Baylor's side, went back to sleep.

I only opened one eye when a few hours more had passed and a badger was walking past me out of the brush, to be replaced by the wolf that was Demon. He curled up then in Piper's vacated spot at Baylor's head. Thus the day passed uneventfully and I was well-rested come the afternoon.

I awoke feeling quite wonderful. Really, I felt like I wanted to run wild across the low rolling hills of heather, chasing rabbits. I realized in some part of me that this was my wolf instinct, setting in throughout the day, but I had no urge to change that. So I exited the brush to find Piper sitting cross-legged outside of it slicing chunks out of a piece of wood with his dagger.

I looked at him that he might see my intent, then turned to go.

"You remain aware, and do not go far." Piper whispered the warning to me as I let loose my instincts and ran.

I had come back three times with three rabbits in my jaws. Each time I had happily received a pat on the head from Piper. He took them and used his dagger to the more productive purpose of cleaning and gutting them, before Demon and Baylor emerged near dusk.

I was just returning with a fourth and Demon was saying to Piper, "You let her go alone?"

He turned then, noticing me as I came up, and dropped the rabbit on his foot. Then I went back to my natural form, almost reluctantly, and only so that I could say something.

"I was very much on the lookout," I said.

I looked him in the eye so that he would see that I was serious and that no further chastising of Piper was necessary. I had been very aware of all that was going on around me.

"I scanned frequently and it's not like I asked for Piper's permission to go," I continued.

When Demon seemed not at all inclined to give up being upset, I added, "You did tell me you wanted me prepared. That I should learn everything I could so as not to have to rely on others, did you not?"

I was using his words against him. Baylor and Piper both chuckled then. As Demon's face went through so many emotions, so quickly it was hard to tell which it would settle for, I saw my win in the making and with their increasing laughter I could not resist one more thing.

"Thank you for dinner, Angel," I prompted starting to laugh myself.

Demon bent down and picked up the rabbit from off of his foot. "You are correct. I cannot shield you from every thing that *may* happen. Please just be very careful of yourself." Then he forced a smile and repeated, "Thank you for dinner, Angel."

He was holding the limp rabbit up before him and I felt awful suddenly, for I had made light of his concern for me. This bothered me, the whole time they were preparing our meal. When at last it was ready and we were all seated around the small fire, eating our meal in a silence that was only increasing my feelings of guilt, I bowed my head and leaned over slightly.

"I am sorry to have worried you," I whispered. "It was wrong of me to make light of your concern. I know you only had my best interest in mind."

He looked at me silently for a moment, then he smiled his acceptance of my apology, giving me yet another heartbreaking glimpse of his slight dimples and somehow making me feel twice as guilty, yet divinely forgiven, all at once.

Then we finished our meal in a more comfortable silence.

~19~

Dover

We gathered up what few things we had with us, putting dirt on the fire, and were off again as soon as we had all finished our meal. We traveled again mostly in silence as the realization of the reason for our travel set in. It was not merely an adventure for the sake of an adventure. Baylor was leaving his homeland behind quite probably for the first time, to lure some evil creature from it that appeared to be hunting him.

Demon was on a mission, to find out what had become of a longtime friend of his, one who had gone quite inexplicably missing. Piper, I am sure, did not see this journey as a source of enjoyment, as he had brought this disturbing news in the first place. Now he was being forced to return to a loved one by this very slow method. He had left Adonia amidst the confusion this disappearance had created, and most likely would rather be at her side right now. I felt a sense of guilt that I should be part of the reason he could not return to her swiftly.

"Piper!" I said, calling out to get his attention.

He had been a little ahead of me as we walked and slowed then to walk beside me.

"What is it, Lass?" he said, glancing at me when I had not yet given reason for saying his name.

"Do you wish to return more swiftly to Rome?" I asked finally.

197

"Yes and no," he said, replying honestly. "I would like to be back at Adonia's side, to help her in this time of confusion. But she is a strong woman and has her brother Adreal for now. I think it better I return with you, seeing I've brought you all safely to her. Rather than allow for the possibility that something could befall all of you, which I might have helped to prevent." He smiled another of his winning smiles. "She would hold me responsible when she found out, as I would myself." Then thoughtfully he added, "No, this is the better way."

His smile when he had spoken of Adonia had let me know Demon had made no mistake in his assessment of Piper's feelings for her. I glanced up ahead to Demon thinking something along the lines of 'I wish Demon smiled like that when thinking of me.' But I kept these thoughts to myself, walking for the moment in silence.

"You love her, don't you?" I said finally.

I was not really asking if he did, only asking for confirmation from him of what I thought was obvious. I was simply making conversation.

"Yes," Piper said.

It was a simple answer but portrayed a far from simple feeling. I drew then on all Demon had told me, glancing ahead again at the one whose words, I was remembering.

"She loves you too," I said.

Again it was a statement, not a question.

"Yes," he replied.

Again it was a simple answer, holding far too many things within it to be as simple as it appeared.

"It will be all right, you know," I said.

I don't know why I said this last. What made me so sure, that these two, if nothing else, would be okay somehow? Maybe I just felt that, after having met him, he would find a way, with or without the Council's approval.

Maybe it was simply some deep need in me to believe that love would work, for at least this one couple, so that I could believe it would work for me someday. I had said it and could not take it back. I would not take it back even if I could. I had to believe. He looked at me then with a calm softness about his eyes that was somehow sad but still hopeful, and it made me somehow feel connected to him.

"For you as well, little Angel. Someday he will set aside the past and begin to see the future," he said.

I blushed then, not knowing how he had guessed so easily those things I had kept even from myself. I took only the first part of his word at that time to store as hope within my heart. It was much later, when we had fallen back into silence and he had moved forward to walk beside Baylor, that the rest of it began to sink in. I remembered the times that I had thought Demon might kiss me, when I had thought I had seen him nod to the painting of his lost betrothed.

I realized then that Demon still held onto Seraphim, even after all these years, and Piper had been encouraging me not to give up. There was a part of me that found these revelations about Demon even more appealing in their romantic nature. I told myself, I would leave things as they were. I had forever to overcome her memory. Maybe I had not been wrong about his desire to kiss me. I need only bide my time and someday his desire would overcome his sense of loyalty to one so long gone.

I painted this beautiful scenario in my mind, of his realizing he wanted me as I had realized I wanted him. I held onto it. I had fallen in love with him. I had recognized it and admitted it to myself. I had to believe that someday he would do the same. This hope I stored with all the rest of my dreams and walked happily through the night.

By dawn of the third day we had come to Loch Ness. Here there was so much beauty and sense of serenity all about it. It made me hope they would choose to make our camp here. Piper walked quietly to the water's edge, squatting down to sweep his hand back and forth in the water.

"This place brings me peace," Piper said. "It reminds me somehow of the one that made me." He turned back to us then, a huge smile on his face like a very happy child. "Let us stay here for the day. I will take the first watch."

Then without waiting for a reply he stood and dove into the shallow water. He changed into a cod as he went, so that his head would not touch the bottom, but rather his small fish form darted away as it hit the water.

We were just finishing our cheese, wine and bread that we had brought with us, when he emerged again still smiling. He turned then and sat facing the water, obviously expecting we had accepted his suggestion, and he was taking up his watch accordingly.

We walked then back into the wood and once within its shade did much as we had the day before. Had any happened upon us, during this time, they would have thought it the strangest of sights; finding a huge black wolf willingly being used as a pillow by an even bigger beast of a man, and another one curled peacefully to his side like a happy little lap dog.

They again took their turns at keeping the watch and I again woke fully rested by mid-afternoon. Once again I went off to hunt for us, and again returned victorious, only this time I had brought for us a young deer. I came dragging it proudly, if not a little awkwardly, between my legs, back to our camp. This had been a hard task, as it seems I now had eyes bigger than my stomach, but not the confidence in my skill to enlarge myself as Demon had. I dropped the thing and sat panting happily for a moment until their laughter made me turn back into myself to inquire as to the reason for their mirth.

"What is so funny?' I asked them, when I again had a mouth to do it with.

"You were drooling like a great happy dog waiting for praise," Baylor said, still laughing.

"You've taken quite a liking for this hunting thing, even if your prey is near as big as you," Demon added.

He was holding his arms out in front of him, swinging them awkwardly; mimicking my difficulty dragging the roe to them, making them all laugh all the harder at his antics.

I looked from one to the other of them, as they finally started to calm themselves. I was about to tell them they could hunt for themselves next time, when something more important occurred to me.

"I was drooling?" I said, aghast at the thought.

They never answered me, they just started laughing again.

This was how we would travel the rest of the way down into and across England. We would walk at night. Sometimes Demon would turn into a huge horse, carrying Baylor swiftly across the miles, as Piper and I ran along side. We rested during the day and laughed and talked while we ate. We would start off again, most times before dusk, keeping to a brisk pace.

We avoided most towns, stopping only occasionally to refill our wine sacks and replenish what few supplies we needed. We went unmolested by the one that had attacked us on our first night and I slowly began to think that maybe Baylor had truly scared it away. I didn't know how long it would take for a Changeling to recover from such a thing and draw itself a new form. I had no real idea as to how Changelings fought, other than Demon's statement as to the need to inflict as much damage as possible, as quickly as possible.

We were nearing Dover, which we had decided would be the best place to make the crossing into France. We would set sail from here and continue again, as we had been, onward into Italy and then to Rome. It was as we were approaching this town, to buy passage to Calais, that these new questions occurred to me. I then picked up my speed that I might fall into stride beside Demon.

"How long does it take for a Changeling to recover from the damage done to it when it fights?" I asked him

"You are wondering why it has not yet come back?" he said, as he turned to look at me.

"Well yes, I suppose, Baylor seemed to heal instantaneously whenever it hurt him," I said, biting my lip then and considering my next question. "But it wasn't killed when Baylor ripped its head off. I felt its soul flee. It's just going to go off, and rebuild and come back better prepared, and very angry."

"It will take some time. All the energy it had collected and made its own was dropped. When enough pain is inflicted, sometimes the soul will flee without thought in desperation to escape it. If one is quick enough and savage enough to shake it loose or rattle its senses, this can happen," he explained. "But unlike calling up a new body to form around your soul when you arrive somewhere, he now has to convince new energies to join with him after having allowed those that were his before to be destroyed. He abandoned them to flee and in a sense the universe doesn't want to be with him right now. Every part of it wants to live by being part of something else, and being part of him was very unprofitable."

He smiled at me, making sure I understood him fully, and then he went on, "Yes, he will be back. He will bend the universe to his will. He is a Changeling and that is what we do. He will also, most likely, not come back alone, but for now we are fine. When he does return, we will be prepared, and if I can snatch him mayhap I can get some answers from him, since he will not want to be forced to abandon his energies again so soon. It would be even harder to gather another form to himself so close on the heels of the last time."

"What questions would you ask of him?" I asked him.

I was only minimally comforted by this response, but curious now to know what question he had for this Changeling. His answer was quite unexpected.

"Which Elder it is I need to thrash," he replied.

The anger suddenly evident in his voice reminded me of how protective he was not only of me but of Baylor as well. I went quiet as I did not like his angry voice and did not want to question him further on anything that might make him even more upset. I was also forced to remember that the other reason for this journey was the disappearance of a friend of his. I knew he had been doing very well in keeping his spirits high, throughout our travel, and I had no intention of ruining that.

We came to Dover very early in the morning and the town was very quite. We made our way to a building near the docks. I caught the occasional look from the sailors that occupied it, but the presence of the three men I traveled with kept their comments to a minimum. We broke our fast here and this was a strange thing to me. I had always taken my meals with Mem and Father Paul. Later I had eaten with Demon and Baylor, but never in a public place such as this tavern.

I was very aware I had not even been around any but other Changelings and Baylor since I myself had been changed. I concentrated very hard on being normal, which is probably what made me fail so miserably.

"Relax, enjoy the meal, nothing is going to happen," Demon said.

He had leaned into me, to whisper in my ear, making me jump. I had to laugh then at myself. I was still with friends and just eating, so what if others were in the same general area? I joined then in the conversation. As they talked I found myself forgetting any one else was around.

"So what do *you* think happened with Edsel?" Demon was now saying to Piper.

"I do not know, as I said his presence is still strong at his villa. But even if he had been wounded grievously," he replied thoughtfully, "he is old and powerful, and he could have pulled himself together in the two weeks we had searched for him. That is another reason why Adonia sent me to you. She feels you are wiser in some respects than the others, having been trained in a different manner. She is hopeful you may make sense of these things with your older wisdom and greater learning than we have been able to."

They were talking in low tones and I found I had to lean forward slightly to hear them.

"Have you spoken to Santon? What is his view?" Demon asked next.

He was barely picking at his food, as was I. It was not nearly as good as Baylor had spoiled me with.

"Santon said he would have been inclined to believe it was a forced ascension, had it not been for the fact that it had taken all of them to accomplish such a thing before. He just didn't see it having been possible without him and Edsel being a joint part in the willing of one," Piper said, looking just as incredulous at his own statement as Demon.

"Do you believe that this forced ascension is even possible? Edsel

203

told me about such, but I never truly believed him," Demon said.

Piper and Demon both had finally pushed their plates away, giving up all pretense of eating.

"I do not know. The way Santon spoke of it, even if it was, it can't be done without at least five very powerful wills combining. So even if it is, I don't see how it was done to Edsel. I cannot believe either of the twins would have helped in such a deed, nor do I think Santon had any part in it. I know I myself did not. That leaves only Cathmore, Lachlan, and, I am sorry to say, your friend, Kynan, that amount to any of age and power in Rome at the time." He looked sadly at Demon. "This is truly beyond me."

We all sat silently contemplating all of this, and I felt I was at a serious disadvantage. I did not know nearly as much about this as they did, and if they were confused by all of it, I was completely baffled.

When at last Baylor was finished, as he seemed the only one of us with any appetite, Demon drew the necessary coins from the purse at his belt. He laid them on the table and we left. We walked down to the docks and I stood safely between Baylor and Piper as Demon purchased passage for us.

So it was that shortly before noon we had left behind any resemblance to all I had known and were well on our way to an entirely different world.

~20~

Hellcat

When we arrived in France, Calais was alive and bustling with energy. People were running back and forth, going about the business of the day. Dock workers were hauling loads of goods on their backs to waiting carts, shouting back and forth to each other. Hawkers were yelling what it was they had that they'd sell, right there, right then, cheaper than if you waited to buy it from another in town. Captains called out to crewmen and sailors and not all boarding for the appointed jobs seemed to want them. I saw women leaning up against the walls of dirty buildings, ignoring the filth at their feet, throwing suggestive looks and words. I couldn't translate all the words, but I understood the general meaning, as would any who might take notice. I wasn't quite sure I wanted to know the full meaning of what these women suggested, because what part I had gotten put me off quite neatly from even looking any longer.

I wanted badly to be quickly away from this place, yet at the same time I wanted to examine all of it. I was very glad of the three men with me, as I was suddenly aware of all the sidelong glances of the dock workers and sailors surrounding us. I heard a couple of them call out things I did not understand accompanied by gestures equally unknown to me, but just as with the women and their actions, I had some idea. I knew simply by the way they quieted, when Baylor or Demon turned to look at them, that it had not been acceptable conversation.

I put my hand to my stomach, feeling suddenly nervous and slightly nauseous; all the smells, all the people, all of it nearly overwhelming me for a moment.

"Have you need of food, Lass?" Baylor's sweet face, looking so concerned down at me, calmed me instantly.

"No, not that. Not here anyway, I'd rather hunt for myself and have you prepare it," I said.

He seemed to understand instantly the cause of my discomfort and turned, saying something softy to Demon. Then we headed quickly for the outskirts of town. It took us longer than I might have liked, to wind our way through the different alleyways and dirty streets, on a route out, but eventually the crowds thinned. Then the buildings and houses as well, then even the farms disappeared, slowly leaving us alone with the world.

As soon as I saw that none could possibly notice, I asked Demon if I could hunt. He paused briefly, probably scanning as I had just done before even asking. Then he nodded that he did not mind. I took off then, turning into the large black wolf I had become so comfortable with, and running at a soft lope for the tree line, escaping all the discomfort I had just been feeling.

I was almost there when I felt it. A great pull from behind me. Our attacker had returned and he was not alone. I knew instantly this was the case. He had also either just arrived from someplace distant or shielded himself well. I turned in mid-stride without thinking about it, once again allowing the wolf in me to take over.

There were three of them now and they were switching forms quickly, some forms I recognized and some I did not. All were hard-pressing my companions. Baylor was doing incredible damage with Bane, they were indeed one in their purpose. Yet he did not have now the advantage he had had as a Werewolf, of being unfazed by the things appearing before him. It kept changing shape and coming at him again and he was slowly being forced backwards. This angered me greatly. It seemed to me to be very unfair and I have always hated when things are unfair.

I did not know if the one Demon fought was the one he wanted to question but he was tearing it apart as though it were. For every form it took he would take one somehow bigger or stronger and tear into it anew. My mind was taking all these things in as rapidly as I was running; working to remember each form and each defense yet at the same time growing angrier every time the one facing Baylor used its abilities to its unfair advantage. Piper seemed quite content to fight his opponent as a man, using his sword as Baylor was. Only he was laughing wildly like it was a wonderful game that he was playing for the sheer enjoyment of it.

As I closed in, I saw Piper swing clear around, cutting his opponent completely through the middle. Then, stopping dead, mid-swing, he came back full force, cutting off the head as well. I felt that one's soul flee as its body fell in three pieces at Piper's feet. I noted that Piper seemed somehow disappointed his fun was over. I then saw Baylor stumble on something beneath his heel, and his opponent again changed form, becoming a panther and leaping atop him as he went down, jaws gaping.

I did not think for even half a second what I would do, or was doing. I only knew that Baylor was my friend, I adored him. I would not allow him to be harmed. I came in, still at a dead lope, launching myself forward and into the air. Taking the great black beast by the neck, from the side, and rolling it with me as I went, I came back to all fours, with its throat still gripped in my mouth, thrashing my head violently back and forth.

"Angel!"

I froze as some part of me recognized the sound of that voice.

"Angel!"

That was my name. I came back to myself then and released the great limp cat from my jaws. I looked up at Demon and there was mixed awe and something else on his face. I could understand the cause for neither. So I did what I had to do. I changed back into my normal self, to ask him.

"What?" I asked.

I saw then that both Piper and Baylor stood behind him, the discarded bodies of two other Changelings before them.

"You've sent him fleeing again!" Demon said.

Still he had the strange look written on his face and a question evident in his voice. He gestured behind me in consternation.

"What?" I said again, turning behind me to see what he was talking about. "Oh!"

It occurred to me then that it was the one who had been attacking Baylor which he had wanted to question.

"I'm sorry, I didn't know which one you wanted to speak to," I said as I looked down at my feet. Then, remembering I had a viable excuse, I added, "But he was on top of Baylor and I couldn't think then anyway."

I had looked up then, daring him to condemn me for trying to help our friend, and was shocked as he swept me up, swinging me around and hugging me.

"I'm not angry, Angel," he said. Putting me down and smiling that wonderful smile of his, he added, "I'll have my answers another day, for now you have amazed me!"

Baylor then came up and patted my shoulder, saying, "I'd have got him eventually but I thank you for caring anyway."

I knew it might have galled him a little, that I had jumped into the middle of his fight. So I did my best to make a joke of it, so he wouldn't be upset at me that I had.

"Well, he may not have refused to tell me a tale but he was intent on harming my favorite storyteller," I said, smiling.

He too gave me a hug then and I thought I might be forced to flee my form as well as he squeezed me a bit too tight. We all walked off then, as though nothing out of the ordinary had happened, stepping over the remains of those Changelings who had dared to take us on. There was in me a feeling of indestructibility, that with these three, I could take on the world. I also had a new confidence, that I could not only defend myself, but even be useful to them as well.

I looked back over my shoulder as a sudden thought occurred to me. It shook my recent feeling of invulnerability. The discarded bodies were long since out of sight but Demon followed my look anyway.

"What is it?" he asked me.

"When Baylor fought the gorilla back home, and we had stayed there, it could not have come to reclaim its body. Can they not simply go back now that we have gone, and call them back, as I did mine at the stream when you first came to me? " I asked. The thought of another fight this soon disturbed me.

"Yes, they will meet with resistance but not as much as with all new bodies," he said softly.

I think he was trying to keep me calm by keeping his voice so low.

"Then why did we not burn them or destroy them in some way?" I asked.

I was even more confused now. Why had we had not taken precautions, if he knew this would make it easier for them to come after us again?

"It is all still energy that recognizes them. We would have only slowed them, not stopped them. Their souls had fled changing the energies now from flesh to ash is a useless endeavor," he replied calmly.

"But then they will come after us forever!" I cried.

I was aghast at the prospect of being on guard and hunted for the rest of my life. Which did not seem would be very short, since the one I was speaking with had been born before Christ.

"I doubt that," he replied, laughing suddenly. "It doesn't matter who's giving the orders, there isn't a Changeling alive who doesn't prefer being corporeal and avoiding pain. They will not perpetually put themselves in a position to lose their bodies. Any Changeling who has been through it will know it only gets harder to convince energy to come to you, if you constantly let it be destroyed. None want to spend a hundred years convincing one little bit of energy at a time that they should be trusted just once more, and assisted in being given form."

"One hundred years!" I was in shock.

"An exaggeration, but it is still a painful process and they'll tire of it,

I promise. One little Werewolf is not worth it and I will see that they realize it." He smiled at me again and I forgot to remind him that I didn't think it was Baylor they had come for.

By the time Piper had picked a spot that he felt would work for a camp I was exhausted mentally. We had walked through the night, crossed the strait, fought a gruesome battle, and then walked again until night. Still I had not slept. I didn't know how they had done so well with all of it, but I was ready to fall down. Piper was building a fire, and I thought maybe I should hunt but I had no energy for it. I simply lay down and slept.

I think I started dreaming immediately. I was the goddess of the painting and Demon was offering me some delicious-smelling meat that he had cooked over an open fire before me. Then something was threatening Baylor and I got up from my seat, turning into the hellcat I had dreamed of before, to defend my storyteller. I fought side by side with him, and he was a Werewolf again. We were doing so much damage that did no good, as our attackers just kept coming back. Then my foot was hurt and I tried to heal it.

I came awake in a rush, realizing the delicious smell of the meat Demon had offered in my dream was real. It was an animal's leg in the fire. The three Changelings we'd battled before were there again and the pain in my foot was real as well. I had been stepped on. My mind was foggy and for some reason I could not understand: if the rest were real, why then was Baylor still human?

I came to my feet in one swift movement, digging my claws into the back of the neck of the one closest to me. It was again the one facing Baylor. I realized I had become the hellcat of my dream and in some part of my mind I thought Demon would be upset again that I had created it for my form. It was done though, and I was in a rage, and didn't care. Would they never leave us? This was the one I had met before, the one Demon wanted. I recognized the feel of it. It was vile to me.

I pulled back on its neck where I had dug in, using all my weight to try and pull it back from before Baylor. Mayhap I was even thinking to pull its head off, as Baylor, when a Werewolf, could have easily done. I was unable to figure out what new beast it had chosen for its form, but it was massive and strong, and the name of it didn't matter to me then. It occurred to me too that Demon wanted to question it but I had no time to figure how to subdue it for such questioning to be done.

Suddenly it knocked Baylor's sword away and grabbed him by the throat. I wanted to scream then that someone must help me protect him. I was suddenly deathly afraid this creature would remove his head and my Baylor would die. I didn't care now to merely subdue it, only to make it stop by whatever means.

Then I felt something puncture my side and I knew I had been wounded. I did not have to look to see my blood pouring from me. I could feel the warmth of it seeping into my fur. It all happened so fast, Demon screamed for me to heal myself, not to flee, but I had no intentions of leaving now, not when they needed me. Baylor needed me. I jumped onto the back of the one I held, the one still facing Baylor as though I were a lesser threat. I dug my clawed feet deep into its back gaining leverage, and drew one of my sharply dangerous hands back, just as Demon grabbed the one that had wounded me from behind, dragging it backwards.

I plunged my free fist, with all my might, deep into Baylor's opponents back, splitting wide its ribs. At the same time I willed that some of its energy come to me and heal me. I yanked my claws back, bringing with it in my grasp, the thing's heart. In that same instant it pulled forward, yanking Baylor's head from his shoulders. I let out a horrified scream, enraged and broken, sounding nothing near to human.

Then the most amazing thing any of us had ever seen or imagined happened. Baylor turned into the Werewolf, snatching back his head from the thing's now limp fingers and placing it back on his shoulders. He turned then and snatched up the legs of the one Demon was still battling, tearing it limb from limb like it was made of straw. It was soon strewn around us in so many pieces, like the random feathers about a chicken pen, when the fox leaves.

I seemed to be taking note of all of these things in slow motion as though I had somehow been left behind and had to now catch up mentally. The one I had just destroyed finished crumpling beneath me. I just stood there still on its back spellbound and frozen. I slowly realized that I had not felt its soul flee. Instead I felt an awesome pull, like the light had felt, only much stronger, and the soul seemed to disappear completely. I felt somehow stronger and mayhap even heavier than I had ever in my life felt before. Even the pull of the light just then, that had been so awesomely powerful and dreadful to me in its greatness before, had merely been another thing to note but not to fear.

The last one of them fled then, leaving us all in a state I can not even name for you. At about the same time, each of us said, "What happened?" then, "I don't know!" Then we all stood in shocked silence for a very long moment. I finally looked at Baylor. It was Baylor the man, not Baylor the Werewolf.

"Have you ever done that before?" I asked.

"Done what?" he said, appearing just as confused, if not more so, than the rest of us.

"Turned into a Werewolf and the full moon still two nights away!" I nearly yelled.

I was shocked even more to think he didn't know he'd done it.

"I did?" Baylor asked and now he looked even more confused than he had before, if that were even possible.

"Yes, you did! And this thing," I said, stomping one foot on the body under my feet, "it tore your head off, and you snatched it back, and put it back on."

I started laughing then, not the happy laughter we usually shared, but nervous, near hysterical, panicked laughter. I couldn't get control for a moment, as I kept hearing my inner monologue, *"Give me that head. No! It's mine."*

"Angel, are you all right?" Demon's voice cut into the argument in my head, and I snapped back to reality.

I jerked my head up and looked at him.

"What?" I asked him.

"I said, are you all right?" he repeated, looking at me like I'd gone mad, which, I must admit, I was probably on the verge of doing.

At this point, though, his look only caused me to look down at myself to see what he was looking at. I found myself still the hellcat I barely recalled becoming, still holding the beast's heart in my claws. Quickly I dropped the repulsive organ and fixed myself, stepping off of the corpse I hadn't realized I was standing on. I thought those things were what had concerned him, but even then he didn't seem any more convinced I was all right, than I was.

"What?" I said again, when he was still looking at me in that same manner a few moments later. "I am fine, just confused. What just happened here?"

I said the first as much to convince myself as Piper and Demon.

Neither of them said anything for the longest time and I looked to Baylor for support. He seemed lost in his own thoughts and not at all able to help me except for maybe by providing a diversion.

"Why don't you look at him like that?" I said.

I waved my hand behind me to where Baylor had just slumped to the ground, dropping his head in his hands and getting lost in thoughts I couldn't guess at.

"He's the one stealing his head back from that thing. What is that thing?" I demanded.

"A Yeti, and you killed him," Demon said, finally speaking to me.

I let out a sigh of relief as some small fear they would just stare at me forever, never saying a word again, finally left me.

"Once again, I am sorry, you will have to ask him next time," I said.

I was exasperated that he should look at me like I was a madwoman for a matter as trivial as that. The thing had had to be destroyed at the time because it was killing Baylor. As Demon had said, he would just have to ask it next time.

"There will be no next time. You *killed* him!" he said slowly.

He spoke as though I were slow-minded and could only follow him if he spoke plainly and slowly, which as of a few moments ago I was almost willing to believe.

"You mean he won't come back for more ever again?" I was very pleased.

"No!" Demon said. "I mean he *can't* come back for more ever again."

~21~

Yelm

"What?" Now I knew I had lost my wits. "I thought you said we couldn't be killed!"

"Well, apparently, Angel, you've proven me wrong," Demon said.

Now it began to dawn on me why he had looked at me so strangely. Why Piper had just stood there, with his mouth agape, saying nothing.

"When? How? I don't understand." I looked at them then with most likely the same look they had given me.

"You don't know?" Piper asked, as he looked at me incredulously.

"If I knew how I'd done it, would I be asking you?" I said shortly.

The shortness that was due to all the stress went unnoticed, except by Demon. He came up to me then and put his arms around me. I was so tired and confused and I don't know what else. I simply buried my head in his chest and started to cry. He held me for some time, then, patting my back, he pushed me out to an arm's length, still holding my shoulders.

"Better?" he asked.

I felt suddenly foolish then as he questioned me like a child. I didn't want him to think of me as a child. I wanted him to think of me as a woman. I stared back at him for a moment, determining I would pull myself together, and we would figure out all this confusion.

"Yes, I am fine now," I said. I started then to try and figure it all out. "It all happened so very fast. I remember I felt a pain in my side,"

"Yes, the bastard I was fighting got through my guard, and missing me, stabbed you," he said, gladly trying to help with what I was trying to work out.

"Then you told me not to leave, but I remember thinking I had no intentions of doing any such thing," I said.

He nodded, showing me he was following me, and Piper stepped closer to make sure he heard every word.

"Then I thought it was going to rip Baylor's head off and I know Baylor does not age but I didn't know if this would kill him. I mean, most Werewolves die if you remove their heads, right?" I asked.

They both nodded whether in agreement or simply to show they were following my line of thought, I wasn't sure.

"Then I was shoving my claws into its ribs, thinking, I suppose, in some morbid corner of my mind, to rip out its heart and prevent this," I continued.

Demon raised an eyebrow at this and Piper nodded his head appreciatively.

"Then I remember pulling back, willing some of its energy to come into me, and heal the hole in my side. Then it crumpled and Baylor put his head back on and now we're here. I don't know!" I wound down the last quickly, as I was beginning to feel the whole accounting was useless, for they had been there as well, had they not?

"That is it!" Demon said triumphantly. "The Yelm! You stole his Yelm!"

"Yelm?" Piper repeated the word like it tasted bad.

"Yes!" Demon was excited now, pouring out his ideas to us in a flood. "My teacher told me that the Yelm is the soul's anchor in this realm. The first piece it attaches to when it comes to earth. He told me to guard it well. Never to leave it, no matter how light I need to be, or how quickly I need to become incorporeal. It is one of the first things a Changeling learns."

He looked to see if Piper and I were following. Then he looked back to Piper, who still seemed a little confused.

"Your teacher may have called it by another name," he said. "But I'm sure she admonished you to never leave it behind. She must have told you something to this effect, right?"

Piper nodded, finally, and again and Demon raced on.

"Now I see why it is so important!" he said excitedly. "I mean yes, we call it an anchor, but I thought it merely like an initial building block for every foundation you might choose to build, a cornerstone for the rest to attach to. I see now it is even more essential than that, without it your soul has nothing to hold it here!"

He was pacing back and forth, apparently rerunning it all in his mind; rearranging his knowledge to accommodate these new facts. Piper was standing there starring at me again.

"What?" I asked him, as his look turned more and more perplexed.

"How is it one as young as you could exert enough will to coax from another the *meadhanan nan cruth*?" Piper asked me.

I guess we were all in a state of confusion because he had slipped into Gaelic. It took me a moment to decipher what he had said from what Mem had taught me.

"The means of form? That is what your teacher called the Yelm?" I said, looking with amusement at him, but he didn't seem to find it at all amusing. "Well, I suppose it is fitting, considering all we've come to figure out. I don't know, maybe it was tired of living with him. He did get hurt a lot lately." But it made no sense to me either so I continued jokingly, "Maybe I had come into contact with it when I put my hand inside him and it could not resist my charm."

This finally succeeded in getting a smile from him, although it quickly faded, as he too began to pace and think. I was simply happy I would not have to deal with that one ever again. I was also hopeful the others would have seen it and thought I'd done it on purpose. Then maybe they would stay away so I couldn't do it to them as well. Then maybe I could curl up and get some sleep.

I remembered Baylor then and turned to find him as I'd seen him last. I walked to him and put my hand on his head. When he didn't look up, I squatted down before him, sliding my hand down to his cheek and lifting his chin so he would look at me. When he finally did, the look he had was pure misery.

"What is it?" I asked him, concerned and confused.

He said nothing. I pleaded then, fearing I would cry again.

"Please, tell me, I can not bear to see you so," I begged.

Finally it seemed he realized I would not leave him.

"I have doubled my curse, by leaving my people again. Now I will change at random with or without the full moon," he said, sounding so broken I could not bear it.

"Not so!" I said, and his look was so instantly hopeful I quickly moved forward. "I think you only changed long enough to save your head, literally. I think if you do change again, outside the full moon, it will only be in another such dire case. Your mother's curse has kept you alive this long, it merely refused in any way it could, to not let you die now. I don't believe you will change at random at all."

I was thoughtful for a moment, then added, "Do not worry over this, for it will not be as you think. The curse seems, in all its aspects, merely to want to keep you alive and capable of defending your people. The Werewolves you are meant to hunt only change on the full moon, hence so will you. As for the rest of the time, it will only try to keep you alive."

He seemed to brighten then, seeing that I was probably right. I smiled at him and pulled lightly on one of his braids.

"Can we sleep now?" I asked.

He gave a short laugh then and lightly pretended to punch my jaw.

"You've a real good chin, Lass," he said.

Then he slid forward off the rock he had slumped down onto, leaning back slowly to rest his head on it. He patted the ground beside him and I took my black wolf form and curled up at his side, sharpening my senses but hoping it would be unnecessary.

When next I awoke, the sun was high in the sky and it took me some moments to realize I had slept the night through, and half the next day as well. It seemed that with none but the three with whom my wolf's mind felt completely comfortable around the rest of me had shut completely down and sunk into oblivion.

The others were arguing, albeit in a friendly manner, in increasingly high tones. I opened one eye and Demon turned immediately toward me. I tried to close it again quickly but I was caught.

"Is that not right, Angel?" Demon said, not fooled. "It is fully possible, that at the point when the soul was about to flee anyway, you pulled the part of it that contained the Yelm from it. The Yelm was then abandoned, if only by accident, as it fled only to find itself sucked into the light."

I gave up being able to sleep any more and sat up, turning back into myself as I did saying, "I suppose."

"Mayhap," he continued still obsessing over this new revelation that a Changeling could die. "That is what happened to Edsel. Mayhap he somehow had his Yelm stolen from him." He paused for a moment. "There is still so much I do not know. I need to find another older, wiser Changeling like my teacher. If I can find no answers in Rome, I will go in search of the old one, whose presence was sensed in Egypt by Lachlan."

"We must hurry!" Piper said, becoming anxious to be gone now. "With all that has occurred and we have come to learn, I do not feel safe that Adonia and Adreal are now left with only Santon. I do not trust the others completely."

He stood, showing he would brook no further argument unless it were while moving forward.

"Then let us be off," Demon said.

So saying, and with a slight pull to gather the extra-needed mass, Demon turned again into a huge horse. It was much in the way of the kind used to labor in the field. Baylor immediately moved to jump on its back. There was no more talk as I took the shape of a huge wolfhound as Piper had,

219

and we left that place at a steady lope. It would have appeared to most that some barbarian from a bygone era had taken his hounds hunting, and they would not have been too far off. We were hunting. We were hunting for answers.

We ran like this until our bodies tired, then we made them new again and ran some more. We did not stop until Baylor was near to falling off in exhaustion, unable as we were to constantly renew. We rested then and the next few days progressed at an only slightly slower rate, as we had to stay far from the roads, allowing Baylor to change then and run along beside us, staying out of sight. When day came he rode, and we stopped only when absolutely necessary.

By the end of the cycle of the second full moon that I had been in his company, we had entered Italy. We finally slowed then and began searching for a sheltered place to sleep. We came at last upon a small grove of olive trees and built in their center a fire. This time it was Demon who brought us our meat and Piper who cooked it.

We rested then, that we would be at our fullest strength and highest awareness when we came into Rome. We kept the watch as usual. A great feeling of excitement was growing in Piper. I could tell as he fidgeted with the sticks on the fire that he wanted desperately to be back with Adonia, and assured of her safety.

I had not met her yet and therefore could only guess from coming to know him that her feelings would be much the same as his so obviously were for her, for how could she not return them? I tried to sleep but my mind seemed to be preoccupied with love again. Once more I was feeling more hopeless than hopeful, as I had swung constantly back and forth throughout our journey.

No further sign had come from Demon, that he might have in him a like want for me. No looks I could take as a desire to kiss me. I had constantly ranged between satisfaction brought on by his occasional close proximity while we were sleeping, to disappointment because it was so rare and never seemed to mean more than that was where he ended up.

Finally I sat up and slapped at Piper's stick with one of my own, holding mine up then as if to challenge him to a duel. He looked at me and smiled as the mock challenge written on my face broke through and amused him. Thus our mutually pensive mood was broken and it seemed we were reassuring each other that all of it would work itself out in the end for both of us.

I curled up then next to Baylor's side as had become my habit, only this time I chose to go back to the wolfhound, as this might not cause such alarm, should any happen upon our camp. I slept deeply, when sleep finally came, and awoke well-rested. Piper was already awake and pacing and Demon was gone.

I was just about to ask where he had gone and for what reason when I felt him returning. It is a feeling I will never forget and will never be matched; when his soul came back to being near me, after being apart. There was about it a comfort and familiarity I had come to cherish.

He swooped into the grove as a falcon and landed before us, answering my questions before I could ask them.

"I have flown as far ahead as I felt I should and felt nothing of any with ill intent. We should travel unmolested at least to the outskirts of the city," Demon said. "But do not for one moment let down your guard."

He looked at me to assure himself I had taken his words to heart. Then he turned and led us from the grove. It was once again as the barbarian hunter, that we traveled and I found it amusing, watching Baylor constantly rub his buttocks to bring some blood back into it. We passed a few wagons here and there and as this happened more frequently I realized we had reached the outskirts of the city. I could see great buildings ahead of me in a style I had only seen in the books of Father Paul. I began to grow excited and did not notice as Demon led us from the road into another grove of olive trees. Once there we all became ourselves except for Baylor, who became a moaning grumpy old man.

"Gavannon's bones, man, couldn't you have gated the beast?" he said to Demon, still rubbing his offended posterior.

"Surely, but then I'd not have the pleasure of listening to you bemoan my lack of value," Demon shot back sarcastically. "Now you may walk."

"Thank the gods for small favors," Baylor replied, then added, "if my legs will even carry me."

So we walked then into the heart of the great city of Rome. I looked about me in awe. Everywhere was beauty. I hardly took notice of those around me. Walking as I was in the center of a triangle of capable men, I allowed myself the freedom to enjoy every sight.

Then I remembered Demon's warning and knew why he had given it. He had known I would be awestruck. I focused my attention then and scanned around me. I found there were a large number of Changelings in this great city. I felt some I withdrew from instantly and a few I thought would be friendly. All in all, I simply shortened my search to my immediate surroundings, and walked as I was in the relative safety of my friends.

Piper seemed to take the lead in his excitement, and we followed him down many winding streets. When at last I had begun to think the city would go on forever, he stopped before an ornate gate. This gave me a view of a beautiful home and a very beautiful young woman. The woman threw the door wide, having obviously sensed our arrival. She was tall, like me, with long black hair as well, so deep and rich it showed nearly blue where mine hinted of cherries. She appeared to be close to my own age, and I could not guess who she might be.

She ran to the gate and threw it wide, launching herself into Piper's arms, and I was thoroughly confused. So also did Demon appear to be, as he looked first from her to Piper, then back again.

"Adonia?" he asked finally.

She turned from Piper then and threw herself into Demon's arms as well, saying, "Demon! It has been so long. I have missed you."

"But, when did you take to running about looking like an adult?" he said, still as confused as I.

The fact that the person I had always pictured as a young girl now

222

stood before us as a young woman made me quirk my eyebrow at Baylor quizzically, as though he might somehow have an answer for me. Just then her perfect match, only in the masculine, came out from the villa and I knew this had to be Adreal.

He too ran forward then and gave them both a hug, and Adreal said, "Well, actually that's an amusing story."

Baylor elbowed me lightly in the ribs and whispered, "I'll lend you my brush again."

We both started laughing then and the others seemed to suddenly take notice of us. Turning as a whole, the group looked back at us. We had somehow been left in the rear, forgotten for the moment, but were enjoying ourselves nonetheless. We hushed ourselves like naughty children who had just been caught stealing pies. Then, clasping our hands quickly behind our backs, we began playing the roles perfectly and awaited proper introductions.

~22~

Getting Lost

After we had all been introduced, which had taken a moment, as Demon had been shocked again by Adreal's appearance, then yet again by Baylor and me, and our antics, but finally we had all been 'well met' and gone inside. The place was much as I had pictured it in my mind. It was spacious and felt wonderful, as if only good had lived here.

The twins led us through a huge room, with chairs and chaise lounges placed here and there among potted plants and small tables, all of them conveniently facing toward the center. It reminded me very much of our home in the Highlands, and I thought Demon had quite probably done this on purpose.

We came out the other end of it into a beautiful garden, and this too was much as I had pictured it. I thought then, I should plant one someday for Demon. The twins had dropped to the carpeting of grass, like the children they no longer looked like, and we all followed their lead. Wine was passed around and questions were circulating just as quickly. Suddenly Adonia raised her hand and Demon and Piper fell silent.

"We are fine. No further events of notice have taken place. We have still found no sign of Edsel, but Santon and we are well. As for our appearance, I will tell you that first, Demon, as it seems you will not stop staring." She said the last smiling at Demon who still had not stopped looking back and forth between them.

"It's just so real! As though you don't even have to think about it at all!" he said, trying to defend his rudeness.

"That is because it is real." His eyes widened again in shock, and she raised her hand again to forestall him. "Let me explain. About thirty years ago Adreal and I had an argument. Now this is a rare thing as you know, so when he called me a big baby I was crushed. I told him I would grow up then and cease my play with him, he would be a big baby by himself. I spent three years refusing to play with him in any way. I would not change my form to fly with him. Nor in fact even leave our room, for more than a meal. I noticed then that I was growing up in truth and so did he."

She smiled then, continuing, "He begged me to stop this, insisting that he took it back, but I refused. So he stopped changing as well, telling me if I were going to get old and die then so would he. I gave up eventually, of course, seeing that I had made my point, and not wanting to truly grow old. Adreal stopped then too, once he had caught up with me in age and appearance. So you see, this is natural to us," she giggled, adding, "and we haven't had an argument since."

Demon finally closed his mouth, then opened it again and took another drink of his wine.

"You managed to age," he said, astounded, "truly age."

It was all he could seem to manage when he could finally speak. He sat silently for a time and I could not guess at his thoughts, but I think Adonia guessed at mine, for when I looked at her she was smiling knowingly at me.

I managed to smile back, wondering if the entire world knew, then she turned to Piper. They began conversing quietly and my stomach knotted up a little at the way they looked at each other. I wanted so much for Demon to look at me that way and speak to me with such adoration in his eyes. Instead he merely addressed the group.

"We need to get down to the business of figuring out what has happened to Edsel," he said.

He seemed to be admonishing himself for delaying in this, rather than really telling us what we needed to do. He stood up then, his wine still in hand, and walked back into the house. Adreal and Baylor got up and followed and so did I. I could feel a presence other than the twins about the place. It somehow reminded me of Father Paul. As I followed the others, they seemed to be walking toward it, for it got stronger as we went. We came to a door, which Demon opened without preamble. It revealed a sleeping chamber and the presence was strongest here.

"He dispersed his energies there." Demon's voice, cutting suddenly into the silence that had fallen, nearly made me jump. "Whether by choice or otherwise, he left all that had been him, here."

He walked along the length of the bed and stood silently before the window for a moment.

"I thought it felt like when you had left your energies all throughout the garden, but I could not believe he would have left us without a word," Adreal said.

Demon seemed deeply saddened to have had his suspicions confirmed. He took a step back, putting his arm around the younger man's shoulders and still looking out the window when he spoke.

"Mayhap he had no choice; do not be hurt by this just yet. He may have been forced by some circumstance to leave quickly and had no opportunity to tell you." But I could see in Demon's face that he too was greatly upset. "There are things I have learned on this journey back to you that you must know. We must consider all the possibilities before we judge him too harshly."

He led us then back to the garden where Adonia and Piper sat with their heads close together, still talking quietly. They looked up as we approached. I could see a slight hesitancy in Adonia's posture that told me she had been well-trained in hiding her feelings for Piper. She relaxed instantly when she realized it was only us, and I could not help but wonder about their relationship.

I could not understand why it was that she did not simply

disassociate with the Council and go her own way with Piper. Then I thought about the Council's minions chasing us from Scotland and into France, and her twin as well. I realized there was probably even more than these things I already knew stopping her.

Demon told them what he had just told us and my mind moved on to the new discussion, slowly leaving my contemplation behind.

"But who could have done him such harm, to cause him to flee, that we could not have sensed?" Adonia questioned. "We have stayed ever aware, as you have warned us we must, and I cannot believe anyone came to our villa unknown by us."

"Then mayhap we must consider it was one known then," Demon replied grimly.

"No, I tell you it is not possible. I like Lachlan no more than you, but none were here," she tried again.

This time she made it clearer that no one at all had been sensed, whether known or otherwise. Also, she seemed to have read all our minds in naming the one we felt most likely at fault.

"Then mayhap we must consider the possibility of a forced ascension. It might…," Demon trailed off, unable to form his thoughts into things resembling sensible statements. He seemed very confused and ill-tempered by it.

"I just don't know. Too many possibilities, too many new revelations, I feel like I am missing some valuable information. In light of all I've recently discovered, I do not even feel I can safely scoff at the idea of forced ascension."

He looked up from his intense investigation of the grass at his feet and his look was very pained. I knew him to be a man who took it upon himself to protect and teach and that it must be tearing him up inside not to be sure that he was in a position to do either. I wanted to go to him and put my arms around him and give him some of the comfort his nearness gave me. But he stood then, yanking up a handful of grass as he did.

Tossing them to the ground, he said, "I'm going to talk with the other Elders. You stay here."

He said the last to me, again as though I were a child, and when he turned to go I sat dumbfounded. Not only that he would go alone to confront those we feared responsible for sending the ones that had hunted us all the way here, and could also be responsible, in some way, for what had happened to Edsel, but also because he would leave me in such a manner.

After my shock had a moment to wear off, I leaped up and ran after him, stopping him near the front door. I did not know what I intended to say or do, I just went. I grabbed his arm as he reached to open it and he swung around to face me.

I forestalled any words he might have spoken to send me back to the others with my own, saying, "I am not a child! I am a woman!" He raised his eyebrows then, looking very surprised, and I rushed on. "I do not think you should do this but obviously you do not care what I think or feel, you haven't even asked. You will do as you see fit, for whatever reason suits you, I see. I know you are older and think you're wiser than the rest of us but that does not give you the right to rush off without allowing us our say. You could be putting yourself in the gravest of danger without considering that we might be able to help." He raised his hand to stop my tirade, but I ignored it and kept going. "What will happen to me if you are gone? I need you. I..."

I shut up then, suddenly realizing what I might have been about to say, and looked at my feet in embarrassment.

"I will be fine, Angel. I can handle myself. It is better that I go alone, and leave Baylor with you and the others. You must help them watch out for him, we do not know what has happened to Edsel and our assumptions do us no good. We can't sit here condemning the Council because they have before shown a harsh judgment upon others; Edsel was one of their own. We are jumping to conclusions that may be quite far off the mark. There may be things they know that can help me to figure out what has happened here. We do, however, know that the Council does want Baylor eliminated and the two of you have made quite a team in keeping him alive."

"But I," I began.

He again cut me off, patting my cheek and pushing me gently back toward the garden.

"No but's," he said.

Then he opened the door and walked out, leaving me once more dumbfounded.

"I will be back, I swear it!" he called back over his shoulder.

But his words left me no peace of mind.

I did not know whether I had been about to say, "But I love you," hoping that would make him stay; or, "But I don't think it is Baylor those creatures were after." Neither statement had made it from my mouth in any event so I stood there agonizing over not only which it might have been, but which might have worked, realizing that I knew neither would have and that he would have left anyway. He would not, as before, have believed me that they could have been after one of us. The pat on my cheek had been enough to remind me that I was no more than a cherished student, and he was still in love with a memory. He was stubborn, and once he had determined to have his answers, nothing would have stopped him.

I was still standing there contemplating whether I should throw caution to the winds, try again, run after him and tell him both of these things, when Baylor came up behind me and put his arm around my shoulders, giving me a squeeze. I looked up at him, trying to smile, but my eyes welled up betraying me.

"Nay, Lass, don't you cry. He will be safe," Baylor told me.

I tried once more to force a smile but gave up, as I was failing miserably anyway and finding that I didn't rightly care.

I poured it all out on Baylor, saying, "He will not listen. I don't know for sure if any of the Elders are responsible for Edsel's disappearance any more than he does. I cannot say one way or another if they are capable of what was done in this place. I do not even know exactly what was done. But I do know it did not appear that the gorilla was after you. I do know we are more capable of protecting each other from anything that may come when we remain together. And I do know I don't want to loss him, I, I…"

"I know, Lass." He cut me off, not so much as Demon had, but merely to express a deep understanding. "Come back to the garden with me now, it seems Adonia wants the tale of our journey."

He spun me gently back in that direction and kept talking to distract me from my pain and anger.

"She's a lot like you, that one," he said, smiling at me. "You must help me to entertain her, lest she beat me with her little book of poems."

I finally gave a short laugh at that. I looked up at him thankfully as he led me through the house, knowing he was the best brother I could have found. We got back to the garden just as Adreal was pinning Piper to the ground, wrestling as Baylor and Demon had done. Adonia was laughing like the happy little girl I had imagined her to be. I tried to enjoy the scene and let go of my worries but found I had not succeeded very well when Adonia looked up at me.

"Did he swear?" she asked.

I was not at first sure what she meant. Then I remembered how they had extracted a promise from him to return.

"Yes," I said, wondering why she would ask me.

"Then don't you worry, Angelica, he has always kept his word. Come sit with me tell me about yourself. How did you come to meet him? How long have you been together? How was the journey?" she asked.

Baylor rolled over on his back in the soft grass and started laughing hysterically at this and I could not help but join him. My present situation was forgotten momentarily as I received a taste of my own medicine. When at last I thought I had control enough to speak, I sat up and looked at her.

Her look was very perplexed and she seemed to be trying to decide if we were insulting her in some manner. Baylor saved us both by explaining to her what we had found so funny; then she too laughed. When we had calmed ourselves I covered a yawn with my hand, trying not to laugh right through it when she asked me another question.

So I spent the remainder of the evening answering all the questions her insatiable mind could come up with. Enjoying my medicine as much as I'm sure Baylor had enjoyed it when I'd begged him for more. Adreal had a few questions of his own but it appeared that she asked the questions, for the most part, for both of them. Time passed quickly as I was occupied in this manner and kept from my brooding by Adonia's constant questions. She was indeed very much like me and I began to wonder if all Changelings might have an insatiable thirst for knowledge and if this might be part of what kept us here.

When I came to telling of the final battle with the other Changelings, she was amazed by my version of a hellcat. I illustrated for her how I had appeared upon waking and she asked me how it felt. I explained it to be like nothing more than changing my clothes. Then they were both even more amazed at my having *killed* one of them.

My yawns were coming more and more frequently as sleep had not been in plentiful supply these last few days, but I had no desire to leave their company. So we talked about my having somehow stolen the Yelm. Sometime during all the debating, Piper excused himself from the confusion to go off in search of more wine. Back and forth the twins and I debated this matter and none of us could come up with any better explanation than Demon's.

Demon. He was still not back and I looked over my shoulder through the villa toward the front door.

"He will return," Adonia said.

I jerked my head back to face her. I had not even realized what I had been doing, let alone that I had been so obvious.

"You are tired Angel. I have kept you up far too late after such a journey," she said, having taken to addressing me as Piper and Baylor did, and I smiled at her fondly, having found in her a kindred spirit.

"I will wait for his return," I said, knowing she would understand.

"And be of little use when he does," she said laughing. "You must get your rest or he'll be scooping you up out of this grass where you crumble." I smiled at her way with words, trying to imagine such a thing, as she continued, "Come, if you sleep now, then when he arrives you will at least be rested enough to understand what news he brings back with him."

She stood then, extending her hand to me and I accepted as she added, "Time will pass more quickly while you are dreaming and he will surely be back when you wake."

I allowed her then to lead me to a bedchamber and sit me on the bed. It felt strange to me that the space should be so large and empty, but sleep came almost instantly and I had no time to be discomforted by it.

I came aware in a panic as I felt again those terrible claws tearing through the space in which my soul had been sleeping. Instantly I knew this was no mere Changeling. I had frame of reference now. I had battled with other Changelings, with vile intent, and this was not one of these. This was unfamiliar in every way, seeming evil and inhuman beyond any of those I had come up against.

I remembered how Demon had assumed what I had felt was a Council spy and been angered they would retract their agreement to leave Baylor to him. How he had thought that it had been searching for Baylor to destroy him. I remembered I had then assumed I had overreacted believing he must have been correct. Apparently we were all wrong.

Too late I realized I was thinking too much of what it was and was not. Too long I tried to put it into working words. Too late I remembered thoughts of the black void. I tried to draw in my breath to scream but suddenly I had no substance to draw it into. I was blown apart, by such an awesome force I cannot describe it to you. Every bit of the energy I had ever called my own had been pushed from me so swiftly I had not even felt it go.

I did not exist and somehow I knew that was not right, but for the longest I could not figure out why.

Part

3

February 10th 1996

~23~

Finding Me

Something was very wrong.

I was in a state somewhere between blind panic and pure hysteria and I knew somehow that I had, quite literally, finally lost my mind.

"*Finally?*"

Now why had I thought that? I didn't know.

"Where am I? Who am I?" I was questioning myself frantically but I could seem to find no answer within me. Then suddenly I heard another voice coming from within the dark confines of my consciousness.

Somehow I knew this was not my voice but I cherished it. It said, "I named you Angelica and I made you my own." Before I could reach out and hold onto it, it was gone. I wanted to scream. I needed that voice. It might have been able to give me more answers. It had before, hadn't it?

"Terrible thing you're a witch's daughter, pretty one." This other voice floated out of the nothingness I seemed to be part of, coming as if to torture me. It was not pleasant. I wanted it gone. I pushed it away.

Then I heard my own familiar inner monologue, with its decidedly English accent, "*Daughter? Sister? Which, witch?*" It started laughing insanely and would not stop.

Then and I yelled, "Stop that!"

"*Why?*"

"Because it makes me feel like I'm losing control and I need control," I said. But truly I was feeling somewhat calmer already, just knowing I had my name.

"I am Angel!" I said happily.

"*An Angel and a Demon took a walk in a field and talked about the universe and how to control it...*"

"That's it! That is important, but why?" I searched frantically through what few memories would come back to me.

"Changeling, Shape-shifter..." Yes! Yes. I knew this other voice. It felt right. It was familiar. I loved that voice. I loved that man. Yes, it belonged to a man and I cherished him deeply.

Suddenly I saw myself in my mind's eye. I was a goddess reclining on a chase lounge. I was being fed plump purple grapes by fat little baby angels. These little angels were laughing and whispering things I could not make out but knew somehow it was necessary that I did.

"I am called Angel too," I said to one of these cherubs as it popped another grape into my mouth, hoping to befriend it that it might tell me the secrets as well. Then I saw a god coming toward me. The most perfect and amazingly beautiful Greek god there ever was, and I knew him.

"I know him," I told these little angels. "His is the voice from before."

He was familiar and right. I loved him. I loved his voice. I loved everything about him. Who was he?

"*Demon?*"

Yes. That was it! I knew that.

"*Then why did you ask?*"

"Demon!" I called out, ignoring my decidedly sarcastic inner monologue. "Where have you been? I have missed you."

But he turned then, when I questioned him, and I cried out again, "Wait, don't go! But I love you! But I..," I wanted to scream then, as he disappeared.

"*Useless words now, silly girl, should have said them before.*"

"Why won't he listen to me? Why won't he love me?" I begged the darkness for answers.

"Because you are not she."

I was angry at my inner monologue that it should remind me of this, because then I was outside of the goddess and she was just a beautiful woman in a painting I had seen somewhere once. I was distraught to see this picture fading from my mind. All the pretty little cherubs and their yummy, yummy grapes disappeared, all the secrets they might have shared fading from my reach. I think somehow I had known all along, that it was only a painting. It had seemed the only recognizable thing and now it was gone, leaving me utterly alone once again.

I was plunged into total darkness.

"Nothing in life is!"

Who asked you?

"Fine!"

Silence and darkness fell in on me. It was becoming too close and constrictive; this feeling reminded me vaguely of another time and a conversation with the woman who named me. I felt I would fall backwards into panic once more.

"You talk to me, not the other way around." I was relieved then that this inner voice had at least not abandoned me as well. It had always been there, especially during times of stress. I welcomed it back now.

"But why?" I said, not knowing which why I addressed but needing to hear the words of any answer, just to be hearing.

"Because I am all you have right now."

Why?

"Chirp...Chirp...Never change the mad or deranged..."

Why?

"Isn't it obvious?"

But I am not mad!

"Oh, truly?"

Well, I was not when he changed me.

"Hum, mayhap, but you are now..."

If I had had eyes I would have cried then. Cried that I had lost control and even my own thoughts would betray me. Cried that I was only myself, and because Demon had left me. Cried simply because I could not cry.

Why can't I cry?

"Because you do not have any eyes, silly girl. No eyes!" Again the voice inside began laughing insanely.

Why not!

"Because you have not created any, foolish little girl."

Stop mocking me.

"You mock yourself."

Right.

"Ha!"

If you're so smart, then how do I create them?

"You are the one who makes the changes, Changeling. You tell me."

I knew. I knew even as I had said it. "Yelm!" I cried out triumphantly, happy I had the answers that the mean little English voice had taunted me with and that I hadn't needed it to tell me. I frantically tried to see or feel if I had my Yelm with me.

There it is! I did have it, as well as another.

I was confused again and I would be taunted for it.

"Which one?"'

Which one, what?

"Which Yelm?"

What? '

"Bad Angel! Angel of Death."

Why do you say such cruel things?

"You killed it!"

It or Baylor, I said as the memory flooded back on me. I did not know I would kill it. I do not even know how I did it. I felt guilty and was trying to defend my actions, if only to myself.

"Chirp...Chirp...Never take from another, those parts which make it whole..."

But why not?

"Murder! Murder, bad little witch!"

But I had no choice! How can defending myself and those I love have been wrong?

"Not wrong, just bad, bad for you!"

But why?

"Obvious! Obvious! So easy, little girl!"

Then tell me!

"Because now you have confused us. We have two Yelms now. Which, witch?"

Use mine. Use both. I do not care, just stop calling me a witch. I was becoming angry with myself now.

"Use ours, it loves us more."

Fine.

"Which is ours?"

The one that feels most familiar.

"Use it for what?"

To begin making me eyes. Now who is being the foolish one?

"Bring me something to do it with, then."

Fine.

This was terribly hard and I cannot begin to tell you how long it took me, but eventually I had eyes and still I could see nothing. I knew I had done it right but still no vision came to me.

Why is it so dark?

"Because you turned away from the light."

Of course I did.

"Of course you did!"

Would you rather have ended our existence there at the stream? We would have never met Baylor and Demon or Piper and the twins.

"And?"

"Oh, that would have been a horrible loss! You mean we might have avoided this pain? Oh no! Please! Please let me live for the pain!"

I ignored the heavy sarcasm and continued.

We would have never seen what wonders we've seen, or done the amazing things that we've done. I tried to convince myself it had all been worth it. More and more memories came flooding back on me as though I had broken through a dam with my slow revelations. Even if Demon doesn't love me, he is still the most wonderful of friends. And Baylor, Baylor, he is my brother! I love him too.

"Love is not the pain. The pain comes from our inability to accept that others do not return our love in a manner we expect. I will accept it, and learn to expect no more and no less than I receive freely. Otherwise we will never find joy in it and will always be let down. I will love him for who he is. It does not matter that I cannot be his beloved Seraphim.'

"Seraphim, you concede the field to a two thousand year old memory"'

You have to admire the loyalty.

"No I don't! I might stand in awe at the scope of his stupidity, though."

Stupidity?

"Yes! Stupidity!"

No, that is his torture. He must come to terms with love and what pain he allows it to bring him. As all of us must. As I am.

"A bit slow isn't he?"

All things in their own time, and more so with those who have no lack of it, I said, still defending him.

"But now we'll miss other wonders. We'll never be married or have a family." It tried another tactic, trying to convince me I had made the wrong decision in turning from the light.

They are our family, a wonderful family, I argued. Besides, what children do dead woman have anyway? I would not be swayed, my decision had been sound and I was still glad I had made it.

"You know what I mean. You can not deny that pain. Chirp...Chirp... Never bear children..."

Yes, I faltered, but why not?

"What would a Changeling womb create?"

I don't know.

"But it's so obvious!"

Not to me!

"Yes, to you. I am you and it's obvious to me."

What then?

"No, no, silly girl, you tell me."

Baylor?

"See! I'm good for something, little girl."

The answer startled me and I started running madly through my newfound memories, looking at them all with my new eyes. I was reexamining everything Baylor had told me. It all made sense now: curses making Werewolves, blessings turning Druids into stags. Blessings, curses, Changelings or Shape-shifters, I felt so incredibly stupid.

Stupid girl!

"Yes!"

I could hear Demon's rich voice in my head: "Do you believe me? Then you have all you need."

Then I heard Baylor's deep baritone: "Old Sara would tell me I was going to grow up big and strong, a powerful warrior...and I believed her."

Yes! Yes, I have to tell him! He needs to know!

"Wouldn't that be a trick? You should have told him when you had a mouth to do it with!"

But I didn't realize then!

"Not a very bright one, are you? Near as slow as Demon!"

I must tell him.

"Tell who?"

Tell Baylor!

"Get about it then, I will be here...Waiting."

I was so excited, thinking, I must tell him about the not-so-blessed Druid who bore him and the curse that wasn't really a curse.

These were the thoughts that brought me back, that helped me to find myself. Knowing that whether or not Demon ever loved me, as he had his Seraphim, that he along with the others were still my family and one of them needed to know what I had figured out. This drove me to begin pulling myself back together, literally.

I do not know how much time exactly it took me to bend the universe to my needs. It seemed to take an eternity to simply convince enough energy to join with me to merely form the smallest of birds. Even then it was dark and I could not see or move and this frightened me terribly.

It came to me, just when I thought I would go into a hysterical panic again, that I was underground. I had created my form under the earth. So I released these energies to the shortest of distances from me, and rose up, calling them back to me quickly for fear if left too long they would deny me again.

~24~

Not As They Seem

I did not know where I was, or when it was, or even how long I had been in my incorporeal state. How long had I had existed on the brink of insanity? How long had I talked to myself, just trying to remember who 'myself' was? It didn't matter now though, what mattered was finding the others. It was evening and the moon shown full above me. I knew then, looking up at that glowing orb, that it had to be at least near to a full month.

I thought again then, of the brother of my soul; how he was being tortured in his spirit, at this very moment, howling his pain somewhere beneath this very moon. I flew up to view my surroundings and see if I might discover where I was. Then I remembered how I had come to be in this state and quickly used the trick the twins had discovered, of projecting my aura as that of only a bird.

Thus disguised I came to a height at which I could see Rome before me. Somehow my soul had avoided destruction, keeping with it the two Yelms, and bringing me to relative safety beneath the earth outside the city. I wondered if it had been the having of two that had kept me bound to this earth. Then I became very frightened. What if the others had experienced the same explosive force as I had? What if they had not survived it? Was this what had befallen Edsel?

Remembering Edsel reminded me of Demon and his leaving to speak with the Elders. I had realized at some point that the power that had put me in this state had not been one I had sensed before when searching out the Changelings of Rome. When I had scanned upon my arrival there had been some whose souls I had not cared for, but none had been like that one. I did not feel now that they had been responsible, at least not directly, for my predicament. I needed to tell the others. I had encountered an entirely different thing than ever before and the others must know that as well.

I flew then into the city over the rooftops, inhaling every smell, foul and fresh, which came from it, simply to enjoy smelling again. I came eventually over a garden I recognized, and knew it to be of the villa belonging to the twins. I landed in the center of it but I was afraid to scan for any of them in case I might be revealed to the powerful evil that had nearly destroyed me in the first place. So I changed into a rat, as it was about the only other form I could manage. I projected the rat's mind and searched throughout the villa in this manner. I could find no one. Again the fear that they had been destroyed, as I had almost been, caused me to have to fight back panic.

I had no choice then, but to scan briefly and carefully throughout the city, but my soul found only those that were unfamiliar to it or it had no desire to meet with. I pulled back then, taking refuge once more in my small rat's mind. Frightened and alone, I sat as I was for a very long time.

The garden was the only source of comfort I had had, in what felt like forever, as I could feel the other's presence here. They had spent much time in this place, so I spent the night in the garden surrounded by what remained of them in the grass and flowers. They had been my family, as it were, short as our time had been, and I slept in the relative peace of their residual company.

When I woke, I was full of renewed purpose, having been fed by that peaceful place. I gathered from it what more energy I could, in spite of a still harsh resistance from the world around me. I had enough now to become a large owl. With this new form and confidence, I rose up into the air, again determined that I would find them. All the things I would tell them when I did, gave my wings new hope.

I could only think that if they were not in Rome then I must have been lost to them for quite some time, mayhap many months, and they had given up their search and gone home. I could not allow myself to believe they had been destroyed. I had to think Demon and Baylor had taken the twins and Piper with them, returning to the relative safety of Scotland.

As I flew, I went over again all Baylor had told me, chastising myself that I had not realized the things I did now, and told him right then. I had to ease up on myself, realizing also that not even Demon had figured it out, and he had been with Baylor nearly two thousand years. I told myself it was the way in which Baylor told his tale that threw us off. Baylor so strongly believed he had been cursed, he had made us believe it too; when really, if I had examined it more closely, I would have seen it clearly.

I looked then below me and there was the olive grove we had made our final camp before heading into the city. I allowed my wings to float me slowly into one of the trees and there I rested. There was no feeling of them left there and I told myself it was because we had not stayed there long. I did not at that time want to believe any great length of time had passed with me unaware. The fear was there though, growing. I had noticed, before leaving Rome, new buildings that had not been there before, and others which had been in disrepair that were now restored. All of this was stored in my mind, where I refused, as yet, to consider it, not wanting to be made to believe it could have been years not months that I had been unaware. I slept there, safe in my denial, telling myself I needed my rest, and that I would find them safe at home in Scotland.

"Wake up, wake up, he's going to get you, silly sleeping girl."

I came awake in a rush as my instincts used my inner voice to tell me to beware. There was a young boy no more than twelve coming toward me with a net. It took me not a full second more to realize what he intended. I flew backwards from the limb on which I had perched throughout the day, taking air under my wings. The net fell just short as he threw it, and I fled into the deepening dusk, as his shouted expletives rang in my sensitive ears.

I took to flying over the road, recalling as much as possible the route Demon had had mapped in his mind. We had traveled at such a speed, and so much of it in a tired daze throughout the darkness hours, I was not sure if I had it right. Why had I not paid better attention? Why had we traveled at night?

"Because Baylor was a Werewolf, you ninny."

Oh! Of course we had had to stay out of sight while making this leg of the journey; it had been during the cycle of the full moon. Having remembered Baylor and his torment, I was brought back to my examination of how it all came about. These thoughts put new strength and speed into my wings as I rushed along eager to find him and help him.

Quite suddenly I nearly fell from the sky, as a new revelation struck me. Was it that I had believed *too* much in what Demon had said? Was it not my belief in my own abilities that made them abilities at all? When he said it was a difficult process to coax new energies to you, after an episode such as mine had been, and my wholehearted belief in his instruction that was making it so difficult for me now? Was my belief all that held me back?

It was full dark now as I left off flying over the road and flew toward the wood. I set down upon the ground just inside the tree line. I told the universe I did not care what it thought. I would have my own form again. Now do not think it was simply an easy thing now, because it was not, but I had my way. I simply refused to take no for an answer.

I stood there, for the first time in a long time, as myself. I looked myself up and down and was not sure for a moment if this was how I looked. It seemed it had been forever. It was the form created for me when I ordered the energies that I commanded to make me who I am, so I accepted it. I had no choice and it did indeed feel comfortable and right.

I took off running then, laughing and twirling through the trees. I did not think to fear anything, man or beast. I felt fairly confident any evil Changeling scanning would come across only a half mad young woman, running happily through the darkened wood. I do not know how long I ran like that, but I was winded when I came upon a stream.

I plunged into it without a thought and began stomping and splashing and throwing water into the air. I had hands and feet to do it with, and this was the most beautiful feeling in the world. Loving the water more than ever because I could feel it soaking into my skin. My skin! To be, simply to have my own form, and be; I was ecstatic.

I had started singing then, serenading the moon with a song of pure joy. I could not tell you now the words, or if there even were any, but I was sure the moon understood me. The moon and I were friends this night; for even though she sat aloof and gloated over my friend's Werewolf form elsewhere, she illuminated my own rightful form for me now. I sat down in the water, letting it flow across my chest and remembering the pool in our bathing chamber.

Our bathing chamber! I had to get back to the Highlands. There was so much to tell them! I jumped up and took to the air again, full of joy. They would be so pleased to hear what news I had. I swooped and dived, spun and soared; everything would be so good when I got home. All would be made well in our world.

I flew till dawn, then I set down again, taking the form of the huge wolfhound I had used so often when crossing this French countryside. It had become second nature to me now to project only the aura of that which I was appearing to be. As I did it then, a new revelation came to me, further explaining why Baylor had remained such an enigma to all of us for so long. As ever these thoughts, which raced through my head so frequently, revealing more and more to me of my friends' condition, put fresh strength into my strides toward them.

I knew, from the Twins, that when you thought of yourself as merely what you were appearing to be, that was all that was sensed when another scanned for you. So it was with a renewed sense of safety I continued in this manner. Knowing if that powerful evil thing, that had separated me from all my energies and my family, searched for me, it would find only a wolfhound. With little thought I also created within my form the instincts and senses necessary, so that I could go the reverse of our prior path. Then I just started running.

There were those occasions when I caught sight of farmers or landowners as I crossed the miles. Though they were as much in wonder of me as I of them, none tried to stop me. I ran much in the manner we had when trying to reach Rome, stopping only when I absolutely had to sleep due more to mental exhaustion than anything within my constantly renewed form. It was not until I had made it nearly back to Calais that I realized I was going to have a new difficulty.

As I drew near to it I recalled that here I would have to cross the channel and I realized I had three choices. I could buck up and do it as a human, taking passage on a ship and taking my chances with interacting as a person with my Changeling abilities. I could hope to avoid somehow any of the accidents Demon had warned me could occur. I would surely have to do it as a man, there was no doubt of that. I was not at all sure I could pull this off but I knew I would not like to do it as a woman. I remembered vividly the leers of the sailors and the men at dockside. Where would I even get the monies to buy passage? Demon had paid for everything we had had need of, seeming to have an endless supply of coin, drawing whatever had been necessary throughout our trip from the leather pouch tied at his side.

I could do it as a bird but then if I tired, where would I come down if I needed to rest? I had never flown for such a distance without a ready place to land available to me. I feared mental exhaustion far more than any the body might feel, for I had no way to combat it. This led to a scenario I disliked, that of landing in the water, which presented the same problem for me as my final option; I could cross as a fish but here I had the dilemma of sharks.

Sharks! When Demon had mentioned them, he had said it in such a manner as to make me think I should dread meeting one. I had forgotten to ask him why. I thought then, that as a human, I would well and truly dread such a meeting, but I was a Changeling. Surely if I met one of them I could become one quickly enough to escape its attack, right? Surely it would leave me alone, seeing I was one of its own. It could not be all that bad, could it? Surely Demon would have said outright if these were creatures to be avoided by our kind for some reason.'

"I'm not sure!"

However, I was not sure, and had reached no clear decision when I came to the outskirts of that city.

I swerved then from my direction and headed for the nearest grouping of trees. Not only to avoid the crowds of the city, as such things seemed to disturb me deeply, but also to avoid the small group of wagons I saw coming up the road toward me. I still had a deep-seated fear I would somehow show myself to be more than human.

I needed to think this through and didn't feel up to doing it near anyone. I was still very worried about the things that Demon had told me. I might be hurt in some way, and unthinkingly heal myself. Or one of those men, who had looked on me so disturbingly before, might try to accost me, frightening me as they had before. I could change to protect myself without thinking, just as I had to fight beside Baylor. I was afraid that I would make some terrible mistake and be seen doing it, ending up in some terrible mess.

I did not know what to do. I sat in the shade of the trees thinking up horrible endings for every choice I hadn't even made yet. I was second-guessing every possible decision and its probable outcome, thus making myself even more afraid of every route available to me. I thought of Demon and how he had told me not to worry.

"Yes well he didn't have to; he was a man, with a purse full of endless coins."

That was it! I could be Demon. I might not know how to be just any man but I was pretty sure I could remember him well enough to help my energies copy his form. Could I not also tell my energies to give me his instincts as I would with any other form, or simply just command them to make me him, as I had when telling them to make me who I am? Would it work?

I pictured him in my mind as he had appeared on our journey, in every detail I could remember, and told my energy to make me him. It worked. I had done it. I looked myself up and down again, as when I had become myself for the first time after so long. I wanted to hug myself then, I had done it so well. I felt my kilt and the soft cloth of my shirt. Then I noticed the pouch at my waist. Just out of curiosity I shook it and amazingly it was heavy and full.

This gave me pause. Did my will to create Demon as I had pictured him extend so far? Had the world bowed itself to me so much, as to have given me some of its precious metals? I opened it and pulled out a hand full of its contents and stood in awe. My hand came out holding more monies than I had ever before held at one time. I dropped them back into the pouch and looked around quickly. Suddenly I had become fearful someone would note such bounty and try to steal it from me.

Then the oddest thing of all occurred. I had a flash of Demon's thoughts on such a matter. He would cut any such attempted thief to shreds. He didn't abide such people, he had a deep-seated dislike, no hatred, for thieves. I didn't know if this had been some of his instinct I had created with his form, but I reached for a dagger, which was not stuffed into my kilt, hidden by my shirt. I had not known he kept one there, but knew just as surely as the reflex had me reach for it that he must have always had it with him. I did not know what his dagger had looked like but I did know how mine, that he had given me, had looked.

I bent down then, taking up a handful of the soft earth at my feet. I pictured that dagger. Thinking of it as if creating a piece of clothing, I told this earth to become for me my dagger. This was slower than becoming Demon had been but it did happen. I look back and wonder if it was only that I had not been sure then that it would work, hence the command had not been as strong as it would be in the future, that had made it take so long.

I took heart as I placed the dagger in my belt. I had Demon's instincts to help me know how to use it and his form to keep most from attempting any action that might make me need to. I felt a new confidence in me as well, and wondered if this came from the fact that between my will and my energy, I had made myself into him in all his aspects. For I knew my new confidence and knowledge of how to use the blade at my side were not really mine, but Demon's.

I began walking toward Calais again, with a new thought that I would retain all of this knowledge and confidence within me, when I again became myself. I enjoyed that I had no fear of the crowds I eventually entered, resting assured in the knowledge I could maintain my guise. When I approached one of those hawkers always present by the docks, I ask him without pause which of those ships in port would leave for Dover soonest.

Though the man looked at me strangely, I had Demon's confidence and I stood still, awaiting his answer.

"There is the one, there at the end," he said, pointing to my left down the way. "The one they're loading now."

I thanked him and he smiled at me quizzically. I walked away, in the direction indicated, not knowing why my question should have confused him but not really caring. I approached the next man with the same easy stride, enjoying being Demon. This one held a sheet of paper and was glancing back and forth from it to the workers walking up and down the gangplank. I took him to be in some position of importance regarding decisions having to do with this ship. I waited politely until he looked up at me.

"Good morning, I'm seeking passage to Dover, have you room for one?" I asked when I had his attention.

"Only one?" he questioned me, looking me over quizzically.

"Yes, just myself," I said.

Saying this gave me a thrill. That I had managed to find a way in which to make the crossing, and was about to do it on my own, gave me a powerful burst of pride. I was still enjoying this feeling when I noticed the man had continued in his staring at me. Just when I was about to lose my newfound confidence, thinking I had made some fatal mistake in my appearance, he replied.

"Aye, as long as it's only you, we'll make space. It will cost you though," he said.

I let out a sigh of relief, realizing he had only been considering whether or not he could fit me on board. I knew I would have to haggle with him over the price but this did not bother me. I had become quite good at bartering while traveling with my mother. Finally a deal was struck and I waited as patiently as I could for the evening tide.

I briefly considered, entering one of the many taverns to pass the time, but set the idea aside. I had hunted that morning and eaten as the dog, not bothering with a fire that might draw attention to me. Since my belly was full, I felt no desire to press my luck any further than I had to. Instead I simply purchased a bottle of the wine these people were so well-known for, from one of those ever-present hawkers. I sat quietly with it at the edge of the pier, until the man called to me to prepare to leave. I jumped up happily and proceeded to the gangplank, passing him the cost of my passage as I went up. My heart pressed its way up into my throat as we got underway. I was going home.

When we came into Dover it was again in the early morning hours, and this reminded me greatly of the others. I recalled vividly our morning meal at the tavern, just there, as I passed it. The conversation Demon and I where having as we traversed these very miles. My heart was singing as I put greater distance between this place and me, drawing ever closer to home and family.

As soon as I was sure my actions would go unnoticed, I again turned into the great wolfhound and set to putting the town at even greater distance behind me. I felt a renewed hurt in my heart at having left Demon behind, if only in changing my form. I had felt a kind of closeness in being him, which though not the same as his actual presence, had done me good. Still, I slept that night very peaceful, though I was alone under a bush somewhere in England. I might not be near him, or any of them, in the flesh, but I was closer to that goal and would attain it soon. I could not and would not allow myself to be brought low by these feelings of loss; I merely had to remind myself that the sooner I found them, the sooner I could tell them all the wonderful things I had come to realize.

~25~

Good Dog

I realized slowly that I really could hear the children's voices, and they weren't just coming from somewhere in my dream. I found myself trying to make sense of the words and this brought me slowly toward wakefulness. Whose children where they? Why were they in our home interrupting my sleep? We were not allowed to have children. Someone was disregarding the Code. I awoke startled, realizing I was not at home, only sleeping with the fervent wish I was.

They were adorable, these children that had woken me. Two little peasant darlings, the older of which was the most beautiful small boy I had ever seen. He stood there with brown hair waving gently in the breeze, huge hazel eyes full of such incredible intelligence for one so young. This gorgeous little boy was leading the other child. Quite obviously this was his younger sister for she was equally beautiful, with the same hair and eyes, only hers seemed to be getting watery as though she were wondering whether or not to cry but finding it hard not to in the interim. He held her hand in one of his, and a basket in the other.

"We will find more," he was reassuring her, trying to keep her from tears, "and even if we don't Mem will understand it was an accident. It is not as though you threw them into the stream. One cannot help it when they stumble. 'tis why its called an accident."

I stood and stretched then, yawning hugely, startling and scaring them. They had stiffened and frozen. Then I had realized my mistake, all those teeth displayed so by my yawn. I would have frozen too. This I quickly tried to repair by wagging my tail and panting stupidly.

"I don't think she'll bite," the young boy said, again trying to reassure his sister whose state had just returned quickly to the near tears of moments before.

Bravely he set his basket down and, putting his hand forward, began making kissing noises at me. I suddenly wanted to laugh at the absurdity of it all but played my part out instead. I came forward nosing his hand and he patted me on the head. Glancing into the basket, I assumed the "more" he had assured his sister they would find was in reference to the herbs they seemed to have been gathering.

"See, she's a good dog, probably just lost her way," he said.

It seemed his words gave her courage once again, as she wiped at her eyes and put out her hand timidly. I licked it to reassure her as well.

"How did you get us into this?" Again, I wanted to laugh at the hilarity of the entire situation.

Answering myself, "I lost my way, even the child knew that."

The little girl was giggling in delight as I continued licking her, happy to see her fear turn to joy and even happier that I had some part in it. The little boy began talking to me as though he expected I would understand him.

"My Mem will not let us keep you and I'm sure your master will want you back in any case. I bet you miss him too, but you can come with us to find the herbs Mem wants for the stew if you'd like," he said.

He had composed his sentences under the assumption my master was a male and I could not fault such a thought process. I was in no position to correct him even if I had wanted to, so I simply walked beside him when he picked up his basket and began to walk again. I was enjoying the human voices speaking so innocently to me of trivial things, I thought to continue with them a moment.

He seemed to expect this, my lumbering along beside him. He continued, "But if you want to come home with us I may be able to slip you some of Gennie's milk. Gennie is our goat. You'll be fitter to find your master then, after a little bit of a meal."

It was all too amusing and I will admit it did me more than a little good. Not only did I manage to lead them right to where the kind of herbs they were seeking would be easily found, but I spent the early evening hours in a barn, in the company of two very wonderful little people and a goat named Gennie. I had been well fortified in the spirit and the belly, and by the time I left there it was with a new confidence in myself not brought on merely by assuming Demon's form. I knew then, full well, that I could resist my subconscious's whims and decisions. I had managed the whole evening and never once turned into myself to laugh with them.

I had left them when their mother had called them in for dinner, accepting the little girl's hugs and kisses with kisses of my own and listening to the young boy's admonitions that I return now to my master, so that neither of them would have to worry about me any longer. I managed a safe distance from their farm before turning into myself and running laughing into the night.

My spirits were high as ever and I soon leaped into the sky, changing as I went into a huge white owl, soaring over the miles in a wonderful state of mind. I would find him all right, and neither of us would have to worry about any of it, any longer. I would solve for everyone the long-standing riddle of Baylor and we would all have a great long laugh over it.

I traveled once more as quickly as I could, resting as I had been only when I had to. This was excepting of course my slightly longer stop at the Loch Ness. Not being able to resist swimming there like Piper had. Piper had been full right about the place, it did feel wonderful and peaceful. I had slept there meaning to be on my way at dawn, but could not resist wading in and swimming around like a happy child for awhile. I was so close to my goal the joy and eagerness mixed, so that I swam laughing for a time, then launched myself up and away. I took this last leg of my journey with amazing speed, my will to be home and safely back with all of them driving my wings like the Devil himself pursued me.

I came down on our plateau near dusk and ran laughing to the door, kicking it at its base. As Demon had done, when returning with the young boar the first night we had hunted together. I could see Baylor throwing the door open and putting his hands out to receive it; to receive me, but no one came to open it. I kicked it again, stepping back a few paces to be sure I was kicking the right spot. The door blended into the face quite well and I had to be sure. Still there was no answer.

I pried at it frantically, realizing I did not know how they opened it from the outside. Why weren't they answering? Again the fear I had pushed to the back of my mind rose up to haunt me. I pushed it back hurriedly. I could not allow myself to believe they had suffered what I had, and not survived it.

Finally I threw off most of my energy, telling it to follow me and seeped in through the tiniest of gaps where the door met the face of the cliff. When I pulled my form back together inside I could see nothing. Here I admit to breaking yet another rule. I gave myself the eyes of an owl, greatly enhanced, so that I could see in the darkness, mixing forms, adding yet another broken Code to my list of wrongs per the Council.

"Chirp…Chirp…Never mix forms…"

"Not now!" I was in shock; the place was a ransacked mess and no one was there!

"They are not here!" I was becoming frantic again now.

"Did you really think they would be?"

"Yes! I had to, they had to survive! I am the youngest and if I survived, surely they did as well. I felt their presence strongly in the garden, they had to have been there recently," I argued, fighting back the panic that was trying to drive me mad yet again.

"Mayhap what you felt was what was left of them. Mayhap they were still talking in the garden and their energies were blown all over it."

"I will not believe it!"

I shut this inner voice out and began frantically picking up the mess and cleaning. I began acting as thought they were on their way home, and I did not want them to find it in such a state. I set all the chairs back upright and exerted my will over the broken pieces, telling them to bind themselves back together. I didn't ask myself whether this should have been possible. I did not care. I just wanted things perfect when they came back. I had to convince myself they were only hunting and would be back soon or I would lose my mind again. I remembered at some point to light all the lanterns and change my eyes so that they would not catch me with my unnatural owl's eyes.

At first I did not even consider how our home had come to be in such a condition, though later many vivid scenarios would play themselves out in my head. I merely set myself to cleaning and repairing everything. There were deep layers of dust on anything and everything it could attach to. A lot more so than a small part of me knew should have been possible in so short a time.

I was pulling and swirling great clouds of it, willing it away from me and out under the door. Gathering the broken pieces of all the many broken dishes and vases that were lying about and telling them to repair themselves as though they were mere extensions of me and must obey. I was angry that this mess should make our home look so uninhabited and inhospitable when it had to be both, for me and for them. We lived here. We would live here still. This was our home, but it felt so empty. I gave up then, when I could find nothing more to clean, and fell down upon Demon's chaise lounge and cried.

Cried that they were all gone and I had looked so forward to seeing them again. I cried that I was still alone after trying so hard to make it home to them. That I could not share with them all I had discovered. Crying because I could not stop the mean little English voice from telling me they were dead, and I was fooling myself. Sobbing all the more, when I realized all of the comfort that I had used to feel of Demon's presence on this couch was gone, just as they were. I even cried for the simple fact I was crying

256

again at all.

I don't know how long I spent in this manner. Going back and forth between the deepest of depressions, crying for hours into Demon's favored lounge, and believing something had occurred to take them away again, for just a week or so, and they would return very soon. Eventually, though, I became desperate and again chanced discovery by whatever power had attacked my person.

I stood out on our plateau nightly, sending out my inner sight as far as I could, repeatedly finding nothing. I then began to think that mayhap I had been mistaken and they had not returned here after all. Perhaps they where still searching me out in Rome and I had only missed them in my searching. I convinced myself this was entirely possible. I had been afraid of being found out myself and mayhap so had they. Possibly they had been shielding themselves as I had.

I would return and search more thoroughly. If I had missed them somehow, I would find them. I would not give up. I would traverse the path from here to Rome as many times as it took to find them at one place or the other. I held this new determination and it kept me sane, for awhile.

I had the presence of mind to leave a letter for them. I did not know what had done the damage to our home, but I thought for sure a letter on my pillow, on my enclosed wooden box of a bed, would avoid its notice, should it return. I had felt no other presence in all my nightly scanning. So I felt relatively safe it had gone. Be it that awesome power I had encountered, or another one of the Changelings that had hunted for us, I doubted it would think to check my bed. If they returned, however, and felt my presence as having been there, they would surely check my bed for sign of me having slept there. I said a small prayer that I wasn't leaving directions as to how to find me for any I was trying to avoid and then set out.

I began to wander again then, as I had in my youth, only now I was alone. I took the path from our home in the Highlands to Rome three times within the following years. Going more slowly each time, to better search, and my hope faded just as slowly. More and more it became harder to

257

convince myself they had escaped any harm.

I had adopted a different way of searching for them each trip, and on this last one I had grown my bravest. Making my way as Demon I had begun stopping in taverns and inns all along the way and asking if any had seen my "twin brother," traveling with a huge red-headed beast of a Highlander. This final time I was crushed upon my return.

I had lost nearly all my hope already but I had stopped at an inn in Aberdeen, asking as I always did the same question. I had received as ever the same answer. I had then accepted a mug of ale, not even tasting it. A great, deep sadness began to completely overtake me. I had run ahead of it for far too long, and it had caught up to me finally.

The young woman who had served me there had returned to check if she could help me in any other way. I had come to recognize such offers as meaning far more than I had originally thought. I had been aware for quite sometime, having used his form for so long, that I was not the only woman to find Demon extremely attractive. As a matter of fact I had learned a lot more about such things, than I had cared to have. It was with as much the resentment of this as my sadness that I replied overly harsh, that the ale would suffice. She had not taken my rude reply to heart, instead she had sat down opposite me.

She said, "He has been lost to you for a long time, this twin you seek?"

I had felt bad then for taking my anger out on her, when she now appeared only to care that I missed my "brother" horribly. I could not muster the will to say much as I looked into my ale.

"Yes," was the best I could do.

"Where did you lose him?" she asked me.

Consolingly she had reached out and put her hand over mine where it sat on the table. I looked at her hand, wondering how I should feel about her action. Finally I had decided I did not care if it was my hand or Demon's she patted. It was compassion and human contact and I was in desperate need of both.

"Somewhere between Rome and the Highlands," I replied.

"That is quite a distance to be searching. How long have you been looking for him? When did you lose him? How?" She had smiled at me and I noticed she was missing one of her teeth.

One part of my mind was sidetracked then, desperate for diversion from the pain, wondering if I could fix her tooth as I had ordered the broken pieces of dishes to repair themselves at home. The other part of my mind was considering her questions sadly. It seemed it had been nearly three years, and I had no real desire to try fixing her tooth, I didn't have much desire left to do much of anything. So I replied to the best of my knowledge.

"I lost him the year twenty-three, in Rome," I said finally. "The how of it is too hard a thing to explain...."

She began laughing then and I could not understand why. I looked quizzically at her from across the table, in the dim light, trying to decide if it should anger me that she was laughing while I was hurting so dreadfully inside.

"Surely you jest!" she said. Seeing I did not understand her amusement, she sobered instantly and continued, now appearing as confused as I. "How old were you then, when you lost him, just new born? Did your parents tell you of him just recently? You have aged well..."

Her confusion was now nothing compared to my own. The inn's main room was suddenly far too small and I could not get enough air to my lungs. I had come to hate this feeling, when rooms would shrink on me and my lungs couldn't expand enough to support my chest. There was suddenly too much smoke and noise, too many people to see me.

"What year is this?" I managed to whisper.

She narrowed her eyes then, maybe beginning to suspect I was completely mad or having a jest at her expense after all. My mind was whirling madly and I was not inclined to disagree with her should she tell me I was losing it.

"The sixty-sixth year," she said.

I stumbled to my feet, knocking my chair to the floor behind me and

259

grabbing the table to hold myself upright. I could not breathe at all and my vision was blurring. I could not faint here. I could not faint at all. I would not faint. I would make it from this place. I would survive this too.

~26~

Searching

I stumbled like a drunkard out into the street, seeing nothing of the world or people around me. Vaguely I could hear her voice calling to me from the door of the inn, asking me if I was all right. I was not. I could not turn to tell her. I took off running then, as fast as Demon's strong legs would carry me. Running from the truth and any that might tell it to me, but I could not escape the voice in my own head.

"I thought it would be something like that."

"What do you mean?"

"We both saw all the buildings in disrepair all over Rome, and the new ones that had not been there before. All the people dressed in unfamiliar fashions, even the farmers in the fields we passed. You have missed the obvious yet again, my sad little girl."

"I did not know!"

"Yes you did! You just didn't want to see it!"

"How?"

"We were quite mad for a very long time, you and I."

"I'm not mad anymore, I came through that..."

"Then why are you running down the street like a drunken fool, talking to yourself?"

"Stop!"

"No, you stop. It took you forever to even ask me who you were. I helped you then, I will help you again. Stop running now. We have been running for far too long. Let us consider all these things. And mayhap more if you are ready...."

I stopped then, dead in my tracks as other things began to slip around and into my mind. The dust! The unusual amount of dust, that had been on everything in our home, it all made sense now.

Surely they had thought me well and truly gone, if I had been incorporeal so long. They would have given up in their searching for me by now and returned home. Mayhap they had returned before and Baylor had flown into a rage when he had found me not there, hence the state of the place. Then they had too gone searching again. Just as I was about to use this reasoning to reestablish my hope and go flying home, I was stopped.

"It has been forty years, they would have been there long before you, had they survived. They would have given up long ago and been there when first you arrived. They would have tried to resume their lives as you will have to."

"No!"

"You are deluding us again. Stop now. More likely that damage to the home was done by the one hunting for you long ago."

"But they are stronger than I," I began with all the old arguments again.

"Must I remind you, little Angel of Death, you had two Yelms to anchor you, and it still took you forty years."

"Then it may take them eighty, but they will return to me! I will go home and they will return. I have forever to wait for them!" I screamed at the infuriating inner English monologue.

"You may have forever but Mem does not."

"Mem!"

"Yes, Mem. If she is even still among the living, she is well into her seventies. We should find her first."

I stood in shock, still, frozen as the terrible realities set in. I was

262

trying desperately to absorb all of this new information. Agonizing that I had known but not been aware and that I had wasted so much time because of that weakness. More so, though, was a new and terrible fear, that I was quite probably well and truly mad and I didn't know how to change or fix that.

Then it set in and I was realizing I had thought I would have plenty of time to return to my mother, my sister, and check on her, telling her I was happy with my life. I had always thought I would learn what I had to, to walk among the people unnoticed, then return and be with her for a time. I realized now I had little or no time to speak again with her, and she was my only link to this life. She was the only person who might tell me more of who I had been, who my father was and how much I was loved, at least by her.

I flew then to our hovel, the last place we had lived together. Blind and nearly broken again, I found it not but a hulk of tumbled and rotten wood. I walked in wounded circles trying to think, through the haze of heartbreak, what to do next. Irrationally I stumbled to the nearest home, knocking upon the door. I remembered, just before they opened it, to become myself but how I cannot tell you.

"I am looking for a midwife who lived in a hut in the woods not far from here. She was my, my grandmother," I stumbled. "Do you know where she might have gone?"

The woman merely narrowed her eyes at me and closed the door. I did not care at all about her rudeness. I was used to such things. I only cared about finding news of my Mem. Still not thinking clearly in my hurt, I went from door to door, checking every farm along the way, until I entered the nearest small town nearing dusk. Then I began asking if any remembered a midwife, who might have appeared an older version of me.

I disregarded the looks of disapproval and the whispers as I went on. Stupidly not realizing, in my blind need to find word of her, what a stir I was creating. Neither did I realize just how badly the church's view of such things had made my questions appear. So it was much as a sheep to the slaughter that I took the two that approached me finally at their word.

I had been randomly asking my questions of those in the

marketplace, when two well-dressed young men approached me instead. They told me that they had news of my "grandmother," if I would follow them. They led me to a church, and I was filled with memories of the wonderful Father Paul. I felt instantly calmer as we approached this structure. I was thinking that mayhap Mem had befriended another kindly priest, and she was now being cared for within these walls by another such as the man we had cared for when I was growing up.

I was led into a small room at the back of the church and asked to sit for a moment while they found the older priest who could better answer my questions. I heard the younger men whispering to someone in the room beyond, but was too desperate for news to care much about what. I heard the last of it as an older man in a long black robe came into view, saying to them, "...tell them to hurry to my council."

He turned then to study me and I felt suddenly uncomfortable in my own skin. His look was not at all kind, as Father Paul's had always been. He closed the door behind him and never took his eyes from me, as he walked around the edge of the small desk at the other end of the small chamber. For the second time that day I had the feeling the place I was in was too small and only getting smaller.

He did not say a word or introduce himself. He simply flipped open a book on his desk and began looking over its contents. Finally I could bear the silence no longer. I opened my mouth to ask him what news he might give me. To remind him that was why I had followed the young men, in the case they had been unclear in telling him my purpose here.

Quite abruptly he spoke first, saying, "So you are a relation of one Elizabeth Marie O'Conner?"

This took me by surprise, for though I had known Mem's given name, having it stored in some corner of my mind, I had never heard it spoken in such a manner.

"Yes. Yes, Sir," I stuttered.

Something about the way he'd said it was making the small hairs at my neck crawl to an upright position. I realized this was no kind priest. My thoughts of the wonderful Father Paul began to fade. I could no longer see Mem being cared for here.

"Did you grow up in any knowledge of her actions?" he asked me, again without preamble, making notes in his book.

"Her actions?" I repeated, confused by the question.

"Did you know what she did?" he said, seeming to be put out, to have to rephrase his question.

"She was a midwife," I replied then, finally understanding.

"Did she teach you any thing about what she did?" he asked then.

He was making another little note in his book and did not look up as he asked this question. I heard the front door open and close again, and excited talking going on in the front of the church. I was wondering what was going on out there when he repeated his question.

"Yes, of course," I replied, still not thinking clearly.

"Are you of any relation to an Angelica O'Conner?"

My mind was suddenly reeling, wondering how he might have known my name. Suddenly it came to me he might have found or at some point had access to Father Paul's notes. That would explain his knowledge of my and Mem's names, but still it did not explain enough to me because I was not thinking clearly. But then I had not been thinking clearly for a very, very long time and it seemed I was not going to any time soon.

"Yes," I stumbled on my words. "She, Angelica, she was my, my mother."

I was still wondering what was going on outside the door as the voices had drawn closer and more excited. He stood then and excused himself, if a bit rudely, exiting the room and closing the door again behind him. I altered my hearing then, heightening that particular sense, and caring little that I was making a habit of ignoring the Code completely. I was desperate, now more than ever, to know what he might know of my Mem.

What I heard then drove me nearly into a blind rage. They were arguing excitedly over having discovered yet another witch. Me a witch? I had admitted to it, unabashedly, if one were to believe the man who had just

265

questioned me and his accounting. By admitting Mem had taught me her "craft" and that Angelica was my mother. This disgusted me; however, it was the last of it that drove me near over the edge of reason.

These unseen voices had become excited. Talking as though they were remembering their favored classes shared at college, passing memories between the three of them. Only these remembrances were of tortures. Tortures they had imposed upon Mem. They began reminiscing, *reminiscing,* like they had the greatest of times. Their voices flew into my ears like bees with poisoned stings as they recounted, in their near jovial manner, which ones and how many times inflicted it had taken to extract such a confession from my mother. Their words only reflected signs of remorse or disappointment when they spoke of how getting a confession from me had proved to be so little work.

The only thing that kept my calm demeanor in place, as they entered and announced my guilt; all that was keeping me seated, as they informed me of my punishments and when they would be dealt out, describing to me in lurid detail and with too much enjoyment what parts I could escape were I to renounce my league with Satan and turn my heart to God, was a terrible need in me to know their faces. I needed to have a vision of the three that had murdered my mother; they that had tortured my sister; these I painted in every detail on the canvas of my mind. I kept them framed, in unspeakable pain, for my future use. I understood then completely the meaning of "with a vengeance." I memorized their every feature and thought terrible thoughts as first my stomach turned to stone, and then my heart, and the great weight they made within me merely strengthened my resolve with the carrying of it to make them pay.

'You always tell me you're no witch, tell them! Tell them Mem wasn't either.'

"No."

'Why?'

"Because I don't care now. And I am become worse, much worse."

'What do you mean?'

"Watch and see."

I said not a word to them, as they asked if I would renounce Satan three times. Three times, I just stared at them, each in turn. They became uncomfortable in their chairs under my unwavering gaze, shifting uneasily more and more frequently in their seats. Finally leaving me and locking the door behind them, they went out into the street, to prepare to bring about their judgment.

I threw off my form then, leaving for them my dagger on my chair. Knowing that they would know what I wanted them to know when they found it. I did not worry then about my rage or the state of my mind it had brought me to. This time I was enjoying the little voice inside, I had turned the tables on it, and it was the one being made uncomfortable now. I did not worry about anything but making them pay dearly for robbing me of my Mem. Mayhap I should have, mayhap I will be made to pay someday, some dearer price than I have been made to pay already, but as Baylor had said once, "That is all just the path behind me now" and I do not know that I would change it even if I could.

I went out from under the door, no longer worried about how I would coax my form back. I had complete control of such things now. I never took no for an answer, not since I'd learned I did not have to. I left out an open window in the adjacent room, taking the form of the dreaded crow, that should not have been dreaded had they the faith they professed. I went to perch upon the steeple's cross, high above the church, high above all of them and watched, waiting for my time.

A crowd had gathered out front of the church while I had been inside. Obviously the word had spread quickly that a witch was being tried. There was a great deal of questions and answers, being yelled back and forth. As people discovered it was the "granddaughter" of the last witch they had convicted, shouts of approval went up and a tall stake was planted in the square below me. Wood and kindling were brought and piled around its base. A table was brought out and set before it, and I assumed this was where the rest of my inducement to renounce the Devil was to take place.

The excitement of the people, as the preparations for such horrible acts were being made, brought a sickness to my stomach. My mind shrank back from all of it; unable to allow me to consider my mother having experienced, even in the smallest part, what these people were describing to one another, with such vulgar enjoyment.

I stayed my perch, choosing to remain the huge black crow I had become on exiting the church. I was digging my claws angrily into the cross I sat on. I was worked up into an even more terrible rage by all of it. However, my only enjoyment for the moment was to be the confusion caused by the discovery of my absence.

When they had gone to get me for this trial before the people, a cheer had gone up. Now the people were angry, confused and fearful. The witch had disappeared, or escaped somehow, leaving the door somehow locked and a dagger in her place. The news spread like wildfire through the crowd, and confused questions and fearful responses replaced the prior topics of torture everywhere. Some departed quickly upon hearing the news, wanting to be far away, should I reappear. Others stayed close together, feeling safer in small groups. The priest tried repeatedly to calm them, telling them that God would see His children safe and His justice served. I watched it all with angry amusement, biding my time.

It was well into the night when the three men I waited on calmed the remaining few and sent them upon their way. The priest then reentered the church and the other two began to walk down the street toward their homes. I left the cross atop the church then, and followed them to learn where they slept. Confident the first to have questioned me would be sleeping somewhere within that building, when I was ready for him.

These other two were very nervous; constantly glancing over their shoulders, and I knew by their actions, that they did not believe all that they had told the people. They did not have that faith they had told the people to rest peaceful in, that their God would protect them. We would see soon enough.

They were right to be afraid.

I flew steadily over their heads until one of them left the other, entering a large house off to my right. This I marked also in my memory as I followed the last man to his home. I came to rest above his door and when he spotted my form, he was suddenly afraid.

"Superstitious? Bad, bad, where is your grand faith now?"

~27~

Vengeance Is Mine

I did not try to quiet my inner monologue now. I let it run where it would. I squawked at him as he fumbled to enter what he felt was the safety of his home. I left him then to settle within, schooling myself to patience. I had no end of time for this, did I? For once it seemed time was with me; mayhap time too enjoys revenge and knew as I did that this man deserved a little of it to wallow in his fear.

When in time I felt he would be readying himself for bed, I flew around the house, finding the shutter with the light shining from under it. I tapped my beak upon it and he came to see what was causing the noise. Jumping back from me in fear, he slammed it closed again and dropped the drapes quickly upon seeing my form, as though this gesture of fear would shield him from me.

I heard him drop to his knees within and begin praying fervently for deliverance. I heard him beginning to plead with the Almighty to save him from the demon at his window, begging that an angel be sent to protect him. Somehow that had amused me, for I was an Angel, was I not? I threw off that form that had freighted his superstitious mind so, and entered through the cracks around his window. If he wanted an angel, he would have one.

"But you don't want this Angel."

"He will not help you," I whispered, taking my own shape before him.

He fell to sobbing frantically then, but I had no pity. I could see him in my mind's eye, doing such things to my mother, I could not have imagined had his own mouth not described them for me.

"Please...mercy," he managed.

"Mercy?"

"Mercy, Angel....Chirp...Chirp..."

"Did my mother plead mercy?" I asked between gritted teeth, ignoring any more gracious thought that might have held my anger in check.

I allowed no expression to come to my face as I walked slowly toward him. I showed only an almost cold curiosity that might bring an honest answer from him. Truly I don't think I could have recognized myself had a mirror been placed before me, and perhaps that is best, but I will never know either way.

"Your mother?" he cried.

He seemed confused now, momentarily stopping in his gibberish and incoherent sobbing.

"Elizabeth Marie O'Conner, she was my mother. You murdered her. You remember, don't you? You spoke of the deed with great relish today at the church." I said this all flatly. "You mentioned a search for me, Angelica. Well I am here!"

I was fighting desperately for control and clenching my jaw to stay myself from spitting the words. He fell then again into his sobbing and begging for his life, and I saw I would have no answer.

"Then ask the next one, but cease this one's pathetic noise."

I did. I released my rage full upon him then. Becoming the hellcat again and relishing the absolute fear and recognition of death in his eyes as I came. I had lost what little fight there was within me for peace and mercy, the battlefield was bloodied.

"Messy, girl, very messy."

I left then, satisfied it would take some time for them to be sure it was him, when they found him here. A great enjoyment infusing me along with the knowledge his discovery would bring the others no end of terror.

I went to roost on the cross again, sleeping well for the first time in a long time. Understanding fully now how Baylor had to have felt when avenging his own mother. Looking forward to more such release and waiting out a good time for it.

I awoke about an hour before the sun that morning to another scene of pandemonium erupting in the square before me. My first victim had been found already, some poor manservant probably having had the misfortune of coming upon him. The people were in a panic, banging relentlessly upon the doors of the church. The priest emerged finally, wiping the sleep from his eyes irritably. Immediately he was besieged by the frightened masses that had gathered.

"The witch has called up the Devil himself to destroy us," someone called out.

This frightened shouting went far in increasing the overall feeling of fear among them. The man I had left safe in his bed the night before was frantically begging the priest for the protection of the church, trying to grasp the priest's hands. That one shook him off, trying to calm the people again and get from them an answer.

"What has happened that you have all lost your faith so easily?" he yelled above the noise.

He managed to get the tale from them in bits and pieces. The people were frightened they would also suffer such a fate, and would not be quieted easily.

"Calm yourselves," he called out again. "Our Lord has reason for allowing his child to have suffered death for him. That one had sat in council with me in such matters many times and served the Lord well. Now his death serves to test your faith. Will you so easily turn your faces from our Savior? Will you allow this witch to damn you all by causing you to lose your faith? She will be found and her evil ended. We will leave the stake here as proof of our faith and she will burn on it as our sacrifice of penance for allowing it to have faltered."

He had finally gotten their attention and they were quieting slowly.

I was in awe of him in some small way, that he was so deluded as to be completely sure of the right of what he had done, and sought now to continue to do. I could not fathom the depth of such fanaticism. That a religion based in so much good and furthered by such normally decent people's belief in it, could do so much evil. I knew from my lessons with Father Paul that, such vile deeds had occurred throughout history in the name of God. In some part of my mind I knew I was only further fueling these evils.

That I was doing evil myself, remembering: "Thou shalt not kill."

"They should not have killed then!"

'Vengeance is mine, sayeth the Lord.'

"Nay, vengeance is mine!"

I found I did not care. They had murdered my Mem and "An eye for an eye" was the only part of this religion I did care for at that time.

"An eye for an eye then!"

"A tooth for a tooth..."

I stayed my perch for a little longer, watching the crowd disperse for a second time. Then I left, flying out of the town and into the woods to hunt. I was hungry, such deeds were hungry work. When I returned it was growing dark already and I found the other man in the church with the priest, afraid to return home.

I am not sure whether it was the priest's desire to be left in peace so that he could get back to sleep, or an actual distaste for the man's serious lack of faith, but he was speaking to him harshly.

"Get you to your home and pray the Lord forgives your lack of faith, that he will deliver you lest he allow you to be delivered into his hands by this witch for denying his capability," he said.

The man left finally and I followed him. He was terrified already and I was reveling in this fact.

'Good boy, run on home, last one there is a dead man!'

I flew ahead of him and waited above his door, squawking as he turned toward it.

    'Beat you!'

He screamed then and turned to run back to the church and I flew again ahead of him, coming before him and swooping down, squawking again. He turned on his heels and ran the other direction, already growing winded. I flew ahead of him again, forcing him to run toward the outskirts of the town.

He was winded and panting and had no voice to scream, as I came down behind him becoming a huge black wolf and chasing him.

    'Faster, old man, I'm going to get you!'

He tripped then before me and I launched myself onto his back, tearing away at his flesh. Every horror they had described that they had inflicted upon my Mem ran through my head. For every despicable thought I tore him anew. The first purple light of dawn made its way in through the leaves above to watch me. He found voice to scream then, as though the sun would save him as the moon had not done for his comrade. It was too late though. By the time the townsfolk came to see what was causing the noise, I had finished with him. He could scream for me no more.

I flew back to the church then, still mad with rage. I did not want to wait any longer to have my final taste of revenge. Yet I schooled myself to patience to let the last one suffer the whole day through, knowing I would come for him soon. I sat my perch the remainder of the day and those superstitious townsfolk who noted my raven presence crossed themselves, taking my form as the sign it was meant to be.

I came in through the priest's window that night, having listened in on him as he suffered his fear in prayer the whole day through. This open window was the one from which I had made my original escape and I found it odd it should still be open. I came to rest on the table beside his bed staring at the man who had murdered my mother. I looked with cold rage upon the man that had stolen my sister from me and I squawked that rage from my crow beak, waking him suddenly from his undeserved sleep. He was very afraid, as the others had been. The fear was a beautiful mask before me.

Some part of me recognized I was well and truly mad then, that I had killed two men and meant to kill another, that I had enjoyed it, but I can't recall caring.

I became myself, looming above him, a young raven-haired madwoman perched precariously on the edge of his bedside table; he sat up screaming. He knew me, he knew why I was there.

"Where's your faith, priest? Where's your god?" I asked him.

He was clawing his way backwards into the corner and his mouth was opening and closing but no words were coming from it. I stood then and jumped off the table, sending it crashing and splintering over onto the floor.

"Elizabeth was my mother, my sister, my friend, my family, my blood," I told him.

I allowed myself to become again the hellcat, beginning slowly from my bare feet up. He watched this in abject terror and I reveled in it. In that moment I was enamored of his fear and I wanted to see more of it. I wanted him as mad from it as I.

"She was good and kind, an innocent, she brought out only the best in me," I whispered then, "I am the one you should have feared, in killing her you have brought the worst of me out."

I was the hellcat now nearly to my chest and as the change reached my hands I launched forward, grabbing him by the hair atop his head. I dug my claws in as he tried to squirm free. I was relishing even more the feeling of my claws as they met the bone of his skull and I dragged him by his head from the corner, hauling him from beneath his covers. I noted with some part of my mind that he had soiled himself but paid it little heed as I dragged him through the church, his screams echoing hollowly of the walls.

As I passed the altar, I reached out without clear thought or purpose and grabbed one of the lit candles from it.

"Scream! Yes, scream!"

Reaching the front doors, I kicked them wide and hauled his scrambling, screeching form to the stake. It seemed so fitting to me that he too should end here. Shoving him toward it, I spoke to the kindling at his feet. Telling those small twigs and branches to bind him to it and they did. I threw the candle then onto the pile and willed it to catch on fire.

He stopped his screams, suddenly voiceless for a moment, fighting frantically to free his feet as the kindling did my bidding and wrapped itself tightly about his ankles, leaving only his arms free and flailing about helplessly. Then as it caught and began to flare up I told him, in a voice I didn't even recognize as my own, "Go now and offer my Mem your apologies, for you have sorely wronged her."

I left then. His screaming started up again and the town's people began to peer from their windows in fear, knowing already what was happening, but unable to resist watching anymore than they could bring themselves to come to his aid. I imagine some saw me depart, dropping to all fours and turning more slowly than necessary from the hell cat to the huge black wolf. Then, on the outskirts of the town, leaping into the air and flying toward the mountains as the crow they had seen two mornings in a row upon their steeple. I did not really care. Mayhap I should have but I was finished with this town. Finished with all of it. Something within me died with the knowledge of Mem's death and the deaths of those men responsible for it.

"That is the path behind us now."

I was drained completely. I flew all the way home then, crying inside. I had nothing left. I wanted to give up then, exhausted in everyway beyond anything I'd ever felt, for I had lost even the strength of my faith. I had searched in vain for the others for years, only to come to the conclusion they were quite probably dead. Then I had searched for my only other tie to this world, only to find she had been murdered as well, and I was truly alone.

I had taken my vengeance for her death and now had nothing more to live for. It was in this great depression that I came down upon the plateau, broken, debilitated and feeling utterly alone. I do not know how long I lay there, simply existing, not eating or drinking, just being.

"Get up. Get up! You cannot give up on us now. Where is that will that told heaven it must wait?"

Being reminded of Demon's words to me made me open my eyes, it seemed as though it had been his voice that had said them. I must have been lying out there on the plateau exposed to the elements for many days because the sun had burned my face badly, my lips were cracked and bleeding. At some point I had reverted to my own form as was most natural to my energy, and that entire form ached. I lay there quite some time soaking up the pain, finding myself oddly pleased by my hunger pains as they made themselves known to me amongst all the others. I didn't feel I deserved to be alive, but somehow I was, and had no choice but to make the best of it. I fixed myself and stood, then walked slowly toward the door. I threw off my form and entered the large chamber beyond.

Re-forming, but still in a kind of stupor, I stumbled into the bathing chamber. I pulled off my clothing as a normal person would, suddenly needing to feel normal and clean. I let myself down into the pool slowly, moving as one in a trance. I relaxed against the edge, feeling the cool water against my skin and wishing it could clean me inside as well.

Eventually I waded to the end where the wine had been kept and pulled a skin from the floor of the pool. I opened it and began drinking the cool liquid straight from the soft container. I realized also that I was very hungry, but having no desire to hunt I simply willed my belly to be and feel filled. I do not know how much of the things I had done recently were normal for a Changeling. I had no reference point to decide if it should have been possible to do these things.

I had not been in contact at all with the kindling when I had told it to bind the priest's feet, and yet it had obeyed me. I remembered my first day as a Changeling, and the things Demon had told me. I recalled him pointing at a distant tree and telling me I had no power over it, but I didn't know then whether he'd said that because its distance from me was too great or if this power I'd found I did have over things at some distance was another new thing even to him; another revelation I'd have to let them all know of if, and when, I found them. None of it really mattered, though, because it did work, the universe bowed to me, rearranging itself to suit me, not just what was in actual contact with me but even that which was merely near to me. I knew

277

on some level I should be intrigued and want to test my range and limitations, it seemed the world was mine for the taking and yet I could make myself want nothing of it but what I didn't know how to make it give me: my family.

Thinking of what I had done in my rage to those three men who had taken one of them from me twisted my insides. Not that I regretted it really, but something in me balked at the realization that I had been no better than they. I had killed as they had killed. In itself the action I'd taken didn't bother me, it was simply that the level of my ability to be heartless when enraged that disgusted me. It was not that I felt they had not deserved to die, by no means, merely that I was appalled by my own intense sense of vulgar enjoyment at being the one to oblige them with those necessary deaths. I realized then that I was rife with such appalling inconsistencies. I could one moment be the laughing, carefree, friend and the next the raging hellcat doing heartless and detached battle with a foe. I had adored Father Paul and delivered heinous death to others of his kind.

In a very strange way it made me realize I was still very human. I loved deeply, protected those I loved fiercely, and sought revenge should any do them harm. I could not damn myself for such actions. I lived for those I loved, in every way. To laugh with them, to fight by their side, to help them solve whatever problems might arise, but they were all gone now and I was completely lost.

"One thing at a time."

Eventually all I could come up with that resembled a reason for existing was that I had made quite a mess here and would have to leave this place. I could not remain in Scotland, the story would spread and people would be looking for me, the witch. I had quite probably worsened the plight of all that even slightly resembled a witch by their activities. The mountains, indeed the entire area, would soon be swarming with those hunting black wolves, crows and seventeen year old girls with long black hair. What had I done?

I sat there finishing my wine, trying to decide what to do, where to go, how to make myself move. Sitting there trying to convince myself it had all been justified and would prove to be fine in the end seemed a useless endeavor. What would I do now, what *should* I do? I could return again to Rome, leaving this place to those who would be coming looking for me, but I had done this so many times, I had lost too much heart for it.

There was still in me that undying hope that those I loved would return someday and find me here, but I also recognized that it was destroying me to wait day by day in vain. I went back and forth so often between believing they had survived and fearing them lost to me forever, it was maddening. Each cycle of the full moon made me want to scream, because I could not help Baylor by telling him what I had come to know. I knew that I was going to drive myself mad again and again, and mayhap someday not make it back, if I did not somehow escape the constant barrage of pain. If I could not find a way to be at peace with all of it, I would completely lose the will to even exist. Mayhap next time there would be no remembering of Demon's words to bring me back.

This is when I decided to go to the New World. To lose myself in the freedom Mem and Father Paul had spoken of with such longing. To escape into those dreams that lived at the wild ends of the earth that had always seemed so unreachable. Mayhap I could begin then to live without the constant barrage of memories. I would not be surrounded constantly then by the things that reminded me so much of those I loved so deeply but couldn't find. Mayhap I could outrun the little voice in my head and forget, finding peace if such a thing truly existed for one with as much to remember as I.

I would leave a final letter on my pillow, telling those I loved that they could come find me there. There mayhap I would not have to live in fear of that awesome power that had nearly destroyed me, and I could allow myself to be myself. They could scan for me and find me, as I had so far failed in finding them. So it was I wrote my letter and said goodbye to our home and the Old World, and began my journey to find a new life in the New World.

~28~

New World

I left the mountains and headed north in the most direct path toward the ocean. I came out on to a beach almost before I knew it. I had traveled here as my favored wolf and its ears had picked up the sounds of the surf, but I had not registered how close I had come, until I broke free from the underbrush and stood upon the sand.

This stretch of beach was beautiful and uninhabited and I realized I would have to follow it until I came to a place with a ship. I had not thought this through very well. I had simply decided to leave, and knowing I would have to cross water, had gone unthinkingly straight to it.

Then I began to think, did I really want to be on board a vessel with no way to escape, being constantly surrounded by people? Reminded constantly of those people I wanted to be surrounded by but could not? Did I feel I could remain disguised and unnoticed for such a long time? I had heard that it took many, many horrible months to make the difficult voyage and suddenly I did not think I wanted to find a ship to take me away at all.

Instead I began to reconsider swimming. A part of me no longer cared if I met a shark and it did indeed prove to be a dreadful bane to a Changeling. I finally came to the conclusion that I would swim and if I met with some horrible fate in the process then so be it, I simply hoped it would be a quick death. I did not care much either way anymore, it was still better than becoming incorporeal again after having been so for forty long years, and could be no worse than being cooped up, en masse, with a bunch of superstitious humans on a ship. If I made some dreadful mistake after such an extended length of time as I would have to be among them, and was thrown overboard, I would end up swimming anyway.

Having decided to swim, I wasted no time allowing myself to back out. I waded into the surf, simply thinking I would keep becoming the biggest fish I encountered. Until I had gathered so much mass, a shark would not bother with me. I ducked my head under the water and copied the first fish I saw and swam off to my new life.

When I encountered what I later learned, to my great amusement, was a shark, I had become that, only to change into something more impressive to me as I progressed. I loved the water and it offered me no resistance, as I became a swifter and larger creature every time I saw one. The water seemed more than willing to bind to me and lend itself to my mass. I stayed mostly close to the surface and when I eventually encountered what I know now was an orca, I was in awe. This creature was to me pure perfection, so I became one and remained one for a very long time.

I traveled in their midst, enjoying their very human sense of play and family structure. I had no sense of how long I did this, but when I would come to realize we where swimming near a ship, I would come up beneath it and adjust my hearing so that I might listen to the people aboard talk. If I discovered that I could either not understand their speech or they were not coming to port in the New World, I would move on with the orcas.

In a way they became a new kind of family or at the very least my companions. I had a sense that time was passing me by but I neglected to care, until one day I heard my desired destination mentioned in the waters above me. I began then to follow that ship more closely and listen to the talk of those on board. I knew it was coming time then to leave the ocean and my orcas behind, and I was saddened and elated all at once. I soon found myself saying my goodbyes to that liquid, peaceful world as well and I took the most direct route toward the shore.

Once again I went through many changes. I became smaller and smaller, until the water was becoming too shallow to bother. Then I simply stood up and walked onto the shore. I knew already that I did not want to stay close to the coast. This would be where the constant surge of humanity would be coming ashore by the shipload, seeking much the same things I sought. Even then I knew some small groups of those that had come before me, concentrated there as though they feared to move further inland. I myself wanted to be away from all of it, everything human, as swiftly as possible. I needed to be wild and free, as I had been in the ocean; I was not yet ready to be human and made to think.

I had determined during my coming here that I would head into this country's heart, searching out the wide open spaces. I had heard of these frequently; such expanses were mentioned often by those people cooped up in their close quarters on ships above; they spoke longingly of them. They would lower their voices and speak of other things this great New World held in store, with fear threading their whispers, but I felt no fear. I don't think I felt much at all then.

I knew Mem had wanted to come here, for she had often brought it up in conversation with Father Paul, but I had pushed those thoughts away back then. The fact that she would have come here had she been given the opportunity was enough for me when it came to remembering things. I had come here to escape those kinds of memories that further thoughts of her or Father Paul would resurrect, I would not begin haunting those graveyards for many more years.

I took the form of a bird and flew inland, coming across new animals and birds all the time. New things to occupy my mind were present always back then and I managed to escape the pain of all my losses for a long time. By living more as these new creatures and losing myself in their instincts, I didn't have to think very often or very deeply. Being less present and human in mind than would have been approved of, I traveled further and further inland.

One day I came upon a great wide-open space while flying in a new form I had discovered. This eagle had amazing sight and I could see all of the world, it seemed, laid out before me. In this world there roamed a great heard of beasts I had never thought to imagine: buffalo. I swooped down and studied them. Then I became one just to feel what it was like. They took no notice of me and I roamed about the great, grassy expanse with them. I had found a small measure of peace in spending most of my time as an animal, so I had half a thought to continue in that manner for some time with them, as I had my orcas, but it was not to be so.

Quite suddenly the herd broke into a dead run and I was swept up in the confusion. I ran with them, as a group of strange men wearing next to nothing, with painted faces and with feathers about their heads, came whooping into our midst. Now, I had heard of Indians and how much fear they had instilled in the people that were coming here, but this unexpected sight of them stunned me nonetheless.

I took off apart from the herd, wanting to be away from them, but one of these men followed me. He threw his spear, striking me in the side, and I stumbled and fell in pain. I did not think then but simply went back to the form I had been in before, that of the eagle, and took flight, quickly escaping the pain that had invaded the buffalo's form. It was the Indian's reaction to this that stayed me in my instinctual flight and held me circling so humanly curious above him.

He had not been afraid. He had not made signs to shield himself as though I were a minion of the devil himself. He had been more reverent and it seemed also very apologetic. I could not understand his words but it was clear they were not spoken in fear but awe.

I longed suddenly to understand him and the only way to do this would be to be one of his kind, to be human again. I actually thought about it for a moment but the others came to join him to see what he was doing, talking to the bird above his head instead of hunting as they had. He began pointing excitedly to the spear that he had thrown, which lay on the ground where I had left it. I watched in awe myself as they all began to speak to me with words I could not understand, dipping their heads in apparent reverence. Seeming to be trying to coax me down to apologize or even worship me. Again I was tempted but I found myself sadly lacking in courage after having grown up in a culture that wanted to burn me at the stake for so much less.

I had flown away then, confused by all of it, needing to sit alone for a moment and think. I came down upon a rock in the middle of a stream, becoming myself, relishing as I had not in so long the feel of simply being myself and thinking. I had not done this in so very long and I think I even giggled as I put my bare feet into the water, wiggling my toes. I though this might not be so bad as long I only thought about the right things.

So I did, and as I did I began to wonder if these people knew about Changelings. Was it possible they accepted them, even revered them? I did not want to be a kind of deity, by no means, but to be accepted and be myself at the same time would be a wonderful thing to experience. If they did accept them, was it because they had known others of my kind, and if so were those ones good or bad? Might they know of the Council or what became of my family of Changelings?

'Oh, careful, these thoughts could lead you back to the consuming sadness.'

I veered off then and began to think again of how the Druids had once been accepted and revered, and how later those who followed their teachings even in the slightest, had been persecuted like my Mem. I began wondering if mayhap these people were not savages at all, simply more closely akin in their way of life to the Celts of old; more of a mindset to be accepting of things in the world around them, even if they did not fully understand them. Could it be they were curious more than afraid, questioning more than condemning, a people more like my mother and Father Paul?

I felt a great desire to find out and to see if I might be accepted. Was it possible I might find in them the same camaraderie I had with Demon and Baylor, Piper and the twins? This last thought was enough to get me up and into the air again. I realized I needed that kind of thing in my life again. I needed to be able to talk and laugh and tell stories with friends. I felt I could handle it, if only a little at a time. I thought I could overcome my own sadness. I was wrong.

When I came back over the prairie they had gone and I was saddened, berating myself that I had wasted the chance. I turned to fly back to the stream and spend the evening bemoaning my lack of bravery. Then I saw him riding slowly back onto the prairie, on the small horse he had before. He looked very different, but it was him none the less, he wore no paint on his face now and had removed the feathers from his head, but I would not forget that face.

His gaze was turned to the sky and he seemed to be looking for me. When he spotted me he held his hands up. Showing me they were empty of any weapons. Getting off his horse and standing beside it very still. I gathered my courage then and flew toward him.

As I said before, he had dismounted his horse and stood beside it, one hand on its mane, like a beautiful statue. They were both stunning viewed like this. He had long shiny black hair, a blue-black like Adreal and Adonia's. He had a strong square jaw, a straight nose, and very dark brown eyes. As I said, I would not forget that face. I realized as I came down toward him that I did not know how I should appear to him. I did not know how a woman of his people would clothe herself.

I thought then mayhap I would not necessarily have to be an Indian to understand him. Could I not, just as easily, when making myself again into me, ask the energies making me up to make the knowledge of his language part of me? I wasn't positive it would work, but many other surprising things had, so why not try it? It had come to me long ago that sometimes the belief that things were not possible was the only thing that made them impossible, when it came to Changelings.

A strange thing happened when I came down beside him. Giving my energies this direction, they pulled the smallest bits of energy from him, to make the knowledge for me. I felt strange in this, for I knew some of the matter now making me up belonged to this young man. I had appeared before him simply dressed in a long skirt and a blouse and he was staring at me open-mouthed, seeming to be torn between dropping to his knees and running away.

"You are a paleface woman?" he said at last.

I was relieved he had not run and that I had understood him, but it seemed I had a different problem now. For the words "paleface" and "woman" had not came out as pleasantries.

"What do you mean?" I asked, feeling strange as the words rolled off my tongue in his language. "I am whatever I choose to be, as you have seen, but I was born with this skin and I am comfortable in it. Would it be more a comfort to you if I appeared as you?"

I was ready to oblige him should he say yes. I saw no need to quibble over skin tones.

"No, no, many apologies," he said. "I simply thought you were the spirit of one of my tribe. I did not know that the palefaces had this ability, too."

He ducked his head in a gesture of apology again and I thought for a moment he would drop to his knees.

"Your people take animal forms?" I was astounded.

Had I found another little cache of Changelings and not known it? He certainly did not feel like a Changeling but then neither had Baylor, and he had changed shape. I was reminded that it was the knowledge within a Changeling's soul of what it was that made it exude such a feeling and made it recognizable as such to others. My questioning of him seemed to keep him from his knees, for he straightened midway, very confused. This encouraged me, for I had no desire to be worshiped.

"Among my people we believe such things are possible," he replied slowly.

Ahh, so this was a belief, not a fact, but where had the belief come from? Were there now or had there ever been Changelings here? My imagination ran away with me as I gestured for him to walk beside me. He fell into step immediately and we walked and I talked, unconsciously heading back toward the stream where I had spent the afternoon.

"Chirp...Chirp...Never allow it to be known what you are by any other than those being changed..."

I knew I was breaking the Code yet again but could not bring myself to care. As I questioned him, I realized how complex yet simple his people's belief system was. I explained I was not a spirit and this seemed the hardest part for him to accept. He had readily accepted all I told him, but the concept that I could be like this and still be flesh and blood was very hard for him. That I had chosen not to die to become what I was, was also difficult to explain but in a strange way it did seem to put him more at ease with me. Now I was merely a strange new entity rather than a kind of deity, a living thing more so than something mystical.

We had been sitting on the bank of the stream for sometime now and he very timidly reached out and pulled my hair.

"Ouch!" I cried, more in surprise than pain.

He jumped back, obviously not expecting I would have felt it, let alone that it would hurt me. Again I feared he would revert to reverence as he bowed his head.

"Many apologies again, I did not think I would hurt you. My spear did you no harm." He said this very quickly, as if to explain himself before I would hurt him for his actions.

I realized just how hard it must be for him to absorb all of this, and applauded him for doing so well in the face of so many revelations. I did not know for sure just how well I was expressing everything I was trying to explain, nor how much of it was merely being blended in his own mind with his own beliefs, but I had no desire to make myself out to be some sort of godlike sprit and tried very hard to make my existence more reconcilable with a natural phenomenon than with a supernatural event.

"I am just a girl with a strange gift," I said, once more trying to put him at ease.

I had to explain to him, then, other things about us and we ended up sitting on the bank well into the night, just talking. Once again I was amazed to find myself in the position of being alone and comfortably conversing with a man for whom I had no name.

I made no such game of it this time, simply asking him, "What is your name?"

He smiled then, giving me to realize I had just given him the opportunity to share with me some wonderful news he was quite proud to relay.

"I was called Limping Gray Wolf," he said, becoming excited. "But I have just received my new name from the Medicine Man."

I cut in here, needing to clarify, whether this was his actual name, and not a nickname.

"You do not limp. Why do they call you that?" I asked.

He then explained to me that sometimes the women of his people named their children after the first thing they saw when they gave birth. He told me that his mother's first sight had been a wounded gray wolf, limping its way to the safety of the woods.

"And your new name?" I said, remembering I had cut in, and he had been about to share that with me.

"The Medicine Man called me Gray Wolf Spirit Hunter," he said proudly.

"And why is that?" I asked, realizing there must be a story behind that as well.

"In his visions, he said, he saw me turn into a gray wolf and hunt with the other wolves that are the spirits of our people," he said simply. "I am to be a great leader."

Of course it was not simple to me for I had to ask him then about visions and this led to more questions. Eventually though I came to realize it had been this vision and the receiving of his name which had brought him back to the prairie to find me. He had thought that I was one of these spirits that would take the shape of the wolf and become his spirit guide.

"Well, I am called Angel," I told him.

I was happy he found no meaning in this or need to ask me if my mother had seen an angel after my birth, or what visions my Medicine Man had experienced. Apparently this tribe had thus far avoided missionaries.

He told me then that he should return to his people and I asked him that he keep my existence a secret, explaining I did not feel comfortable at this time with the thought of so many knowing about me. He had said he would, then asked if we might talk again. We had agreed to meet at the stream two nights hence and he had left then seemingly very happy.

I had sat there quietly feeling a little bit of my old happiness returning to me. I had sat through the entire evening, enjoying the company of another person. I still could not bring myself to care that it had been due to my revealing my secret and abandoning the Code yet again.

I flew off to the large cave I had taken to sleeping in. It had become my new home. It was not nearly as large by even a third as the one I had called home in Scotland, but it was cool and dry. I sat there taking in my view; though not the one I would miss so often, it too was beautiful to me. I watched for a while as the lightning bugs seemed to pop in and out of existence before me, and quietly enjoyed the sound of the crickets as they serenaded each other in the darkness. Allowing myself to be lulled to sleep, I slept comfortably as a wolf safe in this darkness.

We met again two nights later and this soon became a habit. We would meet and talk and soon we even took to hunting together. He was in excellent form, running easily through and over any terrain we chose to hunt, keeping pace with me as I became the wolf to lead the hunt.

He seemed to think this was what he was born to do: to hunt at my side with me the wolf. I understood his acceptance of this, due to what I had learned of his people's beliefs, and eventually ceased trying to be sure he knew I was not a spirit. I did, however, continue to question him often on many other beliefs and found he was no end of new knowledge for me.

He also taught me how to do many things that I would have otherwise only done as an animal. He showed me which fruits, vegetables and roots were good for humans to eat and how to prepare them, doing all of it with a great deal of respect for me. An easy acceptance of my lack of knowledge in these areas did not conflict with his belief I had great knowledge of other things.

He showed me things and places that were beautiful to him. Places where water fell were especially appealing to him. He loved waterfalls, even the smallest of them, and I loved searching them out with him. We would follow even the smallest of streams until we found where they might drop some distance, often jumping off these ledges ourselves and swimming in the large pools they created.

He would point out to me, sometimes, the beauty of the water flowing over the golden rocks. We would sit mesmerized by their twinkling for hours, while telling each other stories. I knew this to be gold but it did not matter then, what need had I for it? Later it would bring humanity here en masse, driving me out, and I would have cause to wish I had gathered it all up and hidden it away from them forever. For now, though, I merely enjoyed, as he did, the way in which the water sparkled over it on its downward course.

He had taken to remaining with me longer and longer, sometimes staying a whole week or even more. I did not know how far he came to keep these meetings with me. I also did not know how old he was or if these long absences left a mother, or even a woman or children, worrying. I finally asked him one evening how old he was and he told me something I understood to mean about sixteen summers. So I had thought that at least the woman and children part was quite unlikely.

I knew I would keep him safe for his mother and ours was a relationship which I was comfortable with, so in the interest of keeping it that way, I never brought up such matters as a wife or children. I also knew either way I simply appreciated his companionship very much and had no desire to jeopardize that by possibly insinuating I felt he was neglecting more important duties to remain with me.

Eventually he managed to convince me to come with him and meet the others of his tribe. We agreed to meet again two weeks later, after he had told them who and what I was, preparing them to accept me as he had. I did not think much about what it was he meant to tell them or how he thought to explain me. He was confident he could accomplish it and that confidence fed mine in him. He did not seem to feel this would be a difficult task for him, and I felt now better prepared to allow him this, as it was all he had ever asked of me.

He obviously thought it a great honor to know me and felt he was withholding this honor from his people, by not having told them of me yet. I felt I owed him this much, for he had pulled me back to myself, by being a friend to me all these many, many months. He left me then, commenting on how this would be a good month for his people, for a trader was to be coming, in fact had probably already arrived. He felt that the trader would bring many new things to further his people's progress and that my visit, so soon after, signaled a new prosperity for his people. He was eager to begin what he felt would be new time of learning and sharing knowledge for his tribe.

I returned to my cave and began to anticipate meeting more of his people. I was elated by my hope that they would all be as wonderful as he was. I thought I would enjoy meeting his mother, for she had raised quite and extraordinary young man. He had come to be a very good friend to me and I began to think of it much as I had thought of meeting Baylor. After knowing Demon I had looked forward to meeting any friend of his. I looked at it like meeting other friends in waiting.

The night finally came and I flew out from my cave with excitement, alighting on the bank of our favored stream. I fidgeted as I waited for him, swishing my bare feet through the water. I waited until my feet had pruned up, and still he had not come. The moon had risen high overhead and still no sign of him. I began to worry then, for he had never missed an appointment with me.

I became the black wolf then and, remembering his scent, I began to search for him. I went in the direction he had always headed when leaving me, and kept my nose down. I came eventually upon the scent of his horse, finding it in the underbrush along a small path where some of the hair from its tail had been pulled out as they passed. I knew then I was on the right path at least for finding where he went, when he went home.

I tracked his route throughout the remainder of the night, coming through the woods back out onto another prairie just as the sun began to turn the horizon a beautiful shade of purple. Yet the beauty of the morning could not hold me, contrasted so sharply with the horror I saw ahead. There, before me, was a huge grouping of teepees and they were almost every one ablaze.

~29~

Gray

I took off at a dead run, not fully understanding why the teepees should be burning, very fearful that this would bring harm to "Gray" as I had come to call him. I had a frightening thought that he was asleep or knocked unconscious in one of these blazing teepees, about to be burned up. I then saw a white man holding a torch, with a horse packed and ready to flee at his back. I flew into a rage, the like of which I hadn't felt in many, many, years. I put my head down then, blind again, and ran directly for him.

It was Gray who saved that mans life. He came into view and, seeing me, raised his hands to stay my wrath. He stepped boldly in front of the man with the torch, shielding him with his own body.

"NO!" he yelled.

I skittered to a halt just short of knocking us all down, and he looked at me sadly, as I fought to comprehend. He seemed to have aged drastically in the two weeks we had been apart, and I could see a sheen of sweat upon his brow.

"Angel, this man is called James. He is helping me to keep the disease from spreading," he explained.

The man appeared not only appalled by the fact he had just narrowly avoided being mauled by a wolf, but also that this Indian had control enough over it to stop it and now spoke to it, calling it by name.

I stood up wanting to laugh at the look this James gave, even more so when he turned impossibly paler upon seeing me turn into a woman, but other matters pressed me harder.

"What disease?" I asked angrily, but I knew. I could smell it all around me. I had smelled this plague before and it was relentless. I was realizing that all the people I had looked forward to meeting must have fallen to this plague, for they were not present and I could smell their flesh in the blazing teepees. Then I realized an even more terrible truth: the plague had already taken root within my friend. I could smell it on him, see it in his sweating brow. It would be ruthless within him now; how he was still standing, I could not fathom. I wished then reverently for the counsel and direction of Mem.

"James says it is called 'smallpox.'" he said, as he turned to see if he had said it right and saw James near to fainting. "She is no evil spirit, Angel will do you no harm," he tried to reassure him.

"When did this happen? Where are your people?" I asked him, afraid I already knew the answer, but hoping desperately that I was wrong.

I was ignoring this man James, not caring if I appeared rude. I was far more intent on trying to understand what had befallen my friend.

"It came with the traders who came for the furs and hides. I thought good things would come of this, but I was mistaken. James thinks it came in the blankets my people traded for. They traded for the carriers of their own death. My people have moved on to the happy hunting grounds," he said.

I knew this meant that they were dead. I was so saddened for him that I felt I would weep as he continued.

"I was spared because I was with you when it came," he said. "I returned to find them all sick and leaving me one after another. James was here caring for them but he could not save them. All he could do was to tell them that the Creator of all things awaited them. I have sent them all on their way and now James says I must also burn our homes. For the sickness still lives inside them."

As he finished telling me this, he took the torch from James's trembling hands. I looked then to this person, wondering if he were one of the traders or a missionary who had arrived with them, and why he had stayed to do such a thing.

"How came you to be here, to even be caring for them?" I asked him.

"I came to share the message of our Lord and Savior Jesus Christ. I wanted to tell these people of the good news of God," He answered me, still more than a little stunned.

I must tell you here, I had no long-standing hatred of the Church or Christianity. After the three who had killed my mother had paid for her torture and death with their own, I had come to view Christians much as Baylor did. I was more for thinking them for the most part good people with good hearts, who were simply sometimes very misled. James was staring at me still, had never taken his eyes from me in fact, so I decided to make it easier for him.

"I am no demon or servant of the devil, I am no witch, so fear not for your soul. I am called Angel for a reason and we will leave it at that," I said pointedly.

He took it as I had hoped, or at least didn't have the courage to question me. Or continue his constant staring. His eyes would wander back to me inadvertently but I pretended not to notice. I watched in sadness as I saw my friend put the torch to all that remained of his people. James excused himself after Gray returned to us.

"I must go now about the work of my Lord, I did all I could do here. I will pray He watches over you and Gray, guiding you and keeping you safe in his love," he said. Then turning to me, he whispered for my ears alone, "I do not think your friend will last much longer, his will is strong but his body is near defeated."

He turned then, mounting his horse and riding away from us. I stood there narrowing my eyes and watching him go, wondering if it had really been traders who had brought the sickness, or if the missionary had brought more than the good book with him. It did not matter now, for I could not change what had happened here. What mattered was that my friend was as alone now as I had been, and I understood his feelings well. I was glad to be there for him in this time of need, and reached out to squeeze his shoulder compassionately when he had finished his sad duties and walked slowly back to me.

He was burning up.

"Gray, are you all right?" I said.

It was a stupid thing to be asking but it was all I could think of. He turned toward me with glassy eyes, trying to focus, his mouth worked to answer me but no words came from it. He fell forward into my arms. I had to alter my strength to hold him upright and I called to his horse, mimicking perfectly the way he would have done it.

It came to me hesitantly, sniffing the sickening air and nickering its fear but unable to see any other course, for its master was in my arms and my will was the stronger. I lifted Gray onto his back, jumping up behind him. I held him up firmly before me and turned the horse towards the stream. The horse knew this route well and we took it at a dead run. The wonderful little beast navigated the path easily despite the unusual amount of weight, as capable as his riders usually were when the one was well and the other a wolf.

We came to the stream sooner than I had expected we would, but it had not been nearly quick enough. My mind had been running far ahead and I was breaking inside all over again. I slid from the winded horse's back before it had even come to a full stop, bringing Gray down in my arms and carrying him with me into the stream.

"Do not leave me, Gray! I am here, stay with me!" I was crying now and could not control it.

"Careful, careful, little girl, you must not change him unless he wants to. Remember! Chirp…chirp…Never force a soul to become a Changeling should it wish to go…"

"He will want to."

"Be sure, if not…"

"Why not?" I demanded, suddenly angry, but I knew.

To be a Changeling, one needed will. If Gray had no will to be here, I could not make him stay with me. It would be a sin against him, not the Code. The Code, the Council, I had obviously quit caring about long ago.

"But you see now, don't you?"

"See what?"

"Why we should never tell."

"Tell what?"

"Don't play the fool now, little girl. You know."

"Why?"

"Probably knew when you were doing it..."

"And? What harm came of telling him what I was?"

"This...You will never know now! Even if he chooses this, you will never know!"

"Know what?"

"Why, whether he had the will within him all along to remain or you invented it within him by telling him it was possible to remain."

I just stood with him, there in the water, crying softly. I was dying inside once again, as slowly and surely as the young man in my arms. Begging him to stay with me, crying that I did not want to be left alone again, and pleading with him to choose to stay. How many times had I cried like that? How many times more would I be brought to it? I could not do this any more. Mayhap I had done it wrong, I had done a lot wrong, but surely it would not cost me this?

He had grown cooler in my arms and I tried desperately to hold onto some small hope he would pull through, somehow fight the fever back, but then I felt the light; that dreadful, powerful light that I had fought for my existence so very long ago. I began to sob then all the harder, begging him to fight it, so heavy then within my soul the light could not have touched me, but then it had not come for me. All the force of will I possessed, the wanting I felt so desperately to fight it for him, was of no use to him, my will was not the one it would answer to on this one count. The universe did not care about my wants or my will then, only his, and all I could do now was cry. I did, crying out repeatedly for him to fight it and to stay, not even sure he heard me but afraid to my core of being alone again and unable to stop.

Suddenly I felt this amazingly beautiful thing, like music had erupted in my soul, and I knew instantly what it was. I do not think that I can describe for you the feelings of that relief, the instantaneous joy that came to replace all the pain in a mere heartbeat. I did not have to think about it at all, I knew, and I went out in my spirit instantly.

"Would you choose to remain with me, then?" I asked.

Relief was flooding over me yet I needed to be sure he would not later damn me for taking him from the light. I wanted to be sure he had the will in him to be what I would make of him. I needed him to shut out for me the doubting little English Judas in my head, drowning it out with his own words. I had no question as to his worthiness for the gift, only as to his want of it.

"Could you teach me to be a wolf then, as the Medicine Man said?" he asked me simply.

I wanted to laugh out loud then, so great was my relief and joy.

"I will teach you to be anything you wish," I told him.

"Then I will stay with you," he said.

I surrounded him then with my spirit, enveloping him in a great hug much as Demon had me. Then I came back from him and began directing him as Demon had me, to right his fevered form and return to it. He was far faster with these first steps than I, not needing the long explanations I lived for. Soon we were standing together in the stream and laughing like children.

I began teaching him then in earnest all that I had learned. Telling him of all the pitfalls I had come to recognize and all the new things I had discovered on my own. I cautioned him to be very aware of his subconscious and not to believe anything simply because he heard it. To always test his limits, because one never knows when he has become powerful enough to bend or break a law of the universe. He became so wonderfully proficient at everything I taught him so quickly, that I knew he had been born for this gift.

He was never limited by his own mind, he had no concept that something should not be possible.

I reveled in his company and we were quite happy to be together. He became as Baylor to me and I think I became a sister to him. I told him of all the things I am telling you here and now. We remained in this peaceful, happy manner for a very long time and I began to believe this was to be my new way of life. I had become comfortable again, living as different animals most of the time, not constantly reminded of all I had lost but rather enjoying all I had gained. The cave had served us well, but then there came a day when he told me he needed to leave me.

He had gone out flying early that morning and not returned until very late. I had just begun to worry for him when he entered and told me he had to leave. He explained that he had sat idly by for all these years doing nothing for his people. That he felt very bad for having done nothing, as their lands had shrunk year by year and the buffalo were being destroyed. He told me his people were starving to death or being killed outright, while fighting for land and a way of life that had been theirs long before the white man had come. He said he had to go to them and help them in any way he could. When I had asked him what he felt he could do about all of this he had smiled at me, telling me he would change the world if he had to.

I had known I could not try to deny him this. For I knew the depth of will in him, and that he had a huge heart for his people's needs. His own tribe might have died long ago, but he was still an Indian and he cared very much about keeping his heritage alive.

I would never ask him to stand by and let his people disappear altogether. Nor would I let him feel he was betraying me in following his heart. Had I not followed my heart and left my Mem? I was thankful that he had come in the flesh to tell me, as I thought now that I had been unkind in telling Mem in a letter. So I told him to go with my blessing but to always remember me, to come sometimes and find me, and we would hunt together as wolves.

He had given me a huge hug in parting and said he would not forget.

He did come back, quite often in the beginning, then less and less, as the world around us changed more rapidly, and his people's needs became greater. I began to discover little things to entertain myself. I took to venturing out on my own again, as I had before finding Gray. I had never truly learned to be content with absolute solitude, needing small things to entertain my curious mind, like a herd to run with or a flock to follow in flight, but always I returned, when I had to escape it all, to my cave.

I was very much in awe and sometimes admittedly disgust, when the white men began to carve for themselves a country from a continent and no one could stand in the way. I began to pay a little more attention to the world around me. When they demanded and won their independence from the English, just as the Scots had, that did not so much disturb me, but there was more destruction to come before prosperity could follow. I was at a loss as to why it should have meant such rampant death to so many; for there was truly so much space, I found it every time I moved on to escape it all.

I look back now to areas that had been ruled by great tribes of Indians, people who quite probably would have been content to be left to live there, in peace, and yet had never been given a chance, and now those areas are just great unpopulated spans between cities. Those wide open spaces of land have become no more than just something one must try to stay awake while driving through on their way to somewhere else. I was heartsick from all of it for so long that I still tried to hide myself away.

Ferries came, with their great smokestacks, belching black smoke into my clean air, and bringing with them more people than I could possibly imagine. There had always been trappers, missionaries, and those brave few who dared to come to the wilder side of the Mississippi, to find their dreams. But gold, gold was a dream they all seemed brave enough to chase.

So sugar cane had become sugar; gold had called out to the masses and a man name Whitney had made cotton such a profitable business that soon I could find little peace anywhere for very long. Especially when other atrocities, such as the appalling demand for more slaves, soon forced me to escape to my cave more frequently, if only to not witness it with my own eyes;

sometimes it felt far too hopeless. Yet eventually even that began to change, degree by degree, and life by life; Americans formed America and I grew to adore their will. The price of progress, I suppose, all we Changelings have had to survive the hurts of change, and learn to simply watch.

War had come again and again and again in the formation of this nation and each time in some way it had pitted brother against brother, and each time it became harder to see the sense of it, especially the last. Families had turned against their own, whether from across the sea or within the borders of their new homeland, and all of it for what? Money, profit, land - and was it so important? Was it worth such terrific sacrifice? Later wars made so much more sense in comparison to that one; that one nearly broke my heart.

I found a moment once, sitting under a moon swaddled in the smoke of a burning town, when things seemed so terribly unfair in their every aspect that I wanted, for the first time in ages, to rage again. To release from within me the hellcat and demand my own payment for being forced to bear witness to such atrocities and useless waste of life. Was not life the most precious of all commodities? Then again, who was I to be passing judgment? Had I not just been thinking of demanding a few of my own in payment for my pain?

At some point in all of this the gold of Gray's favorite stream was also discovered and another rush for the great dream began. People started coming in droves and planting themselves directly beneath the ledge of my cave. I was forced then to remove myself yet again, finding I needed to escape the never-ending onslaught of humanity. Hence I lost myself again as best I could, thinking to spare myself such regretful memories as I would add to the ones I already carried where I to lose a battle with myself one day and release the hellcat on them for some new atrocity they forced me to witness.

I fully understood then why Piper had mourned the destruction of Londinium while applauding the actions of the great Boudicia. How he had been torn by the want of prosperity for the human race as a whole and the prosperity of his own people on a smaller scale.

I moved further and further away, still trying to find the occasional moments of peace in the wild. I was constantly running away from all I saw and heard, as it proclaimed and end to my New World and heralded in the age of the Americans, all to swiftly. Eventually the wild was no longer my wild, but wild in another way, becoming harder to lose myself in. Soon the lake, on whose shores I had made my new home also became surrounded with humanity. There was less and less wide-open space every time I emerged from my new cave. Towns sprouted and took root, growing up all around me.

Time passed very quickly then, as certain things began to interest me again, and not in the sad, sadistic, manner of watching towns that took years to build burned to ash in a single night. Eventually these new things outweighed thoughts of losing my wildness. I put other sadder thoughts behind me and contemplated instead the rapid recovery of my new country from its, what, third war? I found myself, more and more often, going into the towns springing up around me, simply to observe things more closely.

Soon I chose to make Springfield my home, for though I was often drawn to St. Louis due to such wonders as the World's Fair of 1904, the smaller, slightly wilder nature, of Springfield proved more comforting. It still existed in the in-between state that I was in as well. I was becoming more frequently involved, though. Often in awe of the quick progress being made, following so quickly on the heels of such rampant destruction. I wanted somehow to be a part of it all, to be able to heal as this country and its people were healing.

I would sit in the taverns, usually as Demon. Listening to the talk of all that was new, about the entire world I had nearly forgotten completely. It had been developing not only under my nose but everywhere. I was constantly watching the new fashions of clothes the women wore. They looked so pinched, in the middle that I wondered how they breathed at all, let alone walked down the street under the hot sun. I was very thankful back then that I could be a man.

I would enter a coffeehouse to read the morning papers as though

302

my mind had been starved near to death. I would drink endless amounts of their wonderful coffee while drinking in even more information, shamelessly spying and eavesdropping always. I was constantly learning about other things besides war bringing about these changes. I was beginning to appreciate the changes more fully, and learning about the people who had invested so much of themselves in their development. Edison! My goodness, need I say more?

The ferries, then trains, and eventually motorcars, all were a nuisance, making the air smell and taste bad, but they intrigued me nonetheless. They were all tremendous inventions, launching Americans ahead and into a new and hopefully better era. More importantly, they brought me such vast amounts of information, more quickly than I felt at times I could absorb.

I also followed the work of Albert Einstein and learned a lot from him. That my energies had been given a name, "atom," was only one delightful little part. I also paid very close attention to Einstein in the hope he might somehow, someday, inadvertently explain what had happened to my atoms when I had been nearly destroyed. I had recoiled in horror upon seeing the same explosive force unleashed upon mankind, and found nothing good in it, not even in the selfish form of being able to ascertain how it had been done to me; but the fifth war was ended and time marched forward and forgot.

I always bore in mind the powerful being that had done much the same to me. I was constantly on guard should it come again, but it never did. There were times I would forget, for those few peaceful moments when I would become absolutely absorbed in something new. What it had done to me, to us. Why I was here, and why I was alone. Not often though, not nearly often enough. Ahh, but I am losing track of myself again now.

As I was saying, about what pulled me in. Each new medical miracle was also of special interest to me. Total cures for some things, vaccinations for others, preventative measures and other amazing breakthroughs. There was still a great love in me for the art of healing instilled by my mother, and I began to learn all I could of all that was becoming known. There was one company in particular, founded in I believe it was 1847, that I watched with much awe.

I began to make investments with some of the gold that was so easy for me to come by, wanting to further these studies and all their amazing results. I began to enjoy this investing process, feeling it connected me in some way. I would do it whenever I felt strongly about something then, not just the art of healing. I found I had a knack for this kind of decision-making. As I would choose something of interest to me, invest in it, and somehow make more money by the end of this enjoyable process.

Eventually, by simple virtue of my insatiable curiosity and enjoyment of these little things, I was pulled completely into the world. I could no longer be satisfied with living in the wild or with quietly slipping into the coffeehouses by day or taverns by night. I had done it for far too long. I even began to forget why it was I had begun to do it in the first place.

I withdrew some of the money I had put in a banking facility, a place I had overheard was the best to put ones funds, and I bought a house here on Elm Street. Whenever necessary I simply "sold" it to myself, "moving away" if it seemed someone might question why I was not aging. I had a dislike for even appearing old. I did not like the way it felt. I enjoyed being a man back then, but I was very admiring of Miss Anthony and all those like her, working so bravely to make it possible for all women to experience life as I could so easily by simply changing my form.

I would make repairs to my home and add amenities as they came about. I would rebuild or build on as necessary to accommodate me and my ever growing amount of possessions. I brought my home with me, through the depression, into even more splendor than it had been in before. And when the Mississippi River had her own great uprising against those all around her and nearly destroyed it, I started again. I had grown to love the place and the humanity it afforded me and had no intentions of abandoning it.

I took great pride then in furnishing and refurnishing my home with a flair that reminded me greatly of Demon. I even planted the garden I had always wanted to provide for him. Every flower, every color, every scent chosen and arranged just so and then planted and tended with care. I think every Changeling should have a garden; we all seem to love them. We all seem to search such places out, when seeking peace, be they gardens of the modern sense or merely a grove or vineyard. I know I did many times throughout the years.

Once I even commissioned a painting, to be created of all of them who were beyond me. I described them from memories I had avoided for so long, to a talented young man who translated them perfectly into paint, seeming to see them clearly through my words. I hung the painting in my foyer that I might come home to them and touch them upon my every return. It became my favorite thing, of far more value to me than all the many other things I owned. It was to me much as I think the one of Seraphim must have been to Demon.

It might have been my many years of owning absolutely nothing which caused me to become such a collector of things as Demon had been, but in any case this brought me some small measure of painful joy. I think that is when I began making my real mistakes. I believe these are the things that began the most anguishing part of the remembering. Inadvertently I had started reminding myself of all the things I had been escaping for so long. I did not foresee the harm in it. I did it by such small degrees that the effects went undetected for a long time. By the time I had realized my folly, I could not stop the mean little voice inside my head from telling me I was a fool, not just for having allowed it to happen but for so many things: for the garden, for the painting, for listening to it, for not listening; but then I digress again.

So back to the end: I took on many forms back then, both male and female, to learn all I could, again giving my mind other things to consider. Effectively, I was disguising the slow descent into despair that I had begun in the uplifting process that was feeding my curiosity and my own doom. I even attended college when one was established down the street from me. I enrolled three different times, as three different students, and loved every moment. I bought all the books I could find on every subject of interest, filling an entire room of my home with them. I began staying up to all hours of the night, reading everything that was now so readily available to me. It seemed I would never get enough of the endless supply of information.

Beautiful...

~30~

Drawing Me

All of it was so beautiful!

Poets! Oh, the beauty of what was being and had been written! All of it was now so readily at my fingertips. I fell in love with poetry then, as I am sure Adonia will understand. Some of the poetry had disturbingly attractive ways of making me remember things I knew deep down that I should have avoided, much like roses you know will prick you but still find yourself compelled to lean close to and inhale. I had started the downhill slide and could not resist the momentum of it. It was all so very beautiful to me.

The plays, the plays too! Plays and poetry, it was all so very alluring and beautiful to me. I was seduced, filled with wonder, and my soul felt close to bursting with all of it. I think it was that I thought I could feel the emotions of others, without the frightful consequence of those emotions being my own. I thought once or twice to write a poem of my own, but knew better than to try. I knew my own poems might undo me. I think I made myself believe that all would be well within me as long as the tears that came were for another's pain, but I was wrong. I had merely closed my eyes and blithely begun walking toward the cliff's edge.

The world around me had become an amazing place and I was caught up in it for many, many years, absorbing everything I could. I soon came to love the radio. Voices came from the void and sang me to sleep, like ghostly bards in my living room. Then came moving pictures and after that television. I came to adore the television set, when this was invented. I bought one the second I could. It was always bringing me stories from all over the world and eventually just stories period that I did not need to leave my home to see. I was never alone then and I was being sucked into a whirlpool of never-ending knowledge and it felt good for a moment.

Then the ultimate invention of the home computer system with the eventual Internet access captured me completely. I would become lost for days, escaping into it, talking with people all over the world without a single thought of revealing myself. Or even being myself, for that matter. I could access limitless information with the touch of a key and not so much as a word to another human being. I thought it safe and harmless but it was just another well-disguised lure coaxing me to my ruin.

Rental movies were another constant source of momentary pleasure. I could take them home and closet myself away in what I thought was safety. No real human to bond with and bring me new pain, only a small break from reality allowing me into someone else's world. They became the new escape for me, giving me a glimpse into the world through another's eyes, and an idea of the views others around me had without the risk of actual connection. They allowed me to experience things I otherwise could not, or simply was not brave enough to, by pretending for a moment I was one of the characters or at least with them in that place and time. I was always on the prowl for another good movie, for another few hours of feeling like I was in someone else's world, without the constant pain of my own. Until the last one failed me utterly, sending me into the black pit which is my despair by breaking my heart anew.

It was another snowbound, boring evening and I had gone out early to rent some movies. This had become a habit for me in winter. I would bake some cookies and curl up under a blanket in one of those wonderful inventions called a beanbag in front of my fireplace and watch movies. I would gorge on cookies and coffee. Always coffee now, no longer wine, laughing and crying with my television set, living with those characters;

temporarily, not so alone.

The holiday season had become the time when I would become most easily depressed. It had been so advertised and commercialized that I was incapable of escaping it. I was forced to know just how alone I was, by mere virtue of having no one to give a gift to, or receive one from. So already I was ill-prepared for any new sadness, and the movie did not help. At a time when all were gathering with family and friends, I was putting a movie in my new player and settling in for another long night, with only those characters on my television screen for company.

I had become used to being alone, and it did not bother me much. I knew that somewhere an American Indian I called Gray still lived amongst his people and kept me in his memories. It had been many, many years since he had come to find me, but he knew where and how. I knew he was happy, still doing all he could for his people and it was enough for me. I had long ago accepted that the others were probably well and truly lost to me, but I still held out the smallest hope they would find me somehow. As you can see, I am still a creature of appalling emotional contradictions.

I had even thought once or twice of boarding a plane that could return me so quickly to Scotland, but the fear of finding our home an empty shell of rotting furniture kept me here. It seemed easier for me to hold out blind hope than risk being crushed completely. Once more I have shown myself to be not so brave, but back to why I am doing this and writing this now.

The girl behind the desk at the video rental shop had recommended this movie with such enthusiasm. She had excitedly told me it had it all, that it was the most inspiring film she had ever seen, sure to win an Oscar, if not all of them. She had also told me, winking and teasing me, that the actor was one I wouldn't be able to resist. It had sounded perfect. I needed inspiration, right? So I had asked her no more and brought it home.

It turned out to be about Scotland and William Wallace. It had done more than inspire me. It had torn me completely apart. One of the characters had been so much like my Baylor I had wanted to crawl into the screen and hug him, telling him everything of my life and pain without him. Telling him about being Were. There were scenes of fighting so like Baylor and Piper both that I had screamed at the characters to heal themselves. Crying aloud and shouting at my television set. The TV had ignored me, playing on. It began destroying me with its perfect views of my mountains. Kilts were everywhere. Bagpipes were playing in the background.

It was pushing me to the very edge of reason, once more, with every haunting tune. They had played on, a backdrop for those achingly familiar accents. So pure and perfect to me, that when the characters conversed I thought I should have answered them, warned them, or at the very least been there to fight at their side. I had been agonizingly reminded, all at once, of every single heart-rending memory I had ever hidden from myself, ever moved here to escape in the first place.

Then there had been the ending with the torture they had inflicted upon the hero, and I had been stabbed quite cleanly through my already broken heart. I had sat transfixed, unable to make it stop, sharply reminded of all the things I had heard were done to my mother, and all I had done to the perpetrators in turn. Then all the death, all the pain, me the witch, me the Angel of Death, me going mad again, settled over me like a heavy, suffocating blanket.

I could not get any of it out of my head. It had taken me centuries of living mostly as a wild animal to push these memories far enough away to leave me sane. Now I was dreaming nightly vivid dreams of home. Nightmares of how my mother had suffered and how I had made them suffer for it in turn began to drive me mad again. These memories readily mixed with visions of Baylor running free over the mountainsides, sometimes as a man, sometimes a Werewolf. These jolted me awake nightly, screaming for mercy on my mother's behalf or yelling out with all the force of my broken heart to Baylor.

"You do not have to be the Werewolf," I was howling, howling as Baylor had, howling my full understanding of that kind of torment.

Sometimes in my nightmares it would be Demon running over the mountainsides and I would be flying above him, calling to him, but he would not look up, because I was only me, only Angelica, and not Seraphim; only the camera, and good actors never look at the camera, unless the scene requires it. And he never had looked at me like I had so wanted him to.

It was all too much.

I could not escape any of it. Part of me wanted to crawl into these memories, pick the scabs and scratch the scars, allowing them to comfort and seduce me and drive me mad. Another part of me wanted to escape them all, turning once more into some wild creature and running from them blindly for another two hundred years, fearing the insanity such memories would bring far more than any other thing I had ever feared.

In any case, the deed was done, I had rented the video, and it had destroyed my carefully composed new life and there was not enough wilderness left in this world to escape it all again. I cannot stop now the inner voice, with its decidedly mean, English accent, that tells me to just go now. *"Go ahead and give it all up."* Saying to me as ever that you are all dead and lost to me forever. Trying to destroy the little girl that still keeps her faith close to her, the girl I had kept so safely hidden within me all these many years, the seventeen-year-old believer found dying at a stream by a Changeling. The Angel I had been, who had gathered that basket of faith and took that walk into a field with Demon, was being beaten far worse than the day she met him.

This endlessly evil, accented inner monologue is continuously telling me that Gray is too busy with his own life and people to care what I do, and in any case well enough prepared by me to face whatever comes to him. It throws visions and snippets of conversations at me randomly now. I can find no more moments of peace from it. It is trying to drive me mad. I don't want to be mad again. I cannot bear to become lost in all these things. I cannot bear to have endless arguments with myself. I don't want to be lost ever again or any more. I don't want to hurt or worry or wonder for all of time. I don't even want to exist sometimes. I have fought it desperately.

I have won myself this. I have allowed myself this last hope and opportunity, though it has been the final straw in breaking me. These moments at this table, writing my soul to you, have been hell itself, only in my hell it is cold and bagpipes play in the background as accompaniment to a mean little English voice that serenades me with a choruses of "it's all in vain." Yet just as with the letter I left for you on my pillow in Scotland, knowing you may never find it, I am compelled. I have no choice.

You may be gone from this world completely and this may all be in vain. I had to give it one last try, though, just this one last time. We all deserve at least that much, right? We have earned at least that much. I have to leave something of me that I might somehow still exist, at least in this manner, through these words, for one of you to find.

You see, I have come to find that fairness is a purely human, hopeful awareness. I am still very human and that is all right. I suffer still, that final curse on humanity; that as humans we were not only cast from our Creator's divine grace, but have within ourselves an inescapable awareness that we are being denied far better things. We are made to long for things we will never attain. We are forced to live with the knowledge that we are all created for more than what we receive, but we have lost it for ourselves. This knowledge is instinctual, hereditary, and undeniable. It is why we as humans, even Changelings, conceive of such concepts as fairness and justice in the first place and drive ourselves mad trying to make them be.

All men are not created equal. I am blessed beyond most in that I have the will to demand at least this for myself. Not everyone deserves to live, whether as equals or otherwise, and most assuredly, if fairness existed, I'd have died long ago for my sins. As a matter of fact, people deserve nothing but what they earn and demand and forge for themselves. It may not be politically correct, but it is proven and true. The rest, the ability to fantasize otherwise, are all just divine gifts, gifts we no longer deserve, but then that is what makes the gift-giver divine. Good things happen to bad people and bad things happen to good. Good people do bad things sometimes and bad people do surprisingly good things occasionally as well. To think anything else would mean that life is fair and it is not.

Someone once said to me, a professor I had once, I think: "nothing in life is fair, and nothing in life is free." I had said to him, "aye, and what's more, you can't get out of life alive.' I had said it in sarcastic jest, and, laughing, walked away, but the reality of it has made itself well known to me of late. I have walked away from that reality for the last time, I do not think I can escape it anymore; it is too deeply set within me now. The sad irony is that it is usually by the choices we ourselves make that we deny ourselves a more acceptable view of reality and a far better life, thinking it someone else's job to make it better for us.

Like when we love. Most would look at my tale with pity and think to themselves I deserved to have been loved by Demon, and not just as his pupil. They might think him stupid and short-sighted but I do not, I have had that argument with myself and I have won. I merely think he made a choice, as we all do, and it is his right to do so, whether all would agree with it or not. I look at all of this as a lesson for all those who read it. Love *is* all, but it's not *all* good. Nothing in the universe ever said it had to be. Therefore we may choose to focus on the good and try to earn more of it or we may choose to focus on the bad, demanding we deserve better by mere virtue of the fact that we love. Some masochistic few may fall more deeply in love with the torture of not receiving love in return, as they perceive they should, than with the one they say they love. That is not me. Some lucky few will find it is merely an amazing gift given to all humans, in compensation for all of the harsher realities, that we even have such a concept as love instilled within us, and have been given a lifetime to search it out. That *is* me and I love that about me.

It is love which demands I make something a little more right, that I tip the scales with what free, and incredible, will I have been blessed with and make at least one thing a little fairer for someone else. There is one last thing I must do and I refuse to hear different from anyone, including the voice within me.

~31~

Escaping Pain

To Baylor I must tell one last tale of my own, though it is merely an old tale being retold. For you, Baylor, I have held this truth in my heart, a gift I have longed to give. You must know what I came to see so very long ago and tried so desperately to find and tell you.

Long ago, in a time when Druids still took the form of the stag to preside over the rights and feasts of the peoples of Britannia and Erin, there was a Druid who gave birth to a son though she had been forbidden to breed. This Druid whispered her offspring's name with her dying breath, Baylor, she had called him. The rest of the tale, Baylor's tale, well, most of it is superstition, legend, and random bits of truth, so marred by repeated verbal passing, they are hard to recognize. Let me begin to sort it for you my dearest brother.

This Druid, your mother, had been one that had received the blessing of being able to take the form of the stag. In reality, that blessing was merely being made into a Changeling. I have heard tale of other forms some Druids could take but that is a separate issue merely told now to reinforce what I tell you of Druids and their strange way of being Changelings. The Druid that was your mother, however, had never been taught any more about her gift other than that she could take that single form on certain days of the year. For what reasons, I cannot guess, but she

314

was left sadly unenlightened as to the rest of her gift. Your mother had believed that she was otherwise normal, mortal, and would age and die like any other person. Believing was all it had taken. Belief is often all it takes for many things, it is often all that limits us or lifts us up as Changelings.

Your mother's energies responded to her belief, aging her even allowing her to die. I wonder still to this day if her soul went to heaven, or merely ascended, since she had still changed throughout her life, but that is a thing I have yet to find the answer to. It merely became a new dilemma, which I examined at some length in those early years when I had strength to remember and endless hope it would be of use. I supposed, considering that if the body still changed, and the energies where constantly renewed and not truly aging and dying, then they were constantly rejuvenated by the changes, hence only responding to her belief that she would age and only appearing to do so, as she expected. If that is indeed the case, then those blessed Druids merely ascend and don't truly die. This Druid's form of Changeling is very off to me but it makes a strange kind of sense.

If a Changeling were made in the way your mother was, not at the moment of their own eminent death like others, then the will to remain was not necessarily as strong as in a Changeling who had denied the light to become one. When the energies that made it up had made for it an aged and hurting body, as expected of them, then the soul would willingly ascend, thinking it was time to die. At that point the soul within the person hovering over the dying Changeling would meet with the changed soul as it left this realm, and itself be changed. So this "blessing" had been passed on but less and less knowledge of being a Changeling came with it.

I know now why, whenever this kind of "blessing" had first originated, someone had told these chosen Druids not to bear young. It would be difficult to explain to them how to raise and care for a Changeling child without explaining to them more fully what they were. Someone had obviously, a long time ago, felt like keeping most of the gift to themselves.

My mind reeled back then with all of this, and I hope with all my soul that you will find this and it will help you. I swear to you I searched desperately to tell you, meaning to save you all these years of not knowing and suffering the torment of that lack of knowledge, but I couldn't find you and for that I am dreadfully sorry.

You see, Baylor, when this Druid that was your mother had been raped, she had thought something even more terrible would happen. Just as Edana had been told not to breed, so then must have your mother. What consequences for such a betrayal of the Druid trust she had been told she would suffer we may never know but she knew there had to be something bad in the wind when she had been forced to break the rule. She had known there would be terrible repercussions, and in essence she turned those repercussions against the ones who had forced her. In her anger, she had railed at them, telling them they would pay the price with her.

She could not have known the full extent of what she was doing, but she had been very angry and I cannot blame her, and in that anger her will, a Changeling's will, saw to it that things went as she had predicted. Her will to take vengeance had been strong and evident when her soul was blending with the small soul that had taken root inside her. She had unwittingly made her child a Changeling in that initial contact of souls. She probably even unconsciously made it a boy. She had made her words come to pass by making certain that all heard them and took them as a curse, relating it later to the boy-child she had made.

There is a part of me that cannot help but to applauded her that she had managed to find a way, even while believing as she had that it would end her own life, to take her revenge. She saw to it, whether knowingly or not, that a boy child sprang from her full of that vengeance, and that he would be raised on her words by an old woman who would believe them enough to see he did her will.

Baylor, you have been a Changeling from conception, a Changeling child raised on the belief you were your mother's vengeance. You were told that you would grow up big and strong, and so you did. You were told you would be a powerful warrior and fulfill her curse, and so you did. You were told that you would protect her people, and so you had, and most likely still do to this very day. You were a Changeling, after all, who believed and belief was all it took to make it so. Your young imagination had been filled with not only your Druid mothers curse, but tales of the Red Branch and Cuchulain. All of these things had gone into your young Changeling mind, and you made them happen, without even realizing it.

Baylor, you probably, on some subconscious level, which all we Changelings must be aware of and watch out for, made her vengeance come down under a full moon, in a simple desire to add beauty to the tale, like so many of the old tales of the Celts, fulfilling her curse as only a Changeling could have.

Then when you had completed what you had been told you were born to do, you had returned to your people victorious, only to be filled with guilt that you had been absent from them when they had been attacked again. You had stored this guilt in your subconscious, again without knowing it would come back to bite you, literally. When you had gone off in pursuit of those that had attacked your village, the morning of your fateful conversation with Edana, the guilt had been there in the back of your mind.

Edana! The thought of her wounds me for you. If only both of you had known back then what I know now. I wish with all I am that I had been able to find you, but at least I leave you this now. I cannot change the past for you, but mayhap I can put hope into your future.

I recalled back then, on my mad journey home to find all of you, how you had said you had destroyed all of your foes and then fallen yourself, but then how you had not thought you would die. You had believed you would be found or somehow you would recover to still protect your people. You still felt your destiny was to protect those your Druid mother had called her own. This belief had kept you alive, kept your soul in a wounded and dying form, as only a Changeling's will could have.

Then had come the point of your first real change, when you had seen the huge wolf coming to eat you, and you had been delirious. Just as when I had turned unthinkingly from a bird to a woman to speak to Demon on my first day as a Changeling, my energies responding to my will to have a

317

mouth to speak with, so had your energies responded to your will to "eat you first." You had turned yourself into a wolf to save yourself from being eaten and to do the eating instead. Quite probably you had been a normal, if not unusually large and red, wolf at that time.

There was no telling, as you said, how long you had wandered about in this form. It was when you had come upon your village and seen Edana and thought to call to her and ask her why she had not told you of her choice, being so shocked by the knowledge she had chosen the Druid's gift over a life with you, that this desire or will to be able to speak had done to you much as it had me, and turned you back into your own form. You hadn't been instructed, as I had, about clothing, hence you had appeared naked and thus further confused. That, combined with the fact you saw your sword in the other villager's hand and could not recall how you had come to lose it, had understandably scared you and made you stay hidden. And staying hidden only made things worse.

See, there is when it became, quite understandably, messed. Because these superstitious people had been frightened when they had found no sign of tracks leading to the area where they'd found your Bane, they had come up with some outrageous ideas. Thinking some of your foes had turned into wolves, it was outrageous, but what else was there to their minds? The part about the lone tracks that were bigger, and leading away, and the sighting of the huge red wolf with the braids and leather thongs tied in its hair, howling at the full moon, is probably the only fact present in their tales for a while because that was you that had been sighted.

You had run off in terror then, upon hearing their tale, making yourself believe this was some new aspect of your mother's curse. You convinced yourself that, for abandoning your people for a second time, you had been turned into a beast. When you had come out into the glade and the full moon had shown full above you, your subconscious mind responded to these new beliefs their tale had given you, and turned you again into this huge beast of a wolf you had heard described. You would eventually change it into something less wolf and more man as the years and fears progressed, in accordance with the visions the villager's tales would conjure in your frightened and confused mind.

As if these people's superstitions had not done enough damage, the telling and retelling of the tale over the years compounded it, as we know such things will. It probably began as "one terrible night when the moon was full," a party of men that their hero Baylor had defeated had used dark magic in one final attempt to best him. Their hero's foes had become wolves and they had bitten him and, though he had become one of these cursed creatures in the end, he had managed to defeat them despite the change they had inflicted upon him, surviving to roam madly under each full moon.

Then the tale became a warning to any others wandering about at night, that they might encounter you, and you not of sound mind might attack them, and those wayward wanderers would then also be cursed and become wolves during the full moon as well. Eventually the tale had grown, as such tales will, far beyond any truth it had once hidden, and sufferers of such bites became no longer simply wolves. They would become great huge beasts, half man, half wolf, and these men would not recall it. Of course they would not recall it, because it wasn't happening, at least not yet, not until it was told to enough people who believed it.

Then, in time, if any of these believers had run across your path, now that you had made yourself into a beast befitting the visions these circulating tales created, and been attacked, they believed they would be changed, as they had been told, and so they were. The contact between the souls had been made during the attack, so the ability for their beliefs to change them was there, and this is were it truly began.

The story only grew and compounded even more from there, with more and more sightings and even more believers, because now it truly was happening. They began to develop the tale then even more, with the ways to kill these unnatural creatures evolving from the people's adoration of gore and glory, such as beheading a foe, and the poor villagers' lack of ready silver. Of course it had to be difficult or it wouldn't be a good tale.

Yes, it had become a plague eventually, and yes, Baylor, you had felt

319

an obligation to stop it. Sadly enough, you had been spreading the plague without even knowing it. The fact that the tale only grew in credibility with the sightings of those that believed it and were being made did not help you halt its spread. Now that you had become aware and were trying to stop it, it was these new Werewolves spreading it. It is, however, not your fault. I feel the fault lies with either the person who had left your Druid mother in the dark as to the full extent of her gift, or mayhap even the one that started the tale. These are the pitfalls to be found in half truths.

See, when you had come again upon your people retelling the tale, you had believed it as well, changing your own shape accordingly, and reminding yourself not to harm them. It was only by constantly reminding yourself of this need to protect and not do harm that you were different, but it was the fact you had heard the tale in the first place that even made it necessary.

There also is when you stopped aging, Baylor. I thought long on this, because, as with so many things, this was a trait other Werewolves did not share with you. You had believed you would be unchanged and naked just like the first time when you looked down at yourself when coming aware after a long stint in your beast form, so you were, and have always been. It is only that great desire to survive, and protect your people, and the unquestioned belief you would always come back from being a Werewolf naked and unchanged, which has allowed you to live this long. For you had no knowledge otherwise that you would not die, other than the belief you wouldn't as long as there were those who needed protecting.

This too explained, in a very twisted way, why you had not died when the yeti had torn off your head. Your instincts for survival had been so long ingrained that not only did your Werewolf form heal itself instantaneously when it was wounded, but your subconscious had reverted to that form in the first place when needing such swift healing and defense. Your belief that you would not die so long as your people needed you was so powerful in you that you took what form you needed to stay alive. This will to continue with both living and protecting had simply taken control and reverted to a form that it knew would save you, and crazy as it was you took your head back. Your energies acted apart from conscious thought, and survive you did.

I have often wanted to laugh at the complex simplicity of it all, but it is not funny and the ironies seemed never ending. Some Changeling, somewhere, way back in the darkened shadows of the corridors of time, had left another Changeling sadly lacking in knowledge, and a great many have paid dearly, most with their lives. Knowledge truly is power but, for a Changeling, belief in what we know, or think we know, is a far more powerful thing.

You need to know, Baylor, that being Were is only being unaware of what you are. You are a Changeling, dearest brother, now change! Now that you know, know this as well, your not knowing is part of why we couldn't have either. If one does not know he is a Changeling, then he cannot project himself as one. Neither Demon nor I had been able to recognize you as a Changeling because even when we scanned, as Demon did when looking for you on his first trip to Scotland, we found naught but what you felt you were. I found this to be true ages ago, when traveling back to Scotland from Rome, and though it pained me to know I had missed such a thing then, it gave me strength and confidence to continue the search for all of you, without being afraid of being found by that which had originally destroyed me.

So to whoever finds this, please, see that my brother, my Baylor, reads what I have written here. That he may learn all I have come to know of being Were. That it is only being unaware. It is no curse. It is merely not knowing that one is a Changeling, having been raised up by a superstitious people, in a superstitious time. His mother meant him no harm, she just didn't know any better. I am so very sorry I did not see it for him sooner. Tell him, that he may know I love him. I tried for him. I thought of him. He was the very best brother, friend and storyteller ever known to me and he possesses a very large portion of my heart.

I have searched for all of you for ages, to tell you all this that I have written and more. To tell all of you, that in all of this, throughout all this time, I have come to realize quite a few things. Demon was right, more so than maybe even he knew. There is no such thing as fair, this is a thing proven to me over and over again throughout time. There is merely within some few of us a will that makes us more capable at times to combat that harsh reality. That will in me is fading now. I have done what last little bit I can to tip those invisible scales of invented justice and make things as right as I can for Baylor. I blame no one that there was so much none of us knew. I merely pray that my words show you all the will to brave the unknown and break the rules we set for ourselves that have held us back so long.

No longer ask, "Do you believe?" Say "Prove it, show me, and until then do not limit me, for I am change and I will do what I will." Above all believe in yourselves.

I ask this of you who read this, that _all_ of them, should you find them, as I have failed to, be made to know all I have come to learn, that it may help them as they did me, and they may see that I did and do love them very much as well. I know my time with them was short-lived but its impact upon me was not. They were to me my family, my friends, my only reason for so very long. Show them this, that they will see, I did search for them. I truly did. I did not betray their gifts to me. For every laugh we ever shared, and every hope they ever gave me, I pushed myself that one more mile, until the miles near destroyed me. Mayhap I am without spine and should have damned the little voice inside and gone back just one more time, but...

I had to save me too.

Now that it no longer matters, I have one last thing I must say. To Demon I leave you this: I loved you. I love you still. Truly, madly, deeply, outside of reason, and beyond will. I think somehow that I was born to love you. I do not regret or begrudge you. I have walked in your shoes, quite literally, and it has given me strength and understanding the likes of which I can never explain. I have sat wearing your kilt, alone in my garden, and absorbed your will when mine would fail me. I have understood and loved you even more because of this. Knowing and loving you made me who and what I am and I would never change it. I have come to accept that this is not a thing I can change, should I even want to, so I take it with me always, willingly. Love is my Yelm and I will keep it close forever.

Please, do not think me weak, if you do indeed live and this comes into your hands. I still have the will that told heaven it must wait. I simply have no more explanation as to what it waits for.

The Vineyard

There is a vineyard in my soul that produced the sweetest wine.
And I was drunk on love of you.
Dancing truly, madly, deeply through
A moonlit grove of hope; the playground of the blind.

All the grapes were fresh and tender, tended always in my mind.
There was no finer love or substitute,
No purer heart or sweeter fruit,
There was no better spell, this brew, for anyone to find.

There is a vineyard in my soul that produced the sweetest wine.
And all the grapes of all my faith
Now fell unheeded where I'd traipse.
For to everything a season, and to every love a time.

Finding that all my toil and all my tears couldn't undo the design
That had left my effort useless,
And all the vines now fruitless,
That made the vineyard in my soul a place I go to pine.

Angelica

I will put this now in the floor of this room where I have spent so much time reading, and recently writing, over the years. I will leave my energies behind here above it so that they may serve as a guide to its resting-place, marking it plainly for any Changeling to sense.

If someone finds it other than another Changeling, they will think it merely another fantasy novel, left unpublished and collecting dust, and it will not matter. Yet I pray not. Hopefully, it will not be found by any but the kindest of Changelings, one who will sense my presence here, and do this, my final will.

Deliver this for me. Put it into the hands of one of those I've written of here, one of them whom I still adore and love so deeply. I leave you now with my deepest thanks, and all my love. Please, give it to all of them.

Afterward

The odd man who had found and clutched the aged journal in his hands all those long hours launched himself to his feet. Hurling it across the room as though it had caught on fire and burned him badly, he screamed. The journal no longer seemed such a prize.

"No!" he screamed again, "Noooo..."

The scream collapsed into a howl of pain echoing back at him around the empty room as he threw his head back, enraged, screaming out again.

"Why?"

Over and over again he howled his rage at the aged ceiling. Roaring the same words repeatedly, sounding less and less human with each repetition and more just tortured beast. Maybe the spider was right and a madman had moved into town.

Suddenly the raging man narrowed his eyes and lowered his head, turning a menacing glare toward the front door as the knob twisted and it swung wide open. A lesser man would have turned on his heels instantly upon being met by such a sight, thinking he'd opened the very doors of hell, and the Devil himself was there waiting to greet him with pain.

This intruder, however, stood his ground, his massive frame filling the foyer. This man had faced this demon before. His red hair shown with the last of the sun's rays as they caught in it and created for him a halo of fire, and his smile remained unwavering despite the other's obvious rage.

"Has Piper had us buy the wrong house?" he asked, ignoring the holes the other was boring into him with his eyes for having interrupted his outburst.

His only answer was his longtime friend's turning and putting his fist through the wall. Stepping fully into the empty dining room and putting the take-out food he had just entered with in the center of the floor, the great beast of a redhead let out a sigh. He had known his friend would have forgotten such trivialities as food and had come prepared; glancing around, he could tell he had been right. Surely his friend would calm down after eating something, he thought. He straightened back up to his impressive full height then and continued unabated in his conversational manner.

"He seemed quite sure this time that he had felt her presence here."

Finally the other man calmed himself enough to speak.

"Yes, Baylor, it was her house." He gritted it out through clinched teeth, fighting hard not to destroy every wall in sight.

"Then where has she gone now?" Baylor asked.

"She has ascended," came the grinding response.

The man lost his composure again and put his foot through the same wall he had abused earlier.

"Demon, calm yourself, you'll have the neighbors calling the cops about domestic abuse or some such." Baylor tried raising his hands slowly to stay his friend's wrath on the walls. "You know things are different..."

"Calm myself? CALM MYSELF! Did you not hear me? She has ASCENDED!" Demon yelled.

Baylor took a step back, aghast and trying desperately to grasp the words he hadn't caught mere moments before. There was something terribly wrong with what they meant and his heart refused to accept what his mind was trying to process. Demon couldn't be right.

"Surely you are mistaken. Piper said it was strong here, if she had ascended it would have weakened by now, right?" Baylor looked pleadingly to Demon, his eyes begging for a different answer than he knew was coming.

Demon's dear friend was pleading for affirmation of all the faith they had held and that had held them for so long, and for once Demon had nothing to give him and somehow that made the moment even worse. Demon calmed a little then, realizing Baylor had loved her just as much as he had, and a deadness steeled into his eyes and voice as he forced himself to speak.

"No, old friend, it is only the fact that she did ascend," he said sadly, sinking to his knees and rubbing the floor beside him lovingly, "leaving all of her energy behind here, that makes it possible that she can still be felt after all these years."

"But what will we do?" Baylor asked. He was a man through and through and had always prided himself on that, but he felt himself on the verge of tears as he sank to the floor across from his friend.

"I do not know," Demon whispered, barely audible, in his own pain.

"You said once you did not think one can come back from that; are you sure though?" Baylor tried again after some time.

He was still unable to let go the hope that had driven them both for so long. Demon could hear his friend was on the verge of breaking down and he was as well. They both needed hope, now more than ever.

Suddenly he had it. Demon looked from Baylor to the hole in the floor, where the feel of her had been so strong, calling him back to the very spot repeatedly as he had walked through the old house. Then he looked back to Baylor, remembering fully the book, remembering some of the incredible things she had told them.

"What? What are you thinking?" Baylor asked excitedly.

Demon did not answer him, only pointed in the direction of the book he had thrown. Baylor turned then and noticed it in the corner where it had fallen. He was on his feet and there in two long strides, quickly retrieving it. He came back flipping it this way and that, looking at it quizzically.

"What?" he repeated.

"It is a journal she had left for us," Demon replied finally, having come to his conclusions and made a decision. "She said in part of it that she realized some things were not possible only because we believe them to be impossible, or something like that. She spoke of doing some things I have never even considered." He looked his old friend in the eye then. "She figured out some very important things for you as well and you should read it while I'm gone."

"Gone? Gone where?" Baylor asked, very confused now.

"Up! Up where the tired ones go. Up were they escape the pain," Demon said, excitement building in his voice.

"But you cannot leave me now as well!" Baylor nearly yelled.

Baylor felt near to panicking now and he was not accustomed to such a feeling. He had survived more ages and changes than he could currently think, but most of it had been with this one at his side.

"No, I'm not. I am simply going to bring our Angel back." Demon's confidence now was growing, along with his excitement.

"Can it be done?" Baylor asked, excited and apprehensive all at once.

He was fearful of losing his longtime companion, yet couldn't help feeling exhilarated at the same time. With Demon's certainty showing through so vividly, he was quickly believing it would work and he'd have them both back in no time.

"Oh, it *will* be done," Demon replied, fiercely confident he could do it.

He looked again at the book in Baylor's hand. He started smiling then. Becoming again one of those giant children she had described them as. Shifting his weight, he cocked his head and grinned almost stupidly.

"She loved me too, you know," he said, smiling at his best friend.

"Yes, I know," Baylor replied.

"No, I mean she *loved* me," Demon reiterated.

"Yes, I *know*," Baylor also clarified. "Bring both of you back safely to me."

"I will, I swear it," Demon promised.

"Then, until we swear again," Baylor said.

Baylor stood his ground, like the warrior he was, and watched the friend of hundreds of lifetimes disappear. He did not shed a tear or allow his faith to falter. He kept his chin up as he had been bred to and did not think of the darker possibilities. Instead he thought how he must buy some comfortable chairs and furnish this kitchen soon. Because they would return and all must be made comfortable for all the stories they would be forced to tell.

He wandered through the place much as Demon had the previous morning, making mental notes of all that would be needed and who would need to be contacted to accomplish it all quickly. He too found himself drawn back to the main dining hall where the take-out was growing cold and her journal was waiting to be read.

Finally Baylor sat down on the uncomfortable planks and sighed to himself then that all other things would wait, he wanted her words now. He realized then that anything of Angel after all this time would make it all heavenly and, accepting the hard floor, he sat back and began to read what she had figured out for him.

Coming soon

No Ordinary Angel

By C.C. Guice

The First Born Saga

Book Two